R.A. Salvatore's

WAR OF THE SPIDER QUEEN BOOK VI

Resurrection

PAUL S. KEMP

R. A. SALVATORE'S
War of the Spider Queen Book VI: Resurrection

Distributed in the United States by Holtzbrinck Publishing. Distributed in Canada by Fenn Ltd.

Distributed to the hobby, toy, and comic trade in the United States and Canada by regional distributors.

Distributed worldwide by Wizards of the Coast, Inc. and regional distributors.

Forgotten Realms, Wizards of the Coast, and their logos are trademarks
of Wizards of the Coast, Inc., in the U.S.A. and other countries.

All Wizards of the Coast characters, character names, and the distinctive likenesses thereof
are property of Wizards of the Coast, Inc.

Printed in the U.S.A.

Cover art by Brom
First Printing: April 2005
Library of Congress Catalog Card Number: 2004113605

9 8 7 6 5 4 3 2 1

US ISBN: 0-7869-3640-1
ISBN-13: 978-0-7869-3640-3
620-17726-001-EN

U.S., CANADA,
ASIA, PACIFIC, & LATIN AMERICA
Wizards of the Coast, Inc.
P.O. Box 7071702
Renton, WA 98057-0707
+1-800-324-6496

EUROPEAN HEADQUARTERS
Wizards of the Coast, Belgium
T Hofveld 6d
Groot-Bijgaarden
Belgium
+322 467 3360

Visit our web site at **www.wizards.com**

FORGOTTEN REALMS

R.A. Salvatore's

WAR OF THE SPIDER QUEEN

BOOK I

Dissolution

RICHARD LEE BYERS

BOOK II

Insurrection

THOMAS M. REID

BOOK III

Condemnation

RICHARD BAKER

BOOK IV

Extinction

LISA SMEDMAN

BOOK V

Annihilation

PHILIP ATHANS

BOOK VI

Resurrection

PAUL S. KEMP

For Jen,
Roarke,
and Riordan

Acknowledgements

*Countless colleagues and friends deserve my thanks,
but one above all: Phil Athans. Thanks, my friend.*

Eight legs, eight.

Clattering on the stones, ticking, ticking, tapping, tapping impatiently.

They were done with their battle, with their feasting, devouring their siblings, growing stronger with each juicy bite. Bloated and spent, they stood around the octagonal stone, myriad eyes staring into myriad eyes, eight legs eight tapping and clattering.

They could eat no more; they could fight no more. Exhaustion held them in place, as Lolth had desired from the beginning. The thousands became eight—the eight strongest, the eight smartest, the eight most devious, the eight most ruthless. One would fuse with the Yor'thae. One would assume the mantle of a goddess, the deity of Chaos.

Only one, whom the others would serve . . . if the One gave them that choice and that chance. If not, then they, like their thousands of dead siblings, would be devoured.

The spiders knew that they could not influence the choice any longer. The competition was long past, the fight decided, and only She Who Was Chaos could make the final pronouncement. The spiders did not delude themselves with false hubris. They did not deceive themselves with any thoughts that they might undo that which would be done. The broodling war was over.

Eight legs eight tap-tapped nervously on the stone.

Beyond the cocoon of the inner sanctum, the drow were not so accepting. They basked in pride, they placed self above Lolth, they thought themselves worthy or even beyond that peak. They dared presume knowledge of Lolth, of the choice before them all, and they dared plot and connive to deny their rivals their proper place.

Fools, they were, and the spiders knew it. Futility glided in their every step, their fate long sealed.

The plot was scripted by the Lady of Chaos, and that was the most perplexing and tantalizing of all. For any road paved by Lolth would not run straight, nor to any expected destination.

That was the beauty.

The spiders knew it.

The time was approaching.

The spiders knew it.

Eight legs eight clattered on the stones, ticking, ticking, tapping, tapping, patience twisted, stretched and torn asunder.

Eight legs, eight.

Inthracis sat in his favorite chair, a high-backed throne made from bones packed together with a mortar of blood and pulped skin. Tomes and scrolls, the tools of his research, lay open atop the large basalt table before him. The soaring walls of the three-story library of Corpsehaven, his fortress, loomed on all sides.

Eyes stared at him from out of the walls.

Made from the heaped decay of thousands upon thousands of semi-sentient, magically preserved corpses, Corpsehaven's walls, floors, and ceilings could have filled the cemeteries of a hundred cities. Bodies were the bricks of Inthracis's keep. He regarded himself as an artisan, a fleshmason who smashed and twisted the moaning forms into whatever contorted shape he needed. He was indiscriminate in his choice of materials; all manner of bodies had been pressed into the structure of his keep. Mortals, demons, devils, and even other yugoloths had found a home in Corpsehaven's walls. Inthracis was nothing if not a fair murderer. Any being that stood in his way on his rise through the ranks of the Blood Rift's ultroloth hierarchy ended up in one of his walls, decaying and near death but still sensate enough to feel pain, still alive enough to suffer and moan.

He smiled. Being surrounded by his dead and his books always settled his mind. The library was his retreat. The pungent reek of decaying flesh and the piquant aroma of parchment preservative cleared both his cavernous sinuses and his cavernous mind.

And that was well, for he desired clarity. His research had revealed little, only tantalizing hints.

He knew only that the Lower Planes were in an uproar and that Lolth was at the center of it. He had not yet determined how best to capitalize on the chaos.

He ran a mottled, long-fingered hand over the smooth skin of his scalp and wondered how he might turn events to his advantage. Long had he waited to move against Kexxon the Oinoloth, Archgeneral of the Blood Rift. Perhaps the time for action had come, during the Lolth-spawned chaos?

He stared into the bloodshot, pain-filled eyes of his walls but the corpses offered him no answers, only lipless grimaces, soft moans, and agonized stares. Their suffering lightened Inthracis's spirit.

Outside Corpsehaven, audible even through the walls of pressed flesh and glassteel windows, the scream of the Blood Rift's blistering winds sang their song of agony—a high pitched, rising keen, similar to that made by the dozen or so mortals Inthracis had personally flayed. As the sound subsided, Inthracis cocked his head and waited. He knew that a planar tremor would follow hard after, trailing the wind's wail with the same certainty that thunder followed lightning in an Ethereal cyclone.

There.

A slow rumble began, just a soft shaking at first, but building to a crescendo that shook the entire fortress, a paroxysm that caused flakes of skin meal and dried hair to rain like volcanic ash from the high ceiling of the library. Inthracis suspected that the entirety of the Blood Rift, perhaps even the whole of the Lower Planes, was shaking. Lolth had torn the Demonweb Pits free of the Abyss, he knew, and raw, purposeless power—reified chaos—poured into the Lower Planes and sent shudders throughout the cosmos.

The multiverse, Inthracis knew, was in parturition, and the cosmic birthing was rattling the planes. Reality had been reorganized, entire planes moved, and the Blood Rift, Inthracis's home plane, groaned under the resulting onslaught of energies. Ever since Lolth had begun her . . . activities, the barren, mountainous plane had suffered a plague of volcanic eruptions, blizzards of ash, and thunderous rockslides that could have buried continents on the Prime Material. Fissures opened at random in the mountainous, rocky landscape, swallowing leagues of earth. The churning, gore-filled flow of the Blood River, the great artery that fed the body of the plane, roiled in its wide channel.

Given the upheaval, Inthracis had several times increased the magical protections that shielded Corpsehaven from such threats, but still the danger gave him pause. Corpsehaven sat on a level ledge sculpted from the otherwise precipitously steep side of the Blood Rift's largest volcano, Calaas. It would not do for an unexpected landslide or volcanic spasm to send Inthracis's life's work skidding down the mountainside.

The wind outside rose again, a low whine that grew to an unbearable keen before beginning to die. Behind the wind's wail of pain, Inthracis could just make out the conspiratorial whisper of a word. He sensed it as much as heard it, and it was the same word he had been hearing intermittently for days:

Yor'thae.

Each time the gust hissed its secret, the corpses in his walls moaned through rotted lips and decayed arms loose from the wall squirmed to reach bony hands for rotted ears. With each utterance of the unholy word, the entirety of Corpsehaven wriggled like a hive of abyssal ants.

Inthracis knew the word's meaning, of course. He was an ultroloth, one of the most powerful in the Blood Rift, and he was versed in over one hundred twenty languages, including High Drow of Faerûn. The *Yor'thae* was Lolth's Chosen, and the Spider Queen was summoning her Chosen to her side. It infuriated Inthracis that he had not been able to learn why.

He recognized that Lolth, like the Lower Planes, was undergoing a transmogrification. Perhaps she would be transformed, perhaps the process would annihilate her. The calling of the *Yor'thae* presaged events of significance, and the word was in the ear, on the tongues, and in the minds of all the powerful in the Lower Planes: demon princes of the Abyss, archdevils of the Nine Hells, ultroloths of the Blood Rift. All were positioning themselves to take advantage of whatever outcome resulted.

Despite himself, Inthracis admired the Spider Bitch's temerity. Though he did not fully understand the stakes, he did understand that Lolth had gambled much on the success of her Chosen.

Such a gamble should not have surprised him overmuch. At her core Lolth was the same as any demon—a creature of chaos. Senseless risk and senseless slaughter were her nature.

Which is why demons are idiots, Inthracis decided. Even demon *goddesses*. The wise took only well-calculated risks for well-calculated rewards. Such was Inthracis's creed and it had served him well.

He tapped his ring-bedecked fingers on the polished basalt table, and sparks of magical energy leaped from the bands. The legs of the table—human legs grafted to the basalt top—shifted slightly to better accommodate him. The bones of his chair adjusted to more comfortably sit him.

He looked upon the collective knowledge gathered in his library, seeking inspiration. Desiccated hands and arms jutted from the walls of flesh, forming shelves upon which sat in orderly rows an enormous quantity of magical scrolls, tomes, and grimoires, a lifetime's worth of arcane knowledge and spells. Inthracis's multifaceted eyes scanned them in several spectrums. Multifarious colors of varying intensities emanated from the tomes, denoting their relative magical power and the type of magic they embodied. Like the dead in his walls, the books offered him no ready answer.

Another tremor rattled the plane, another wail trumpeted the promise or threat of Lolth's *Yor'thae*, another agitated rustle ran through the dead of Corpsehaven.

Distracted, Inthracis pushed back his chair, rose from the table, and walked to the library's largest window, an octagonal slab of glassteel wider than Inthracis was tall and magically melded with the bones and flesh around it. A lattice of thread-thin blue and black veins grew within the glass, a byproduct of the melding.

The veins looked like a spider's web, Inthracis thought, and he almost smiled.

The grand window offered a wondrous view of the heat-scorched red sky, a panorama of Calaas's side and the rugged lowlands of the Blood Rift far below. Inthracis stepped close to the window and looked out and down.

Though he had flattened a plateau half a league wide into Calaas's side, he had raised Corpsehaven right at the edge of the plateau. He had chosen such a precipitous location so that he could always look out and be reminded of how far he had to fall, should he grow stupid, lazy, or weak.

Outside, the unceasing winds whipped a rain of black ash into blinding swirls. Arteries of lava, fed from the eternal flow of the plane's volcanoes, lined the lowlands far below. Fumaroles dotted the black landscape like plague boils, venting smoke and yellow gas into the red sky. The winding red vein of the Blood River surged through the gorges and canyons.

Here and there, swarms of larvae—the form mortal souls took in the Blood Rift—squirmed along the broken landscape or wriggled up Calaas's sides. The larvae looked like pale, bloated worms as long as Inthracis's arm. Heads jutted from the slime-covered, wormlike bodies, the only remnant of the dead soul's mortal form. The faces wore expressions of agony that Inthracis found pleasing.

Despite the ash storm and roiling landscape, squads of towering, insectoid mezzoloths and several powerfully muscled, scaled, and winged nycaloths—all of them in service to one or another of the ultroloths—prowled the rockscape with long, magical pikes. With the pikes they impaled one larva after another, collecting souls the way a spear fisherman hunted fish on the Prime. The stuck larvae squirmed feebly on the shafts, overwrought with pain and despair.

To judge from the heads on some of the nearby larvae, most of the souls appeared to be those of humans, but races of all kinds found their way to the Blood Rift, all of them damned to serve in the furnaces of the plane. Some of the souls would be transformed into lesser yugoloths to fill out Inthracis's or another ultroloth's forces. Others would be used as trade goods, food, or magical fuel for experiments.

Inthracis looked away from the soul harvest and gazed down and to his left. There, barely visible through the haze of ash and heat, built into a plateau in Calaas's side not unlike that upon which Corpsehaven sat, Inthracis could just espy the pennons of skin that flew at the top of the Obsidian Tower, the keep of Bubonis. The ultroloth immediately below Inthracis in the Blood Rift's hierarchy, Bubonis coveted Inthracis's position as much as Inthracis coveted Kexxon's. Bubonis too would be scheming; he too would be planning how to use the chaos to further his ascent up Calaas's side.

All of the Blood Rift's elite ultroloths laired on Calaas. The relative height of an ultroloth's fortress along Calaas's side indicated the owner's status within the Blood Rift's hierarchy. Kexxon the Oinoloth's fortress, the Steel Keep, sat highest of all, perched among the red and black clouds at the very edge of Calaas's caldera. Corpsehaven sat only twenty or so leagues below the Steel Keep and only two or three leagues above the Obsidian Tower of Bubonis.

Inthracis knew that the day would come when he would face a challenge from Bubonis, when he would himself challenge Kexxon. For the hundredth time in the past twelve hours, he wondered if the time had come. The thought of throwing Kexxon's corpse down the Infinite Deep amused him. The Infinite Deep descended to the center of creation, and its rocky sides were so sheer, so unbroken by any shelf or ledge of significance, that when things fell there, they fell forever.

Without warning, darkness descended on the library, darkness so intense that even Inthracis's eyes could not penetrate it, though he could see in virtually all spectra. Sound quieted; the wind seemed to offer its wail as though from a great distance. Inthracis could hear the walls squirming in the darkness. His hearts beat faster.

He was under attack, he realized. But who would dare? Bubonis?

The words to a series of defensive spells rose to the front of Inthracis's mind and he whispered the syllables in rapid succession, all while weaving his fingers through the air in a series of intricate gestures. In the span of three breaths, he was warded with spells that would protect him against mental, magical, and physical attacks.

He slid from his cloak a metal wand that fired a stream of acid upon command. Then he levitated toward the high ceiling and listened.

The walls of Corpsehaven rustled with a wet susuration. Decayed hands reached down from the ceiling to paw his robes, as though seeking reassurance. Their touch gave him a momentary start. He heard nothing save his own soft breathing.

It occurred to him then that someone or something had managed to penetrate the intricate wards set about Corpsehaven without triggering any alarms. He knew of no one, not even Kexxon himself, who could have done so.

Worry took hold of him. His grip on the wand tightened.

Within the darkness, a sudden heaviness manifested, a palpable presence of power. Inthracis's ears popped; his head throbbed; even the corpses in his walls uttered a cracked scream.

The darkness seemed to grow substantive, to caress him, its touch lighter than that of the corpses, more seductive but also more threatening.

Something was in his library.

Despite himself, Inthracis's three hearts hammered in his chest.

With sudden certainty, he realized that he shared the darkness with a divine power. Nothing else could have so easily invaded his fortress. Nothing else could have so terrified him.

Inthracis knew that he was overmatched. Fighting would be pointless. A god, or perhaps a goddess, had come for him.

He lowered himself to the floor. While it was not quite in him to abase himself, he managed to offer the darkness a stilted bow.

"Your respect is insincere," said a soft, oily male voice in High Drow.

At the sound of the voice, another irritated rustle ran through the corpses, another moan escaped their decayed lips.

"*Their* respect, however, is genuine," said the voice.

Inthracis did not recognize the speaker by voice, but given the word on the wind outside, given the speaker's use of High Drow, Inthracis could infer the speaker's identity. He chose his next words with care.

"It is difficult to offer the proper respect when I do not know to whom I am speaking."

7

A chuckle. "I think you know who I am."

At that, the darkness lightened somewhat, enough that Inthracis's eyes could pierce it. Sound too returned, and the howl of the wind rose.

A masked male drow sat atop Inthracis's basalt table, legs dangling off the edge and not quite reaching the floor. Shadows alternately lightened and darkened around the drow's lithe form, swallowing parts of him in blackness for one moment before coughing them back up to visibility the next. A short sword and dagger hung from his belt, and leather armor peeked out from under his tailored, high-collared cloak. Long white hair, highlighted with red, surrounded an angular, vengeful face. He wore a haughty smile on his thin lips, but it did not reach the holes of his eyes, which were visible even through his black mask.

Inthracis's eyes registered the arcane power emitted by the drow's blades, the armor, his very flesh. He recognized the avatar, and it was as he had suspected.

"Vhaeraun," he said, and was irritated that he did not quite keep the awe from his voice.

He looked upon Vhaeraun the Masked God—Lolth's son and Lolth's enemy. His hearts hammered still more, and his legs felt weak though he managed not to show it. In the flitting shadows around the drow, he saw that the avatar's hand was severed at the wrist. The stump seeped blood onto the table.

Inthracis did not care to contemplate how a god might have been so wounded. He also did not care to contemplate why Vhaeraun would be manifesting in Corpsehaven. Inthracis rarely had contact with drow, living or dead, mortal or divine. Drow souls did not typically end up in the Blood Rift.

Vhaeraun hopped off the table and sniffed the air. His dark eyes narrowed.

"Even the air *here* stinks of spider," the god said.

To that, Inthracis said nothing. He dared not speak until he knew exactly what was happening. A dozen possibilities danced through his mind, none of them desirable.

"I require a service, yugoloth" Vhaeraun said, and the whisper of his voice went hard.

Inthracis stiffened. Not a favor, not a request—a service. It was worse than he had feared. He ran his long forked tongue over his lip ridges while he tried to formulate a suitably vague response.

The darkness swallowed Vhaeraun, and in the next heartbeat the avatar stood behind Inthracis, his breath hot in the ultroloth's upper left ear.

"Would you refuse me?" Vhaeraun asked, his soft words dripping menace.

"I would not, Masked Lord," Inthracis answered, though he would have if he could have. While yugoloths *were* mercenaries, even they had their limits when it came to patrons. Inthracis had no desire to get involved in whatever divine conflict Vhaeraun may have been engaged in with his mother.

The next moment Vhaeraun was no longer behind him but across the room near one of Inthracis's bookshelves. The corpses in the wall recoiled as much as their contorted forms allowed at the nearness of the god. Dead eyes stared out of the wall in horror. Even those dead whose hands and arms formed the bookshelf tried to squirm back into the wall, and a score of priceless tomes clattered to the floor. Vhaeraun eyed them and tsked.

Inthracis wondered how his corpses perceived Vhaeraun's appearance. Surely not that of a drow male.

Vhaeraun looked up and said, "Listen." He cocked his head to the side and his eyes went hard. "Do you hear it?"

The wind outside rose and fell, carrying its message of Lolth's Chosen. The corpses near Vhaeraun moaned again.

Inthracis nodded. "I hear it, Masked Lord. *Yor'thae.* It says *Yor*—"

Vhaeraun hissed and held up a hand, silencing Inthracis. The eyes of the corpses in the walls went wide at the demonstration of divine pique.

"Once is enough, ultroloth," said Vhaeraun. "So you hear the word, but do you know its meaning?"

Inthracis nodded slowly, fear growing in his gut, but Vhaeraun went on as though he had answered in the negative.

"The *Yor'thae* is the chosen vessel of the Spider Bitch. And this, all this—" With alarming suddenness, the avatar again stood behind

Inthracis, hissing angrily in his ear as the fortress shook once more—"is the effort of the Queen of the Demonweb Pits to summon her Chosen and transform herself."

Inthracis gulped, sensing the god's rage, sensing the danger he was in.

Vhaeraun reappeared in the shadows across the room, and Inthracis allowed himself a breath. Vhaeraun reached out with his good hand and ran his fingertips along the bodies in the wall. They squirmed, moaning anew. Vhaeraun's fingers came away glistening, and he smiled.

"What do you want of me, Masked Lord?" asked Inthracis, though he knew he would not like the answer.

In an instant, Vhaeraun stood before him, teeth bare, face hot with rage.

"What I want, you insignificant insect, is my mother's heart fed to demons and shat out for my amusement! What I want, you speck of a creature—" he brandished the stump of his wrist before Inthracis's face—"is Selvetarm's obsequious brain torn from his foul head so that I can use his empty skull as a piss pot."

Inthracis said nothing, merely stared, stood rigid, and held his breath. He was an instant from death. Even the corpses stood still and silent, as though too terrified even to moan.

Vhaeraun took a breath, visibly calmed himself, and offered Inthracis an insincere smile.

"But first things first, Inthracis the ultroloth. Let me be direct: there are three potential candidates for *Yor'thae*. See them now."

"Wait, Masked Lord—"

But Vhaeraun did not wait. The avatar closed his eyes, and pain knifed through Inthracis's brain. Through the pain an image of three drow females formed in his head, and three names: Quenthel Baenre, Halisstra Melarn, and Danifae Yauntyrr.

The pain subsided, though the image remained, burned into his brain with a divine brand.

Vhaeraun said, "Each of the three are trying to find their way to the city of the Spider whore. My mother is calling them, you see, drawing them to her, testing them as they come. One will be Chosen, one will be her—"

The wind howled anew, and another tremor shook the plane. The word *Yor'thae* sounded once more through the chamber.

"Yes," Vhaeraun said, and an irritated tic caused his eye to spasm. He focused on Inthracis and said, "What I require of you is that you kill all three of the candidates."

Once again, Vhaeraun was suddenly across the library, behind a large lectern.

Inthracis could do nothing else, so he nodded. Privately, he wondered why Vhaeraun could not kill the three drow mortals himself.

The answer occurred to Inthracis a moment after the question: since the so-called Time of Troubles, the Overgod had forbade the gods from directly affecting the existences of mortals. Thus, Vhaeraun needed an ally unbound by the Overgod's edict, a non-divine ally.

The mercenary in Inthracis started to overcome his fear. He saw opportunity and took it.

"And for me, Masked Lord?" he asked, with the proper amount of deference.

Vhaeraun vanished from behind the lectern to appear beside him. Inthracis looked straight ahead, not daring to face the god.

Whorls of shadows curled around them both, black snakes that slithered along Inthracis's leathery skin. Vhaeraun held his unwounded hand before Inthracis's face, and Inthracis saw that the arm was as incorporeal as a shadow up to the elbow. With a smile, Vhaeraun reached *into* Inthracis's body and clutched one of his three hearts. It stopped cold.

Agony raced through Inthracis; his breath caught, and his muscles spasmed. He arched his back, gritted his teeth, but dared not move farther or protest.

"For you?" Vhaeraun whispered in his ear. "For you this: my gratitude, something that is beyond price."

Vhaeraun clutched Inthracis's second heart, stopping it.

Inthracis's vision went blurry. He struggled to draw breath.

"Oh," Vhaeraun said, "and also the destruction of Kexxon and your ascendance to the position of Oinoloth and Archgeneral."

Hearing those words, Inthracis could not contain a grin.

Despite the agony, he managed to hiss, "You are most gracious, Masked Lord."

Still wearing the same smile, Vhaeraun set Inthracis's hearts again to beating with two flicks of his forefinger and withdrew his arm, which became instantly corporeal. Inthracis inhaled sharply, sagged, and kept his feet only through sheer pride.

After he had recovered himself, Inthracis located Vhaeraun— across the room at the desk again—and asked, "What size force is appropriate, my lord?"

"An army," replied Vhaeraun with a derisive wave. "Muster on the new Demonweb Pits, on the *Ereilir Vor*, the Plains of Soulfire. My mother is not yet sensate enough to muster her own forces to stop you."

Inthracis debated with himself before asking, "And what of Selvetarm, Masked Lord?"

Vhaeraun's face twisted in anger, and he said, "He will not trouble you. My mother has removed the Pits to their own location in the multiverse and sealed them against entry by the divine—*any* divine. Events there are beyond the reach of other gods, now. I cannot enter to destroy her, but neither can Selvetarm enter to protect her. Unless he has guessed at my ploy—" Vhaeraun's contemptuous tone indicated that he did not think Selvetarm could guess the sum of two and two—"you will face the mortals alone."

Inthracis dared one more question: "What will occur if the *Yor'thae* reaches the Spider Queen?"

Vhaeraun's eyes narrowed. "Because they will not reach her," he replied, "the answer is irrelevant."

Inthracis said nothing but took Vhaeraun's reply to mean that even the god did not know what would occur. That did not bode well.

He bowed and said, "It is my pleas—"

Vhaeraun vanished without further words.

The red light of the Blood Rift refilled the room. Inthracis took several deep breaths. Even the corpses in the wall seemed relieved. All that remained of Vhaeraun's presence in the room was a smear of blood on the basalt table and lectern. Inthracis summoned an invisible servant armed with a cloth, caused it to absorb the blood, and teleported the cloth to his laboratory. He was certain he could use divine blood as a component for one spell or another. The exercise helped calm him.

He gathered himself and prepared to send word to his generals to sound a muster. Vhaeraun had said to assemble an army. Inthracis would use his best shock troops, the Black Horn Regiment.

Despite the underlying fear of what might occur should he fail Vhaeraun, the ultroloth felt a certain exhilaration. If he was successful, and if Vhaeraun kept his word—a large *if*—Kexxon would be destroyed and Inthracis would unseat him as the Archgeneral of the Blood Rift.

Even as those seductive thoughts coursed through his mind, a more sober voice advised caution. It occurred to him that all of Vhaeraun's scheming might have been in accordance with Lolth's plan. The Masked God had said that Lolth was testing her priestesses as she called them toward the Pits. Perhaps Inthracis and Vhaeraun would be doing nothing more than creating another challenge for the *Yor'thae* to overcome? Or perhaps Vhaeraun was mistaken and none of the three priestesses was to be the *Yor'thae* at all?

Perhaps, Inthracis thought and sighed.

Caught between one god and another, though, he knew he had no choice but to obey. He would do as Vhaeraun had demanded because to do otherwise would result in certain death. Or worse.

Outside, the wind howled its message.

An unbroken line of drow souls extended before and behind Halisstra as far as she could see, a ribbon of Lolth's dead stretching across the infinite, featureless gray aether of the Astral Plane. With Lolth's power apparently returned, the souls were at last free to float toward the Spider Queen's plane, where they would spend eternity.

One after another the souls streamed along in a procession as straight as that of marching soldiers. The orderliness of the line struck Halisstra as strangely incongruous for souls heading into the arms of a goddess who embodied chaos.

Formerly as drab as the gray aether in which they floated, Lolth's reawakening had sent a surge of power through the line of souls, through the Astral Plane, and perhaps through all of the other planes as well. The Spider Queen's stirring had painted the dead in hues reminiscent of life, had reawakened the souls even as Lolth had herself reawakened from her Silence. By reinfusing them with color and purpose, Lolth had marked each of the souls as irrevocably and irretrievably hers.

The words bobbed uncomfortably in Halisstra's consciousness: Irrevocably and irretrievably Lolth's. . . .

Floating in the same gray aether, as anchorless as the souls drifting past, Halisstra looked at her slim black hands. On them, she saw the blood of the countless screaming victims she had sacrificed in Lolth's name. Did not their blood mark Halisstra as irretrievably Lolth's, the same as the souls around her? Wasn't her soul too colored, stained crimson?

She clenched her fists, and looked past the souls and out into the gray nothingness. The same hands that had murdered in Lolth's name were to wield the Crescent Blade of Eilistraee. With it, Halisstra was to kill Lolth.

Kill Lolth. The thought excited her, repulsed her.

Halisstra saw her course clear before her, a path as straight as the line of souls, but she still felt lost. She *was* marked by a goddess, by two goddesses, and at the moment she was not certain whose mark she preferred.

The feeling shamed her.

She felt both Lolth and Eilistraee pulling at her, tugging her in opposite directions, stretching her as thin as parchment. Lolth's reawakening had roused in Halisstra something she had meant to leave for dead in the silver moonlight of the World Above, when she had given herself to the Dancing Goddess.

But it had not died, not really. Could it ever? Lolth's inexplicable pull on Halisstra remained, a troublesome, seductive memory of power, blood, and authority. Halisstra had only her infant faith in Eilistraee with which to shield herself from a lifetime of indoctrination. She did not know if it would be enough. She did not know if she *wanted* it to be enough.

She had spent her life in service to the Spider Queen—killing, *ruling*—and had turned her back on all of it in less than a fortnight. How could that have been a genuine conversion? She had been Houseless, her city destroyed, everything she knew gone. Turning to Eilistraee had been an impulse, almost flippant, and driven by fear of an uncertain future.

Hadn't it?

She did not know, and the uncertainty shook her.

Even while Eilistraeen prayers filled Halisstra's mind, she found herself looking longingly at the manifestations of Lolth's reawakened power that surged through the endless gray of the Astral.

After the Spider Queen's power had traversed the line of souls and revivified them, the Astral Plane itself had exploded in chaos. Maelstroms of colored energy formed here and there in the aether, churning vortexes of violence that spun rapid circles for a few heartbeats or a few hours and dissipated into glorious, acrid showers of sparks. Jagged bolts of black and red energy several leagues in length intermittently knifed across the void, ripped it into pieces for a moment, and raised the hairs on Halisstra's arms and head. Lolth's power fairly saturated the plane.

And it felt different than Halisstra remembered—more vital, but also somehow incomplete.

Halisstra found the flashing storms of power a tantalizing suggestion of the Spider Queen's might, a seductive reminder of different prayers, of a different kind of worship. Lolth's power was everywhere around her. Lolth herself seemed everywhere around her, knowing her, tempting her, whispering to her.

And always the whispers were the same: *Yor'thae.*

The word was promise, threat, and imprecation all at once.

Halisstra did not know whether to smile or cry each time she heard the word sigh across the Astral winds. As a *bae'qeshel*, she was trained in lost lore and knew what the word meant. Its etymology came from two words in High Drow: *Yorn*, meaning "servant of the goddess"; and *Orthae*, meaning "sacred." The *Yor'thae* was Lolth's Chosen, her sacred servant, the vessel through which Lolth would . . . do something.

But Halisstra did not know what the something was. Though she knew the meaning of the word, she did not understand the word's meaning *for her* or for Lolth. More uncertainty.

Halisstra knew the power of words—her *bae'qeshel* magic depended in part upon words for its power. And like a *bae'qeshel* spell-song, the whispered recitation of *Yor'thae* had enspelled her, had wormed its way into her soul and there planted the seed of doubt. She was at war with herself and struggling to stay whole.

She and the two priestesses of Eilistraee, Uluyara and Feliane, had been following the line of drow souls for what felt like an eternity. A trio of the living trailing an army of the dead, they propelled their bodies through the endless gray mist of the Astral Plane through the force of their will.

The aether appeared to extend forever in all directions, the gray emptiness broken only by the line of souls, occasional islands of floating, spinning rock, and the colorful, whirling maelstroms of Lolth's returned power. Swimming through emptiness, Halisstra felt her senses dulled by the uniformity. Time and again she had to fight down a sense of vertigo, though she couldn't tell whether its source was the infinite space under her feet or the internal struggle taking place in her soul.

"We must be getting closer to the portal," Uluyara said from behind her.

Halisstra didn't turn, only nodded.

With each passing moment, the three priestesses moved closer and closer to their goal, yet with each passing moment Halisstra also became less and less sure of herself and their cause. Hours before, Seyll, a former priestess of Eilistraee, had sacrificed her own soul to shield Halisstra from the infusion of power the reawakened Lolth had sent surging through the Astral aether. Seyll, a woman Halisstra had murdered in life, had chosen the annihilation of her own soul so that Halisstra could complete her charge to kill Lolth with the Crescent Blade of Eilistraee.

But Halisstra was beginning to think she was charged with something else too, something she could not yet see.

Yor'thae, whispered the aether, and Halisstra's body went weak.

She began to suspect that Seyll had allowed herself to be annihilated not so much to protect Halisstra from something but to prevent Lolth's power from touching Halisstra and communicating something to her, something profound. Seyll had gone to oblivion in service to Eilistraee, not Halisstra.

She felt herself standing on the edge of a mystery, at the precise moment just before understanding dawned. If only Seyll had allowed Lolth's power to reach Halisstra she would have—

"No," she said. "No."

But the word sounded as empty as a void.

Halisstra's course had seemed so obvious when she had been staring into the steady crimson eyes of Seyll, when she had heard in the dead priestess's words the promise of hope and forgiveness through worship of Eilistraee, sentiments Lolth and her faithful would have deemed weak. But then Halisstra had encountered Ryld Argith's soul in the Astral. He had been standing in line with the rest of the dead, colorless, awaiting his eternal fate. She had stared into his dead eyes, listened to his listless words, and felt her certainty of purpose crumble. Old feelings had bubbled up from the bottom of her soul. She had wondered, she still wondered, what would happen to Ryld if she somehow did kill Lolth. Would he, like Seyll, be condemned to annihilation?

The thought of it made her chest tight. She would not condemn her lover to nothingness; she *could* not! But what then? The fact that she felt genuine love at all she owed to Eilistraee, and the Dark Maiden had charged her to kill Lolth, had put into her hands a weapon that prophecy said could do it.

But the proximity of Lolth's power quickened Halisstra, tempted her, spoke to her. Halisstra heard Eilistraee calling to her heart, but she felt Lolth calling to her soul. It both appalled and delighted her.

She was terrified.

Yor'thae, said the nothingness.

She closed her eyes and shook her head.

"What do you want?" she whispered.

She was distantly conscious of her body slowly sinking in the aether but did not care. She had forsworn Lolth—she had! She'd made herself a willing apostate. She had embraced Eilistraee's faith, sworn herself to the Dancing Goddess under the light of the moon on the surface of the World Above.

But . . .

But her conversion had occurred at the end of a sword's point. She had been implicitly threatened with death by the priestesses she had come to call sisters. Was it not all a sham then, driven by the need of a homeless drow priestess without access to her spells to find acceptance and a home somewhere, *anywhere?*

No, she thought, and pressed her fingers hard against her brow as though she could drive them into her brain and pluck out that part of her that still longed for Lolth. Her conversion *had not* been forced. It had been willing, beautiful, soul opening . . .

A hand, a *steadying* hand, closed gently on her bicep, stopped her descent, and pulled her around. She opened her eyes and found herself staring into the intense red eyes of Uluyara. The drow High Priestess of Eilistraee looked comfortable in her mail and forest green tunic. A sword hung from her hip, a war horn from her neck. A host of magical tokens—feathers, buttons, and pins—hung from her tabard. Her full mouth wore a look of genuine concern for Halisstra, but behind the concern, deep in her eyes, lurked something else—something Halisstra could not quite identify.

"Are you all right?" Uluyara asked. She gave Halisstra a gentle shake. "Halisstra, are you all right?"

Beside them, the parade of souls continued to stream past, so quickly they looked blurry. Black lightning split the aether neatly in two. Maelstroms churned. The voice whispered. Uluyara's white hair waved in the Astral wind. Her armor, weapons, and clothing appeared dull compared to the color of the souls. They all looked dull compared to Lolth's dead.

Halisstra blinked, managed a nod, and said, "Yes. I'm just . . . troubled, from seeing Ryld."

Uluyara's eyes showed understanding, though her hard expression held little sympathy. Halisstra knew that the death and afterlife of Ryld Argith little concerned Uluyara. The High Priestess was focused on their goal of finding and killing Lolth; nothing else mattered to her.

Yor'thae, whispered the Astral.

Hearing the word again, Halisstra felt her cheeks burn. She looked for a reaction from Uluyara, but the High Priestess showed no sign of having heard anything.

"Did you not hear that?" Halisstra asked, fearful of the answer.

Uluyara stiffened, cocked her head, and looked around warily. Her eyes came back to Halisstra.

"Hear what?" she asked. "The souls? The lightning? There is nothing else."

Before Halisstra could answer, Feliane floated beside Uluyara and put a gentle hand on Halisstra's mailed shoulder. The slight elf priestess wore a suit of fine mail and a small round helmet out of which her long brown hair streamed. A thinblade hung from her narrow hips. She looked like an armed child sent off to do battle. Was Eilistraee so desperate?

"It is the murmur of the souls as they journey to their fate," Feliane said. She looked upon the dead and her round eyes were sorrowful. "Nothing more."

Uluyara nodded agreement. The souls did mutter as they streamed past, a low, barely audible hum, but Halisstra knew the whisper of *Yor'thae* was something else, something audible only to her.

"The damned of Lolth do not go quietly to their fate," Uluyara said, and unlike Feliane, Halisstra saw no sorrow in the High Priestess's red eyes. In her own way, Uluyara was as merciless a priestess as any servant of Lolth. "Perhaps they sense at the last the mistake they have made."

Halisstra jerked her arm free of Uluyara and glared into the priestess's eyes.

"I loved one of those damned," she said and could not keep the bitterness out of her voice.

Uluyara stiffened; her eyes flashed, but she said only, "I had forgotten. Forgive my insensitivity, sister."

Halisstra heard no sincerity in Uluyara's voice.

Feliane, her voice gentle, said, "Peace, sisters. We're all tired. You especially, Halisstra, since you carry so heavy a burden. Uluyara and I will help you bear it, but you must let us. Eilistraee too will help you bear it, but you must also let her." She paused before adding, "Do you believe that?"

Her grip on Halisstra's shoulder tightened.

Halisstra looked from Uluyara and Feliane and was suddenly aware of the looks-behind-the-looks on the faces of the Eilistraeeans. She floated between them, speared by their gazes, their expectant expressions. She realized then what she had seen moments before in Uluyara's eyes: doubt.

They doubted her or were beginning to doubt her.

She felt a flash of anger, but it dissipated almost immediately; she also saw genuine concern in their eyes. They loved her and accepted her as a sister despite their doubt. Halisstra's mind turned to Quenthel and Danifae, her former "sisters" in faith, both so different from Uluyara and Feliane. Quenthel would not have abided doubt; and Danifae . . .

Danifae Yauntyrr stood on the same precipice on which Halisstra recently had stood, teetering between Lolth and Eilistraee, torn between the habits of an old life and the hope of a new one, afraid to take the next step. Halisstra believed that Danifae too could come over to the Dancing Goddess, if only she *would*.

In a visceral way, Halisstra *needed* Danifae to submit to the faith of Eilistraee. Through the Binding, she had come to know Danifae well. They were very much alike, Halisstra and her former battle-captive. She knew that Danifae too could be redeemed, that she could be turned from Lolth, and she knew too that Danifae's redemption would validate Halisstra's own.

"Halisstra?" Feliane said.

Halisstra looked from one to the other of her sisters and forgave them for their doubt. How could she be angry at them for doubting her when she was beginning to doubt herself?

"Halisstra?" asked Feliane again, her hazel eyes soft but her grip hard. "Do you believe what I have just said? That we and the Dancing Goddess will help you bear your burden?"

Halisstra looked into Feliane's eyes and managed a nod. "I believe it," she said, but was not sure that their help would be enough.

Uluyara blew out a breath and said, "Perhaps we should make an offering to the Lady before venturing farther?"

"A good idea," Feliane said, still eyeing Halisstra.

Uluyara took from around her neck a pendant of silver, upon which was engraved a sword encircled by a swirling ribbon—Eilistraee's holy symbol. She cradled it in her palms.

Yor'thae, hissed the aether, and Halisstra detected a note of anger in the wind's voice.

"This is an ill place for a dance," Feliane said, looking around at the souls and gray swirls.

"True," answered Uluyara, "but let us at least take a moment to pray."

All agreed, and together the three worshipers of the Dancing Goddess, two drow elves and a moon elf, gathered into a circle and asked Eilistraee for strength and wisdom while the souls of Lolth's damned streamed by, while the storms of Lolth's power raged around them. Halisstra felt like a hypocrite throughout.

Afterward, with doubt still stabbing at her, she asked her sisters, "Are we certain that we can we do this?" She had asked them the question before, but she needed to hear the answer again. She put her hand to the hilt of the Crescent Blade, scabbarded at her waist. It felt warm against her flesh. "This is only a blade. And we are only three."

Uluyara and Feliane shared a look of concern before Feliane said, "That is the Crescent Blade, Halisstra, consecrated by Eilistraee. It will serve. And you must not think that our strength is measured in numbers. Our strength is measured in faith."

Halisstra was not sure that her own faith would provide much strength. Still, she looked into her sisters' eyes and saw firm resolve there. She took what strength she could from them.

Uluyara nodded at the line of shades moving past and said, "Let us continue. Our path remains clear. The gates to Lolth's domain are now open. The souls will lead us to her."

Halisstra tried to imagine what it would be like to stand before Lolth, to do battle with the goddess she had worshiped for almost her entire life. She could not conceptualize it. It seemed absurd. And yet . . .

Perhaps it was possible.

"She is awake but I am not certain that she is fully returned," Halisstra said. "She is calling across the cosmos for her *Yor'thae,* her Chosen."

Feliane and Uluyara stared at her for a long moment.

"Yor'thae," Uluyara said, tasting the word on her tongue and crinkling her forehead at its flavor. "How do you know this?"

"I heard the term once, long ago," Halisstra lied.

Uluyara bored into her. "That's not what I mean, Halisstra Melarn. I mean: How do you know that she is calling for her Chosen now?"

Halisstra felt her whole body flush. She knew that she had just increased whatever doubt they harbored. Shame warred with defiance within her, and defiance won.

With effort, she recovered the dignity and assurance that had been trained in her from birth as the First Daughter of House Melarn.

"By my soul," she said, with as much certainty in her tone as she could muster, "I serve Eilistraee the Dark Maiden. Do not doubt it. Lolth's voice is an echo in my mind. A distant echo."

Her sisters continued to eye her. Feliane was the first to speak. Her angular, pale face wore a soft smile.

"I hear truth in your words," she said and looked to Uluyara. "That is enough for me."

"And me," Uluyara said and looped her pendant around her neck. "Forgive us, Halisstra. It just seemed strange that Eilistraee would choose one so recently separated from the Spider Queen to bear her blade. That strangeness made me . . . concerned." She took a breath and straightened. "But it is not for us to question the will of the Dark Maiden. You *are* the bearer of the Crescent Blade. Come. We'll follow these unfortunates to Lolth and do what we came to do."

With that, the three set out again, following the line of the dead. Uluyara's words bounced over Halisstra's brain, and she could not help but wonder what exactly it was that she had come to do.

Yor'thae, said the wind into her ear.

As they flew through the fog of the aether, the energy bolts and power maelstroms grew more common. Halisstra's entire body felt charged, energized.

"We're getting closer to the source of Lolth's power," she said, and Feliane and Uluyara nodded. Only afterward did it occur to her to feel alarm that proximity to Lolth's power quickened her soul.

A short time later, they saw ahead a huge whirlpool of black and viridian energy, slowly churning. Its eight spiral arms extended out into the aether to almost the length of a crossbow shot. The whole of the maelstrom reminded Halisstra of a stylized rendering of a spider. She found its slow rotation hypnotic. One after another the souls streamed into it and vanished.

"That is the doorway to Lolth's plane," Halisstra said.

A bolt of ochre lightning split the emptiness.

Her companions nodded, eyeing the maelstrom. Feliane looked more pale than usual. The weight of their charge was settling on all of them.

"Are you prepared?" Halisstra asked, as much of herself as her comrades. She drew the Crescent Blade from its scabbard. In her other hand, she held her small steel shield—*Seyll's* shield.

Face grim, eyes fixed, Uluyara nodded. She drew her own blade, put her horn to her lips, and sounded a short blast that echoed through the Astral. The souls showed no sign of having heard.

Feliane drew her thinblade and readied her round shield. She looked so small.

"Follow me," Halisstra said and propelled herself toward the whirl-pool. She was careful to look none of the souls in the face.

She realized as she entered the portal that they should have taken a moment to offer a prayer to the Dark Maiden before entering Lolth's domain. She was certain the oversight had been accidental.

Almost certain.

As the energy of the gate took her, she felt herself being pulled between the planes. As she came apart, the word *Yor'thae* sounded once more in her ears.

As he stepped through the portal, Pharaun felt for a moment as though he were being stretched between two points, elongated across a vast distance until he was drawn as thin as the finest parchment. For a fraction of a heartbeat, though he knew it to be absurd and illogical, he felt as if he existed in two places at once.

Then it was over. He snapped forward in space and caught up with the rest of himself at the portal's destination. Healed and refreshed from Quenthel's and Danifae's spells, he stood under a nighttime sky on the rocky ground of the Demonweb Pits, Lolth's domain.

Quenthel stood to his right, regal and serene. Danifae and Jeggred stood to his left, a small, dangerous spider and her hulking draegloth. A cool wind blew from the . . .

Pharaun frowned. He had no sense of direction and nothing from which to gain his bearings.

Danifae looked around, one hand absently tangled in Jeggred's filthy mane. The wind pressed the former battle-captive's *piwafwi* against her body, tracing a sensuous line along the curve of her hips and the fullness of her breasts. She smiled and started to speak, but Quenthel interrupted her.

"We have arrived," Quenthel said in a hushed voice, looking out over the landscape. "The goddess's name be praised."

That seems a bit much, Pharaun thought but did not say. He saw little worthy of praise. Lolth might have moved the Demonweb Pits from the Abyss to its own domain, but the plane remained little more than the same blasted wasteland. He recalled that other gods in the drow pantheon—among them Kiaransalee and Vhaeraun—maintained domains somewhere in the Demonweb Pits. Pharaun could not see where. From what he could see, the whole of the plane was Lolth's.

They stood in the darkness atop a low rise overlooking a rolling plain of rocks that extended to the limits of their darkvision. In the distance, lakes of some caustic substance bled thick smoke into the air. Great chasms and gorges scored the landscape, open wounds in the earth whose depths Pharaun could not determine from afar. Caves, pits, and craters opened everywhere in the soil, like burst boils, or perhaps screaming mouths. Pharaun saw no vegetation of any kind, not even scrub or fungus. The land appeared dead, blasted as if from a great cataclysm.

Thin, curiously curved and kinked tors of black rock jutted at odd angles from the earth. The smallest of them stood as tall as Narbondel but half as big around, and the wind and weather had left each as pockmarked and hole-ridden as the corpses that had littered the streets of the Braeryn a decade before, when black pox had run rampant among Menzoberranzan's poor. There were hundreds of them, and several had toppled over the years. The broken chunks lay strewn over the ground.

Pharaun studied them for a few moments more, struck with something about their shape. They were reminiscent of something. . . .

"Are those the petrified legs of spiders?" he asked and was certain of it even as the words left his mouth.

"Impossible," Jeggred said with a snort.

But Pharaun knew better. The spires of black stone poking out of the ground were the weathered legs of petrified spiders, spiders that must have been as large in life as the stalactite fortress of House Mizzrym. The Pits had buried their bodies long ago, leaving only the legs exposed. Pharaun imagined the bloated stone bodies that must lie below the surface. He wondered if the spiders had died and been turned to stone in whatever cataclysm had left the Demonweb Pits a wasteland.

"If Master Mizzrym is right," Quenthel said, eyes flashing, "we would have been blessed indeed to have seen such servants of the Spider Queen in life."

Pharaun thought that he had seen more than enough servants of Lolth already. He put the huge, dead arachnids out of his mind and examined his surroundings more closely.

Webs covered everything, some of ordinary size, some of enormous proportions. They hung like silvery curtains between many of the spires, blanketed the tunnel mouths, shrouded the open ground, blew over the landscape in sticky balls, and floated on the wind like the snow Pharaun had felt on the World Above. Some were larger than the calcified webs of Ched Nasad.

"Her webs encase all," Quenthel said.

"And the world is her prey," Danifae added.

Behind them, there was no evidence of the portal. The journey from the old Demonweb Pits to the new had been one way. Spells would have to return them home, *if* they returned home.

The wind picked up into a gust, spraying dirt and webs. An eerie keening gave Pharaun gooseflesh.

It took him a moment to pinpoint the source of the sound: some of the webs, thick-stranded, silvery nets strung here and there, vibrated when the wind passed through them. The vibrations caused a haunting scream that rose and fell with the breeze. The spinners of the webs were head-sized, long legged, elegant looking spiders with narrow red-and-yellow bodies.

"Songspider webs," Quenthel said, following Pharaun's gaze. A hint of awe colored her tone. "The voice of Lolth."

She held her viper-headed whip in one hand and the five red and black snakes swayed to the keening, as though hypnotized. Quenthel leaned an ear toward the serpents and nodded at something they mentally communicated to her.

"The webs call to Lolth's Chosen," Danifae added, eyeing Quenthel.

"Indeed," Quenthel said, giving Danifae a veiled look.

Pharaun thought "Lolth's Chosen" a poor choice of words. Even he knew that the Spider Queen did not so much choose as offer. The one who seized her offer—Quenthel, no doubt—would become her Chosen.

In any event, he heard no words in the keening of the webs, though he did not doubt Danifae's claim. Lolth spoke only to her priestesses, not to males.

He looked up to see a cloudy, starless night sky roofing the ruined landscape. Through a single hole in the cloud cover, like a window, a cluster of eight red orbs glared earthward. Seven burned brightly; one was dimmer. They were grouped like the eyes of a spider, like Lolth's eyes. Pharaun felt the weight of them on his back.

Below the clouds but still high in the sky, green, yellow, and silver vortices of power churned and spun. Some lasted a breath, some longer; but all eventually dissolved into a hissing explosion of sparks as new vortexes formed. Pharaun took them to be a byproduct of Lolth's reawakening, the remnants of divine dreams, perhaps, or the afterbirth of chaos. Often, one of the vortices would eject what Pharaun assumed to be a soul.

The glowing spirits thronged the night sky, a semi-translucent, colorful swarm flitting through the dark like a cloud of cave bats. Most of them were drow, Pharaun saw, though he saw too an occasional half-drow, draegloth, and even a rare human. They paid no heed to Pharaun and his company—if they could even see them from so high up—but instead fell into a rough line and flew off in generally the same direction.

"A river of souls," Jeggred said.

"Which appears to have a current," Pharaun observed, watching the souls form up and flow as one toward some unknown destination.

"Lolth has broken her Silence and now draws her dead to her," Danifae murmured. "They are nothing but shadows now, but they will be re-clad in flesh if their petition is accepted."

Quenthel stared at Danifae with a look of such contempt that Pharaun could not help but admire the expressiveness of her features.

"Only if they reach Lolth's city and are found worthy, battle-captive," Quenthel said. "That is a journey that I, and only I, have already made once."

Danifae answered Quenthel with an impertinent stare. The expression did nothing to diminish the beauty of her face.

"No doubt the Mistress of Arach-Tinilith was found worthy as a shade," Danifae said, and her tone made the words more question than statement. More importantly, her choice of honorific suggested that she did not acknowledge Quenthel to be the highest ranking priestess in attendance.

Quenthel's eyes narrowed in anger, but before she could respond, Danifae said, "And no doubt the *Yor'thae* too must make the journey to Lolth's city to be found worthy. Not so, Mistress Quenthel?"

Another strong breeze excited the webs near them and set them again to singing. In the keening, Pharaun fancied he heard the whisper of *"Yor'thae."*

Quenthel and the serpents of her whip eyed Danifae. The Mistress of Arach-Tinilith tilted her head at something projected into her mind by her scourge.

"Can you not answer that question without the aide of your whip, aunt?" Jeggred said with sneer.

The heads of Quenthel's weapon swirled with agitation. The high priestess kept her face passive and strode up to the draegloth and Danifae. Both priestesses seemed lost in the shadow of Jeggred's bulk.

Jeggred uttered a low growl.

"Did you say something to me, nephew?" Quenthel asked, and the serpents of her whip flicked their tongues.

Jeggred stared down at his aunt and opened his mouth to speak.

Danifae placed a hand on the muscular forearm of his fighting arm, and the draegloth held his tongue.

"You spoke out of turn, Jeggred," Danifae said and lightly slapped his arm. "Forgive him, Mistress Quenthel."

Quenthel turned her gaze to Danifae while her whip serpents continued to regard Jeggred with cold menace.

Quenthel stood a full hand taller than Danifae, and with the strength granted her by her magical belt she probably could have snapped the younger priestess's spine with her hands. The battle-captive kept her hand clear of the haft of her morningstar.

"For a moment, it seemed as if you had forgotten yourself, Danifae Yauntyrr," Quenthel said, in a tone of voice reserved for scolding children. "Perhaps the planar travel has disoriented you?"

Before Danifae could answer, Quenthel's gaze hardened and she said, "Allow me to remind you that I am the High Priestess Quenthel Baenre, Mistress of Arach-Tinilith, Mistress of the Academy, Mistress of Tier Breche, First Sister of House Baenre of Menzoberranzan. You are a battle-captive, the daughter of a dead House, a presumptuous child lacking the wisdom to temper your snide tongue." She held up a hand to forestall Danifae's response. "I will forgive your presumption this time, but consider well your next words. When Lolth's decision is made, her Chosen may feel compelled to right previous insolence."

Beside Danifae, Jeggred's rapid respiration sounded like a duergar's forge bellows. The powerful claws on the ends of his fighting arms clenched and unclenched. He looked at his aunt as though she were a piece of meat.

In answer, the heads of Quenthel's whips hissed into his face.

Out of prudence, Pharaun called to mind the words to a spell that would immobilize Jeggred, should the need arise. He knew where his loyalties would lie if the rift between Quenthel and Danifae became an open battle. Quenthel had just recited her title to Danifae. Pharaun would have added one more: *Yor'thae* of the Spider Queen. Lolth had brought Quenthel back from the dead. For what other purpose would the Spider Queen have done so?

To her credit, Danifae stood her ground in the face of Quenthel's anger and showed not the least fear. Her striking gray eyes revealed nothing. She lifted her hand and made as though to raise it to Quenthel's face, perhaps to stroke her cheek. When the whip-serpents turned from Jeggred to hiss and snap at her fingers, she jerked it back.

"Those days are past," Quenthel said, through a tight jaw.

Danifae sighed and smiled. "I seek only to see that you fulfill your destiny, Mistress of Arach-Tinilith," she said, "and to do the will of the Spider Queen."

While Pharaun mentally dissected the reply for the meaning within the meaning, Quenthel said, "We all know what is the will of the Spider Queen. Just as we all know who will be the Spider Queen's Chosen. Speaking names is unnecessary. Signs will bespeak the *Yor'thae*. Let each interpret those as they will. But an unfortunate fate awaits those who misinterpret."

Danifae's beautiful face adopted an unreadable veil but she held Quenthel's eyes. "An unfortunate fate indeed," she said.

Quenthel gave Danifae a final look, turned back to the draegloth, and asked, "And you, Jeggred. You have had an opportunity to reconsider your course. Is there something you wish to say to me now?"

Pharaun could hardly contain a grin. Quenthel Baenre had arrived in Lolth's domain a new woman. No longer was she the whispering, diffident female who spoke only to her whip; she was once again the Mistress of Arach-Tinilith who had led them from Menzoberranzan, the First Sister of the most powerful House of the city.

In that moment, Pharaun thought her more sexually appealing than even Danifae.

In the next moment, he realized he had been too long away from his paid harlots.

Jeggred too must have sensed the change in his aunt. Had Pharaun ever pitied anything in his life—he had not, of course—he might have pitied the draegloth. Instead, he found Jeggred's obvious discomfiture amusing and deserved. The half-demon had thrown his allegiance to Danifae and was facing the consequences of that mistake. Quenthel would not be forgiving.

Jeggred started to speak, but Danifae, still staring at Quenthel, shook her head, once only, a small gesture that quieted the draegloth as effectively as a silence spell.

"Softly," Danifae commanded.

Jeggred deflated and said to Quenthel, "No . . . aunt."

He did not make eye contact. His four hands went slack to his sides, and his eyes dropped.

Pharaun cocked an eyebrow in appreciation. By referring to Quenthel by her familial instead of her formal title, Jeggred had avoided directly offending Quenthel further yet had not contradicted anything implied by Danifae. Perhaps the half-demon was but a half-oaf instead of a whole.

While her whip kept vigil over Danifae and Jeggred, Quenthel turned to Pharaun, insulting Danifae by showing her her back.

"And you, Master of Sorcere," she asked, "have you any thoughts on this matter?"

Pharaun knew she didn't really want his opinion; he was only a male, after all. She wanted him to make his loyalties clear. He considered evading the question but quickly decided against it. House Baenre was the First House of Menzoberranzan; Gromph Baenre was his superior; Quenthel Baenre was or soon would be Lolth's Chosen. The time had passed for vagaries. Perhaps as a reward for straightforwardness Quenthel would allow him to kill Jeggred.

"Mistress," he replied, and his use of the title gave his answer to Quenthel's question, "it appears that Master Hune has taken his leave."

Quenthel smiled and her gaze showed approval.

Behind the Mistress of Arach-Tinilith, Danifae glared hate at him. Jeggred licked his lips and the promise of violence in the draegloth's eyes was clear.

"Hune served his purpose, Master Mizzrym," Quenthel replied, "and his absence now is of no moment." She turned back and looked at Jeggred and Danifae. "All will serve Lolth's purpose, before the end. All."

"The world is her prey," Danifae answered.

Quenthel smiled indulgently, turned on her heel, and walked away a few steps to survey the landscape. She touched her holy symbol and whispered a prayer. Four of the serpents glared over her shoulder at the former battle-captive and draegloth. One, K'Sothra, hovered near her ear.

Danifae stared impassively at Quenthel's back, then turned to sneer at Pharaun.

You are a fool, as ever, she signed.

Pharaun made no reply except a smirk that he knew to be infuriating.

Jeggred too stared at Pharaun, his expression hungry. Pharaun met his gaze and smiled insincerely.

The mage looked around at the blasted realm and said to Quenthel, "Hardly hospitable, is it, Mistress? I think Master Hune may have shown unparalleled wisdom in avoiding this leg of our little journey."

Quenthel made no reply, but Jeggred uttered a growl and snarled, "I should have killed that mercenary and eaten his heart."

In Jeggred's words, Pharaun saw an opportunity to reinforce his loyalty to Quenthel. He took it, knowing the draegloth would be easy to manipulate.

"Eat his heart?" he asked. "As you did Master Argith?"

The half-demon bared his fangs in a grin.

"Exactly like Argith," said the draegloth, smacking his lips. "His heart's blood was delectable."

A gob of yellow saliva dripped from the corner of Jeggred's mouth and splattered in the scree.

Ryld Argith's death bothered Pharaun not at all, but he could use it, and Jeggred, to make a point to Quenthel. Besides, he enjoyed jibing the half-demon.

"Surely you are not so intellectually infirm as to think that Master Argith's death excites my sentiments?" he asked.

Jeggred growled, flexed his claws, and advanced a step.

Pharaun continued, "I am, however, stunned that one of your obviously limited intellectual gifts even knows the meaning of 'delectable.' Well done, Jeggred. At least something you've said this night befits a Baenre."

Quenthel responded with a single laugh, and Pharaun knew he had made his point.

Jeggred lurched forward, his fighting arms outstretched. Danifae clutched his mane and restrained him, her eyes on Pharaun.

"Hold, Jeggred," Danifae said, her voice and manner both as calm as a windless sea. "Master Mizzrym's play is transparent to all but fools."

That last, Pharaun knew, was meant for Quenthel.

"I'll have another heart before this is done," Jeggred promised Pharaun, though he did not pull away from Danifae.

Pharaun put his hand to his chest and feigned a wound.

"You've scarred me, Jeggred," he said. "I offer a compliment to your intellect and what do I receive in return? The threat of violence." He looked past the draegloth to Quenthel as though for support. "I am pained beyond measure. Mistress, your nephew is an ungracious brute."

Quenthel turned and said, "Enough of this. Follow me. Lolth calls."

She started slowly down the rise. Danifae whispered something to Jeggred and released his mane.

To Pharaun, she said, "You should be cautious, Master Mizzrym. My hand grows tired on the leash, and things may not be as clear as you think."

Pharaun gave her his smirk. "I am always cautious, Mistress Danifae," he said, choosing the title with deliberateness. "And things are what they are. That too is plain to all but fools."

To that, Danifae said nothing, though her jaw tightened. She turned and followed Quenthel.

Pharaun and Jeggred were alone atop the rise.

The draegloth's eyes burned into Pharaun. His wide chest rose and fell like a bellows, and his bare teeth dripped saliva. Even from five paces, Pharaun caught a whiff of Jeggred's vile breath and winced.

"You are an effete fool," the draegloth said. "And our business is unfinished. I *will* feast on your heart before all is said and done."

Without fear, Pharaun stalked up to the hulking draegloth, the words to a spell that would strip all the skin from Jeggred's body ready in his mind.

"No doubt it will improve your breath," he said.

With that, he walked past the draegloth.

He could feel Jeggred's eyes burning holes in his back. He also could feel the baleful stare of the eight satellites in the sky above.

At a dignified hurry, he moved nearer to Quenthel and Danifae. Jeggred followed, his breath and heavy tread audible five paces behind Pharaun.

When he reached Quenthel's side, he asked, "Now that we are here, where exactly are we to go?"

Quenthel looked into the sky, to the glowing river of souls that shone like the gem-encrusted ceiling of Menzoberranzan's cavern.

"We follow the souls to Lolth," she answered.

"And?" he dared.

Quenthel stopped and faced him, anger in her face. The serpents of her whip flicked their tongues.

"And?" she asked.

Pharaun lowered his gaze but asked, "And what, Mistress? Lolth calls her *Yor'thae* but what is the *Yor'thae* to do?"

For a moment, Quenthel said nothing. Pharaun looked up and found that her gaze was no longer on him.

"Mistress?" he prompted.

She came back to herself. "That is not a matter for a mere male," she said.

Pharaun bowed, his mind racing. He wondered if even Quenthel knew what it was that the *Yor'thae* was to do, what it was that was happening to Lolth. The possibility that she did not troubled him.

Quenthel offered nothing further, and they began again to walk.

Pharaun looked behind him and met Danifae's gaze. She licked her lips, smiled, and pulled up the hood of her cloak.

Around Gromph, hundreds of fires crackled and burned. Black smoke poured into the air, casting the bazaar in a surreal haze. Abandoned shops and booths lay in charred heaps of rubble. The blackened, petrified forms of drow merchants—turned to stone by the touch of the lichdrow Dyrr, shapechanged into the form of a black-stone gigant—lay scattered about like castings. Some of the petrified drow had run like candle wax in the heat of the Staff of Power's explosion; they would never be restored to flesh. Gromph gave their fate no further thought.

Wide, deep scorings from the gigant's thrashings marred the otherwise smooth floor of the bazaar.

Still dazed from the destruction of the staff, Gromph sat in a heap on the cool stone floor with his legs stretched out before him. Smoke leaked from his clothes. His mind moved sluggishly; his senses felt dull.

But not so dull that he was not conscious of his pain. A lot of pain.

Much of his body was burned. He felt as though a million needles were stabbing his skin, as though he had bathed in acid. His once-severed leg still had not fully reattached and sent shooting pains up his thigh and hip. His non-magical clothes—thankfully, not much of his attire—had melted into his flesh, turning his skin into an amalgam of burned meat and cloth. He could imagine how the exposed flesh of his face must look. He was surprised he could still see. He must have closed his eyes—his captured Agrach Dyrr eyes—before the explosion.

He held two charred sticks in his hands. He stared at them, dumbfounded as to their purpose. In appearance, they reminded him of his forearms—thin and burned almost beyond recognition. It took a moment for him to realize what they were: the remnants of the Staff of Power.

With a wince, he uncurled his ruined fingers from the wood and let the pieces of the staff clatter to the ground.

Seeing no movement in the bazaar except Nauzhror, who squatted beside him and clucked nervously, Gromph thought for an absurd moment that the staff's destruction might have annihilated everyone else in Menzoberranzan.

The stupidity of the thought made him smile, and he instantly regretted even that small movement. The charred skin of his lips cracked, causing him an excruciating stab of pain. Warm fluid seeped from the wound and into his mouth. He gave expression to the pain only with a soft hiss.

Gromph was no stranger to pain. If he could endure his own rat familiar eating out his eyes and a giant centipede severing his leg, he could abide a few burns.

"Archmage?" Nauzhror asked. "Shall I assist you?"

The rotund Master of Sorcere put forth a hand as though to touch Gromph's arm.

"Don't touch me, fool!" Gromph hissed through the charred ruin of his face. More blood leaked into his mouth. Pus ran from burst blisters.

Nauzhror recoiled so fast he nearly toppled over. "I-I meant only to aid you, Archmage," he stammered.

Gromph sighed, regretting his harsh tone. It was unlike him to let his emotions rule his words. Besides, the beginning of a plan for dealing with what remained of the lichdrow was taking shape in his mind. And with Pharaun away on the mission to the Demonweb Pits, he would need Nauzhror.

"Of course, Nauzhror," Gromph said. "We must let the ring do its work for a moment more."

"Yes, Archmage," answered Nauzhror.

Gromph knew that the magical ring he wore would heal his flesh. The process was painful, itchy, and slow, but it was as inexorable as the rise of light up Narbondel's shaft. No doubt Gromph could have benefited from a healing spell—which his sisters could again cast, it seemed—but it galled him too much that Triel had already saved him once. The lichdrow had beaten Gromph, turned him to stone, and he would have died or remained a statue forever but for his sister's intervention.

No, he could not ask her or any of the Baenre priestesses for healing or any other aid. Lolth's grace once more abided in them. Things would soon return to normal, and Gromph wished to be no more beholden to the priestesses of the Spider Queen than was absolutely necessary. He knew too well the price. Instead, he would endure a few more moments of agony while the ring regenerated his flesh.

I am pleased that you survived, Archmage, said Prath in his head. The telepathy spell was still working, it appeared.

I share your pleasure, Prath, Gromph answered. *Now be silent.*

Gromph's head ached, and he no more wanted the apprentice's voice rattling around in his head than he did a dagger in his eye.

In only a few moments, his skin was itching all over. He resisted the urge to scratch only with difficulty. After a few more moments, dead flesh started to fall from his body and new, healthy skin grew in its place.

"Archmage?" asked Nauzhror.

"A few more moments," Gromph answered through clenched teeth.

He watched, wincing with pain, as clumps of blistered skin fell from his body and traced his silhouette on the ground. Gromph imagined himself as one of Lolth's spiders, molting its old form and pulling a larger, stronger body from the dead shell. The battle with the lichdrow had taxed him, but ultimately it had not beaten him.

Of course, he reminded himself, the battle was not quite over.

When he felt ready, when most of his dead skin had sloughed away into a grotesque pile on the bazaar's floor, he extended his still-tender hand to Nauzhror.

"Here, help me rise."

Nauzhror took Gromph's hand in his own and pulled him to his feet.

Gromph held still for a moment, gathering himself, testing his regenerated leg, controlling the last vestiges of the pain.

Nauzhror hovered near him, as attentive as a midwife but not touching him.

"I'm quite capable of remaining on my feet," Gromph said but was not sure that he was.

"Of course, Archmage," Nauzhror answered but stayed close.

Gromph took a deep breath and let his shaking legs grow steady. Through his stolen Dyrr eyes, he surveyed the wreckage around him, surveyed the whole of the city.

Except for the smoking ruin of the bazaar, the center of the city remained unaffected by the siege. The great spire of Narbondel still glowed, tolling another day in the life of Menzoberranzan the Mighty. Gromph could not remember if he had lit it or if another had.

He cocked his head and asked Nauzhror, "Did I light Narbondel this cycle?

"Archmage?" Nauzhror asked.

"Never mind," Gromph said.

Only the fact of Menzoberranzan's empty thoroughfares testified to the fact that the city was embattled. The ordinarily thronged streets were as still as a tomb. The Menzoberranyr had confined most of the fighting to the tunnels of the Dark Dominion, the Donigarten, and Tier Breche. The city's center remained untouched by any battle except that between Gromph and the lichdrow.

But that battle had nearly leveled the bazaar.

Gromph turned and looked across the cavern to the great stairway that led to Tier Breche. There on that high rise stood the spine of Menzoberranzan's power, the triad of institutions that had kept it strong and vital for millennia: Arach-Tinilith, Sorcere, and Melee-Magthere.

Flashes, explosions, and smoke illuminated the schools in silhouette. The siege of the duergar from the north continued unabated. Gromph knew that each of the schools was scarred and burned by stonefire bombs, but he knew too that each *stood*.

And soon, the duergar would find the spells of Lolth's priestesses bolstering the defenses, strengthening the counterattacks, and rejuvenating the fallen.

"The duergar are stubborn," said Nauzhror, following his gaze.

"More likely, they are ignorant of Lolth's return," Gromph replied. "But ignorant or stubborn, they soon will be dead."

In Gromph's mind, the battle for the city was already won. The siege of Menzoberranzan soon would end. He allowed himself a moment's satisfaction. He had done the part allotted him, and his city would live.

"Agreed," Nauzhror said. "It is only a matter of time, now."

Gromph turned and looked to the other side of the cavern, where rose the high plateau of Qu'ellarz'orl. If Sorcere, Arach-Tinilith, and Melee-Magthere were Menzoberranzan's spine, the great Houses of Qu'ellarz'orl were the city's heart.

House after House lined the plateau, with House Baenre dominating by far in both size and power. Squatting in House Baenre's shadow along the rise, barely visible from such a distance, were the fortresses of the city's other great houses—Mizzrym, Xorlarrin, Faen Tlabbar, even Agrach Dyrr.

Gromph's eyes narrowed when they fell upon the stalactite wall of the traitor House. Occasional flashes of power and explosions of magical energy lit the Dyrr fortress. The siege by the Xorlarrin mages continued. Gromph imagined that it would for some time. With Yasraena and her underpriestesses once more wielding Lolth's power, the siege could take a long while.

"The Xorlarrin are also stubborn," Gromph observed.

"And greedy," Nauzhror said. "With House Agrach Dyrr defeated and removed from the Ruling Council. . . ." He trailed off.

Gromph nodded. When Agrach Dyrr fell, no doubt House Xorlar-rin hoped to take its place on the Council. Nauzhror observed, "The fall of House Dyrr too is only a matter of time."

Gromph nodded again and said, "But I cannot wait."

Within House Agrach Dyrr, he believed, was the lichdrow's phylactery, the receptacle of the lichdrow's immortal essence. Gromph had to find and destroy it if he was to fully and finally destroy the lichdrow. Otherwise, the surviving essence of the undead wizard, embodied in the phylactery and driven by Dyrr's undying will, would bring itself back together and reincorporate a body within a matter of threescore hours. Were that to occur, the battle between the lichdrow and Gromph would begin anew.

And Gromph no longer had a Staff of Power to sacrifice in order to win.

Another fireball exploded along the parapet of Agrach Dyrr's wall.

"What are you thinking now, Yasraena?" he asked softly.

Gromph knew that the Matron Mother of House Agrach Dyrr already would have learned of the lichdrow's fall; likely she was scrying Gromph even then.

Like Gromph, Yasraena would know that the lichdrow was not fully dead until and unless his phylactery was destroyed.

"Did he confide its location to you, Matron Mother?" he whispered.

"Archmage?" Nauzhror asked.

Gromph ignored Nauzhror. He thought it unlikely that the lichdrow would have shared the location of his phylactery with Yas-raena. He imagined that the relationship between the lichdrow and the Matron Mother would have been a tense one, not unlike that between Gromph and his sister Triel. Likely, Yasraena no more knew the location of the lichdrow's phylactery than did Gromph. But like Gromph, Yasraena would look first to her own House, the most likely hiding place.

She already would be looking for it, Gromph knew. He had little time. He would have to find a way through the defensive wards of one of Menzoberranzan's great Houses while it was under siege and while its Matron Mother and her underpriestesses—all once more armed with spells from Lolth—would be awaiting him.

He almost laughed. Almost.

"Come, Nauzhror," Gromph said. "We return to my sanctum. The war for the city is won, but there is a battle or two yet to be fought."

Prath, he sent to the young Baenre apprentice. *Meet us in my offices.*

Yasraena stood over the marble scrying basin and watched the image of Gromph Baenre waver and fade as he and his fellow mage teleported away from the ruined bazaar. There was no sign of the lichdrow. The undead wizard's body had been utterly destroyed.

But not his soul, she reminded herself, not his essence, and that reminder gave her hope.

Though her heart pounded in her chest, Yasraena kept her expression outwardly calm. With the lichdrow . . . absent, she was the true and only head of House Agrach Dyrr. It would not do to show alarm.

Two of her four daughters, Larikal and Esvena, the Third and Fourth Daughters of the House and each a lesser priestess of Lolth, stood to either side of her. Her First and Second Daughters were occupied supervising the defenses of the House against the besieging Xorlarrin forces, so it fell to Larikal and Esvena to gather intelligence and spy on the House's enemies. Both were taller than Yasraena, and Larikal bordered on heavyset, though neither was as strongly built as their mother. But both *had* inherited Yasraena's ambition. Both were as eager as any drow priestess to kill their way to the top of their House.

Three males too stood in the chamber, on the other side of the basin. All were graduates of Sorcere and apprentices of the lichdrow. They seemed stunned that their undead master had been defeated. Slack hands hung limply from the sleeves of their *piwafwis*. Yasraena saw fear in their stances, uncertainty in their hooded red eyes. It disgusted her but she expected little better from males.

"The Archmage has retreated to his sanctum," said Larikal. "He is beyond our ability to scry."

Yasraena vented her frustration on her daughter. "You state the obvious as though it were profound. Be silent unless you have something useful to say, fool."

Larikal's thin-lipped mouth hardened in anger but her crimson eyes found the floor. The male wizards shifted uneasily, shared surreptitious glances. Yasraena gripped her tentacle rod so tightly in her hand it made her fingers ache. She would have strangled the lichdrow herself, had he stood before her.

Look where his plotting had gotten her House!

She stared at the dark water of the stone basin and tried to think.

The battle for the city was over, or would be soon. When the great Houses mustered their priestesses—priestesses again capable of casting spells—the tide of battle would turn rapidly. The duergar and tanarukks would be routed. Her House would stand alone against the combined might of all of Menzoberranzan.

Despite the dire situation, Yasraena held onto hope. After all, House Agrach Dyrr had single handedly annihilated several noble Houses in recent centuries, both under her stewardship and that of her sister Auro'pol, the previous Matron Mother. The Dyrr knew how to fight.

For a heartbeat, she entertained other options.

She could flee the city, but where would she go? Would she become a Houseless vagabond, wandering the Underdark or the outer planes with her hands out? The thought appalled her. She was the Matron Mother of House Agrach Dyrr, one of the great Houses of Menzoberranzan, not some beggar!

No, she would live or die with her House. She would withstand the siege, find a way to make her House useful to another great House, and ultimately arrange a truce. House Agrach Dyrr would be forced to step down from the Ruling Council, of course, and would have to endure a few centuries of ignominy, but she and it would *survive*. That was her only goal. The House would climb back onto the council in time.

But to realize her hope, she needed the lichdrow. Without him, the House would not withstand the siege much longer. She knew that the undead wizard would reincorporate in only a matter of hours so long as his phylactery remained safe.

Unfortunately, no one seemed to know exactly where the phylactery might be. Her own divinations had been unable to locate it, though she assumed it to be somewhere in House Agrach Dyrr—the lichdrow spent virtually all of his existence within the House. He would not have secreted the phylactery anywhere else. Yasraena knew that Gromph Baenre would make the same assumption and would come for it. She had to find it first, or at least prevent Gromph Baenre from finding it at all. To do the latter, she needed to know what Gromph Baenre was doing at all times.

In the past, her daughters' and the House's wizards' scrying spells had been unable to pierce the wards around Gromph Baenre's sanctum within Sorcere, despite frequent attempts. But they had to find a way to do it, and so they would. Yasraena needed to know when the Archmage was coming.

She looked across the basin to Geremis, the aging, bald apprentice to the lichdrow. At that moment, his hairless head irritated her beyond measure.

"Scour your memories for any clue, Geremis," she commanded. "Or I will extract your brain and sift it with my own fingers. Where would the lichdrow have hidden his phylactery?"

Visibly shaking, Geremis shook his head and did not meet her eyes. "Matron Mother, the lichdrow shared such information with no one. Please. Our divinations have—"

"Enough!" shouted Yasraena, and stomped her foot on the stone floor. "The time for excuses is past. Larikal, you and Geremis organize a team to search the House. By hand, on all fours if necessary! Perhaps an ordinary search can find what spells cannot. Keep me informed on the hour."

She knew that Geremis sometimes shared Larikal's bed. Both were ugly, and the thought of their coupling made her ill.

"Yes, Matron Mother," answer Larikal, not daring to argue. To Geremis, Larikal commanded, "Follow me, male."

Both hurried from the scrying chamber, eager to get out of the way of Yasraena's wrath.

After they had gone, Yasraena looked to Esvena. "You, find a way to penetrate the wards around Gromph Baenre's sanctum within

Sorcere." She eyed the two remaining males, both homely, middle aged wizards; she did not even know their names. "You two, assist her. And bolster our own defenses. If you cannot get through the Archmage's wards, or if he or any Xorlarrin piece of dung breaches ours, I will be displeased."

She let the threat linger in the air.

One of the males cleared his throat and began, "Matron Mother—"

Yasraena lashed out with her tentacle rod. Two of the black, rubbery arms at its end extended themselves and wrapped around the throat of the wizard. He gagged and clutched at the tentacles. His red eyes went wide; his mouth moved but no sound emerged. With a mental command, Yasraena ordered the rod to squeeze the male's throat harder.

"You will speak only when I command it," she said and looked into the face of the other male. He did not meet her gaze. "As I said, the time for excuses is past. Do what needs to be done."

Esvena looked on with a cold smile.

With her free hand, Yasraena backhanded her daughter across the mouth. The younger priestess stumbled back, bleeding from her lip and glaring hate at her mother.

"Do not dare smile in my presence," Yasraena spat. "The fate of our House is at stake. Indulge your petty pleasures after we have defeated our enemies."

Esvena wiped the blood from her lip and lowered her eyes. "Forgive me, Matron Mother," she said.

Yasraena knew the apology to be insincere but would have expected nothing else. She released the male from her rod. He fell to his knees, before the scrying basin, gasping and choking.

"We all live or die with this House," Yasraena announced. "Should I so much as *suspect* treachery or half-efforts, you will be flayed to death, resurrected, and flayed anew. That process will continue indefinitely until my anger is sated. Do not doubt my resolve."

She eyed her daughter, and Esvena's eyes showed real fear. The males did their best to grovel.

"Proceed with the attempt to scry the Archmage's offices," Yasraena said, "and do not stop until you succeed. Gromph Baenre will be coming and I must know when. I will check back on the hour."

As she turned to leave the scrying chamber, a tremor shook the House, a byproduct of the Xorlarrin onslaught.

Telepathically connected to her First and Second daughters through the magical amulets they wore, she projected, *Anival, what is happening?*

Her First Daughter's calm mental voice returned, *Xorlarrin ogre shock-troops bearing a magically augmented battering ram attempted the gates. All of them are dead and the ram ruined. The wards hold, and the Xorlarrin cannot gain even the moat. They appear to be regrouping. Another House may join them soon, Matron Mother.*

Yasraena knew, but to her First Daughter she replied with only, *Very well. Continue on and keep me apprised.*

Yasraena did not know how long her House could withstand the continued siege of the Xorlarrin wizards. Wards and protective spells sheathed the House's moat, bridge, and adamantine wall—some of them Yasraena had cast, some her forbears, many the lichdrow—but wards could be broken. So far, the Xorlarrin had not been able to breach them, but sooner or later, given enough time, they probably would.

Yasraena silently prayed to Lolth that the wards would hold for just a short time longer, long enough for the lichdrow to reincorporate and again stand at her side. That was all she would need to save the House. Unless . . .

Perhaps there was another way. It galled her, but it might save her House.

She would contact Triel Baenre. At the very least, she might be able to give her House more time.

Without another word, she left her underlings behind and headed for her private chambers. As she exited the scrying chamber, she heard Esvena berating the male wizards.

FIVE

Traveling the rocky, uneven terrain proved difficult. Pits, gorges, and smoking lakes of acid forced Pharaun and his three traveling companions to weave a circuitous route. They picked their way around gorges and holes, between the tall, black spires of petrified legs. Pharaun particularly disliked walking in the shadow of the petrified spider legs. He felt at any moment that they would return to life and catch them up in their embrace. Spiders and webs thronged the petrified limbs, darting into cracks and crevices.

The wind fought against them as they moved, and it whistled through the songspider webs. Pharaun was sweating. He felt exposed.

"Mistress," he said to Quenthel. "The passage of hours may bring a dawn. We are under open sky."

Pharaun had no desire to experience the blinding light of another sunrise like he had seen in the World Above.

Quenthel did not look at him. One of her whip vipers—Yngoth,

Pharaun was certain—hovered near her ear for a moment. Quenthel nodded.

"A sun *will* rise over Lolth's Pits," she said. "But it is dim, red, and distant. You have nothing to fear, Master Mizzrym. We will find traveling under its light as easy as traveling by night."

Jeggred snorted and asked, "Do the snakes of your whip fill the holes in your understanding of the Spider Queen's realm, aunt?"

Danifae snickered, or perhaps it was a cough.

Over her shoulder, Quenthel answered, "Sometimes, nephew. They are demons—bound by *me*—and have some knowledge of the Lower Planes that I require them to impart. Perhaps Mistress Danifae can fill in the rest of our understanding?"

She stopped, turned, and looked at Danifae.

The battle-captive did not lower her hood. "When I have something to add," she said, "I will offer it."

Quenthel smiled at her nephew and started again to walk.

"Perhaps we should use spells to transport us, Mistress?" Pharaun suggested to Quenthel, though he did not know exactly where they were going.

Quenthel shook her head and replied, "No, mage. This is the Spider Queen's realm, and she wants us to experience it. We will walk until I say otherwise."

Pharaun frowned but made no other answer. He could have flown, of course, using the ring he had taken from Belshazu, but decided not to provoke Quenthel. For him, the new Demonweb Pits was an obstacle to be overcome. For Quenthel, it was a religious ordeal to be experienced. Circumventing it would have been heresy.

Throughout their nighttime trek, the eight stars of Lolth peered down at them through a hole in the clouds that moved with the satellites across the night sky. Pharaun felt the Spider Queen's gaze pressing into his back like the tips of eight spears. Lolth's voice, in the form of the keening of the wind through the songspider webs, hummed in his ears. Pharaun found it maddening but kept his thoughts to himself.

High above them, the river of souls streamed silently onward. Sparking power vortices continued to dot the sky and vomit forth the spirits of the dead.

Pharaun marveled at the number of drow souls. He knew that all of them must have died after Lolth had fallen silent. Where had they all come from? How many worlds did Lolth's children populate? He hoped many. Otherwise, he feared he would return to find Menzoberranzan as empty as the space between Jeggred's ears. The fact that Gromph had stopped responding to his sendings did not allay his concerns. Possibly the Archmage was too preoccupied with the siege of Menzoberranzan to reply; possibly, Gromph was dead.

He shook his head, pushed away the doubt, and focused on the now.

Pharaun's magical boots allowed him to stride and jump with more ease than the rest, but even he found the footing treacherous. Jagged rocks edged as sharp as daggers, boulders as large as buildings, sheer drop-offs, hidden pits, and shifting fields of loose scree challenged their every step. Most of the pits turned out to be web-lined tunnels that snaked down into the darkness under the landscape. Pharaun assumed that the whole plane must have been honeycombed with them. The stink of rot and a soft, barely audible insectoid clicking floated up from the black depths of the holes. He did not like to think of what might be lurking under their feet.

After a few hours travel, they stopped for a moment to eat their rations of fungus bread, cheese, and cured rothé-meat near the edge of a pit as large across as an ogre's arm span. A disturbing clicking sound emerged from somewhere deep in the darkness of the hole. A musty stink wafted out of it.

"What is that sound?" Jeggred asked above the wind, around a slobbering mouthful of meat.

"What is that smell, you mean," Pharaun corrected. "It's almost as bad as your breath, Jeggred. And I mean that in a brotherly way."

Jeggred answered him with a glare as he tore into another shank of rothé meat.

From under the hood of her cloak, Danifae whispered, "The sound is the voice of Lolth's children."

"Breeding pits, I would guess," Quenthel said by way of clarification and bit into a piece of dried meat.

She held forth her whip, and the serpents snaked their heads downward into the pit and hissed.

The clicking stopped. At the same time, the wind died, and the keening of the songspider webs went silent. The night grew still.

Pharaun's skin went gooseflesh, and the four of them sat motionless, staring into the pit and waiting, expecting a horror to crawl forth. It didn't, and after a time the wind started anew and with it, the keening.

Pharaun hurriedly finished his repast, rose, and said, "Shall we continue?"

Quenthel nodded, Jeggred stuffed another mouthful of cured rothé into his jaws, and they left the pit behind them and moved onward. As they walked Danifae smiled from under her hood at Pharaun with undisguised contempt. She obviously found his discomfort with the plane amusing.

Pharaun ignored her and thought he had never imagined he could so miss Valas Hune. No doubt the mercenary guide could have led them along the path of least difficulty. Or perhaps it was Ryld he missed after all, who would have at least provided a nice partner for conversation. Quenthel and Danifae, on the other hand, simply trekked along under the souls in silence, oblivious to the difficulties of the terrain. And Jeggred was worth speaking to only to taunt.

Webs were everywhere, growing increasingly more common. They coated everything, from the ordinary-sized traps of a black widow to the monstrous, thick-stranded curtains of silver as large as the skinsails on the Ship of Chaos. Pharaun's shoes were caked with webs. The air itself, thick and irritating to his throat, seemed infested with invisible strands.

After several more exhausting hours of travel, webs coated them all in a sticky sheathe. Pharaun had to continually remove the delicate strands from his face so that he could breathe. He felt as though the whole plane was really a giant spider, cocooning them all so slowly that they would not realize their peril until they were wrapped up, immobile, and awaiting the bite of fangs.

Pharaun shook his head and put the image out of his mind.

Despite the many large webs hanging between the boulders and tors, up to then Pharaun had seen only ordinary-sized arachnids, ranging in size from a fingernail to the size of a head. The narrow-bodied, long-legged songspiders were the largest spider he had seen, though he knew there had to be larger ones somewhere. Spiders lurked over, under, and between every rock and hole on the surface. The ground was acrawl with them. Pharaun assumed that the originators of the largest webs must have laired in the tunnels underground, where he hoped they would stay, at least for the time being. The small spiders were enough of an irritant.

Though he knew that not even the smallest of the creatures could sneak through the magical protections of his spells, Sorcere ring, and enchanted *piwafwi*, Pharaun could not shake a constant crawling sensation on his skin.

Danifae and Quenthel, on the contrary, appeared to enjoy allowing the spiders to crawl freely over their skin and hair. Jeggred, of course, seemed as oblivious to the spiders as he was to most everything, though even the half-demon took care not to willfully squash any of the creatures while he walked.

As they picked their way through yet another field of petrified spider legs, Pharaun caught a flash of motion from near the top of one of the tallest of the spires. He stopped and watched, but the motion did not repeat itself.

Curious, and otherwise bored, Pharaun activated the power in his ring and took flight. He rose rapidly into the air up the face of the tor. He spared a look down as he rose and saw his traveling companions looking up after him. He knew then how they all must look to Lolth's eyes—small and meaningless.

When he reached the top of the stone spire, he stopped and hovered in mid-air, the words to a spell ready in his mind.

The wind gusted, rustling his hair and cloak. Farther above him floated the glowing, translucent line of souls, the lowest of which were almost within arm's reach. The spirits did not respond to his presence so he ignored them. Power vortices swirled in the heavens, raining green and blue sparks. Acrid clouds of smoke peppered the air.

From below, Quenthel shouted something, but he could not make it out in the wind. Still, he could imagine what she was probably saying.

He ignored her and focused on the object of his curiosity.

Irregular outcroppings of rock covered the otherwise flat expanse of the tor's top, as if the spider's leg had been hacked off before it had been petrified. Thick webs hung between every outcropping, blanketing the surface in silver.

Hanging there in Lolth's air with Lolth's dead, Pharaun felt inexplicably comfortable, as though soaking in a warm bath. The Demonweb Pits stretched large and alien below him; the sky extended vast and strange above him, but he did not care. He thought that it might be almost comfortable to lie amongst the webs, to wrap himself in their warmth. He floated forward, desperate for a rest.

Within the strands, he saw, prey struggled—large prey. He could not make out their forms because they were covered entirely in webs. The prey nearest him, perhaps agitated by his presence, wriggled, struggled, and some of the web strands parted to reveal an open eye.

Aliisza's sending had hit Kaanyr Vhok like a lightning bolt. The words still bounced around his head.

Lolth welcomes home the dead. She lives.

Then nothing more. Kaanyr had expected Aliisza to return to him, but she had not, nor had she communicated with him since. He found her behavior surprising.

For a moment he had convinced himself that the alu-fiend was lying about Lolth's return, but he knew he was deceiving himself. He had heard no falsehood in her mental voice, and he knew her well enough that he would have been aware had she been telling a lie. She could have been mistaken, so he would confirm her missive, but in his core he knew it to be true. Soon, he and his men would be facing not only Menzoberranzan's soldiers and wizards, but also its priestesses of Lolth. Lots of them.

He had warned Nimor already of Lolth's return, though the drow had not so much as acknowledged the sending.

The ungrateful ass, Kaanyr thought.

According to Kaanyr's spies, Nimor had fled the battle with the Archmage of Menzoberranzan, leaving the lichdrow Dyrr to face the Baenre wizard alone. Details were few, but it appeared that the Baenre wizard had at last prevailed. Apparently, the city's bazaar had been leveled and many Menzoberranyr destroyed or petrified.

At least the lichdrow had done something worthwhile, Kaanyr thought.

Kaanyr evaluated his situation. First, the lichdrow was destroyed and House Agrach Dyrr was closed up and under siege. Second, Nimor Imphraezl had fled. Third, and most importantly, the Spider Queen lived and her priestesses could again cast spells.

The evaluation allowed only one conclusion, and the conclusion settled over him like a shroud.

He had lost the battle for Menzoberranzan.

The realization sat heavily on him. He'd had to turn it around again and again in his mind before he came to accept it.

Sitting on a luxuriously upholstered divan in the magical tent that served as his headquarters, he held a goblet of brandy to his lips and drank. He barely tasted it, though he ordinarily savored its sweetness. He sighed, set the goblet on a nearby table, and sagged back into the cushions of the divan.

He had been so tantalizingly close to victory. So close!

His Scourged Legion had fought well and hard in the tunnels along Menzoberranzan's southeastern border, and in the Donigarten, amidst the dung-fed forests of fungi. He had lost five score of his tanarukks but killed half again that many drow, along with several score of their fighting spiders and a drider or two. For a time, it had appeared that his tanarukks would force their way through the drow lines, penetrate all the way to the great mansions perched on Qu'ellarz'orl, and lay siege to House Baenre itself.

But then he had received Aliisza's sending.

He could not win the battle; he knew that. All that was left was to ensure that he did not lose his hide, and that would require quick action. He had no doubt that the drow and their priestesses were planning counterattacks even then.

Fortunately, Kaanyr Vhok had a plan. He would use Horgar and the duergar to cover the retreat of his Scoured Legion. The stinking, incompetent little waddlers had done nothing in the battle for the city other than hide behind siege walls and lob their stonefire bombs at Tier

Breche. If the duergar forces actually had gained and held even a single defended tunnel, Kaanyr would be shocked.

At least now they will serve a purpose, thought the cambion. They will die so that I will live.

He took up his goblet and offered a mock toast.

My gratitude, Horgar, you little vermin, he thought. May you find an ugly death, since you were so ugly in life.

He drained the glass and smiled. Only then did his mind turn again to Aliisza.

Did her silence mean that she was leaving him?

He snorted derisively and shrugged. He did not care if the alu-fiend left him—their relationship had been one of convenience—but he would miss her physical gifts. He did wonder at her motives, though. Could she be in *love* with this drow mage she had spoken of? He dismissed the possibility and settled on a more likely solution: her fascination with the Master of Sorcere had grown into infatuation. She often fancied weak things, the same way a human woman might a pet.

She would be back eventually, he figured. She had left him before, even for decades at a time. But always she came back to him. Randomness was in her nature; structure in his. She was drawn to him, though, so she would not be away long. She simply wanted a new plaything for a time. Vhok did not begrudge her that.

He smiled and wished the Master of Sorcere well. Aliisza could be exhausting.

Of course, the mage must have had something of substance to him, since it appeared that he and his ragtag bunch had managed to wake up Lolth. Kaanyr had thought their quest a fool's errand until it had actually worked.

He sighed, stood, strapped on his rune-inscribed blade, and called out of the tent, "Rorgak! Attend me."

In moments, his tusked, towering, red-scaled lieutenant parted the curtains and entered the tent. Blood still streaked Rorgak's plate armor. He wore a collection of drow thumbs on a thin chain of hooks around his thick neck. Kaanyr counted six.

"Lord?" Rorgak asked.

Kaanyr gestured Rorgak close and said in Orcish, "Lolth has returned. Soon the spells of her priestesses will strengthen the city's defenses."

Rorgak's black eyes went wide. Despite his brutish looks, he was reasonably intelligent. He understood the implication of the words. He asked, "Lord, then what do we—"

Kaanyr silenced him with an upraised hand and a soft hiss. "We are removing our headquarters back to Hellgate Keep," he said. He could not quite bring himself to call the withdrawal a retreat. "Inform the officers. Make it appear to the drow as though it is a tactical withdrawal to consolidate forces for a counterattack."

Rorgak nodded and asked, "And the duergar?" His tone suggested that he already surmised the answer.

Kaanyr validated his guess by answering, "Kill the hundred or so intermixed with our forces, but be certain to allow no word of it to travel back to Horgar and the main body of his forces. Let them continue with their attack on Tier Breche."

"Horgar and the dwarflings will be slaughtered when the priestesses of Arach-Tinilith join their spells to the forces defending the Academy," Rorgak said.

Kaanyr nodded, smiled, and said, "But that final battle will occupy the drow long enough for the legion to move far from Menzoberranzan. Go. Time is short."

Rorgak thumped the breastplate of his plate armor, spun on his heel, and hurried from the tent.

For an instant, Kaanyr wished that Aliisza stood near him. He could have used some comforting.

It took Pharaun a moment to realize what was ensnared in the web.

One of the souls, a drow soul.

Presumably, the other wriggling forms were more trapped drow souls. They must have ventured too low, or the web's creator might have been able to snatch them from the sky. And perhaps the same creature could snatch Pharaun himself from the sky just as easily.

Pharaun didn't like the mental image that last idea evoked.

He cleared his head and scanned the outcropping for the spider or spiderlike creature that had spun the web but saw nothing other than the doomed spirits.

Still, something had affected his mind. . . .

The trapped soul near him, perhaps sensing his presence, struggled against the web and freed more of its face. It was a drow male. Opening his mouth in a soundless wail, the soul pinioned Pharaun with his terrified eyes. He wriggled more and set the entire web atop the tor to vibrating.

As though agitated by the movement, the other cocooned souls too wriggled more. All to no avail. The webs held them fast.

Another shout from below drew his attention, but he ignored it.

Fascinated and horrified, Pharaun called upon the power of his Sorcere ring to allow him to see emanations of magic and invisible things. As he'd expected, the web glowed a soft red in his sight. The corporeal web possessed magical properties that allowed it to trap and hold incorporeal souls. He wondered at the arcane mechanism behind that spell when his augmented sight revealed an otherwise invisible creature crouched in the center of the web, near one of the bound souls. Except for the eight black eyes in the center of its face and the fangs poking out from under its lips, it appeared vaguely reminiscent of a drow whose body had been crossed with a spider and stretched thin on a torturer's rack to twice its normal length. It crouched, watching him, on the web strands, naked, its clutching fingers half as long as Pharaun's forearm. Patches of short, bristly hairs jutted in patches from its skin. Periodic tremors coursed along its body, as though it was wracked by pain. A horrid fluid leaked from its mouth. Spinneret holes opened in its legs.

I see you, Pharaun thought as he called to mind a spell.

He must have stared a moment too long. The creature realized that it had been seen. It opened its mouth and coursed over the web toward him. As it moved, a voice sounded in Pharaun's head, a reasonable, persuasive voice augmented by magic.

Here is comfort, here is warmth. Come closer.

Pharaun felt the suggestion sink into his brain and pervert his will, but he resisted its pull and floated backward, incanting a spell the while.

The creature bounded forward, hissing. When it reached the end of the web, it spun a flip and turned its legs toward Pharaun. Web filaments shot from its spinnerets and hit Pharaun in the chest. He barely felt the impact on his flesh, but the webs seemed to reach through and into him.

His breath nearly left him. He felt himself separating in two, like curdled rothé milk. The web was pulling his soul from his body. The creature hissed again and began to pull.

More shouts from below. Quenthel's voice, angry.

Pharaun maintained his concentration—barely—and finished his spell in a whisper. The magic powered his voice, gave it strength, potency, and with it he uttered a single word of power.

The magic of the spell shredded the web strands attached to Pharaun and struck the creature like a hammer blow. The force blew it backward along its webs where it lay still.

The trapped souls struggled for freedom from the partially destroyed webs. The male drow nearest him managed to squirm himself free of the web. The soul did not so much as look at Pharaun. Instead, he simply headed skyward to join the other souls on their way to Lolth.

"Thanks are unnecessary," Pharaun shot after him, in a voice more like his own.

Below him, Quenthel was still shouting.

Pharaun shook his head to clear it and checked his body to ensure that he had suffered no permanent damage. Satisfied that he had not, he removed a leather glove from his cloak and voiced another spell.

An enormous hand of magical force took shape before him. At his mental command, it retrieved the stunned body of the arachnoid creature and gripped it tightly, taking care to ensure that the hand's grip covered the creature's spinnerets. Pharaun voiced another spell, temporarily dispelling the creature's natural invisibility.

Pharaun descended, trophy in hand, so to speak. He did not spare even glance at the other trapped souls.

The moment his boots touched stone, an impatient Quenthel demanded, "What in the Nine Hells were you doing?"

She had barely looked at the creature enwrapped in the huge fingers of his magical spell.

"Investigating, Mistress," Pharaun answered.

Before Quenthel could reply, Danifae threw back her hood and said, "I did not hear you ask for permission to investigate, male. Nor to kill one of Lolth's creatures."

Pharaun glared at Danifae and might have advanced on her had Jeggred not offered a threatening growl.

"I have not been in the habit of asking *your* permission, battle-captive. And this creature attacked me."

"Relearn your habits, Master Mizzrym," Danifae snapped, her eyes narrow and cold. "You are a resource of a priestess of Lolth, nothing more. Your disobedience borders on impudence and heresy."

To Pharaun's surprise, Quenthel said, "She is correct. The next time you divert our mission without my command, you will be punished. Lolth awaits her *Yor'thae*. We will not waste time with your trivial investigations."

As if to emphasize her point, the serpents extended to twice their ordinary length and flicked their tongues against Pharaun's flesh.

The Master of Sorcere swallowed his anger, stifled his pride, and set out to control the damage.

He offered Quenthel a bow and said, "Of course, Mistress. Forgive my presumption." To Danifae, he said, "And I was not aware that you now spoke for the Mistress."

Quenthel's jaw clenched at that. She glared first at Pharaun, then at Danifae.

"No one speaks for me," Quenthel said, and Pharaun lowered his gaze.

Danifae said, "I seek only the Spider Queen's will, Mistress of Arach-Tinilith."

"As do I," Quenthel said, and turned away to study the route ahead.

When she did, Pharaun met Danifae's eyes. She offered him a small smile—no doubt she thought she had driven some wedge between Quenthel and Pharaun by pointing out that the mage had acted without the high priestess's permission. Her gaze promised Pharaun an ugly death should the wedge result in a wide enough gap.

Pharaun smiled back at her. He felt reasonably comfortable that he had mitigated the damage by suggesting that Danifae had acted presumptuously by speaking for Quenthel. And if blades came to blood, it would be Danifae who would suffer the ugly death.

The thought gave him a momentary start. Kill a priestess of Lolth? True, Danifae was Houseless but she was still a priestess. Such a thing would not even have occurred to Pharaun before Lolth's Silence. He realized that while Lolth might have returned, her Silence had changed something fundamental about the relationship between male and female drow—for at least some males, priestesses would no longer seem so untouchable. Their weakness during the Silence, albeit temporary, had removed some of the social controls that underlaid their rule. He wondered how that would play out in future years.

The creature held in his magical fist stirred and groaned. Pharaun's spell had left it only temporarily stunned.

"As is her wont," Pharaun said to Quenthel. "Mistress Danifae has misconstrued the situation. I have not *killed* one of Lolth's creatures. I have merely brought it to you, Mistress, to do with as you wish. Perhaps to question it?"

Quenthel belted her whip and turned. Pharaun saw approval in her eyes. The serpents of the whip went slack. She eyed the creature closely for the first time then stepped forward, took its fanged jaw in her hand, and squeezed.

"Speak," she said to it. "What are you?"

"Be wary, Mistress," Pharaun warned. "It has the ability to implant a suggestion. That is how it lures souls to its web, offering them comfort."

Quenthel squeezed, and the creature wailed. Danifae smirked at its pain. Jeggred eyed it as if trying to determine how it might taste.

"If you attempt it," she said. "I will squeeze your head until it bursts."

"Not do," the creature whimpered in a high pitched voice. It spoke in an archaic form of Low Drow. "Not do. Mistook him for a soul. But not a soul. Living."

Quenthel shook its head and asked again, "What are you?"

The creature attempted to shake its head but Quenthel's strength held it immobile. Spittle and hisses rained from between its lips.

"The cursed of the Spider," the creature said at last, its voice difficult to understand.

"The cursed of Lolth?" Quenthel asked, eyebrows raised. "You do not serve the Spider Queen?"

Phlegm and drool leaked down the creature's face. Its forehead furrowed.

"The Spider hates me, but I feed on her souls. Eat many."

Quenthel relaxed her grip on the creature and looked to Danifae, then to Pharaun.

"This useless creature has nothing to tell us," she said. "Kill it, Master Mizzrym."

Pharaun did not hesitate. He caused his magical hand to squeeze, and squeeze. The creature screamed, bones cracked, and drool and blood exploded from its mouth.

"The Teeming will take you," it wailed, then it burst into a shower of gore.

"The Teeming?" Pharaun asked while he dispelled his magical hand and let the bloody pile fall to the ground.

Neither priestess responded to his question or seemed interested in the creature's threat, so he said, "It appears that the Spider Queen is not without a sense of irony. She rewards her followers for a lifetime of service by allowing them to be captured on the way to her and made food for whatever spun those webs."

Quenthel scoffed, eyeing him with contempt. The serpents of her whip lazily flicked their tongues at him.

"Master Mizzrym," Quenthel said. "You understand as little as most males. Faithful worship in life is not a guarantee of safety in death. This whole plane is a test for Lolth's dead. Surely even you can see that?"

Danifae looked at Quenthel and said, "Then does that not make this creature a servant of Lolth after all, Mistress Quenthel?"

Silence fell. Quenthel seemed dumbfounded by the question.

Before the high priestess could reply, Danifae looked to Pharaun and said, "Lolth winnows the weak always, even among her dead. If a soul is weak or stupid, it is annihilated."

Pharaun shrugged and said, "How pleasing for her."

Quenthel whirled on him. "Pleasing indeed, wizard. Are you concerned for the safety of your own hide?"

At that, Jeggred smirked.

Pharaun almost laughed at the absurdity of the question. He was *always* concerned for his own hide.

Instead of answering Quenthel directly, he said, "One might think the Spider Queen would make an exception to her tests for the *Yor'thae* and her escort, at least."

"Exactly the contrary," Danifae said and tucked her hair behind her ears.

She held her hand before her face and watched a small red arachnid with overlarge mandibles crawl along her fingers. She kneeled and let it scurry safely onto a rock; only then did Pharaun see the pinprick of blood on her hand from where the spider had bitten her. She had not even winced.

Danifae rose and said, "Lolth subjects herself to the same laws to which she subjects her servants, mage." She eyed Quenthel with a sly smile. "Only the strong or the intelligent will survive. Only one who is both can be her *Yor'thae.*"

Quenthel answered the former battle-captive's stare with an icy glance.

Returning her gaze to Pharaun, Danifae continued, "Were Lolth to select an unworthy priestess as her *Yor'thae,* no doubt something unfortunate would happen to the failed candidate. And her escort."

Quenthel's whip was in her hand, the serpents fully awake.

"It is well that she will not choose wrongly then," Quenthel said.

The serpents of Quenthel's scourge rose up, and five sets of small red eyes fixed Danifae with a hateful glare. Quenthel cocked her head and nodded, as though the whips had spoken to her.

"Has she not yet chosen, then?" Danifae asked, all innocence.

Quenthel's eyes flashed, perhaps in anger at herself for such a poor choice of words. She walked toward Danifae and stomped on the red arachnid that Danifae had just released onto the rocks.

Danifae's eyes flashed surprise, and she took a backward step. Even Jeggred seemed aghast.

"To kill that cursed creature is no crime," Danifae blurted, indicating the twisted form on the ground, "but to kill a spider is blasphemy."

Quenthel scoffed, ground her boot against the stone, and said, "That was no spider. It only appeared to be one. That is how it survived. For a time, at least." She eyed Danifae with meaning and said, "Killing those things that pretend they are more than they are is consistent with Lolth's will."

Danifae's mouth tightened as she took the sense of Quenthel's insult. Without a word, she snapped up the hood of her cloak, turned, and walked away. Jeggred glared at Quenthel and stalked after Danifae.

Quenthel smiled at their backs and Pharaun could not help but wonder why she left Danifae alive—there would be no consequences for her murder. Danifae did not belong to any of the Houses of Menzoberranzan, and Lolth reveled in internecine slaughter between her priestesses.

"Come," Quenthel said to him. "More obstacles await us before we reach the mountains."

And in those words, Pharaun heard Quenthel's explanation.

If indeed the whole of Lolth's plane was a test, as both priestesses had averred, then likely more challenges awaited, challenges that might require allies to overcome, even for Lolth's *Yor'thae*. Quenthel did not kill Danifae for the simple reason that she might need her later.

He hurried after the Mistress. As he walked past where Quenthel had been standing, he caught sight of a small red arachnid that looked very similar to that which Quenthel had squashed.

Had she only pretended to squash it?

He could not be certain, but her words to Danifae sounded in his head: *Killing things that pretend they are more than they are is consistent with Lolth's will.*

Who is pretending? he wondered.

He pushed the question from his mind and followed after.

While Larikal and Geremis led the search for the lichdrow's phylactery, Yasraena decided that she would attempt to buy her House peace, or failing that, time.

She sat on the stone throne of her reception hall—a locale that Triel Baenre could easily pinpoint with a spell—and hoped that the Matron Mother of the First House would respond.

She gathered her thoughts, held her holy symbol in hand, and spoke the words to a sending. The spell would allow her to speak and send to Triel Baenre a statement of not more than twenty-five words. Defensive wards had no effect on a sending, mostly because the spell did nothing other than transmit the speech of the caster. It could carry no spells or words of power.

When she finished the casting, she spoke Triel's name to denote the recipient and recited her message.

"Matron Mother Baenre, Matron Mother Agrach Dyrr wishes to discuss situation. I am in Dyrr reception hall. Scrying wards are lowered. Do same. Mutual clairaudience."

With that, Yasraena spoke the triggering word to lower the anti-scrying ward in the reception hall, and contacted Anival telepathically through the magical amulet at her breast.

Matron Mother? Anival answered.

Send one of the House wizards to my throne room, one skilled in divinations. Now.

Yes, Matron Mother, Anival answered, and the connection went silent.

While Yasraena waited from the House wizard to attend her, she cradled her holy symbol in her hand and recited the words to a minor spell that allowed her to see scrying effects. If and when Triel's House wizard placed a clairaudience sensor in Yasraena's throne room, Yasraena would know.

In less than a fifty-count, one of the House wizards, Ooraen, a recent graduate of Sorcere, entered through the far archway of the reception hall. He made obeisance and hurried down the aisle to the throne.

"How may I serve you, Matron Mother?"

"You know how to cast a clairaudience divination, I presume?" she asked.

The wizard nodded.

"For the time, stand beside my throne and be silent. When I command it, you will cast the spell at the location I designate and leave me."

The male bowed and stepped beside the throne.

Yasraena drummed her fingers along the haft of her tentacle rod and waited. And waited. Nearly an hour passed, and she grew increasingly impatient.

A small magical sensor materialized in the throne room, a fist-sized, red globe that would have been invisible but for Yasraena's augmented eyes.

"I see it, Matron Mother Baenre," Yasraena said to the sensor.

At the mention of Triel's title, Ooraen gave a visible start. Yasraena turned to him and said, "Cast your clairaudience spell in the reception hall of House Baenre."

Yasraena knew that Ooraen had never seen the inside of House Baenre but that did not matter. An adequate verbal description of the desired location would serve.

After only a moment's hesitation, Ooraen removed a tiny metal horn from his cloak, held it to his ear, and recited the words to his spell. When he completed the divination, Yasraena heard Triel's voice through the sensor: "Greetings, Yasraena."

That Triel had called her by her given name rather than her title was an intentional slight, but Yasraena gulped down her anger. She waved Ooraen from the chamber, and the wizard fled down the aisle.

"Greetings, Matron Mother Baenre," Yasraena replied.

"How fares House Agrach Dyrr?" Triel asked, and Yasraena heard the sarcastic smile in the voice.

"Well," Yasraena answered, defiant. "House Agrach Dyrr fares well."

Triel's laughter carried through the sensor.

Yasraena ignored it and said, "Matron Mother, I sought this communication so we might discuss a settlement."

"Indeed?" Triel answered.

"Indeed," Yasraena replied and wasted no further time with conversational niceties. "House Agrach Dyrr's alliance with the forces besieging Menzoberranzan was undertaken in secret by the lichdrow.

By the time I learned of it, the plot already was in motion. Since then, I have endeavored to quietly undermine the lichdrow's plots at every turn. Now that his body is destroyed—"

"Now that your ambition has proven far too large for your capabilities," Triel interrupted, "you wish to sue for peace. Is that not so, Yasraena?"

Yasraena could not keep anger from her own voice. "You mistake me, Matron Mother Baenre. I—"

"No," Triel interjected. "You mistake *me*. You seek to save your House by blaming your own failings on the lichdrow. Even if what you said was true, it simply demonstrates your own incompetence to rule."

Yasraena gripped the tentacle rod so tightly in her hand that her fingers ached. Anger burned in her, and she almost exploded at Triel. Almost.

Instead, she calmed herself and answered. "Perhaps you speak some truth," she said, slightly emphasizing the word 'some.' "Which is why I wish to make you an offer."

Silence. Then, "Speak it."

"House Agrach Dyrr is made a vassal House to House Baenre for five hundred years, the arrangement to be ratified by the Ruling Council. My House will be removed from the Council—" temporarily, Yasraena added to herself—"and in the meanwhile will be under Baenre rule and protection during that half-millennium period. I and it will be at your disposal, Matron Mother."

Yasraena knew the offer to be a bold one. It had been long since any of the city's Houses had been made a formal vassal to another. But it was not unheard of, and she had few other options.

A long silence followed, during which Yasraena held her breath. No doubt Triel was mulling the possibilities.

At last, Triel said, "Your offer has some small potential, Yasraena."

Yasraena exhaled.

Triel continued, "To show me your sincerity, you will destroy the lichdrow's phylactery."

Yasraena had expected nothing less. "Of course, Matron Mother.

I am in the process of locating it but the siege makes it difficult. As does what I presume to be the inevitable assay of the Archmage. Temporarily halt the siege and restrain your brother. When I have the phylactery, I will contact you again and provide evidence of its destruction."

Triel laughed. "Do not be foolish, Yasraena," she said. "You will demonstrate your worthiness to be a vassal House to House Baenre by finding and destroying the phylactery even while House Agrach Dyrr is under siege by the Xorlarrin. And if the Archmage decides to try your defenses, then you will abide that too. Or you will not. And if not, then destruction is what your House warrants."

Yasraena bit back the angry words that flew to her lips. She had little choice but to accept.

"Your terms are reasonable," she said through gritted teeth.

"I'm pleased you find them so," Triel answered. "Do not contact me again, Yasraena, unless it is to provide evidence of the lichdrow's destruction."

With that, the connection went quiet. A heartbeat later, the sensor in Yasraena's reception hall dematerialized.

Yasraena sat in her throne and thought, her mind racing. She had made her play but was not sure how it would unfold. If she did in fact locate the phylactery, she was undecided whether she would honor the terms of the deal or instead safeguard it until the lichdrow could reincorporate. A part of her very much desired the permanent destruction of the meddling undead wizard, but the pragmatist in her knew that she weakened her House, if not her own personal position within it, by destroying the lichdrow. But to throw herself on the mercy of House Baenre. . . .

Yasraena shook her head. She had no decision to make if her House fell to the Xorlarrin or Gromph Baenre found the phylactery before her. She rose and went searching the halls for Larikal.

Silence reigned for the next several leagues of travel as Pharaun and his cohorts picked their way through the towers of stone and the

blasted ground. The entire plane, the very air, felt restive and stretched, as though about to explode.

Over the hours, the wind grew steadily more forceful, with intermittent gusts so strong that Pharaun had to lean forward to avoid being blown off his feet. The gusts howled between the towers of stone, set the songspider webs to screeching, and stirred up a blizzard of spiders, dirt, webs, and loose scree. Jeggred protected Danifae from the living hail with his hulking body. Pharaun shielded himself with his magical *piwafwi*. Quenthel merely smiled into the storm and held her arms outstretched to provide a haven for any spiders that blew onto her. After a time, spiders teemed in her hair and on her *piwafwi*.

She was home, Pharaun realized, and pulled the hood of his magical cloak lower to protect his face. The *Yor'thae* was returning home.

The gusts grew more frequent and still more intense with each passing hour. An increasingly powerful hail of pebbles, webs, and spiders pelted them, like a blizzard of sling bullets. The keening webs sounded more and more like the agonized wail of a creature in pain. Pharaun had little experience with surface weather patterns, but even he could smell a storm on the wind.

"Perhaps we should find shelter," he said above the shrieking winds.

"Faith is our shelter, mage," Quenthel answered back, the wind whipping her hair around her face. A small black spider crawled over her eyelid, down her nose, and over her lips. She only smiled.

Danifae put back her cloak hood and cocked her head as though she heard something. Red spiders thronged her hair too, and her face.

"Can you not hear it in the keening, mage?" Danifae shouted. "The Spider Queen calls us onward. We continue."

Pharaun squinted into the wind, looked from one priestess to the other, and said nothing. He heard nothing in the wind but the abominable screech of the webs. And as for faith providing a shelter? He knew better than that. He had seen Lolth's faithful trapped in a web atop a tor, waiting to be fed upon. That was the shelter provided by faith in the Spider Queen.

Still, he bit his tongue and trudged forward, bent against the wind and hurtling debris. Time passed; fatigue dulled his mind and body.

The storm and winds continued to build as the hours dragged on.

When the sky to his left lightened enough to afford a better view of the landscape, he decided to call that direction "east." Despite Quenthel's assurance to Jeggred that the sun would not harm them, Pharaun found himself squinting, bracing for its impact.

To the west, perhaps another five or six days' of foot travel away, were mountains. The great triangular peaks soared high into the sky, forming a wall of dark stone with sides as sharp, sheer, and craggy as fangs. Caps of red ice crowned them. So too did storm clouds, an expanding bank of black as thick and as dark as demon's blood—a storm the likes of which Pharaun could never have imagined.

And it was moving toward them. The cutting wind and screaming webs were its prophets.

The line of souls, unbothered by the swirling wind and gathering storm, poured toward the base of one of the mountains. There, they congregated at a dark point, perhaps a valley or a pass, between two of the largest peaks.

"Lolth's web and city sits on the other side those mountains," Quenthel said above the wind, above the screeching of the webs.

Danifae held her hair back from her face and looked to the far horizon. The distant look in her eyes reminded Pharaun of a mad prophet he had once seen in Menzoberranzan's bazaar.

"All the souls are massing in that gorge at the base of the mountains," Pharaun said, not certain everyone had seen it.

"It is not a gorge," Quenthel answered, her voice barely audible over the wind.

She offered nothing more, and Pharaun didn't like the haunted look in her eyes.

"The sun rises," said Jeggred, shielding his eyes with one of his huge fighting hands.

Pharaun turned to see the lip of a tiny red orb creep diffidently over the eastern horizon. It cast little more light than the silvery nighttime satellite of the World Above when it was full. The light from Lolth's sun formed a clear line on the landscape, a border between darkness and light, that oozed toward them as the orb rose higher. Just as Quenthel had said, the light caused only minor discomfort.

Pharaun lowered his hand from his eyes and watched the first sunrise of his lifetime.

To his surprise and alarm, where the dim light touched, movement occurred. At first, Pharaun thought the sunlight was causing the earth to ripple, but then he realized what was actually occurring.

The plane was birthing spiders. Millions of spiders.

Crawling, scuttling, clambering, they moved from the darkness of their fissures and caves and into the light, summoned by the dawn. All had eight legs, eight eyes, and fangs, but there the similarities ended. Some were the size of rats, some were the size of rothé, and a few that clambered forth out of largest fissures had bloated bodies as large as giants. Some leaped, some phased in and out of reality, some pulled their bloated forms along on overlarge pedipalps or swordlike legs, others tumbled or flew on the gusting wind.

As the sun's light moved across the landscape, the pits, tunnels, and holes that it lit vomited forth their arachnid denizens. A ponderous but visible wave traveled across the earth as the sun slowly trekked higher into the sky. The ground was acrawl.

The light was moving toward them. They watched in awed silence.

Pharaun had lived with and amongst spiders his entire life but he had never before seen anything like the seething, roiling mass of arachnids that was beginning to blanket the surface of the plane. They coated everywhere the light touched, a seething blanket of legs, eyes, and hairy bodies.

At first, little occurred other than the birthing. The spiders that emerged from their holes seemed content to sit in the light as the birthing line moved across the world. But soon, first one, then another, then a hundred, then a million of the spiders attacked the others and fed upon the fallen. A slaughter trailed the birthing line by a few hundred paces, and there the surface of the plane erupted into a roiling, chaotic mass of fangs, pedipalps, and pincers, all biting, cutting, and tearing. Hisses, screeches, clicks, and the sound of ripping bodies filled the air, a wave of sound that followed hard after the sunlight. Severed legs dotted the rocks; huge carcasses flailed and bled; ichor stained the earth.

It was purposeless slaughter, madness made flesh, chaos given substance.

Lolth must have been smiling.

Pharaun could see plainly that anything caught in the midst of the bloody tumult would be fortunate to survive. He spared a glance under his feet, and saw pits and holes gaping like open mouths all around them. Even above the wind he could hear the scrabbling of feet coming from within them, the eager clicking of fangs, the tapping of legs on stone. In his mind's eye, he pictured another million arachnids lurking just inside the darkness of the holes, waiting for the touch of the dim sun to set them free of their underground prisons. Pharaun had no idea how such an ecology could sustain itself and did not care. Though born in a city where slaughter was commonplace, even he found the level of violence repulsive.

And soon they would be in the midst of it. The sun was rising. The light was coming.

"Goddess be praised," Quenthel said, a rapturous look on her face.

The wind gusted, pasting his robes to his body. The webs keened in answer. Pharaun thought the Baenre priestess must have lost her mind.

Danifae emerged out from under her hood to greet the sun, not unlike the spiders emerging from their caves. Pharaun counted not less than seven tiny red spiders crawling in her hair,

"Do we intend to simply stand here and wait?" he asked above the noise.

Neither priestess replied, and he decided that was answer enough.

"Afraid?" Jeggred asked, smirking.

Pharaun ignored the draegloth and mentally activated the power of his ring of flight. With a silent command, he surreptitiously lifted his feet half a handspan off the earth. If the priestesses had a plan, that was well. If not, he saw no need to remain earthbound in the face of the madness.

Together, the four of them watched as the light and violence churned its way toward them. As it grew closer, the clicking and screeching from the caves and pits around them grew louder, more eager, hungrier. The arachnids within sensed the approach of the light.

Jeggred answered those sounds with a low rumble in his chest. He stepped before Danifae and assumed a fighting crouch. The priestesses did not even look at the ground around them. They had eyes only for the approaching slaughter.

Pharaun decided to try again. "Mistress," he said to Quenthel, "would it not be wise to take shelter?"

Quenthel looked at him sidelong and said, "No, mage. We must stand in the midst of this and bear witness."

From around her neck, she removed her holy symbol of Lolth—a jet disk inlaid with amethysts arranged to look like a spider. The serpents of her whip stood upright and watched the wave of spiders approach. Quenthel chanted a prayer, the words in a language even Pharaun could not understand.

Pharaun bit back the cutting reply that came to his mind, content that he could take flight if and when the need arose.

Danifae put her hand on Jeggred's fur-covered back.

"It is the Teeming," she said to no one in particular, recalling the words of the soul-eating creature Pharaun had taken prisoner. Awe colored her tone.

Pharaun didn't care what it was called. He knew only that soon the sunlight would reach them, light the pits around them, and . . .

He imagined his body buried under a mountain of bloated bodies, jointed legs, mandibles, and unforgiving eyes.

Quenthel and Danifae both appeared lost in rapture, temporarily mad perhaps. Each held her holy symbol in her hands; each wore the wild but assured expression of an ecstatic.

Pharaun knew that ordinary spiders answered the priestesses' commands, but he did not know whether the arachnids native to the Pits would. Besides, the priestesses' powers were limited. They could not command *millions* of spiders, could they?

Pharaun liked the situation less and less. He reached into his *piwafwi*, removed a ball of sulfur-soaked bat guano, and held it between thumb and forefinger—just in case. Ordinarily, he would not have considered offering violence to Lolth's children, at least not in the presence of her priestesses, but if it came to killing spiders or dying himself under a heap of hairy bodies, the choice would be an easy one.

As ready as he would get, he waited.

The sunlight slid across the rockscape, birthing more spiders, closer, closer . . .

When it reached them, motion exploded all around. Thousands of spiders boiled from their holes like steam from a heated beaker, hissing and clicking. From a large tunnel to Pharaun's right, rothé-sized masses of hairy spider legs issued forth—five, ten, a score. His heart hammered between his ribs. The creatures had no bodies as such, no heads. They were nothing more than a clumped, disgusting, squirming mass of legs, each of which was longer than Pharaun was tall, and eight of which ended in a pointed claw of chitin as long as his forearm.

"Chwidencha," Pharaun said. "Two score or more."

Chwidencha—he'd heard them called "leg horrors"—had once been drow, or perhaps drow souls, but they had failed Lolth, and as punishment had been transformed by the Spider Queen into that twisted form. The Demonweb Pits did not appear to Pharaun to be a paradise for the Spider Queen's faithful. It looked more like a prison for her failures.

The chwidencha's rapid, undulating movement was enough to cause Pharaun a wave of nausea. Impossible clusters of long, jointed legs, like a nest of vipers, squirmed a greeting to the red light of the dawn.

Though they had no eyes that he could see, the chwidencha immediately noticed the companions. Forty or more mouths offered muffled hisses from orifices buried under nests of legs.

"I see them, Master Mizzrym," Quenthel said, turning around, but her voice lacked the same confidence it had held a moment before.

The thousands of spiders boiling from the holes around them did not come near the chwidencha and left the companions unmolested, a small island of sanity amidst the chaos.

Lolth's damned appeared to command a certain respect, or fear.

With alarming speed and coordination, the chwidencha pack encircled them at a distance of perhaps ten paces.

The four drow closed ranks a few steps, a reflexive action. Pharaun called to mind the words to his fireball spell but held off casting. He shared a look with Quenthel but could not read her face. Jeggred's chest rose and fell heavily, and his fighting claws flexed. The draegloth interposed himself as best he could between the arachnids and Danifae but it was little use. They were surrounded. His growls answered their hisses and tapping claws.

Outside the ring of Lolth's damned, the spiders that had boiled forth stood still for a moment, like arena fighters gathering their strength. Then the urge to slaughter reached them, and they erupted into violence. Thousands upon thousands of spiders engaged in an orgy of dismemberment and feeding. Squeals, screeches, and hisses rang through the morning air. The ground vibrated under the volume of violence.

Within the ring, the tension grew. The chwidenchas' legs churned sickeningly, as though they were agitated or somehow communicating. Though he could see no eyes, it was clear to Pharaun that the chwidencha were regarding them. He felt the weight of their looks, the heaviness of their malice, the depth of their hate.

"Well—" he started to say.

At the sound of his voice, the chwidencha pack hissed as one. The smaller legs sprouting from what would have been their faces writhed, squirmed, and parted to reveal fanged mouths larger around than Pharaun's head. Finger-length fangs dripped a thick, yellow venom.

To all of them, Quenthel said, "We will not harm any of Lolth's children."

Pharaun could see that Quenthel was sweating as badly as he was, though her voice was calm.

"These are more like stepchildren," he answered and ran through the inventory of spells in his mind.

"They are neither," Danifae said, raising her holy symbol—a red spider encased in amber—before her. "These are her damned."

At the sight of Lolth's brandished symbol, the chwidencha pack emitted a high-pitched screech that made the hair on the nape of Pharaun's neck stand on end. As one, they spasmed in anger, legs churning and squirming. The claws on the ends of their legs cracked rock, and Pharaun could not help but imagine what they could do to flesh.

"They do not appear to be the religious type, Mistress Danifae," Pharaun said.

Danifae did not lower her symbol.

The wind gusted, set the songspider webs to screeching, a sound that temporarily rose above even the cacophony of the Teeming.

This entire plane of existence is mad, Pharaun decided. The priestesses are mad. I am mad.

The chwidencha answered the song of the webs with another screech of their own. Pharaun didn't care for the look of their open, fanged mouths.

"Mistress," he said to Quenthel, "perhaps you could discourage further discussion with these creatures? I find them poor conversationalists. Mistress Danifae?"

For that, Quenthel turned to look at him just long enough to stare daggers. Danifae smirked.

Quenthel raised her jet symbol at the chwidencha, mirroring Danifae's gesture and eliciting a similar response.

Venom dripped to pool on the ground. Hisses answered their movements.

Quenthel pronounced, "Leave us now, damned of Lolth! We are servants of the Spider Queen about her will. You will not impede us."

"Back to your holes!" Danifae commanded, offering her own symbol.

A palpable wave of divine power went forth from both the priestesses.

Pharaun expected to see the chwidencha turn and flee into their tunnels but the leg horrors did not move, at least not away from them. More hisses answered the priestesses' command; legs squirmed and writhed. As one, the chwidencha took a slow step forward, and the circle of safety shrank.

While Danifae wore an inexplicable smile, Quenthel's uncertain expression told Pharaun everything he needed to know.

SIX

As she stepped through the portal, Halisstra felt spread across a distance vast and deep. In only a fraction of a heartbeat, the portal moved her from the relatively calm gray nothingness of the Astral to—

She found herself in mid-air, falling.

Before she could activate the levitation power of her brooch, she dropped five paces and hit the ground with a grunt. She managed to keep her feet and found herself standing under a dim sun on blasted ground in the midst of a nightmare.

Spiders surrounded her, swarmed her, engulfed her, from hand-sized arachnids scurrying underfoot to horrid monsters twice her height. The creatures tore each other to pieces all around her. Hisses, clicks, and squeals filled her ears; black, brown, and red ichor stained the ground and splattered her face.

Halisstra was aswim in an ocean of Lolth's maddened children. The Spider Queen must have caused Halisstra to arrive in the midst of the chaos as penance for her apostasy.

She steadied her stance, brandished the Crescent Blade, and took in her environment with only a single glance. She stood on a bleak, pit-ridden rockscape in the shadow of a slim spire of unusual looking rock, a tor of black stone that looked as though it should have toppled of its own weight in the gusting wind. The whirlpools of Lolth's reawakened power dotted the cloudy sky. She had been ejected from one such and thanked the goddess that it had not been higher off the ground. A line of souls streamed through the heavens, all of them floating in the direction of a distant mountain range, drawn there by the lodestone of Lolth's power.

An eerie keening rang in her ears, the sound of songspider webs whistling in the blustery wind, like some obscene attempt to mimic the sound made by Seyll's songsword. In it, she heard the echo of the word she had heard on the Astral, the word that made the hair on the nape of her neck stand on end:

Yor'thae.

She had no time to consider the sound further. The spiders around her noticed her. A sea of frenzied fangs, pincers, legs, and hairy bodies broke around her. Arachnids scuttled over rocks, over each other, over her. She slashed and cut but there were too many. They bit and tore indiscriminately, killing and devouring anything in their path. Spider bodies thumped into her; fangs tried to bite through her mail; claws sent her spinning, knocked her to her knees.

She refused to die on her knees.

"Goddess!" she screamed and swung the glowing Crescent Blade in a wide arc.

As if in answer, Feliane and Uluyara appeared in the air through a short-lived gate that appeared perhaps twenty paces to her right and five paces high in the air. They fell to the ground, and she saw them for only an instant more—both wore expressions of surprise and horror—before they too were buried under a mass of writhing, leaping spiders.

From her knees, Halisstra swung blindly, hitting spider flesh with every pass. Ichor sprayed, splattered her face and hands. Hissing and clicking filled her ears; squeals of pain.

She fought her way back to her feet, impaling a large blue spider on the end of her blade. She slipped in its gushing fluids and nearly fell. A huge, black, hairy arachnid leaped on her back and sank its fangs into her shoulder, but her mail withstood the attack. She flung it from her and stomped its thorax to mush as another huge spider reared before her, lunged forward, and bit at her legs. She dodged backward and fended it off with the Crescent Blade. She felt as though she were up to her waist in the creatures; with each step, she crushed half a dozen small spiders under her boots. She saw no way out, no way she would ever get free. She would die under their fangs, and her body would be left a desiccated husk blowing in the screaming wind.

"Goddess!" she cried again, hacking wildly with the Crescent Blade.

The enchanted steel killed where it struck, slicing arachnid flesh easily, but there were thousands of them. Eilistraee had no particular power over the creatures, and in her desperation Halisstra almost fell back into her old habit of channeling Lolth's power to command spiders. It would be so easy to simply order them back to—

Uluyara's horn rang, and Halisstra latched onto the sound with the desperation of the drowning. She remembered the first time she had heard its clear call, on the World Above under the silver light of the moon. She centered herself, at least for a time, and with effort resisted Lolth's pull.

If she were to live, she would have to save herself with the tools that Eilistraee, and only Eilistraee, had put into her hands.

Holding the Crescent Blade in both hands, Halisstra slashed about her with an abandon born of hopelessness, sending legs and spider flesh flying. Her small shield made her two-handed grip on the Crescent Blade a bit awkward, but she managed. She wanted the extra force to her swings.

Fangs clamped on her arm, her leg, and pierced her mail and flesh. Agony raced through her body, and warm poison throbbed into her veins. She grabbed the hairy blob on her forearm and squeezed it until it popped. She stabbed downward at another spider, impaling it, cross cut to her right, and took the mandible from another. She found it strange that killing Lolth's creatures did not elicit the same elation she had felt back in the forest of the World Above when she had killed the phase spider in the name of Eilistraee.

Instead, she felt out of balance, dirty, guilty.

"I'm sorry," she murmured as she killed but was not sure what she meant. The words just seemed to fit. Spider blood splattered her hands, her cloak, her face. "I'm sorry."

Despite her words, she hacked her way through the roiling mass of bodies, legs, mandibles, and ichor toward where she had last seen her fellow priestesses. To her relief, she saw that both Feliane and Uluyara had found their feet and their blades. They dodged nimbly amidst the chaos, slashing and stabbing. They looked as though they were dancing—they leaped, spun, twirled, and tumbled, serving the Lady of the Dance even while they slaughtered. Both sported cuts and bites, and Feliane had a dark puncture on her bare forearm. Still, Halisstra thought them beautiful. Their blades whistled through the air, an answer and a challenge to the strange keening. Halisstra caught Feliane's eye as both cut their way through the never-ending tide of spiders.

"Halisstra!" Feliane called. Cutting, chopping, her round face was splattered with blood and ichor.

Uluyara whirled a circle beside the elf priestess, her blade a blur, and met Halisstra's eyes for a moment.

"Here!" Halisstra answered.

Without stopping, she opened the abdomen of a spider, then another and another. She was fifteen paces from her sisters.

From out of the maelstrom of bodies a brown sword spider leaped high above the fray. Time slowed for Halisstra.

Easily as large as a pack lizard, the creature's eight arms ended in claws that looked like short swords and killed just as effectively. Halisstra's breath caught as the creature reached the apex of its leap. She had seen sword spiders fight in the basement arena of House Melarn, cutting down out-of-favor male warriors with bloody, brutal efficiency.

As the sword spider descended toward Feliane, it clustered its swordlike claws together to form a single impaling blade, pointing downward at the slight elf priestess.

"Above!" Halisstra shouted but could not be sure that Feliane heard her. "Feliane!"

A large spider appeared before Halisstra, and she hacked off two of its legs with the Crescent Blade.

The shadow of the descending sword spider must have blotted out the dim red light of the sun. Feliane looked up, saw it, slipped to the side, and tried to raise her blade defensively. She was a heartbeat too slow. The sword spider crashed down on her, knocking her blade aside and driving her to the ground, flat on her back. Its clustered legs sheared through her armored shoulder and sank into her flesh. She screamed in pain, and blood spouted. Her sword fell from her hand, skittered away, and was lost under a throng of arachnids.

The sword spider straddled her small form, caging her in its bloody legs. She struggled beneath it, punching with her good arm, kicking, but she was already growing weak from blood loss. The blows crunched into the spider's huge body but seemed to have little effect other than to elicit an angry hiss.

A pack of giant tarantulas drove Uluyara from Feliane's side, and Halisstra lost sight of the High Priestess.

Halisstra shouted again and cut her way toward her sisters, hacking mercilessly at anything in her path. She left a trail of severed legs and pedipalps in her wake. Fourteen paces, twelve, ten. She killed with every step. Ichor covered her; soaked her. Small arachnids teemed over her exposed skin, her face, and her hair. She devoured those that got near her mouth and spat the pieces to the ground.

She knew that she would not reach Feliane in time.

The swords of its claws still glistening red with the elf's blood, the sword spider pinned the dying Feliane with three of its legs and raised its forelegs high in a strike that would lay open her chest and pierce her heart.

Uluyara materialized out of the madness to the sword spider's right, blade held high. The High Priestess charged forward, calling on the Dark Maiden, and swung her blade in a crosscut designed to split the sword spider's abdomen from head to spinneret.

But the spider saw her coming. It shifted slightly atop the wounded Feliane, parried Uluyara's blow with one of its claws, and lashed out with another. The blow hit Uluyara squarely in the chest, sent mail links flying, and drove her backward. She stumbled, tripped on the carcass of a large spider behind her, and was instantly swamped with smaller arachnids.

The sword spider returned its attention toward Feliane. The arachnid again raised its forelegs high and drove them into Feliane's chest. They split mail links, broke bones, and drove into the organs and flesh beneath. Feliane's back arched with the agony, and blood pooled around her.

"Feliane!" Halisstra cried and cut down another spider and another.

She was five paces from the elf. Too far.

The elf's eyes were still open but glassy. Blood poured from her chest and dribbled from the corner of her mouth. The sword spider bared fangs as long as knives and sank them into Feliane's flesh. Her head sagged to the side. The spider made as though to pick the elf up and carry her back to its lair.

Halisstra had no time to think, so she did the only thing she could. She forced back the spiders near her with a flurry of vicious slashes, reached back over her head—a difficult maneuver with a shield slung on her arm—and flung the Crescent Blade with both hands at the sword spider.

The blade flew true, point first, and sank halfway to its hilt into the thorax of the huge arachnid. The creature uttered a hiss of agony, and its entire body spasmed. It withdrew blood-slicked fangs and claws from the elf's flesh and started to turn toward Halisstra. The Crescent Blade stuck out of its flesh like a pennon. Another spasm wracked its body, another hiss escaped its fanged mouth, and it collapsed atop Feliane, dead.

Feliane did not move.

Using her shield, Halisstra bashed another spider in its face as it lunged for her. She jerked Seyll's songsword from the scabbard on her back. With its fluted hilt whistling a counter melody to the eerie sound of the wind, she slashed another spider, another, and rushed to Feliane's side.

She kneeled, and blew a sigh of relief when she saw that Feliane was unconscious but alive—barely. Halisstra had no time to take a longer look. She whirled around and beat back a trio of giant widows, opening a long slash in one. Afterward, she turned, bent, and heaved the sword spider carcass off of the elf.

Unmolested for the moment by any spiders, Halisstra flipped her grip on Seyll's sword and put the hilt to her lips. Placing one hand on Feliane's wounded chest while still trying to keep an eye on the arachnids around her, she blew a single, soothing note. The sound served as a focus for her *bae'qeshel* healing magic.

The punctures in Feliane's chest closed to pink dots, and her breath came easier, though she did not regain consciousness. Halisstra could not risk another spell amidst the swarming spiders. She took the hilt in her hands as three spiders the size of rats landed on her back. Their fangs could not penetrate her mail, and she pulled them from her as she rose and stabbed each in turn.

Standing over Feliane, she scanned the madness for Uluyara.

The High Priestess fought nearby against a red and black spider as large as a rothé. Already she had severed two of its legs.

"Uluyara!" Halisstra screamed. "Here!"

Uluyara spared her a glance, and nodded. The High Priestess unleashed an overhead cut at the spider, drove it backward a step, turned, and raced for Halisstra. The creature bounded after her with astonishing speed.

Halisstra reversed her grip, put the hilt of the songsword to her lips, and blew a series of dissonant notes. The *bae'qeshel* sent a wave of sound over Uluyara's head and blasted the spider with its discordance. The power of the spell flattened the enormous arachnid, opened its exoskeleton, and a host of smaller spiders leaped upon it to feed.

Uluyara wove and danced her way through still more arachnids until she reached Halisstra's side. She looked at Feliane, concern in her eyes.

"She's alive," Halisstra said, breathing heavily, "but we must get out of here now!"

Uluyara smiled fiercely, put a hand to Halisstra's shoulder, and said, "Give me a moment's protection."

Halisstra nodded agreement, and while the high priestess chanted a prayer beside her, Halisstra used Seyll's songsword and shield to slice and smash any arachnids that came near. The violence of the slaughter nauseated her. Spider parts lay everywhere, and blood stained the ground dark.

When Uluyara finished her prayer to the Lady, a ring of silvery blades took shape around them. Thousands of magical blades, all of them spinning and buzzing, formed a ring ten paces high. Two spiders caught in the wall as it materialized were slashed to gory ribbons.

"The Lady's spells serve us well even in the Demonweb Pits," Uluyara said, her voice and eyes hard.

Halisstra nodded, though only then did she realize that it had not occurred to her during the combat to cast one of the spells granted her by Eilistraee. She wondered why but feared the answer too much to consider the question overlong.

Perhaps two dozen spiders remained within Uluyara's ring of blades. Halisstra knew a spell that would finish them, but an unexpected reluctance caused her to hesitate.

"We should go," she said.

"First, these," Uluyara answered, stepping forward. "Eilistraee has put them in our hands. We must finish them."

Uluyara brandished her weapon, but Halisstra caught her arm and stopped her advance. She eyed the hairy wolf spiders prowling within the circle of blades.

"I'll do it," she said.

Uluyara hesitated but finally nodded and said, "You bear the Crescent Blade."

With effort, Halisstra pushed through her reluctance, put her fingertips to the symbol of Eilistraee on her chest, and prayed. She had a terrifying moment when the words momentarily escaped her, but she recalled them presently and her voice grew in strength. When she finished the incantation, an invisible, circular wave of power went forth from her. It hit all of the spiders and drove them, scrabbling and hissing, backward into the wall of blades. All two dozen of them vanished in a spray of legs and slashed flesh.

Halisstra felt sick and elated all at once.

She turned to find Uluyara looking at her, head cocked. The high priestess seemed to want to say something but instead gave Halisstra a nod of approval and kneeled beside Feliane. She took the elf's face in her hands and whispered healing words. After a few moments, Feliane's remaining wounds closed completely, color returned to her face, and her eyes fluttered open. Uluyara helped her to her feet and held her steady.

"The Lady watches her faithful," Uluyara said to the elf, and Feliane nodded.

The slight elf warrior-priestess eyed the carcass of the sword spider. She looked thanks at Halisstra.

Halisstra gave her an absent half smile but found her gaze reaching out, beyond the wall of blades. There, the slaughter went on unabated. Spiders bit, clawed, tore, and devoured one another in a nonstop orgy of violence. From time to time, one ventured or was carried by the combat into Uluyara's wall of blades, where it vanished in a spray of gore.

In a way that made her sick to admit, Halisstra found the slaughter somehow rational. The strong would devour the weak and become stronger still.

She knew that she was looking upon the pith of Lolth's doctrine made flesh, a metaphor for the Spider Queen's entire creed.

"This has to end sometime," she said. "We should hole up until it does."

Feliane, recovering her blade from the ground, asked, "Where will we go?"

"There," Halisstra replied, and nodded at the spire of stone looming over them. Few spiders prowled its sheer, strangely angled heights. They would be able to hold their ground atop it until the madness came to its bloody end. "We'll fly."

Seeing agreement in the eyes of Uluyara and Feliane, she again touched the medallion affixed to the chest of her mail and whispered a prayer to Eilistraee.

"Halisstra," Uluyara interrupted, her voice low and urgent. "The Crescent Blade."

The words to the prayer died on Halisstra's lips, and she felt her cheeks burn. She had left Eilistraee's blade in the carcass of the sword spider.

She had forgotten it.

PAUL S. KEMP

"Of course," she said, in a poor attempt to cover her neglect.

Without meeting Uluyara's or Feliane's eyes, she sheathed Seyll's songsword in the scabbard over her back, walked over to the dead sword spider, and withdrew the Crescent Blade. She cleaned it on the spider's carcass before putting it back in the scabbard at her waist.

When she turned, she saw the doubt in Uluyara's eyes and the embarrassment in Feliane's. She chose to ignore them both.

"You're wounded," Uluyara said, and pointed at the seeping wounds in Halisstra's legs and the holes in her arm.

Halisstra had forgotten them too. She was certain she had been poisoned by the bites. The magical ring she wore allowed her to sense as much, and yet she showed no ill effects. She didn't want to acknowledge why that might be.

"It's nothing," she said and began her spell anew.

When she completed the prayer, her body and gear and those of her fellow priestesses metamorphosed into an insubstantial gray vapor. She could still see, though her field of vision seemed to swell, contract, and roll. She could somehow still feel her body, or at least *a* body, though it felt thin and stretched, not unlike her soul.

The gusting wind tugged at her but she resisted its pull and willed herself into the air. Feliane and Uluyara, both appearing as vaguely humanoid clouds of vapor beside her, followed after.

Free of her flesh for at least a few moments, Halisstra felt free of her doubt, of her inner struggle. She felt unburdened by the world, as light as one of Lolth's souls streaming through the sky high above. She wished she could feel that way forever.

Flying up the sheer, rocky side of the black, twisted outcropping, she looked for a likely place to wait out the slaughter. She was pleased to see no webs anywhere on the spire—though other tors had many—and the gusting wind seemed to keep the spiders from reaching its heights.

At its top, the spire looked as though it had been sheared off by a keen blade, forming a round, featureless plateau twenty paces in diameter. The wind would whip at them there, but they would be sheltered from the violence below.

Halisstra alit on the plateau, waited for Feliane and Uluyara to follow, and dispelled the magic. As one, the three priestesses regained their normal forms. Halisstra's doubt returned with her flesh. The gusting wind nearly lifted her from her feet.

"We'll need shelter," Halisstra said above the wind.

Even there, the keening webs called to her. *Yor'thae*, they whispered.

In the distance, she could see ominous clouds forming over a distant mountain range and moving rapidly in their direction—a storm was coming.

"Gather here," Uluyara said, pulling Halisstra and Feliane into a circle.

Wrapped in the arms of her fellow priestesses, Halisstra felt a sense of sisterhood that reassured her, at least for the moment.

"We will form a sanctuary together," Uluyara said above the wind. "A place of safety in the midst of this obscenity."

Feliane and Halisstra nodded, though Halisstra did not understand exactly what she meant.

Uluyara stepped back from their circle, removed her silver medallion from under her mail, and spoke a prayer to Eilistraee. The wind swallowed her words, but when she was done, she joined her hands, pointed them at the stone of the tor as through they were a knife, and parted them.

The stone answered her gesture. Her magic turned the rock malleable, and she shaped it as though it were clay in her hands. Moving with precision, she used the spell to raise two walls from the flatness of the plateau. They met at a right angle and shielded them from the wind. She stepped forward and shaped them more carefully with her touch, smoothing them as best she could with her palms.

"Now you," Uluyara said to Feliane.

The elf smiled, nodded, and mirrored Uluyara's casting. She raised a third wall, and a fourth, leaving a narrow archway in the middle of one to serve as the doorway.

"And you," Feliane said to Halisstra.

Halisstra spoke the prayer that allowed her to shape stone to her will. When she finished, her hands felt charged, as though they were attached to the earth. She moved them gently, as if she was a potter, thinning the walls and drawing the excess up into a flat roof to form a crude, boxlike shelter.

She felt pleasure in working so closely with her fellow priestesses. They were *creating*. When priestesses of Lolth worked together, it was always to destroy, though Halisstra knew that sometimes—*sometimes*—destruction too brought pleasure.

When she finished her work, she and her fellow priestesses shared a smile. The wind whipped their hair into halos.

Inspired, Halisstra unsheathed the Crescent Blade and with its tip etched Eilistraee's symbol into the still-malleable stone above the open doorway.

"A temple to the Lady in the heart of Lolth's domain," Uluyara said, her voice defiant above the howling wind. "Well done, Halisstra Melarn."

Halisstra saw that the doubt that previously had clouded the expressions of her sisters was gone. Under their accepting gazes, the doubt in her own soul shrank until it was little more than a tiny seed in the center of her being, barely noticed.

At that exact instant, a knife stab of pain raced up Halisstra's leg. Her vision blurred. She grimaced and would have fallen had she not caught herself on Eilistraee's temple.

The spider poison.

Uluyara and Feliane crowded around her, concern in their expressions. Uluyara examined Halisstra's wounds, found the blackened holes in her leg.

"Poison," Uluyara concluded.

"Let me," Feliane said and took Halisstra's hands in her own.

Feliane sang to the Dancing Goddess above the howl of the wind, and her song purged the poison from Halisstra's veins.

Halisstra felt as though something else might have been purged from her veins too. She thanked Feliane, who hugged her.

Afterward, the three priestesses of Eilistraee entered the temple they had raised. Uluyara quickly walked the interior, holding her holy symbol medallion and chanting the while.

When she was finished she looked at her two companions and said, "This is hallowed ground now, reclaimed from Lolth in the name of the Dark Maiden. At least for a time."

Halisstra could not help but smile. The interior of the temple did feel different, cleaner, purer. Within its rough walls, she felt sure of herself for the first time in days.

All three priestesses sank to the floor, spent, their backs to the wall, their legs extended. Exhaustion showed in both Uluyara's and Feliane's expressions. But elation too. They had reached the Demonweb Pits and survived the attack of a spider swarm.

After a few moments' respite, Uluyara healed them all of their minor cuts, scrapes, and bites. Feliane conjured a meal of vegetable stew and fresh water into some small bowls she carried in her pack.

After the repast, Halisstra said to them, "We should take watch in shifts, just to be safe, while we wait. I doubt the spiders will dare the top of this spire in the wind, but we cannot be sure. When things grow calmer below, we can continue on. I'll take first watch."

Uluyara nodded, shifted against the wall, and closed her eyes. She vented a sigh and soon was in Reverie. Feliane followed her quickly.

Both were seasoned warriors, Halisstra realized, taking rest wherever and whenever they could.

Halisstra quietly positioned herself near the open door. She drew the Crescent Blade, laid it across her thighs, and settled in for her watch.

Outside, the wind railed against the temple for the effrontery it was. In its angry wails, Halisstra still heard it calling to Lolth's Chosen, but she knew—or at least she thought that she knew— that it was no longer calling to *her*.

"I'm coming for you," she softly promised. "Soon."

Being little more than nests of legs, the chwidencha charged forward with alarming rapidity. Pharaun willed himself into the air as they closed and his ring answered. In one hand, he still held the ball of guano; with the other, he pulled a bit of flakefungus from a cloak pocket and shouted the words to a spell. As he uttered the last word to the incantation, he crushed the flakefungus in his hand and cast the powder in the direction of one of the charging chwidenchas. It uttered a squeal of agony as the magic engulfed it, flensed it of flesh, stripped it of its carapace, and left nothing more than a shapeless pile of gore.

The rest of the pack did not so much as slow.

Jeggred bounded forward in front of Danifae and met three onrushing chwidenchas with a charge of his own. He caught the first of them in mid-jump, plucking it from the air in his powerful fighting arms and tearing off its legs by the bunch while the creature squealed and slammed its remaining claws against the draegloth's flesh, leaving bloody welts. Ichor sprayed, coating the draegloth, mixing with his own blood. In three heartbeats, the draegloth had disarticulated the creature, leaving only a round lump of hair and flesh.

Two other chwidenchas leaped atop Jeggred, one on his back and one on his side. Their weight knocked him to the ground and the three fell in a snarling tangle of legs and claws. Jeggred still clutched a handful of the legs from the first chwidencha he had killed. Chwidencha claws rose and fell like miners' picks, churning earth and flesh. Fanged mouths tried to penetrate the iron of the draegloth's flesh. Jeggred roared and answered with his own claws. Pieces of chwidencha flew high into the air.

The rest of the pack continued forward and swarmed the priestesses. Danifae barely had time to pocket her holy symbol and free her morningstar before the chwidenchas were upon her. She careened backward and struck one with the spiked weapon, snapping some of its legs. She spun away from a claw swipe from another and slammed the head of the weapon into another chwidencha's front, but a third leaped high and landed atop her. She tried to utter a spell, but the creature wrapped its legs around her as tightly as a cloak and tried to drive her to the ground. She turned a circle, its weight causing her to stumble, all the while offering a muffled chant. Finally she went down, and five chwidencha swarmed over her. Pharaun could barely see the priestess under the squirming mass of legs and claws. Claws pounded into her mail, her flesh.

To his surprise and to her credit, Danifae did not stop fighting. She pulled a dagger from a belt sheath and fought from the ground, kicking, stabbing, screaming, driving the dagger repeatedly into the flesh of chwidenchas that coated her. Pharaun figured her for dead and put her out of his mind.

Below and to Pharaun's right, Quenthel's whip cracked. All five serpents extended to twice their ordinary length and clamped their fanged mouths onto the legs of a chwidencha. Almost instantly, the creature's legs went rigid, and it fell over dead from the whip's venom. Unperturbed, its fellows trampled over it. Chwidenchas closed on Quenthel from all sides.

Quenthel uttered a hasty prayer to Lolth and instantly grew to half again her size. A violet glow suffused her flesh, the power of Lolth made manifest. Using her magical buckler as a weapon, and driven by her spell-enhanced strength, she smashed its steel face into the front of a chwidencha, snapping a mass of legs like twigs. Three claws from a chwidencha to her right slammed into her in rapid succession, driving her backward but seemingly doing no real harm. Her whip struck again, driving back one of the creatures. She caught another chwidencha in her buckler hand, gripping two thick legs in her fist, and threw the creature across the battlefield.

Before Pharaun could shout a warning, another two chwidenchas leaped onto Quenthel from behind. She bore the weight better than Danifae, tried to throw them over her back, but six others rushed forward. Claws thumped against her armor and tore gashes in her exposed flesh. Her serpents lashed out but missed. She fell, buried under a pile of seething, churning legs and claws.

Pharaun heard Danifae shout a warning, he turned in mid-air—

And saw only a curtain of legs, claws, coarse hair, and an open, fang-filled mouth before the creature was upon him. A chwidencha had leaped high enough into the air to reach him. It hit him full force in the chest and wrapped its legs around him. The impact drove him backward and down, despite the power of his ring of flying. He hit the earth in a heap, entwined with the creature, his breath gone. The chwidencha wrapped him up with some of its innumerable legs, while it bit with its dripping fangs and flailed with its free claws like a mad thing. Blows slashed against Pharaun's sides, his arms, his face, into the earth around him.

Only Pharaun's enchanted *piwafwi* prevented the claws from disemboweling him, but he still felt blood flowing down his torso, and the impacts to his head nearly knocked him senseless.

He tried to fend off the blows with his hands and feet and roll out from under the chwidencha, but it was too heavy and too determined to hang on. Unable to fly, he mentally summoned his rapier from his ring, remembering too late that he had lost the ring to Belshazu. The chwidencha's fangs ground against his magically armored cloak again and again, trying but failing to penetrate the garment and open his gut.

Pharaun struggled to regather his senses and his breath.

The chwidencha raised one of its claws high and drove it toward Pharaun's face. He tried to squirm aside, failed, and the claw hit him with enough force to split rock. His protective enchantments prevented his face and skull from splitting open but the impact still exploded his nose and drove his head hard against the rocky ground. For a horrifying moment, consciousness started to slip from him. He grabbed at it and reeled it in with the entire force of his will.

Dazed and increasingly angry, he realized that he still clutched in his right hand the ball of bat guano.

"Here's a treat," he mumbled through a blood-filled mouth.

He mouthed the words to a spell that would turn the chwidencha and the entire area into cinders. He swallowed down the blood leaking into his mouth from his ruined nose and spoke the words clearly. He would have to hope that the inherent drow resistance to magic would shield him and his companions; that, or he would have to hope they could take more punishment than the chwidencha.

Just as he was about to utter the final syllables of the spell, the creature's fangs penetrated his *piwafwi* and sank into the skin of his chest. A bolt of pain caused his body to spasm but Pharaun did not lose the cadence of his spell. He had trained in Sorcere, cast spells as an apprentice while his Masters had held candle flames to his bare flesh. A bite from one of Lolth's failures could not break his iron concentration.

He finished the spell as the chwidencha reared back to take another bite of his flesh. Gritting his teeth, Pharaun closed his fist around the tiny ball of guano and shoved it into the chwidencha's open maw.

Reflexively, it clamped down on his hand.

Pharaun closed his eyes just as his universe exploded in orange light and searing heat. He felt some of his hair melt, felt the flesh of his arm, chest, and face char. He could not contain a scream.

The force of the blast blew apart the chwidencha atop him, reducing it instantly to ash. Hisses, growls, and screams sounded all around him, audible above the explosion. He smelled the stink of burning flesh. His own, no doubt.

It was over in one agonizing heartbeat.

He opened his eyes and found himself staring up into the dark sky above. For a moment, he had the absurd thought that his spell had charred the clouds, but then he realized that the storm was gathering above them.

Blinking, dazed, he shook the charred chwidencha pieces from his body—they were little more than chunks of seared flesh—and slowly sat up. He wiped the blackened blood from his face and nose and blinked until his blurry vision cleared. His hand was a blackened, seared piece of meat. It did not yet pain him, but it soon would.

He looked around and saw that the fireball had wrought a perfect sphere of devastation. A circular swath of blackened and partially melted rock denoted its boundaries. He had not burned the sky, but he had nicely burned the earth. He took a professional's pride in the damage it had done.

Within the circle, Jeggred sat on his four hands and knees, chest heaving, eyes blinking. A seared chwidencha corpse lay in pieces under his claws, and chwidencha legs dangled from his mouth. Bleeding but only mildly burned, the draegloth eyed Pharaun coldly as he spat the legs to the ground and climbed to his feet.

"You'll need to do better than fire, mage," the draegloth said, his voice raspy.

To Pharaun's surprise, Danifae and Quenthel both had survived too. They were burned and smoking, and minor cuts and bruises covered them both, but they lived. Quenthel stood on the far side of the blast radius, returned to normal size. Her serpents, covered in ash, hissed at Pharaun. He frowned, wishing he had at least put them down.

Danifae stood on the other side of the blast, leaning on her morningstar for support. She must have regained her feet and her weapon during the combat.

PAUL S. KEMP

A score or so chwidencha carcasses, charred, smoking, and stinking, lay scattered about the battlefield.

"What in the Abyss did you do?" Danifae demanded, then she coughed. Claw scratches crisscrossed the fireball-pinked flesh of her face.

Saved your hide, unfortunately, Pharaun thought but did not say.

Instead, he replied, "A spell went awry, Mistress Danifae."

"Awry?" Quenthel asked. Much of her hair was singed, but she otherwise looked to have avoided most of the effect of the fireball. "Indeed." She coughed. "If your spell went awry, mage, then you merit no credit for ending the combat."

Pharaun smirked through his broken nose and bowed as best as his wounded body allowed. The bite wound in his stomach throbbed, and his hand was in agony.

Danifae glared at him and added, "Next time, male, you are to provide a warning before another of your spells . . . goes awry."

Pharaun snorted with disdainful laughter and instantly regretted it. Blood shot from his nose, and pain wracked his face.

At that, Jeggred offered a snort of his own.

Through his pain, Pharaun said to Danifae, "And you might have warned me a bit earlier than—"

A scrabbling from outside the circle drew Pharaun's eye, and he trailed off.

All of them followed his gaze.

The Teeming continued around them but that was not what concerned him.

Nearly a score of chwidenchas rose smoking from the rocks outside the blast radius. All had twisted legs and melted flesh and hair, but they too had survived the blast. They hissed, raised their front claws, and started tentatively forward.

"Perhaps the combat isn't ended, after all," Pharaun observed and took some satisfaction in the acid look Quenthel shot him.

Quenthel cracked her whip, and the serpents offered a hiss at the chwidenchas. Danifae brandished her morningstar and stepped near Jeggred. The draegloth threw back his head and uttered a roar that shook stones.

Pharaun let his companions dangle for a moment before he said, "But then again, perhaps it *is* over." He'd had his fill of chwidenchas for the day. "Draw near," he said to them, and looked directly at Danifae. "You are hereby warned."

His companions shared a look and hurriedly backed near him as the chwidenchas slowly scuttled forward. Pharaun took a pinch of phosphorous powder from the inventory he kept organized in his *piwafwi's* pockets, cast it in the air, and spoke the words to a spell. When he finished, a semi-opaque curtain of green fire whooshed into being, a ring of flames twenty paces tall that burned between them and the chwidenchas. It danced merrily, casting them all in a sickly green light.

"That should keep them a while," he said.

His companions offered no thanks, but he took some satisfaction when even the whip-serpents sagged with relief.

With nothing else to be done for the moment, Pharaun said, "Pardon me, all," before he pushed one nostril closed with a finger, blew out a gob of blood and snot, then did the same for the other side.

He was a bit embarrassed by it all—it was something Jeggred might do—but he had little choice. He could hardly breathe. Pharaun shook his throbbing head to help clear it and drew a handkerchief from an inner pocket and wiped off his face as best he could. The white silk came back black with ash and red with blood.

Through the ring of flames, Pharaun saw the chwidencha circling, watching them through the breaks in the fire. Beyond the chwidencha, he still caught glimpses of the violence of the Teeming.

"How long, mage?" Quenthel asked.

"Not long enough, unfortunately," he answered. "Perhaps a quarter hour. How long does this Teeming last?"

Quenthel belted her whip and shook her head. Pharaun wasn't sure if that meant she didn't know or simply didn't want to answer.

"It lasts as long as Lolth wills it," Danifae offered, belting her own weapon. She ran her fingers over the scratches on her face, checking their depth.

"Hardly helpful, Mistress Danifae," Pharaun said. "And how

convenient for us that her will caused it to occur just after we arrived here."

"Tread carefully, mage," Quenthel warned.

"Indeed," Danifae said, eyeing him.

Pharaun was tempted to ask then and there why the chwidencha had answered neither Quenthel's nor Danifae's commands, but one look at Quenthel's whip made him think better of it.

Instead, he said, "I think it ill-advised to travel overland while this continues. Chwidencha may prove the least of our concerns. It appears the Spider Queen has decided to make the Teeming part of her test."

The priestesses said nothing but looked out through the curtain of green fire, their expressions distant and unreadable. Perhaps they too were wondering why the chwidencha had not responded to their power.

Finally, Danifae said, "We should take shelter for a time, let the Teeming run its course. Then we can travel overland again."

Jeggred eyed the chwidencha with hungry eyes. "The wizard said the wall of fire will last only a quarter hour. What shelter will we find in so short a time?"

"The caves," Pharaun said.

All of them looked first to Pharaun, then at the ground, to the holes that surrounded them.

"Why not atop one of the tors?" Danifae asked, pointing at one of the innumerable spires of black stone that dotted the plane. "Few spiders seem able or willing to scale their heights."

"Look to the sky, Mistress Danifae," Pharaun answered. Already the sun was invisible behind a wall of black storm clouds. "I think it would be safer and more comfortable, underground."

Besides, Pharaun had already encountered one horror atop a spire. He had no desire to encounter another.

"The caves," Quenthel said, nodding.

"Yes, Mistress," hissed one of the female heads of her whip. "The caves will be safer."

"Silence, Zinda," Quenthel gently admonished her whip.

"Safer?" Jeggred said and sneered. "Safety is the concern of cowards, timid priestesses, and weak mages." He eyed Quenthel and Pharaun meaningfully in turn.

Pharaun smiled at the draegloth, turned his gaze to Quenthel, and said, "I would remind your nephew that it was Mistress Danifae who suggested that we seek shelter to avoid the danger of the Teeming. Does that mean you think her timid, Jeggred?"

Pharaun took a moment to enjoy the look of consternation on Jeggred's face before he said, "Perhaps not, then. But in any event, it appears you would prefer to linger on the surface until we return. I think it an excellent idea. Thank you, Jeggred. Your bravery will be remembered in song."

He offered the draegloth an insincere bow, and Jeggred snarled and bared his fangs.

Pharaun ignored the oaf—showing a dolt to be a dolt brought him only small satisfaction—and eyed the open mouth of the chwidenchas' hole.

To Quenthel, he said, "I can seal the cave opening behind us with a spell, and we can wait for as long as need be. When the storm passes and the violence ends, I can get us back through, and we can travel then."

Quenthel nodded, and said, "An excellent idea, Master Mizzrym."

Jeggred snorted with contempt, and Quenthel fixed him with a stare that could have frozen a fire elemental. The serpent heads of her whip rose up and offered the draegloth a stare of their own.

"Nephew?" she said and made the word sound like an insult. "You wish to say something more, perhaps?"

Jeggred opened his mouth, but Danifae's hand on his arm stopped him from saying whatever words he had thought to offer.

Instead, Danifae smiled her disarming smile and looked to Pharaun.

"Master Mizzrym has offered sage counsel," she said, as though to Jeggred but really to Quenthel. "And Mistress Quenthel is wise to heed it." She let that sit a moment before she cocked her pretty head and frowned. "Though, I've never before seen a male demonstrate such persuasion over a priestess of Lolth."

Pharaun almost laughed aloud at the transparency of the play. Danifae hoped to weaken the relationship between Pharaun and Quenthel by intimating that the high priestess relied to an unseemly degree upon Pharaun.

"Hardly persuasion," he replied. "But perhaps if she were not the only priestess in this little band to have demonstrated wisdom, she would not have to rely on the paltry suggestions of a mere male."

Jeggred glared at him, fangs bare. Pharaun stared back at the oaf.

Danifae showed no sign that she had heard Pharaun. She had eyes only for Quenthel.

The Baenre priestess met Danifae's stare with one of her own, gave a tight smile, and said, "Some males serve a purpose, battle-captive." She too let that sit a moment before adding, "Of course, one must be careful in choosing which males best suit the purpose at hand." Then she let her gaze settle contemptuously on Jeggred. "A priestess with a poor eye for choosing her male servants is often a dead priestess. Perhaps your draegloth has some sage counsel of his own to offer on the matter?"

"Counsel?" Jeggred snarled. "Here's my counsel, you—"

"Jeggred," Danifae interrupted and patted one of the draegloth's fighting arms. "Be silent."

The draegloth said no more.

"Your dog is well-trained," Pharaun said, and Jeggred started to lunge at him.

Danifae caught his mane, and he halted in mid-stride. Pharaun held his ground and smiled.

Again, Danifae did not acknowledge Pharaun, instead saying to Quenthel, "No, Jeggred has nothing to say at the moment. He is a male and offers his counsel only when solicited by me."

Pharaun could see the anger brewing behind Quenthel's eyes. She walked up to Danifae—not even Jeggred dared get in her way, though he did stay beside the battle-captive—and stared down at the smaller female.

"My nephew has never been known for his intellect," she said.

Danifae smiled and stroked the draegloth's arm. "No, Mistress Quenthel," she replied. "Just his loyalty."

Quenthel's expression hardened. She gave Danifae one last glare before turning to Pharaun and saying, "And I rely on only Lolth, male."

When he heard those words, Pharaun knew that Danifae had accomplished exactly what she had hoped.

"Of course, Mistress," he said, and nothing more, for there was nothing more to say. The damage was already done.

Behind Quenthel, Danifae offered him a knowing smile through the cuts on her face. Jeggred offered him a snarl of undisguised hate.

He ignored them both and said to Quenthel, "The cave, Mistress?"

She nodded and replied, "The cave. But first. . . ."

The high priestess withdrew from an inner pocket of her *piwafwi* the wand of healing that she had stolen from Halisstra Melarn back in Ched Nasad. She touched it to herself and whispered the command word. The cuts on her face closed, the burns diminished, and her breathing grew easier. Afterward, she walked over, and without asking permission, touched it to Pharaun and repeated the process. Much to his relief, his nose healed, the charred mess of his hand regenerated, and the innumerable cuts and scratches on his torso closed.

"Thank you, Mistress," he said with a bow.

Quenthel did not acknowledge his gratitude. She put the wand back in her cloak, turned to Danifae, and said, "No doubt, you will tend to yourself and your loyal draegloth."

Pharaun offered Danifae a sneer. Likely, Danifae could tend to no one. Though Lolth had reawakened and both priestesses had spells at their command, it was rare for a priestess of Lolth to store many healing spells in her mind. Priestesses of Lolth destroyed, they did not heal. Quenthel could heal herself and Pharaun fully only because she had Halisstra's wand.

To his surprise, Danifae smiled at Quenthel and said, "Lolth will tend to us. As always."

"Quite so," Quenthel replied with a cunning look.

Pharaun straightened his robes. At his feet, the cave mouth yawned. It sank almost vertically into the rock. Webs lined its walls, and stink leaked from it.

"After you, Mistress Danifae," he said and gestured down at the cave, all the while thinking, After all, there might be something dangerous down there.

Danifae twisted her beautiful face into a sneer and said, "Come, Jeggred, Master Mizzrym remains timid."

The draegloth took her curvaceous body in his inner, smaller arms and lifted her from her feet.

"How quaint," Pharaun observed.

The draegloth stared holes into the mage.

One of Danifae's legs escaped her cloak. She wore tight-fitting breeches, and the curve of her thigh and hip drew Pharaun's eye, despite himself. She caught him eyeing her and did not cover her leg.

"Descend," she said to Jeggred, all the while smiling seductively at Pharaun.

Jeggred touched his House Baenre brooch and levitated down into the cave mouth.

For Quenthel's benefit, Pharaun signed after Danifae, *Whore.*

He looked up to find Quenthel staring at him, her expression unreadable. She drew her whip and stepped to the cave opening.

"Seal it behind us, mage," she said.

She touched her own brooch and followed Danifae and her nephew down, whip bare and ready in the event of an ambush.

Pharaun stood a moment at the edge, watching the top of Quenthel's head sink into the darkness. Quenthel had said to Danifae that *some* males served a purpose—he needed to make certain that she continued to think him one such.

For a moment, for a single tempting heartbeat, he considered abandoning her, abandoning the quest, but quickly dismissed the idea as ill-advised. Lolth was awake, and her priestesses again wielded the power of their goddess; things were returning to normal. Besides, Pharaun would be answerable to Gromph and House Baenre upon his return to Menzoberranzan for any direct or indirect harm he caused Quenthel.

With nothing else for it, he touched his House Mizzrym brooch and stepped out over the cave mouth. For a moment, he hovered there, listening to the darkness below, wondering whether Danifae and Jeggred would actually dare an ambush. He heard nothing and so descended until he floated just below the cave mouth. There, he withdrew from his pocket a round piece of polished granite, a stone he had purchased from a curio vendor in Menzoberranzan's bazaar, long ago. He cradled it against his palm with his thumb, flattened his hands palms downward, and recited a series of arcane words.

When he finished the incantation, the magic formed a wall of stone over the cave mouth. Its borders melded with and into the surrounding rock, blocking the light from Lolth's sun. The brewing storm and the seething Teeming disappeared behind the wall. The cave fell into welcome darkness, to which his eyes quickly adjusted.

He put the granite back in its place and descended the rest of the way down the shaft. It wove a bit here and there, but moved ever downward. He heard no sounds coming from below and assumed that nothing dangerous lurked there—other than his companions. To be prudent, he pulled another chip of flakefungus from his pocket and readied himself quickly to cast the flesh-flensing spell. He thought of an ancient drow adage: Keep allies within reach of your sword, but keep enemies within reach of your knife. He saw the wisdom of it. Pharaun never felt more uncomfortable than when Jeggred and Danifae were out of his sight.

It was clear to him that Danifae was trying to undermine Quenthel's claim that she was the *Yor'thae*. Perhaps she thought to take that title for herself? As absurd as it sounded, Pharaun thought it to be true.

For his part, he was beginning to think that neither priestess was or would be Lolth's Chosen.

Chapter

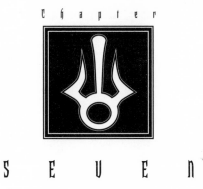

S E V E N

Amidst the smoking ruins of Ched Nasad, Nimor stood on the cracked balcony of a once luxurious noble manse. The house's structural wards had saved much of it from destruction when it had fallen to the bottom of the chasm, but it still lay broken and askew on the rocky floor.

Most of Ched Nasad rested in ruins around him. Heaps of rubble and chunks of stone lay scattered and broken about the chasm's bottom like the grave markers for a race of titans. Once, the city had hung over the chasm on thick calcified webs. Then the duergar had come, the webs had burned under the gray dwarves' stonefire bombs, and the city had fallen.

Nimor smiled at the destruction. He had returned from Chaulssin to look once more upon what his people had wrought.

High above him hung those few of the city's webs that had survived the duergars' attacks bombs. A number of intact buildings dangled in the broken, calcified strands like trapped caveflies, twisting helplessly over the abyss. A handful of minor noble houses, built into the chasm's walls rather than on the webs that once had spanned the abyss, remained largely intact.

Nimor knew that the Jaezred Chaulssin had begun to rebuild the city in their image. Drow in service to the Jaezred Chaulssin worked at the bottom of the chasm, along its walls, and in the surviving webs near the top. The beat of shadow dragon wings whispered in the cavern's depths, and many of the ruined buildings that lay at the bottom of the chasm had already been melded into the Shadow Fringe. Oily, impenetrable clouds of darkness shrouded the areas that existed simultaneously in both planes.

The transformation would go on for decades, Nimor knew, centuries perhaps. But when it was complete, Ched Nasad would be another Chaulssin. The resurrected Ched Nasad would be one drow city that contained nothing of the Spider Queen or her servants.

Nimor smiled, but softly. The sting of his failure lingered still, overwhelming whatever satisfaction he otherwise would have felt. He had hoped to see not only Ched Nasad transformed but also Menzoberranzan.

He eyed the magical ring of shadow on his fingers, a band of liquid black that wrapped his digit like a tiny asp. Of his many magic items, only his ring and his House brooch had retained their enchantments after Gromph Baenre had cast his spell of disjoining during their combat over Menzoberranzan's bazaar. Nimor had not yet replaced any of his lost items. He regarded his penury as penance for his failure.

Menzoberranzan. He saw the city in his mind's eye, imagined it lying in ruin about him like Ched Nasad. . . .

He shook the image from his head. Menzoberranzan stood, and Lolth had returned. Nimor had failed, and he was no longer the Anointed Blade.

He sighed, fingering his ring.

Patron Grandfather Tomphael had ordered Nimor to return to Ched Nasad and Menzoberranzan one final time, to look alternatively upon the scene of the Jaezred Chaulssin's success and the scene of their failure. Nimor, of course, would obey the patron grandfather.

Besides, certain matters in Menzoberranzan—a certain bald matter and a certain half-devil matter—required his attention.

"Here is success," Nimor said to himself, taking one final look around. "Now, on to failure." Without further ado, Nimor called upon the power of his shadow ring to remove him to the Fringe. When the magic took effect, ruined Ched Nasad vanished, replaced by a shadowy ghost of itself. Only those portions of the city that had been removed to the Plane of Shadow appeared substantive.

Nimor willed open a path along the Fringe to Menzoberranzan, and it opened before him. He stepped onto it, beat his wings, and took to the air. Unbound by the physical rules of the Prime Material Plane, the Shadow Fringe allowed rapid travel. Swirling ribbons of shadow surged past and through Nimor. The power of the ring and the nature of the Fringe turned a journey of days into a journey of less than an hour.

Presently, he found himself within the shadow correspondent of Menzoberranzan, a ghostly, dead image of spires, towers, and stalagmite structures. With an effort of will, he pierced the veil between the Fringe and the Prime and found himself hovering in darkness near the top of Menzoberranzan's cavern. Darkness enshrouded him, rendering him invisible even to the otherwise discerning eyes of any drow who might look up. He gazed down on his failure.

The Jaezred Chaulssin had scried the city, to keep tabs on events even after Nimor had fled. He knew what those scryings had shown: The forces that he had so meticulously marshaled to conquer Menzoberranzan were falling into disarray.

Vhok and his Scourged Legion were beginning to withdraw, fighting retreating actions through the caverns east of the fungus gardens. No doubt the tanarukks would flee back to their warrens under Hellgate Keep with their hides, if not their dignity, intact. Horgar and his ridiculous duergar forces would not be so fortunate. The duergar had left the rock of Tier Breche a pockmarked, melted, blackened waste, but they had failed to break through—Melee-Magthere, Arach-Tinilith, and Sorcere all remained in the hands in the Menzoberranyr. The battle there continued still. Explosions and blasts of magical energy denoted the ferocity of the ongoing fight. Nimor knew it to be futile. Lolth had reawakened; the opportunity to conquer the city had passed. The Spider Queen once again answered the prayers of her priestesses, and when Arach-Tinilith spat out her daughters and they bolstered the Menzoberranyr forces with their newly regained spells, the duergar would be routed. Few of them would ever leave Menzoberranzan. Unlike Vhok, Horgar was too blind or too stupid to see it.

Nimor let his eyes linger long on the high plateau of Tier Breche, in particular on the soaring spires of Sorcere. Somewhere within, he knew, was Gromph Baenre. Thinking of the Archmage caused Nimor's blood to seethe. Gromph had destroyed the lichdrow Dyrr—the bazaar was still a smoking ruin from their spell battle—and had been instrumental in thwarting the entire invasion. Nimor both hated and respected him.

Nimor beat his wings and looked to his right, to the great spire of Narbondel. Its base glowed red in the darkness, a defiant beacon proclaiming to the whole of the Underdark that Menzoberranzan remained standing. Nimor wondered if Gromph Baenre himself had lit the beacon's fires.

With startling suddenness, Nimor's emotional control slipped. An unbearable wave of frustration washed over him. He clenched his fists and swallowed down the roar that threatened to escape his throat.

He had fought well, schemed his best, and *nearly*—within a rothé's hair—conquered the most powerful drow city in the Underdark. The trophy of Ched Nasad would have paled in comparison to the jewel of a conquered Menzoberranzan.

Of course, he knew that *nearly* was insufficient, *almost* a paltry substitute for success, both for him and for the Jaezred Chaulssin. *Nearly* won him nothing. *Nearly* had lost him his place of honor as the Anointed Blade of the Jaezred Chaulssin.

That was the lesson the patron grandfather had wanted him to learn in returning—Nimor was to taste of failure, to gag on its flavor so much that he would never allow it to happen again. A tiny amount of humility took root in him and tempered his habitual arrogance.

You promised to cleanse Menzoberranzan of the stench of Lolth, Patron Grandfather Mauzzkyl had said to him. *Have you done that?*

Nimor had answered truthfully—he had not done it. He had only *nearly* done it, and the bitter taste of *nearly* had all but choked him.

There will be other opportunities, Patron Father Tomphael had promised. *If you learn wisdom.*

Lesson learned, Tomphael, Nimor thought.

He fixed his gaze on Tier Breche, where the battle still raged, on the quiet Donigarten, where drow soldiers prowled amongst the giant mushrooms. He thought of Horgar, of the little princeling's failings. . . .

Nimor had a lesson of his own to teach. Horgar would be his student.

With his mind made up, he looked down upon Menzoberranzan a final time. He stared at the soaring, elegant spires, the tall towers, the twisting architecture of the great manor houses—all of it a silent testimony to the unbearable arrogance of the Menzoberranyr. Perhaps they too had learned to temper their arrogance with humility.

Or perhaps not.

Nimor looked down on the city and offered it a grudging nod of respect.

It had beaten him.

This time.

With a minor exercise of will, he moved into the bleakness of the Shadow Fringe.

The chwidencha shaft dropped down a spearcast before ending in a round chamber from which a wide horizontal tunnel extended. Old webs covered the walls, and the dried husks of dismembered spiders lay cast about here and there, no doubt the remains of the chwidenchas' meals. Jeggred kicked at them absently. The dry air stank of must and decay.

Pharaun lowered himself to the ground beside Quenthel. Her whip flicked its tongues at him.

Danifae and Jeggred stood apart, eyeing them. Danifae ran her fingers over her holy symbol.

Pharaun could not help but think that not all of them would be returning to the surface. As a precaution, he still held the piece of flakefungus hidden in his palm.

To Quenthel, he said, "The tunnel is sealed above us, Mistress."

She nodded, looked down the horizontal tunnel, and said, "We will continue on for a bit longer. Find a more suitable spot to rest."

No one protested, and Quenthel started down the tunnel. The rest of them fell in beside her. The cavern was wide enough to accommodate the four of them walking abreast, and they did exactly that. None wanted to show their backs to the others.

Here and there, smaller tunnels branched off of the main corridor and extended away into the darkness. Pharaun wondered if all of Lolth's plane was hollowed out with tunnels, possessed of an Underdark of its own. He thought they might have escaped the chwidencha and the Teeming only to find themselves facing something worse in the depths.

Nothing for it now, he thought, but he kept his hearing attuned for sound from ahead.

He heard nothing other than Jeggred's respiration and the scrape of their boots over the rock. The draegloth shouldered aside any carcasses in their way, but they encountered nothing alive. With the chwidencha pack on the surface, it appeared that at least the main horizontal tunnel was empty.

After a short time, they came to another roughly round chamber, one littered with more desiccated spider husks and the hollowed out molt shells of the chwidencha. The shells, each as thin as fine parchment, looked like dozens of chwidencha ghosts. Jeggred clutched one of them by its leg, and the entire shell crumbled away in his grasp.

A few small pools of green acid dotted the chamber and bubbled smoke and stink into the air. It vented through cracks in the low ceiling. A natural archway in the far side of the chamber opened onto another large tunnel.

"Perhaps here, Mistress?" Pharaun ventured. "We are not vulnerable to attack from behind"—at least not from the chwidencha, he thought—"and can set a watch in the tunnel ahead. A rest would allow me time to study my spellbooks and replace those spells I've cast."

He knew that it would also allow the priestesses, after a brief Reverie, to refresh their own spells from Lolth. He could use the benefit of one or two of Quenthel's healing spells.

Quenthel eyed him with cool disdain, obviously displeased that he had offered yet another "suggestion." Still, she said, "Here is as good a place as any. We will eat, rest, and pray to Lolth."

Hearing no protests, Pharaun found a choice rock and collapsed atop it.

"Jeggred will take the first watch," Quenthel said.

The draegloth, crumbling yet another chwidencha molt, looked to Danifae, who nodded.

"Very well," Jeggred said to Quenthel and stalked across the chamber to take a position at the mouth of the tunnel before them.

Quenthel watched him go with anger in her eyes. When he seemed situated, she said, "Not there, nephew. Up the tunnel a ways. It does me no good to learn of danger after it is already upon us."

Jeggred offered her an irritated growl and looked again to Danifae. The former battle-captive hesitated.

"Are you concerned to be alone with me?" Quenthel asked Danifae, letting contempt drip from her tone.

Danifae looked at Quenthel with a challenge in her startling gray eyes. "I have yet to see a reason why I should be," she replied.

Quenthel smiled. Still holding Danifae's attention, she waved dismissively at Jeggred and said, "Be off, nephew."

Jeggred held his ground until Danifae gestured him up the tunnel with a flick of her fingers.

"I will not be far," Jeggred warned, for the benefit of everyone.

Even after the draegloth had prowled up the tunnel, Quenthel continued to stare at Danifae. The former battle-captive studiously ignored Quenthel, examined her wounds, shook out her gear, and stripped down to a tight-fitting tunic and breeches. Scratches, cuts, and bruises from the battle marred her skin but did nothing to diminish her attractiveness.

Pharaun again was struck by the sheer physicality of the woman. Men had fought and died for things much less beautiful than Danifae's form.

It was unfortunate she would have to die. Hopefully, soon.

After a time, Quenthel too began to tend to her gear while her serpents eyed Danifae. Pharaun took that as a truce and settled in himself.

Each of the three rested as far from the others as the chamber allowed, their backs pressed against the web-covered tunnel wall. They ate in silence from the stores Valas Hune had procured for them long ago and brooded in silence amongst the chwidencha molts.

To occupy himself, Pharaun inventoried and organized his spell components in the many pockets of his *piwafwi*. Afterward he took one of his traveling spellbooks from the extradimensional space contained in his pack and replaced the spells he had cast by committing to memory the arcane words to new spells. Thinking that he might have to use his magic against Jeggred and Danifae, he chose his spells with care.

By the time he had finished, both priestesses had closed their eyes and entered Reverie. Pharaun assumed that both had surreptitiously cast alarm spells around them to warn of anyone approaching too near. He activated the power of his Sorcere ring and saw the soft red glow of a ward spell in the area around both priestesses. He smiled.

For creatures of chaos, he thought, drow certainly were predictable.

Unlike their mistress, Quenthel's whip serpents remained awake and alert. Two of them—K'Sothra and Yngoth, Pharaun believed—extended outward and kept their eyes on the tunnel in which Jeggred hulked. Two others kept their eyes on Danifae, while one of them, the female Qorra, kept her eyes on Pharaun.

Vaguely offended that he warranted only one watch-serpent, Pharaun stuck his tongue out at Qorra. She flicked her own in answer.

Pharaun ignored it, stretched out his legs, and settled more comfortably on his rock. He was tired but not yet ready to enter Reverie. For a while, he watched the rise and fall of Danifae's breasts. He did not allow himself to fantasize about her overmuch—he knew how well she played male lust to her advantage. Besides, it was only a matter of time before Quenthel disposed of her.

Pharaun finally decided that he too should spend an hour or two in Reverie. But first, he would cast a ward on his person similar to that which the priestesses had cast. It would alert him should any creature get closer than five paces.

Just as he began to whisper the arcane words to the spell, Pharaun felt a familiar tingle in his mind. He recognized it immediately, and a more pronounced tingle coursed through his flesh. He aborted the casting, delighted that the alu-fiend had tracked them down again.

Well met, Master Mizzrym, Aliisza purred, her mental voice like velvet in his brain.

Despite himself, Pharaun grinned like a first-year apprentice at the gentle touch of her mind on his. While he knew she had her own reasons for tracking him and his companions, he could not deny that he enjoyed her attentions.

Aliisza, my dear, he projected back. *We do meet in the strangest locales.*

The times are strange, dearest, Aliisza replied. *And strange times make for strange bedfellows.*

One can only hope, he answered, and grinned still more widely.

Quenthel's watch serpent hissed at his smile. Pharaun let it fade from his face, turned, and looked past the serpent.

Up the forward tunnel a stone's throw, he saw the outline of Jeggred's muscular form. The draegloth sat in a crouch, watching up the tunnel, his broad back to Pharaun and rising and falling with each stinking breath. Pharaun could not tell whether the draegloth was awake or asleep. Unlike the drow, Jeggred required actual sleep.

Quenthel and Danifae both were in Reverie, though both wore scowls. Pharaun was pleased. He would have only to deal with Quenthel's whip serpents.

The priestesses you accompany rest ill at ease, Aliisza said.

It is a racial trait, he answered, sarcastic as always.

They simply need a little something to tire them out first, she said.

A little something? Pharaun answered, playing at being offended. Aliisza laughed.

What is the Yor'thae? she asked.

The question gave Pharaun a start, but long practice kept it from his face and his surface thoughts. How did Aliisza know anything of the *Yor'thae?*

Apparently sensing his agitation, the serpent watching Pharaun uttered a soft hiss. Pharaun pretended not to have heard it and settled more comfortably onto his rock.

How do you know that word? he asked.

She let her mental fingers caress his brain playfully. *The Lower Planes resound with it. It's in the wind, the screams of tortured souls, the rush of boiling water. What is it, dear heart?*

Pharaun heard none but the usual guile in her tone so he answered her truthfully: *The* Yor'thae *is Lolth's Chosen.*

Oooh, Aliisza said. *Which is it, the pretty one or the big one with the whip?*

Pharaun could only shake his head.

Maybe it's neither, Aliisza said.

To that Pharaun made no comment, though her statement disquieted him. Her words too closely echoed his own recent thoughts. He decided to change the subject.

Where are you? he asked.

I am invisible. Look around and find me, she answered with a mental smile. *If you do, you'll win a prize.*

With a simple exercise of his will, Pharaun attuned his vision to see invisible objects and creatures—an effect that he had made permanent to his person. Casually, so as not to alarm the whip serpent whose eyes still glared at him, he looked down the tunnel opposite the one in which Jeggred sat, back the way they had come. There, he saw her.

You win, she said.

Aliisza leaned suggestively against the tunnel wall, back arched, arms back, batlike wings furled so as to reveal her lean body—the sensuous curve of her small breasts, the length of her legs, the turn of her sleek hips. Her long ebony tresses flowed down her back. She was looking at him and smiling. Pharaun found her small fangs more alluring than he cared to admit.

Greetings, lady, he said. *I'll just be a moment.*

It is ungentlemanly to make a lady wait, she said, a smile in her voice. *You will have to make it up to me.*

Again, Aliisza, he answered, *one can only hope.*

Her giggle managed to sound both girlish and sexually provocative all at once. He found it thrilling. He looked at the serpent that was eyeing him. It flicked its tongue again.

He leaned back on his rock and closed his eyes as though preparing for Reverie. Fortunately, he knew an illusion that required no material component.

Moving only his fingers and whispering under his breath, he cast a sophisticated glamour. The spell affected the entire area in which he reclined. To the serpent, it would appear that Pharaun remained on his rock deep in Reverie, while the real Pharaun could do whatever he wished in the affected area under cover of the illusion.

After completing the spell, he looked at the serpent—Qorra showed no sign of noticing anything amiss—and climbed silently to his feet. The serpent's gaze remained fixed on the illusion, on the false Pharaun.

Smiling, Pharaun pulled from his pocket a strip of fleece and whispered the words to a spell that rendered him invisible—a necessary precaution, because when he left the affected area of his spell, the illusionary image would no longer screen him. He knew that Aliisza's demon blood allowed her to see invisible creatures so she would have no problem seeing him.

In his mind, Aliisza giggled again, and the sound sent a charge through him. Strange that the presence of a demon, albeit a beautiful one, brought him such pleasure.

Clever, dearest, she said.

He started quietly down the tunnel toward her, leaving behind him an image of himself reclined on a rock, lost in Reverie.

My, but you look horrid! she said as he drew near.

He knew. He had been through the Shadow Deep, the Abyss, and the Demonweb Pits, all without bathing. He had used cantrips to mitigate his stink and keep his clothes mended, but the minor spells could do only so much.

The journey has been a hard one, he replied. *Perhaps you would enjoy an illusory Pharaun more?* He jerked his thumb back up the corridor.

No, dearest, she said and stretched languidly, to show her body to best effect. Her green eyes danced over him suggestively. She held out her arms. *I'll take the real thing.*

The moment he got within arm's reach, he took her in his arms. Her wings unfurled and enfolded them, her perfume intoxicated him, and her skin and curves stirred him. He allowed himself a moment of pleasure, greedily ran his hands over the smooth skin of her body, then—with great effort—pushed her to arm's length.

How did you find us? he asked. *Why are you back?*

She pouted and her wings fluttered. *Such questions, Master Mizzrym! I found you by looking. You are not hard to locate. As for why I'm back . . .* Her face grew serious and she looked directly into his eyes. *I wanted to say good-bye.*

To Pharaun's surprise, a pit opened in his stomach. *Good-bye?* He let his fingertip trace a line along her hip.

She looked away for a moment. *I fear we will not see each other again, dear heart, and I needed to look on you one last time.*

He did not believe a word of that last, though he very much wanted to.

You've finished your charge and now return to Vhok's embrace? Is that it? He was surprised by the bitterness that leaked into his tone. His hands on her body grew less gentle.

She smiled, reached up, and ran a long-nailed finger down his jaw-line. *You are so jealous, my mage. No, I will not return to Kaanyr. I have told him all that I was charged to tell, and now I am done with him. At least for now. I have grown interested in a different kind of man.*

Pharaun ignored the implicit compliment. *What did you tell him of us?* he asked.

Everything, she replied. *That was my charge.*

Pharaun had expected nothing different, but the answer still pained him distantly.

If you will not return to him and your charge is complete, why would we not see each other again? he asked her. The question betrayed a certain weakness, and he hated himself for asking it, but he could not help himself.

She smiled, and her eyes grew as sad as her demonic blood allowed. *Because I do not think you will survive what is coming*, she answered.

For a moment, he could think of nothing to say. Her candor surprised him. Finally he managed a smile.

What is coming?

She shook her head and said, *I don't know. But this plane is dangerous and stinks of . . . something.*

He dropped his hands from her. *You are mistaken,* he said.

She looked at him in a way she had not done before. *Perhaps I am. I can always hope. But if I am not, may I have something to remember you by? A token of my gallant drow mage?*

Pharaun wondered if a token freely given was what Aliisza really was after. He knew what a skilled spellcaster could do with such a prize. A part of him wished it were otherwise, but he had seen through her.

Before that, tell me what is happening in Menzoberranzan, he demanded.

Aliisza frowned, as though the fate of Pharaun's city was an afterthought. *It stands,* she replied. *Lolth's power has returned to the priestesses. Kaanyr is in retreat, and the duergar soon will be.*

Pharaun felt a surge of relief at the news. Menzoberranzan still stood.

Odd, he thought, that he felt such attachment to a place when he felt no such attachment to any of the persons in it.

Distantly, he wondered if Gromph had survived the siege. If not, "Archmage Pharaun Mizzrym" sounded pleasing. And since House Baenre would be selecting Gromph's replacement, he had all the more reason to ally himself closely with Quenthel.

A memento? Aliisza prodded. *Something small. A lock of your hair?*

Pharaun smiled at her, a hard smile. *No, Aliisza. No token. I think I'll keep all of me to me.*

She took his meaning; her brow furrowed in genuine anger.

You misunderstand, she protested. *I—* She looked over his shoulder and behind him. *It seems your absence has been noted. Farewell, beloved.*

With that, Aliisza kissed him as though she never would again and vanished, teleporting away without a sound and leaving him staring at the wall. The smell of her perfume and the remembrance of her last word lingered in the air.

Before Pharaun could do anything further, his invisible flesh erupted in purple flames. Faerie fire. A flutter went through his gut.

The stench of rotting meat overwhelmed the last lingering aroma of Aliisza—Jeggred's breath. Pharaun quickly rehearsed an excuse in his mind, even while he thought through the incantation that would trigger one of his more powerful spells, a spell that required the utterance of only a single word.

Grabbing two fingers' full of web from the wall, he dispelled his invisibility spell, turned, and found that his nose nearly touched Jeggred's heaving chest. The draegloth had moved behind him with the silence of an assassin.

"Jegg—"

With breathtaking speed, Jeggred grabbed him by the throat with one of his fighting claws and lifted him from the ground until they were face to face. Pharaun gagged—partially from his proximity to the draegloth's breath, partially from the clawed hand squeezing his windpipe.

"A spell to cover your absence?" the draegloth asked, nodding back at the chamber where the illusory Pharaun still reclined. Jeggred sniffed the air thoughtfully. "What is it you're doing down here, mage?" His red eyes narrowed. He extended his arm and slammed Pharaun against the cave wall.

Pharaun's magical *piwafwi* and rings prevented the impact from cracking his ribs, prevented even Jeggred's incredible strength from closing his throat, but only just.

"Release . . . me," Pharaun demanded.

His anger was rising, partially at Jeggred, partially at the fact that he feared he might have mistaken Aliisza's motives. Still, he considered it beneath his dignity to flail about, so he remained still.

Jeggred squeezed Pharaun's throat harder and held his other fighting claw before Pharaun's face. With his inner, human hands, the draegloth took hold of Pharaun's arms by the wrists, presumably to prevent him from casting any spell that might require gestures to complete. Pharaun tested their strength for a moment and found them more than a match for his own. Scraps of old meat hung between Jeggred's yellow fangs.

"She is manipulating you," Pharaun croaked, and both of them knew he meant Danifae.

"No," Jeggred said and sneered. "She's manipulating *you*. And my aunt." He spat the last word as though it tasted foul.

"You're a fool, Jeggred," Pharaun managed. "And time will show it."

The draegloth exhaled a cloud of vileness into his face and said, "If so, you will not be alive to see it, because you, wizard, are out of time. This has been long in coming."

Jeggred looked back up the cavern to see if either Danifae or Quenthel had stirred. Neither had. Pharaun's illusionary image sat on its rock in blissful Reverie.

To Pharaun's surprise, the serpents of Quenthel's whip—all of them—stared silently down the tunnel, watching the confrontation.

Pharaun understood it then. If the serpents were watching the confrontation, then Quenthel was watching it too, at least indirectly. She wanted to see what Pharaun would do when confronted with her nephew. Another test. He was growing tired of tests.

Jeggred, of course, saw nothing other than the opportunity to kill an irritating rival. With an unexplainable illusion of Pharaun sitting in the campsite, the draegloth probably believed that he could concoct any story he wanted about Pharaun's treachery.

Jeggred leaned in close and his rancid breath made Pharaun wince.

"You see it now, don't you?" the draegloth asked. "Go ahead and scream. You'll be dead before they awaken. I'll explain it as the execution of a traitor and feed on your heart. My aunt will shout, but she'll dare nothing more."

Pharaun could not help but smirk. Jeggred truly was a dolt. He had all the subtlety of a warhammer. It surprised Pharaun that the draegloth possessed any drow blood at all, so inept was he at scheming. Of course, having met and killed Belshazu, Pharaun knew that Jeggred's demon bloodline was something less than spectacular.

"Your death amuses you?" Jeggred whispered, leaning in close.

Pharaun twisted his head to the side so he could more easily speak.

"No, you do."

With that, he whispered a single word of power, one of the most powerful he knew.

The arcane force in the word hit Jeggred like a titan's maul. Foul breath blew from the draegloth's lungs, and he released Pharaun—who managed to keep his feet when he hit the ground—staggered, uttered a spit-fouled stutter, and sank to his knees.

Pharaun knew the word of stunning would leave the draegloth incapacitated for only a short time. He knew too that the spell likely would not ordinarily affect Jeggred at all, but the draegloth's battle with the chwidencha had left him weakened and vulnerable.

Of course, Jeggred knew no more of that than he did of Quenthel's tacit permission to Pharaun to teach the oaf a lesson.

With exaggerated dignity, Pharaun smoothed his *piwafwi* and straightened the stiff collar of his shirt. When he noticed that Jeggred's claw had torn a slash into the chest of his shirt, his anger burned hotter still.

"Oaf," he said and cuffed Jeggred in the head. It felt good. He cuffed him twice more.

The draegloth sat on his knees before him, drooling, moaning softly.

Pharaun looked up the tunnel to see ten slitted eyes still watching in silence. He knelt down to look into Jeggred's slack face.

Pharaun thought of offering the draegloth the excuse he had prepared—I was gathering material components. The illusion was to avoid alarming anyone who might stir in their sleep and find me gone. The invisibility is one of my ordinary precautions when acting alone—but decided against it. Quenthel wanted to test Pharaun and at the same time teach a lesson to Jeggred. Pharaun would push it as far as the high priestess wanted it to go.

He took Jeggred's slack face in his hand and said, "Remember this moment, demonspawn. This is me doing better than fire, not so? If I desired it, I could drag you to one of these acid pools and dip your head in. Imagine that, dolt. The spell I used to incapacitate you was of middling power. If I wished you dead, I could strip the flesh from your bones in an instant, or stop your heart with a word." He punched the draegloth in the face again, more angry at himself over Aliisza than at Jeggred. He decided that he would burn out Jeggred's eyes before killing him. He started to cast—

But the crack of a whip froze him.

"Master Mizzrym!" Quenthel called, her voice sharp.

With effort, Pharaun controlled his anger. He leaned in close to Jeggred's vile face and said, "Serve your mistress and I'll serve mine. We'll see who has the right of it at the end of this. Meanwhile, I'll place a contingency spell on my person. Perhaps you do not know what 'contingency' means? It means that if you put one of your stinking hands on me again—"

"Mage!" Quenthel called again. Pharaun licked his lips, looked back up the tunnel, and slowly stood. Lesson learned, apparently. He wondered if he had passed her test.

Quenthel stood over the illusionary Pharaun, looking down the tunnel at the confrontation between the real mage and Jeggred. Danifae stood behind and beside her.

"Explain yourself," Quenthel ordered.

Pharaun held up the webs and recited the lie without hesitation: "I was gathering material components, Mistress. I used an illusion of myself to avoid alarming your serpents, lest they disturb your sleep."

At that, the serpents hissed, and Qorra drifted up near Quenthel's ear and hissed something. The high priestess cocked her head and nodded.

Danifae's hooded gaze went from Quenthel, to the stunned and drooling Jeggred, to Pharaun. Despite her obvious vulnerability at that moment, she showed no fear. The Master of Sorcere wondered if Quenthel would take the opportunity to kill the former battle-captive.

"Not this," the Baenre priestess said. She passed her hand through the illusion, which vanished, then she pointed the haft of her whip at Jeggred. "Explain that."

Pharaun looked down on the draegloth, who seemed at last to be recovering from the effects of the word of power. All four of his hands reflexively clenched and unclenched. His moans grew louder, and his drool pooled on the tunnel floor.

"Ah, *that*," Pharaun said, and aimed a smile at Danifae. "Without the two of you available to mediate, your nephew and I found ourselves engaged in a . . . doctrinal dispute. I'm afraid the force of my arguments has left him stunned." He patted the draegloth's head the way he might a pet lizard. "My apologies, Jeggred. All is forgiven now though, not so? We'll simply agree to disagree."

Jeggred managed a growl, and his fighting hands pawed at the hem Pharaun's *piwafwi.*

"Yes, well . . . *ahem,*" Pharaun said, and backed up a step. "There we have it. Friends again."

He walked back up the tunnel and bowed before Quenthel.

"Forgive me for disturbing your Reverie, Mistress," he said.

Quenthel stood silent for a moment before saying, "You did not disturb me, Master Mizzrym."

Hearing those words, Pharaun understood that he had passed her test. He smirked at Danifae and called to mind another spell as he watched Jeggred come back to himself. Just in case.

The effect of the word of power vanished quickly. Jeggred's breath came hard, and his hands dug furrows into the stone. He climbed to his feet, shook his head to clear it, and fixed his baleful stare on Pharaun.

"I will tear your head from your shoulders!" he roared as he stalked up the tunnel.

"Stop," Quenthel commanded but to no effect.

It was Danifae's raised hand and soft word that halted Jeggred's charge. He stood in the tunnel, staring hate and rage into Pharaun.

"All things in due time," Danifae said and offered the mage a smirk of her own.

"Indeed," Quenthel answered, eyeing her nephew coldly.

Pharaun forced a smile, just to irk the draegloth, though when he looked at Quenthel and Danifae, he heard Aliisza's troubling words in his mind. Maybe neither of them was the *Yor'thae.*

Nimor found Crown Prince Horgar at his field headquarters—a large, rough-walled, stalagmite-dotted cavern in the Dark Dominion not far from the battle lines at Tier Breche. The chamber stank of sweat, blood and the thick smoke from stonefire bombs. Nimor hung near the ceiling of the cavern in his half-dragon form, invisible by virtue of one of his spells.

Squads of duergar streamed in and out of the cavern, coming and going from the battle, their blocky armor ringing, their dusky skin smoke-blackened and bloody. Some were still enlarged—duergar possessed an innate magical ability to double their size—so Nimor presumed they had just come from the battle.

They spoke to each other in their inelegant language, their voices deep and gravelly. In the conversations, Nimor caught the ripple of a faint undercurrent of fear. Perhaps the duergar forces at last had encountered the spells of a priestess of Lolth. If so, even the tiny intellects encased in their small bald heads must have understood the implications.

Two elderly clerics, each as bent and twisted as a demon's heart, tended the wounded. Nimor didn't know the name of the deity they served and did not care. Occasional explosions in the distance—stonefire bombs and spells, no doubt—occasionally shook the cavern and rained rock dust on the inhabitants.

Prince Horgar stood to one side of the table, bent over a low stone table, looking at a makeshift map of the approaches to Tier Breche and issuing orders to two of his commanders who stood to either side of him. After a few moments of exchanged words, nods, and gestures at the map, the two bald commanders offered agreement with whatever Horgar said, gave him a salute—by thumping their pick hafts against the cavern floor—and stalked off.

Horgar stood alone over the table. He stroked his chin, staring at the map, lost in thought.

Horgar's scarred bodyguard stood near the Prince. He held a bare warhammer, but his slack stance indicated that he expected no threat to his lord. Nimor smiled without mirth and flexed his claws. With the keen senses gifted him through his dragon heritage, Nimor studied the chamber. Duergar also possessed an innate ability to turn invisible. Nimor wanted no surprises.

As he had expected, he sensed no one in the cavern other than those duergar he could already see.

Horgar stood upright and stared at the cavern wall, no doubt still wrestling with some problem or strategy that plagued his pathetic little mind. He put a hand to his axe haft and rubbed the back of his bald head.

Calling upon the power of his brooch, Nimor levitated down until he stood directly behind the unsuspecting Horgar. The little dwarf was muttering in his awkward tongue.

Lesser races, Nimor thought with contempt.

Nimor might have said something to Horgar before killing him, might have shown himself, might have evoked fear, but he did none of those things. He was the former Anointed Blade, an assassin without peer. When he killed, he did so without fanfare.

Moving with a rapidity and ease born of long practice, he reached around Horgar and tore open the dwarf's throat. He turned visible the moment he struck.

The hole in the prince's throat sprayed blood across the map, across the cavern wall. Horgar gagged and fell across the table, his muttering becoming a fading, wet gurgle. The prince tried to turn to see his attacker, but Nimor had split his throat so thoroughly that the muscles of the gray dwarf's neck would not function.

Nimor grabbed Horgar by the top of his head and jerked his face around, partially to let Horgar see who had killed him and partially to ensure that the crown prince was beyond the ability of the duergar clerics to help. Horgar's eyes went wide, and Nimor satisfied himself that the gaze had flashed recognition even as the duergar's life blood pumped from the gash in his throat. The prince's gnarled body began to spasm in its death throes. The clerics would be unable to save him.

Shouts of surprise and rage erupted around Nimor—the stomping of boots, the clank of armor, the ring of weapons. He looked up to see duergar charging him from all sides, rushing to their fallen prince. Some were enlarging as they charged, growing taller and broader with each step. Others called upon their innate ability to turn invisible and vanished from his sight.

No matter. Nimor smiled, swallowed, triggered a reaction in his lungs, and exhaled a cloud of billowing, viscous shadows that nearly filled the whole of the cavern. He poured all of his pent up frustration, anger, and shame into the exhalation. The cloud of darkness engulfed the onrushing duergar and siphoned energy from their souls. Nimor heard them shouting in pain, cursing, shrieking. He stood unharmed in the midst of the cloud, grinning at the death around him.

The shadows dissipated quickly. Duergar lay scattered around the cavern, some of them dead, some of them dying, some of them weakened so much that they could no longer stand. A few, perhaps, would live.

Unless a drow patrol happened upon them.

Nimor located Horgar's scarred bodyguard. The duergar lay to Nimor's right, still holding his warhammer. The gray dwarf's eyes were unfocused, and drool dripped from the corner of his mouth. Nimor stepped to him, knelt, and looked him in the face.

"You should have chosen your master with more care," he said and slit the guard's throat.

He found the death pleasingly cathartic. It always did him good to kill.

Without another word, Nimor rose, shifted back into the Shadow Fringe, and left the cavern of dead and dying duergar behind him. He wanted to see Kaanyr Vhok before he returned to Chaulssin.

🕷   🕷   🕷

Inthracis walked the flesh-lined lower halls of Corpsehaven. The walls squirmed in his wake. Nisviim, his jackal-headed arcanaloth lieutenant, walked beside him.

The screams of mortal souls sounded in the distance, audible through the walls. No doubt some of his mezzoloths were feeding soul larvae to his canoloth pets.

"Shall I sound the muster for the Regiment, Lord?" Nisviim asked.

Despite the arcanaloth's muzzle and overlarge canines, his voice and diction were impeccable. His heavy robes swooshed with each step. He toyed with one of the two magical rings on his hairy fingers as he spoke.

"Soon, Nisviim," Inthracis answered, "but first we must attend to a small matter in my laboratory."

The arcanaloth cocked his head with curiosity but kept his questions to himself.

"Very well, Lord," he said.

Nisviim was as skilled an enchanter as Inthracis was a necromancer. Ordinarily, an arcanaloth of Nisviim's power would not have been content to serve as a second to Inthracis, but Inthracis had long ago learned Nisviim's true name. With it, he kept Nisviim obedient and subservient. The only alternative to service for Nisviim was pain.

They approached the flesh-and-bone door that led to one of Inthracis's alchemical laboratories. Two hulking, round-bodied, four-armed dergholoths stood silent guard outside the door, both of them dead, both of them animated by Inthracis's spells. Recognizing their master, the guardian dergholoths made no move to stop Inthracis's advance.

Inthracis telepathically projected the password to suspend the wards on his door. The doors flared green as the wards dispelled. Decaying hands reached from the jambs to swing the portal open. The stink of rot, pleasant to Inthracis, wafted into the hallway.

Inthracis and Nisviim walked through the dergholoths and entered. Corpsehaven's dead pulled the door closed behind them.

Animated hands, arms, and claws crawled the floor of the laboratory—the aftereffects of some of Inthracis's experiments. All of them scrabbled out of the ultroloth's path. Several immobilized and magically silenced barbed devils lay on tables, all of them partially dissected. Beakers and braziers covered the multitude of bone workbenches. The handkerchief with which Inthracis had daubed Vhaeraun's blood soaked in an enchanted beaker filled with shadow essence. A bound fire mephit chained to the beaker held his tiny, flaming hand under the glass. Inthracis hoped to turn the blood into a distillate strongly resistant to Shadow Magic.

"Follow, Nisviim," he said.

They crossed the laboratory to the opposite wall, where Inthracis spoke a word of power. The corpses in the wall rearranged themselves at its utterance, squirmed wetly aside, and formed an archway. A small, secret, heavily warded chamber lay beyond. With a mentally projected series of words, Inthracis temporarily deactivated the wards.

The ultroloth walked through, as did his lieutenant.

The arcanaloth believed that he had never before seen the chamber, but Inthracis knew better. Nisviim had been in the chamber many times, but he remembered none of them.

Within the room, reclined in a clear case of glasssteel, was Inthracis's body. Or at least one of them. As a matter of prudence, he kept at all times at least one clone of himself in temporal stasis. Were his current body to die, his soul, and his memories and knowledge, would immediately inhabit the clone. Upon being released from stasis, the clone would live; Inthracis would live.

He had been through three cloned bodies already, and the process had served him well. He'd died under devil claws before Dis's gates in battle with the forces of Dispater, and he'd been consumed by a caustic ooze on the fungus-filled thirty-fourth layer of the Abyss.

"A clone, Lord," Nisviim observed.

Inthracis pushed aside the memories of his earlier deaths and nodded. The time had come.

Without preamble, he spoke aloud Nisviim's true name: "Heed me, Gorgalisin."

Instantly, Nisviim's body went slack, his eyes vacant. The arcanaloth stood perfectly still, as much an animated corpse as the dergholoths outside the laboratory. At that moment, Inthracis could have commanded Nisviim to do anything and the arcanaloth would have done it without question. Indeed, had he desired it, Inthracis could have used the invocation of Nisviim's true name to wrack the arcanaloth's soul or stop his heart.

He did not desire it, of course. A bound, named arcanaloth was too valuable an asset to waste with an amusing death.

Instead, Inthracis said, "In the event that you gain knowledge of my death or if I do not return to Corpsehaven within a fortnight of this day, you will enter this chamber—" and Inthracis telepathically projected into Nisviim's mind the words to bypass the wards of his laboratory and the secret clone chamber—"and dispel the stasis on this body. Thereafter, you will return to your quarters and forget that any of this ever occurred. Nod if you understand."

Nisviim nodded.

"Return now to your quarters," Inthracis said, "and let slip from your consciousness all that has transpired during the last hour. Thereafter, sound the muster and summon the regiment to the Assembly Hall."

Nisviim nodded, turned, and walked slowly from the chamber.

Inthracis watched him go, content that even if he died in combat with the drow priestesses, or if Vhaeraun betrayed and murdered him, he would live again.

In a thoughtful mood, he studied his hand, compared it to that of the clone in stasis. He wondered for a few heartbeats as to the nature of identity. Was the vivified clone still *him?* Was Nisviim still Nisviim when commanded by his truename?

For a moment, Inthracis felt as much a construct as Corpsehaven, no more truly alive than the dead who prowled its halls.

The storm railed against the temple for hours. Feliane and Uluyara sat in peaceful Reverie throughout, untroubled by the angry scream of the wind and the blistering patter of the smoking, acidic rain. Halisstra allowed them their rest.

Within only a few hours, the storm abated, as though the plane itself was too exhausted to continue its tirade. Even the ever-present wind died down somewhat. Halisstra offered a prayer of thanks to Eilistraee, rose quietly, and exited the makeshift temple.

She stepped forth into the fall of night. Lolth's tiny sun was just vanishing behind the distant horizon, casting its last spiteful rays of blood-red light over the landscape. The violence below too had abated, and Halisstra took a moment to enjoy the silence—no storm, no keening webs, no whispered, *"Yor'thae."*

She felt free of Lolth, entirely free. She closed her eyes for a moment and breathed deeply, a clean breath.

She turned and saw that the walls of the temple were pitted from the rain, but that the symbol of Eilistraee over the door remained intact, untouched by the storm.

Our goddess is stubborn, Halisstra realized with a smile.

High above her, the river of souls flowed on toward their eternal fate. Looking at them, she felt a pang for Ryld. She hoped he had found at least some peace.

The souls flowed as one toward a range of craggy mountains that soared so high they looked like a wall between worlds. Halisstra noticed that while vortices of power still churned in the sky, there were fewer than before.

She felt as though events were settling down, consolidating before the final resolution. Unfortunately, she did not know just what the final resolution would be. She pressed the flat of the Crescent Blade against her palm and tried to keep her heart calm.

Feeling small but still determined, she walked to the edge of the tor and looked out and down on the Demonweb Pits.

The sight nauseated her.

Evidence of the destructive violence had survived the storm. Legs, torn carcasses, and pedipalps lay strewn across the broken land for as far as she could see. Ichor stained the rocks, even after the rain. Gorges, holes, and pits marred the surface of the landscape; webs spanned every opening; lakes of acid steamed poison into the air.

Soon, she knew, the wind would return and with it, the keening of the songspider webs and the call to Lolth's *Yor'thae*.

Why did Lolth need this *Yor'thae*, Halisstra wondered? What was the Chosen supposed to do?

With effort, she pushed the questions from her mind. Lolth's schemes no longer concerned Halisstra.

She touched the symbol of the Dark Maiden embossed on her breastplate and smiled. She felt that she had stepped on a new path, that Lolth's voice would no longer pull at her soul. She was free of the Spider Queen.

For now, said a stubborn voice from the depths of her brain, but she pushed it back down.

The sun sank behind the mountains and its light faded entirely. Halisstra felt a painful itch between her shoulder blades, as though she had been poked with needles. She turned and saw, through a convenient hole in the clouds, eight red stars rising into the sky. Seven were bright, one dim. Clustered like a spider's eyes, the stars looked down on Halisstra with palpable malevolence.

She answered their gaze with a defiant stare and a raised blade.

*   *   *

Gromph sat behind the enormous, polished dragonbone desk in his office in Sorcere. A dim green glowball cast the room in viridian and threw long shadows on the walls. Various trinkets, weapons, sculptures, and paintings decorated the office, the magical flotsam Gromph had gathered over the course of his long life.

His magical ring had almost fully regenerated his flesh. The burns were entirely gone; the blisters healed. He tapped his fingertips on the desk—the skin was still slightly tender and tingly—and thought about his next steps.

Though he'd had little time to spare, he had managed a quick meal of spiced mushrooms and cured rothé meat while he and Nauzhror had awaited Prath's arrival. Gromph had not taken the time to bathe or change his attire, so the stink of filth and smoke still oozed from him. More conscious of the smell in the close confines of his office, he crinkled his nose, spoke the words to a cantrip, and used the minor magical power to mend his clothes and clean himself up, at least a bit.

A knock sounded on the zurkhwood door that opened onto the hallway.

"It is Prath, Archmage," the apprentice called.

With a flick of his finger, Gromph temporarily suspended the wards on his door.

"Enter," he commanded, and Prath did.

The wards reengaged when the door shut.

Prath nodded to Nauzhror, who sat in one of the two cushioned chairs opposite Gromph's desk, and crossed the room.

"Sit, apprentice," Gromph said and indicated the second chair.

Prath sank into it, saying nothing.

Gromph studied the two wizards, thinking the apprentice overly muscular and fidgety, the Master overly fat and ambitious. Neither yet understood exactly what Gromph proposed to do.

Gromph's personal office was perhaps the most secure location in the city, the haven from which he could begin in secret his assault on House Agrach Dyrr. A series of wards—far more than those that simply prevented entry through the doorway—sheathed the room to prevent not only physical intrusion but scrying and other magical surveillance. Gromph perceived the wards in the room around him as a tickle on the newly regrown hairs of his arms, a slight charge in the air.

Of all the mages in Menzoberranzan, only the lichdrow would have had a chance to penetrate Gromph's ward scheme, and only maybe.

Of course, the lichdrow was no more than dust at the moment. Gromph intended to ensure that he stayed that way.

A half-full chalice of fortified mushroom wine sat on the smooth, white desktop beside the remains of Gromph's meal. Near the chalice and silver plate sat one of Gromph's two personal scrying crystals. Unlike his crystal ball, unlike the great lens in Sorcere's scrying chamber, the crystal on his desk was not smooth surfaced, but rather was a head-sized, irregularly-shaped piece of brown, black, and red banded chrysoberyl. Those in the World Above called it "cat's eye," and its properties as a scrying medium were highly valued.

Unfortunately, a chrysoberyl scrying crystal typically did not have the range of most other types of crystals. Still, for close work, there was nothing better. And Gromph's crystal had an added benefit: He could cast certain types of spells through it.

The crystal sat cradled in a triangular stand of unusually-textured gray stone. An eye motif decorated the stand. Gromph had sculpted it from the spheroid body of an eye tyrant that he had petrified in battle long ago.

"An unusual scrying crystal," Nauzhror observed. "I have never seen its like."

"It is of my own making," Gromph replied. "And I have never recorded the process of its creation."

Nauzhror only nodded, eyeing the crystal.

Gromph took a sip from the mushroom wine. The bitter taste left a pleasant tang on his tongue. The wine fortified his will. He put his fingertips to the faceted surface of the crystal. It felt cool, though the magic within it sent a charge through his hands. He moved his fingers over its surface, tracing its edges, attuning it to his will.

Nauzhror and Prath watched in expectant silence.

Gromph closed his eyes and let his mind see the lines of power that flowed within the chrysoberyl. He waited for the connection between the stone and his mind to coalesce.

There.

He smiled, feeling the crystal as an extension of his own mind, his own senses. He opened his eyes, still connected to the crystal, and gave a satisfied nod. The bands of color in the crystal had bled together to turn the crystal black. As he watched, the black gave way to a misty gray.

"It is ready," he said, as much to himself as to Nauzhror and Prath.

"Indeed," said Nauzhror. "Are we to be of assistance, Archmage?"

"Yes," Gromph answered. "But not with this. Be patient, Nauzhror."

Prath leaned forward in his chair, elbows on his knees. He eyed the swirling gray mists in the crystal, and asked, "Archmage, I presume you will scry House Agrach Dyrr. Why not use the Scrying Chamber for this task? The crystal there is—"

Before Gromph could answer, Nauzhror answered in the same tone he might use with a particularly dense student, "Because only Baenre are to know of this. There may be spies other than Vorion within Sorcere's walls."

Gromph cocked an eyebrow. Nauzhror's analysis impressed him; the Master wizard saw much. Soon, Gromph would have either to move him up Sorcere's ranks or, if his ambition proved too great, kill him.

"Master Nauzhror offers one reason among several," Gromph said, giving the Master of Sorcere a look of reserved approval. "Another is that I know my offices to be shielded from Yasraena's scrying. I cannot be as certain regarding the wards around the scrying chamber without first performing a thorough check. We do not have time for that. Still a third reason is that I will need you both here, in my office, to further my deception."

"Deception?" asked Prath.

"Need?" Nauzhror asked.

Gromph regretted his word choice the moment it exited his mouth. Nauzhror's expression showed an ill-concealed eagerness at Gromph's declaration of "need." Even Prath looked mildly taken aback.

Gromph sealed the breach.

He stared coldly into Nauzhror's pudgy face and said, "My need is one of convenience, Nauzhror. Nothing more. *Any* Baenre mage will do. Perhaps another would be better suited than you. Do you wish to be dismissed?"

The multitude of possible meanings for which "dismissed" might be a euphemism hung in the air between them.

Nauzhror shook his head so rapidly that his paunch shook. "No, Archmage," he replied. "Not at all. I am honored to be of any small assistance in these weighty matters. I merely want to understand what it is you are planning."

"And you will," Gromph replied. "In time and only in part."

Gromph eyed Prath, whose expression showed no challenge whatever. Gromph was mildly disappointed.

"I am pleased to be of service too, Archmage," said the apprentice unnecessarily.

"I know," Gromph replied. Hours before, Prath had shaved off his own flesh to supply Gromph with a needed material component. He still bore a divot in his finger from the wound.

Prath was loyal, but Gromph had little love for loyalty. It was too fickle a sentiment, easily shattered, easily manipulated. Gromph demanded not loyalty but obedience, and he ensured it through fear of his power. He decided that he would have to keep a close eye on Prath going forward, though the apprentice would be useful over the next few hours.

"Well enough, then," Gromph said. "Let us first determine the nature of the challenge."

He concentrated on the crystal, and whorls of color began to swirl within the gray mist. Prath and Nauzhror watched intently. Both pulled their chairs closer to Gromph's desk.

"The lichdrow's phylactery must be within House Agrach Dyrr," Gromph said, speaking his thoughts and his hopes aloud. "Or at least it must be accessible through House Dyrr."

"A reasonable supposition, Archmage." Nauzhror scratched his cheek and said, "But even if the phylactery is in the House, will it not be too heavily warded for divinations to locate it?"

Gromph replied, "It will."

Gromph pictured House Agrach Dyrr in his mind—the moat, the bridge, the wall of stalagmites and adamantine, and the adamantine keep within. He had been within House Agrach Dyrr many times in the past. He called upon those memories to focus his vision.

"Then how do you propose to find it?" Nauzhror asked.

Gromph smiled through his concentration and said, "I'm not going to find it." He let his underlings share a confused look before he added, "I'm going to find everything but it."

Confusion stayed written in Prath's expression, but Nauzhror's face showed dawning realization.

"Cunning, Archmage," Nauzhror said, and Gromph heard genuine admiration in his voice.

Gromph did not acknowledge the compliment but instead let his mind sink farther into the crystal, let his consciousness float on its many facets.

"What is he going to do?" Prath whispered to Nauzhror.

He need not have kept his voice to a whisper. Gromph could maintain concentration while holding a conversation or while burning in the Hells' fires.

"Excluding the possibilities," the Master of Sorcere answered. "Watch and learn, Prath Baenre."

Prath seemed to want to ask another question but held his tongue.

The mists in the crystal parted, and House Agrach Dyrr took shape in the facets. Nauzhror and Prath leaned farther forward, put their elbows on Gromph's desk.

Gromph forced the crystal to change perspective and saw the House as though from the ceiling of Menzoberranzan's cavern.

House Agrach Dyrr was built in a series of concentric circles, with a domed temple of Lolth centermost. A wide moat in a deep chasm surrounded the complex. The chasm ended at the very edge of a high, worked wall of nine stalagmites, each as thick around as a giant's waist and as tall as a titan. Walls of adamantine stretched between the stalagmites. A second, lower adamantine wall ringed several inner structures.

Gromph moved the scrying eye downward, near the moat chasm, and saw that bodies floated face down in the water, burned, bloated, or cut down. Many were drow, some were orc and ogre, some were unrecognizable.

"Xorlarrin casualties," Nauzhror observed.

Gromph nodded agreement. "And perhaps a few Dyrr dead too," he said.

The moat was useful primarily as a way to channel an attacker's forces. Skilled mages could span it with a magical construction or fly over it, but it would be difficult to attack the walls in more than a few places at once without expending substantial magical resources. And even after crossing the chasm, an attacker would be faced with the foreboding outer wall of House Agrach Dyrr.

Atop that outer wall of stone and metal the Dyrr forces massed— drow soldiers, ogres, trolls, mages, a few of Yasraena's priestesses. They gazed down at the besieging Xorlarrin forces through narrow gaps in the stone parapets. To Gromph, they looked like insects crawling about their hive.

A single adamantine bridge, a narrow slab of metal without guardrails and wide enough for only two or three men abreast, spanned the moat. Gromph presumed the bridge was designed to be dropped into the chasm, if the need arose. At the bridge's end stood the massive adamantine and mithral doors that provided the only access through the stalagmite wall. A group of eight ogres lay in burned pieces in the shadow of the doors. The metal battering ram they had carried lay askew across the bridge. Gromph knew the doors would not show even a scratch from the ram. Like all drow noble manors, the doors, walls, bridge, moat, and the structure of House Agrach Dyrr itself would be warded with a series of protective spells and enchantments, all of them cast by the lichdrow and a long line of powerful Matron Mothers.

House Agrach Dyrr would stand for as long as the wards remained. Gromph knew that the wizards of House Xorlarrin, despite their deserved fame, would be hard pressed to dispel a ward put in place by the lichdrow. Until those wards were dispelled, Xorlarrin spells would harm the walls of House Agrach Dyrr about as well as a candle flame would harm a fire elemental.

"The siege will be long and bloody," Nauzhror said.

The Master of Sorcere and Prath leaned out over Gromph's desk so far that their heads almost touched Gromph's.

"Longer and bloodier still if the lichdrow returns," Gromph said, and the lesser mages shared a look.

"How long do we have, Archmage?" asked Prath.

"I am uncertain" Gromph admitted. "But not as long as I would like."

Prath's brow wrinkled, and he sagged back into his chair.

Gromph returned his focus to the scrying and saw that the bulk of the Xorlarrin forces massed on the far side of the bridge, just out of easy crossbow and spell range.

There, Gromph saw spider cavalry, drow infantry, a score or more of the robed Xorlarrin mages, a handful of priestesses, and a multitude of the soldiery of lesser races. The siege seemed to have quieted for the moment, as though House Xorlarrin was planning a new strategy.

Gromph moved the image over the stalagmite wall and drew in closer. Within the walls stood the squat, interconnected buildings that made up House Agrach Dyrr itself. The temple of Lolth dominated, a domed tabernacle set in the center of a complex that looked from above like the silhouette of a spider.

"Let us see what we have," Gromph said and whispered the words to a spell that allowed him to see magical emanations, their strength and type. He could have simply activated the permanent dweomer on his person that allowed him to see such emanations, but he wanted his underlings to see the wards as well.

When he finished and the spell took effect, Nauzhror drew in a sharp breath.

"Lolth's eight legs," Prath swore, and Gromph forgave him the heretical oath.

Layer upon layer of protective wards sheathed the structure of the house, the bridge, and the moat. More even than Gromph had expected. Gromph's divination translated the wards as a network of glowing lines, a matrix of veins that ran along and within the stone of the fortress, pulsing with power. The magical energy flowing through the walls, floors, and ceilings of House Agrach Dyrr nearly matched that of Gromph's own chambers. The lichdrow and the Dyrr priestesses had been busy over the centuries.

Some of the wards glowed ochre and viridian, some a deep blue, and some glowed a hot crimson. Most of them were designed to prevent physical entry, to bolster the structural strength of the House, or to dampen or negate magical effects, but many were designed to prevent scrying within the walls. It was those that Gromph was most interested in, at least at the moment.

Interspersed among all of the various types of wards were a series of spell traps, killing spells, and alarms that would be triggered by the disruption of a ward.

"One step at a time," Gromph said, both to himself and his under-mages.

He whispered a series of arcane words and modified his divination slightly so that it showed him only the glowing blue lines of the anti-scrying wards. They made a complex network that surrounded the fortress. Various sub-networks covered only certain buildings or rooms within buildings.

"It's as fine as a smallfish fisherman's net," Prath observed.

"True," said Nauzhror. "There are alarms, but I see no killing spell traps set amongst the scrying wards."

"Nor do I," said Gromph and was pleased.

The spell traps set in the anti-scrying wards that surrounded his own offices, if triggered, would trap the soul of the would-be scryer or drive him mad. House Agrach Dyrr had not been as thorough.

Gromph took a long moment to study the structure of the wards, searching for a backdoor. Unfortunately, he saw none. He settled in for a long assault.

He took a calming breath and said, "Let us begin."

✹   ✹   ✹

The Scourged Legion was in full retreat, Nimor saw. Already it had entirely withdrawn from the fungus fields of the Donigarten, and only a token force held the tunnels to the east of the city. Within those tunnels, Shobalar spider cavalry prowled and infantry from House Barrison Del'Armgo and House Hunzrin massed.

Invisible once more, and also using the shadows and darkness as cover, Nimor avoided detection by the drow forces as he moved through their lines. He could see they were preparing for a counterattack against the tanarukks. He was tempted to kill a few as he passed, just out of spite, but decided against it. His business with the Menzoberranyr was finished.

The counterattack that the drow were so carefully planning likely would find no enemies. Before Narbondel climbed another hour, the Scourged Legion would have vanished into the Underdark and be scuttling its way back to the warrens under Hellgate Keep. The war-weary drow were unlikely to pursue, Nimor thought, especially with the duergar still battling at Tier Breche. Nimor found it ironic and amusing that Vhok had shown more effectiveness in retreat than he had in attack.

After flying over and through the drow lines, Nimor moved through a long series of mostly empty tunnels, encountering only an occasional stealthy drow scout. To judge from the marks in the stone, much of the combat between the Scourged Legion and the Menzo-berranyr had occurred within those tunnels. The passage of many hobnailed boots had scored the floor; blood stained the stone here and there; severed body parts and spider carcasses dotted a few of the rooms; broken weapons, shields, and links of armor littered the floors; and burn marks from magical energies blackened walls.

Nimor saw no actual bodies until. . . .

A winding, narrow, tertiary tunnel opened onto a large cavern in which lay the bloody corpses of forty or so duergar footmen. They looked as though they had formed against the far, dead-end wall and fought to the last. Broken weapons, dented armor, and cloven shields littered the cavern's floor. Blood slicked the floor, still tacky to the touch. The duergar had been hacked to bits—the work of tanarukk axes and swords, not elegant drow blades.

"Well done, Kaanyr," Nimor said.

It seemed that Vhok, like Nimor, had decided to clean up his duergar association before retreating. It seemed that Vhok no more left ends untied than did Nimor.

Vhok had planned his escape well. He would flee the siege of Menzoberranzan with hardly a scratch, and if it mattered, scavengers would strip the cavern clean of duergar bodies within a tenday. Meat, dead or alive, never went unconsumed in the Underdark. No evidence of Kaanyr's betrayal of the duergar would be found by anyone but Nimor.

Nimor left the dead duergar behind and continued his invisible flight through the caverns. After a time, he began to encounter pockets of the withdrawing tanarukk forces. Squads of scaled and horned tanarukks—creatures with the savagery of orcs and the cunning of demons—trooped through the winding tunnels, weapons bare, bloodshot eyes intermittently checking behind them for pursuit. The ring of their boots, weapons, and armor resounded off the stone. Nimor moved over and through them like a specter, and only the breeze from his beating wings betrayed his passage.

For perhaps half an hour, Nimor trailed the retreating tanarukk forces through the tunnels. The demon-orcs moved with a purpose, probably toward a pre-determined mustering point, and Nimor hopped from one group to the next. He knew he would eventually happen upon Vhok.

Nimor heard the cambion before he saw him—coarse voices, the thump of dozens of boots, and the ring of heavy armor sounded from ahead, as did the occasional barked order by Kaanyr Vhok. Nimor beat his wings, sped forward, and spotted the cambion at the front of a large column of torch-bearing tanarukks. Vhok's close aid Rorgak, a tusked tanarukk broad-shouldered by even the standards of his own kind, stood at his side as they marched. Vhok had apparently retreated ahead of even the token force that he had left behind in Menzoberranzan.

Nimor smiled at the light that shined into Vhok's character—the cambion was a loud bully but ever a quiet coward.

Still, he commanded an army and had his uses and might yet again. And cowards were easy to manipulate, if not to rely upon.

Nimor swooped in front of the column, alit on the tunnel floor, and allowed himself to become visible.

Snarls and shouts of surprise ran through the tanarukk ranks, a low, dangerous rumble. The column surged to a halt. Vhok and Rorgak had their blades in their hands within a heartbeat.

Rorgak, greatsword in hand, lunged toward Nimor. Several of the tanarukks behind Vhok moved forward, blood in their eyes.

Vhok halted all of them with an upraised hand and a barked order.

"Hold," the cambion commanded, and they did. Even Rorgak.

Dozens of red eyes fixed on Nimor, hungry eyes.

Nimor held up his hands to show that he bore only a smile, though he knew his wings and fangs must have appeared disconcerting. Vhok and his tanarukks had never before seen him in his half-dragon form. If it proved necessary, Nimor could quickly flee into the Shadow Fringe.

"Nimor," Vhok said and raised his pointed eyebrows. "I hardly recognized you. You look different than last we met." He sheathed his rune inscribed blade and offered Nimor a hard look. "You take a chance showing a lone drow face to my men and me."

The tanarukks near Vhok growled agreement. Rorgak continued to stare at Nimor, his blade still bare.

Nimor flapped his wings and let shadowstuff leak from his nostrils. "As you can see, Kaanyr, I'm no more drow than you are human or they orcs."

At that, Vhok smiled and tipped his head to acknowledge the point. A few of the tanarukks chuckled.

"What then?" the cambion asked. "Do you have yet another wondrous scheme to offer me?" He gestured at his battle scarred, retreating column. "You see the result of your last."

Vhok's men laughed at that, but it was forced laughter. No doubt their retreat shamed them.

Nimor kept his smile, though it was difficult.

"Perhaps," he said. "But I would speak of it privately. Your tent?"

Nimor knew that Vhok's command tent was a magical structure that formed and collapsed into a fist-sized ball of cloth upon command, so it was always a convenient bit of private space.

Vhok studied Nimor's face for a moment before he said, "Very well." To Rorgak, Vhok said, "Have the legion take a meal. I will not be long."

Vhok added something else in a low tone, speaking to his lieutenant in Infernal. Though Nimor could not understand the language, he understood the meaning. Vhok was instructing Rorgak to stand ready in case Nimor attacked Vhok in the tent.

Nimor merely stared at Rorgak as the big, red-scaled lieutenant nodded to Vhok then headed back into the ranks, barking out orders. The tanarukk column broke ranks for a meal, but many bloodshot gazes stayed on Nimor.

Vhok pulled the magical wad of cloth from his pack, picked as level a spot as he could find on the tunnel floor, and cast it to the ground, uttering a command word in a harsh, forgotten language.

The cloth unfolded itself time and again until finally it sprung up into the pennoned, red-and-gold command tent that Nimor knew well. Vhok gestured him in, his breastplate shining in the torchlight. He kept one hand on his blade.

Nimor furled his wings and entered. Within, he found the tent fully furnished with a fine wooden table, a luxurious divan, and a plush couch. The decanter of what Nimor assumed to be brandy—one of Vhok's indulgences—sat on the table with two empty glasses beside it.

"Furnished and stocked," Nimor said, turning a circle. "An excellent magic item, Kaanyr. You need only dancing girls. Speaking of which, where is your little winged sweetmeat?"

Vhok snorted derisively, but Nimor heard the affectation in it.

"Gone," Vhok said. "At least for now."

"Ah, fickle women," Nimor said, and decided not to press further. "May I sit?" he asked.

Vhok indicated the couch. Nimor crossed the tent and collapsed onto it.

"We did not have to lose this fight, Kaanyr," he said.

"Only one of us actually fought this fight," Vhok answered. "The other fled when things got difficult."

Nimor struggled to retain his smile.

From outside the tent, near the flap, Nimor's keen hearing betrayed the quiet scrape of a boot on stone—Rorgak, no doubt.

Only when he had full control of his tone of voice did Nimor say, "Lolth's return alone saved Menzoberranzan. That and an unfortunate choice in allies."

Vhok looked at him sharply.

"Not you," Nimor said. "The duergar."

Vhok's expression relaxed and he nodded. "True, that," he said.

To Nimor's surprise, the cambion poured two small chalices of the liquor from the decanter and offered one to Nimor.

Nimor took it, but he did not drink. Vhok remained standing.

"Our little princeling is dead," Nimor said, swirling the brandy in his goblet.

Vhok raised an eyebrow. "You?"

Nimor nodded. When Vhok sipped from his brandy, Nimor did the same. The liquor had traveled well.

"Serves the little fool right," the cambion said. "Duergar are useless creatures."

"We are in agreement on that at least, Kaanyr," Nimor said. "The gray dwarves are a race of imbeciles." After a pause, he added, "I tracked you down to thank you for warning me of Lolth's return during my battle with the Archmage."

Vhok smiled around his goblet and said, "We were allies."

"Indeed. And as far as I'm concerned, we still are."

When Vhok did not reply, Nimor filled the silence by raising his glass in a toast and saying, "To grand undertakings."

Vhok raised his own glass half-heartedly and took a sip, eyeing Nimor over the rim. Afterward, he asked, "Is there something else, drowling? Or did you return only to express your gratitude and drink my brandy?"

Nimor decided to take Vhok's obnoxiousness as a jest and laughed it off.

He leaned forward to refill his chalice. As he poured, he said,

"There will be other battles, Kaanyr. Perhaps not tomorrow or the next day, but someday. As I said, I still regard you as an ally. We were effective together and would have triumphed but for some unanticipated contingencies."

" 'Unanticipated contingencies'?" Vhok said with a snort. "That's what you call Lolth's return?"

Nimor shrugged, sat back, and took another gulp of brandy. "Call it what you will," he answered. "Do you deny that we made an effective team?"

Vhok considered it while he drank.

"I don't deny it," said the cambion, "but at this moment, I wish we'd never met and that I'd never seen that cursed drow hive."

Nimor nodded as though in understanding.

"But feelings change with time and distance," Vhok said. "And I am always open to a future opportunity. Provided it involves no duergar."

He laughed and Nimor joined him.

That was the answer Nimor had wanted to hear. Vhok could be a valuable ally in his quest to regain his status as Anointed Blade.

"I know how to find you," Nimor said.

Vhok set down his chalice and stared at Nimor, his smile hard.

"A threat?" Vhok asked.

Again the shuffle from outside the tent.

"An observation," Nimor replied. "We'll see each other again, Vhok. I have no doubt of it."

With that, Nimor activated his ring, slipped back into the Shadow Fringe, and left Menzoberranzan and its environs far behind.

Prath and Nauzhror watched, their eyes fixed on the image in the scrying crystal as Gromph began his attack on the wards of House Agrach Dyrr.

Gromph whispered the incantations to a few preparatory spells meant to augment his magical sight, then began.

He found it surprisingly easy to breach the outer network of wards that surrounded the fortress. Without disrupting the grid, without breaking any of the interconnected lines of power, he gently bent a few aside, created a conceptual opening in the layers of the net, and slipped his scrying eye through.

"Well done, Archmage," said Nauzhror, exhaling loudly. Prath only smiled.

A second layer of interconnected wards awaited him—stiffer magic that he couldn't bend without triggering alarms. After a few moments of study, he opted for a different approach. But he would need to work quickly.

Conscious that he was sweating, Gromph cast two spells in such rapid succession that they might as well have been a single incantation. First, he sealed off a tiny section of the network. With his next breath, he rapidly dispelled the sealed section, opening a hole in the net, and sent the scrying eye through. He turned his perspective and held his breath as he released his first spell.

He watched in alarm as the entire network quivered, the interconnected flow of magic momentarily disrupted by the tiny hole he had fashioned.

He allowed himself to exhale slowly as the magic redirected itself around the hole and flowed anew. It had self-corrected. Gromph had succeeded. He was in.

"Daring," Nauzhror breathed.

Gromph moved the scrying eye to ground level, within the walls of House Agrach Dyrr. He took a moment to gather himself.

He knew that he would face only pockets of wards of varying power, sub-networks guarding this or that room or building. Most of them were unconnected to the larger grid of defenses.

He held onto the image while he took one hand from the crystal and drained the rest of his mushroom wine. Prath looked around the office, found the bottle on a nearby table. He retrieved it, returned, and refilled the chalice.

Gromph moved through and around each of the wards in turn. He could have dispelled them easily enough, but eventually that would have been discovered. For those he could not work through, he dispelled them, but after examining the building or room to his satisfaction, he replaced the ward with a similar one of his own casting.

"No tracks," Prath said.

"No tracks," Gromph agreed. Not yet, anyway.

Presumably, the magic shielding the lichdrow's phylactery was masked from his scrying eye. He would "see" it only when he bumped up against it. Accordingly, he could locate the phylactery only through the process of elimination—eventually, he would attempt to view an area that appeared open to scrying but which he would not, in fact, be able to scry. That would be where the phylactery was located.

Of course it was also possible that the phylactery was not in the stalagmite fortress at all. If so, Gromph would never locate it before the lichdrow reincorporated. The thought gave him pause. He put it out of his mind.

Methodically, he moved his scrying eye through each of the buildings of House Agrach Dyrr, one room at a time.

Nauzhror crowded his head closer over the image until a look from Gromph backed him off.

"Apologies, Archmage," Nauzhror muttered.

Gromph moved the image through dining halls, shrines, training rooms, bedrooms, laboratories, slave quarters, kitchens, amphitheatres, always seeking an invisible wall that would block his scrying eye. Troops, mages, and priestesses hurried through the halls. He could not hear them, though their expressions showed their agitation. He did not let his scrying eye linger long on any one person, lest they sense the divination.

Sweat from his forehead dripped onto the scrying crystal, blurring the image. Prath wiped it away with the sleeve of his *piwafwi*.

Gromph moved the image down another hallway, past another group of—

"Larikal," he said, recognizing the short-haired, uncomely Third Daughter of House Agrach Dyrr. She led a group of three male mages that Gromph recognized as graduates of Sorcere. He let the image linger on the group for a time. His spell showed that each of them bore a variety of magical items: wands, rings, cloak pins, brooches, a staff in Larikal's hand.

"Geremis, Viis, and Araag," Nauzhror said, naming the wizards. "Sub par students, the lot of them."

Gromph nodded and kept the scrying eye with them, keeping a mental count in his head; he moved the image off of each person before he reached twenty.

Larikal barked orders, but Gromph could not read their lips. The mages moved from room to room, hallway to hallway, casting spells and concentrating for a time. Gromph kept the scrying eye just above and behind them, each in turn. Though he could not hear the words uttered by the mages, he studied their gestures.

"What are they doing?" Prath asked.

"Casting divinations," Gromph said, a fraction of a heartbeat before Nauzhror said the same thing.

"Powerful divinations," Nauzhror added, watching as Geremis finished his gesticulating and put a hand to his brow in concentration.

Realization struck Gromph. "They are looking for the phylactery," he said. "They must be."

All of them understood the implication: Yasraena did not have the phylactery in her possession, and she too thought it was hidden somewhere in the House.

A good sign," Nauzhror said.

Gromph nodded. He needed to hurry.

Seeing nothing else of import, he moved the scrying eye away from Larikal and her pet wizards and continued to move through the Agrach Dyrr complex. The process was time-consuming but he endured. He took the time to study each room with care, to cast additional divinations designed to root out the lichdrow's masking spells. Again and again he found nothing, nothing but a desperate drow House under siege and fighting for its life.

"Could the phylactery not be in the fortress?" Nauzhror finally asked, after hours of fruitless searching.

Gromph didn't even bother to look up. "Silence," he commanded.

It had to be there. The lichdrow would not have allowed the phylactery to be far from him. The risk was too great.

Gromph continued the search. He scoured each building thoroughly. In an isolated portion of the complex, he found the lichdrow's alchemical laboratory, library, and quarters. Shimmering gem golems carved in the shape of drow wizards stood rigid guard at every door.

"His laboratory," Prath said, eyeing the uncountable number of beakers, braziers, chemicals, and components. The room was disordered, as though someone had searched it roughly.

Thinking that the lichdrow's laboratory or quarters were a likely hiding place for the phylactery, Gromph moved carefully through the lichdrow's wards and pored over the rooms. His frustration mounted when he found nothing. He went over it again, certain that somewhere was the telltale spoor of a masking spell. Again he found nothing.

He was exhausting his spells, exhausting his body. Between his spell duel with the lichdrow and his scrying of the fortress, he had spent fully half of his repertory. If he did not find the phylactery soon, he would have to rest, restudy his spellbooks, re-memorize the incantations that slipped from his fatigued mind one by one as he cast them. By then, Yasraena might have located the phylactery herself.

He sighed, mopped his forehead, and moved on. He had only the temple to Lolth and a few other structures remaining.

The temple first.

With minimal effort, he slipped past the elaborate wards that protected the temple of Lolth. No doubt Yasraena herself had cast them. Gromph thought her spellcraft paltry. Her wards were no match for him.

The interior of the temple appeared much the same as the temples to Lolth maintained by other great Houses. A sacrificial altar, limned in violet faerie fire and dotted with candles, sat in the apse at one end of the large, oval nave. Behind the altar towered the enormous sculpture of a spider, carved in lifelike detail from smooth basalt or perhaps jet.

Gromph knew it to be a guardian golem that would animate should anyone enter the temple without authorization.

High-backed, ornate stone benches lined the nave, facing the apse. Transparent gossamer curtains, made to look like spiderwebs, hung across the temple's faerie fire limned windows. Spider motifs appeared on everything, from the black altar cloth to the carved door jambs to the armrests of the benches. Spiderwebs hung in every corner, the silvery threads and their small black creators regarded as blessings from Lolth.

A depiction of the Spider Queen in her hybrid form—a beautiful drow female head and torso jutting from the bloated body of a giant black widow—decorated the underside of the temple's domed ceiling. Gromph wondered in passing whether Lolth appeared the same since her return, whether Lolth *was* the same.

Almost the whole of the temple glowed in Gromph's sight, alight with enhancements and protections cast by Lolth's priestesses. Otherwise, the nave was empty.

Gromph blew out a frustrated sigh and prepared to move on, but something rankled him. He kept the scrying eye on the temple, looking, thinking.

"What is it, Archmage?" asked Prath, excitement in his voice. "Have you found it?"

"Silence," Nauzhror admonished the apprentice, though the Master's voice too betrayed a certain eagerness.

Gromph shook his head. He saw nothing out of the ordinary, but . . .

The spider golem!

His scrying eye did not show it as magical, yet it should have detected as such—strongly—unless the Agrach Dyrr priestesses had replaced the former golem with a normal statue. He deemed that unlikely.

An excited charge ran through him. He caused the scrying eye to draw nearer to the golem until its image filled the viewing crystal. He pored over it, inch by inch. Was it standing atop a secret panel in the floor? He cast another series of divinations, attempting to get even an inkling of whether or not the golem's magic was being masked.

At first he met with no success, but he persisted.

Finally, and for only an instant, he caught a flash of a faint red glow, like light squeezed from under a closed door. In that single instant, the golem flared in his sight, as befitted the latent magic that would animate it, but a still brighter glow flared from *within* the golem.

Nauzhror smiled, Prath gasped, and Gromph could not contain a chuckle.

"The golem," Nauzhror breathed.

The Master of Sorcere sounded as exhausted as Gromph, though he had done nothing other than observe.

"The golem is masked," Gromph said, nodding. He could not believe the lichdrow's temerity.

"The *golem* is the phylactery?" Prath asked.

Gromph studied the construct for a while longer, confirming his suspicion with a series of spells.

When he finished, he said, "No, but the phylactery is embedded within it."

Despite the evidence they had seen in the crystal, Prath and Nauzhror's faces showed disbelief.

"Within the temple's guardian golem?" Prath said. "It is heresy."

"It is ingenious," Nauzhror countered.

Gromph agreed. The lichdrow, a male, had not only hidden his phylactery within House Dyrr's temple of Lolth, he had hidden it within the body of the temple's most powerful guardian. Gromph had located it only because he had known the spider sculpture to be a golem that *should* have glowed in his magic-detecting sight. That it had not had caused him to look more closely, and he still had almost missed it.

With a slight exertion of will, Gromph let the image in the scrying crystal fade. It moved to gray, then to black.

The archmage leaned back in his chair and stretched his arms over his head. His entire body ached, his temples pounded, and sweat soaked him. Unfortunately, he could not take time to recover. Getting through the anti-scrying wards and finding the phylactery had been the easier of his two tasks. Next he had to get himself physically into House Agrach Dyrr, into Lolth's temple, and destroy first the golem, then the phylactery.

"You should rest first, Archmage," Nauzhror said, reading his expression and knowing what would come next.

Gromph picked up his chalice and gulped another mouthful of wine. Enough. He did not want a light head when he assaulted House Agrach Dyrr.

"There is no time," he said. "Yasraena or her daughters may happen upon the phylactery. It will be easier to take out of the golem than it will be to take from Matron Mother Dyrr's hands."

Nauzhror could not help but nod agreement with that. He asked, "When, then?"

"Within the hour," Gromph replied and blew out a tired sigh.

Prath and Nauzhror digested that. Gromph closed his eyes and tried to still the pounding in his head.

"The wards will be challenging," Prath said at last.

Nauzhror backhanded Prath across his mouth and snapped, "The archmage is aware of the challenges, apprentice."

The rebuke drew blood. Prath sank back in his chair, daubing his broken lip. His eyes burned, but he said nothing. Gromph was pleased to see the anger in Prath's face.

Gromph *was* aware of the challenges. He had just seen them; they all had.

An intricate network of wards, an altogether different layer of protections at least as complex as those he had just bypassed, would attempt to prevent his physical entrance into the fortress. The combined power of all of the mages of House Xorlarrin had so far been unable to breach those wards. Gromph was no mere Xorlarrin wizard, of course, but neither was the second layer of wards likely to prove as easy to bypass as the anti-scrying protections.

And triggering a ward while he was physically present put him at risk for injury and death, not merely detection. He remembered well the glaring red glow of the spell traps.

"Shall I accompany you, Archmage? asked Nauzhror.

"No," Gromph replied, and massaged his temples. "I have other plans for you two. You, Nauzhror, are to stay within my offices and help me attempt to scry House Agrach Dyrr."

Nauzhror's fat face pinched in a question. "Help you scry? You did exactly that. What do you mean?"

Gromph eyed Prath, who also looked confused.

"I mean," Gromph said, "that I will be in two places at once, Master Nauzhror."

Gromph let his words hang in the air without further explanation.

After only a moment, realization showed on Nauzhror's face.

"Prath will remain here in your guise," the Master of Sorcere said.

"Yes," Gromph affirmed. "And I in his, at least for a time. You will remain here too, Nauzhror, as though assisting me with my divinations."

Prath's expression showed understanding but also a question. "Why the ruse, Archmage?" he asked. "Yasraena and her mages cannot scry into your office. No one can."

"No," Gromph agreed, "but no doubt she is trying. She knows I must move against her House, and she will want to know when I am coming. We will mislead her. You and I will change forms to appear as the other. I will decrease the power of the wards around my office enough to allow Yasraena and her wizards to finally get through. When she does, she will see Gromph and Nauzhror attempting to scry House Agrach Dyrr, as though in preparation for an attack yet to come. The actual attack, however, will already have begun."

Nauzhror smiled.

"Very clever, Archmage," he said. "Might it not be easier, however, for *me* to take your form?"

Gromph had expected as much from Nauzhror. He eyed the master coolly and said, "I think not. And be careful, Nauzhror, lest I find your eagerness to sit in my chair unseemly."

Nauzhror's eyes found the floor. "I meant no presumption, Archmage," he explained. "I merely thought that I might be better able to mimic you than would an apprentice."

Gromph decided to let the matter rest. He had made his point to Nauzhror. "Prath will serve. Besides, having you, a Master of Sorcere, assisting me will further the deception."

Nauzhror accepted that with a submissive nod.

The archmage rose from his chair and said, "Time is short. Let us begin."

With that, Gromph removed his magical robes and the most well-known of his magical trinkets, including the ring worn only by the Archmage of Menzoberranzan. Nauzhror watched the ring slip from Gromph's finger with poorly disguised hunger.

Prath too rose and stripped himself of clothes and gear.

Presently, Gromph stood in the overlarge *piwafwi*, robes, and other accoutrements of an apprentice wizard, and Prath was in those of the Archmage of Menzoberranzan.

"They may fit you someday," he said to Prath.

The apprentice blanched. "Mine do not fit you," he said, embarrassed.

Gromph almost laughed, thinking of how he must look. He had not been so humbly attired in centuries.

He looked to Nauzhror, indicated Prath, and said, "Master Nauzhror."

Nauzhror nodded and spoke the words to a minor glamor. When he finished the incantation, an illusionary image of Prath took shape beside the actual apprentice, a magical portrait to serve as a frame of reference.

"An excellent likeness," Prath observed.

Gromph agreed. He opened a lower drawer of his desk and withdrew a scroll scribed with one of his most powerful spells. To Prath, he said, "Apprentice, should you err in the casting of this spell, it could have most unfortunate results."

The archmage would have cast the spell on Prath himself, but the magic could affect only the caster. Prath would have to do it himself.

Gromph continued, "After completing the incantation, look upon me and will yourself to take my form. The spell will do the rest."

Prath took the scroll in a hand that, to his credit, did not shake. He unfurled the parchment, studied the words, looked once more at Gromph and Nauzhror, and at their nods, began to cast.

Gromph listened with care to the apprentice's pronunciation of the words. To Gromph's satisfaction, Prath read with confidence. When Prath pronounced the last word, the scroll crumbled in his grasp and his body started to change.

"The sensation is not painful," Prath said, his voice already changing.

Prath's body thinned, his eyes sank deeper into their orbits, his hair grew longer, and his eyes changed from his own crimson to Gromph's blood red. Prath studied Gromph's features as the magic wrought its change, mentally shaping the transmutation. The magic of the spell filled in the necessary details and after only ten heartbeats, Gromph was looking upon his double.

"Well done," Gromph said to Prath.

The apprentice beamed.

"In my uppermost right inner pocket is a jade circlet," Gromph said to Prath, nodding at his robe. "Give it to me."

Gromph would need the component to cast the same spell on himself, not from a scroll, but from his memory.

Prath reached into the pocket of the archmage's robes, found the circlet, and handed it to Gromph.

Gromph placed it on his head, and spoke the words and made the gestures that would allow him to assume any form he wished. When the magic took effect, a tingle ran through his flesh. His skin grew malleable and at the same time somehow thickened, like wax.

Using the illusionary image of Prath as a model, Gromph caused the magic to morph his body and features into those of Prath. Gromph felt no pain throughout, merely a strange sense of his flesh flowing. When he felt his body solidify, he knew the transformation was complete. The spell's magic would continue for several hours, during which Gromph could call upon the spell to transform him into virtually any shape he desired.

"It is done, Archmage," Nauzhror said, studying him. "The likeness is nearly exact."

Nauzhror dispelled the illusory image of Prath.

Gromph nodded. To Prath, he said, "The remainder of my components, apprentice."

Prath mumbled acquiescence, reached into the magical pockets of Gromph's robe, pulled esoterica out of the extra-dimensional spaces in the pockets of Gromph's robes, and set it all on the desktop. Among the items was the soul-stealing duergar axe. Shadows swirled along its head, suggesting faces, implying screams.

Gromph took the multitude of components and secreted them in his robes. He took the axe too, and hung it from his belt. It felt heavy at his waist, but he had no extradimensional pocket in Prath's robes in which to carry its weight.

He reached into another drawer in his desk and withdrew several potions, a scroll, and a milky-colored ocular on a silver chain—looking through the ocular would allow Gromph to see through certain types of illusions. He also removed several wands, all of them of bone, all of them capped with the petrified eye of a keen-eyed slave. Having cast so many of his own spells, he would need the ocular's and the wands' powers to supplement his repertory.

When he had everything he needed and had organized it to his satisfaction, he looked to Prath and gestured at his high-backed, bone chair.

"Take your seat, ur—Archmage," he said with a smile.

With obvious reluctance, Prath stepped around the desk and sank into Gromph's chair.

"No hesitation, and no reluctance," Gromph admonished him. "Yasraena will see it. Until I return, you *are* the Archmage of Menzoberranzan."

Prath looked Gromph in the face, set his jaw, and nodded.

Gromph then had only one thing more to do.

Though Nauzhror and Prath were both Baenre, Gromph knew better than to rely on familial ties to assure obedience. He needed to instill fear. Once he entered House Agrach Dyrr, he would be vulnerable to an easy betrayal. Nauzhror, and perhaps even Prath, would be tempted to do so unless Gromph made the cost of failure higher than the benefit of success. A simple lie would do.

"Other than you two, I have shared this plan via a sending with only Master Mizzrym," Gromph said. "In the event that I fail, I have ensured that Pharaun will alert Matron Mother Triel and investigate the causes of the failure very carefully."

Neither Nauzhror nor Prath uttered a word. Gromph's message was clear—betrayal would be punished, and harshly, even if Gromph was dead.

Nauzhror said, "Yasraena will never be aware of the deception."

"Good fortune, Archmage," Prath said.

"Maintain the illusion until I return or you know me to have failed," Gromph ordered.

Both nodded.

Satisfied, Gromph spoke words of power and used them to weaken the more powerful wards that surrounded his office. Yasraena's wizards soon would find their way in.

Swallowing his pride, he bowed to his "superiors" as would any young apprentice.

"Masters," he said and backed out of the office.

The shapechanging spell would continue in effect for only about two hours. He would have to do everything that needed done within that time.

The real work was about to begin.

NINE

Still in the shape of Prath, Gromph exited his offices and moved through the vaulted halls of Sorcere. The tapestry-festooned corridors stood mostly empty. Almost all of Sorcere's masters and apprentices were occupied in finishing off the surprisingly stubborn duergar forces in the northern tunnels. Gromph did encounter one master, Havel Duskryn.

As he passed, Gromph bowed and said, "Master Duskryn."

"Prath Baenre," the tall, thin Master replied, rubbing his weak jaw and obviously too involved in whatever troubled him to query "Prath" about his business.

Gromph hurried through hallways lined with paintings, sculpture, and framed magical writings until he reached the apprentices' wing of the complex. There, he encountered two of the new class of apprentices searching for a tome in the apprentices' library. Neither spoke to Gromph, and he made his way to Prath's austere quarters.

Like all apprentices, Prath lived alone out of a stone-walled room five paces on a side. His sparse furnishings consisted of an uncomfortable looking sleeping pallet and a small zurkhwood desk and chair. Books, papers, ink, a glowball, and three inkrods were neatly organized upon the desktop. Prath was surprisingly fastidious. Gromph's own chambers as an apprentice had always been in disarray.

Gromph walked through Prath's doorway and pulled the door closed behind him. The moment the latch caught, a magic mouth whispered, "Welcome back, Master Prath."

Gromph smiled. An apprentice could be flogged for casting spells frivolously, though the masters usually turned a blind eye to the practice. In truth, using spells for pranks and entertainment made an apprentice's otherwise harsh existence a bit more bearable. It also encouraged creative thinking in the use of spells. When Gromph had been an apprentice, he had kept an invisible wine service in a corner of his quarters, complete with an unseen servant to pour it at his command. Smuggling the wine into Sorcere had been a difficult challenge. Prath's violation looked minor compared to Gromph's.

Gromph slid into the chair behind the desk and leafed through Prath's papers. He saw from the notes and formulae written there that the apprentice was in the process of learning a series of progressively more complicated augmenting transmutations. Gromph spent a moment reading over Prath's observations.

He decided first that Prath had potential; he decided second that it was time to get on with his work. He had several preparatory spells to cast. He pushed the papers aside.

Gromph's own magical robe had extradimensional pockets that organized their contents according to his mental urgings. Prath's robe contained no such enchantment, and Gromph found sorting through his spell components an unfamiliar chore. Still, he took it in good spirit, found the various items he would require, and cast.

He first sprinkled a pinch of diamond dust over his head and whispered the words to a protective spell that would ward his person from detection. The spell was not as powerful a shield against scrying as a stationary screen, but it would serve to defeat most scrying attempts.

Next, in preparation for the spell traps he would encounter in the fortress of House Agrach Dyrr, he cast a series of wards that protected his flesh for several hours against negative energy, fire, lightning, cold, and acid. If the spell traps did more damage than his wards could absorb, his magical ring eventually would regenerate it, provided the damage did not kill him outright. Not even his ring could bring back the dead.

Third, he withdrew from his pocket a tiny vial of glassteel containing a dollop of quicksilver. After pricking the tip of his finger on the edge of the duergar axe at his belt, he squeezed a few drops of his blood into the vial. He then smeared the tips of his fingers with the admixture and incanted the words to one of his most powerful spells, a dweomer that would whisk him back to his offices should certain contingencies—contingencies that he would have to articulate as part of the casting—occur.

His fingers traced glowing lines in the air as he recited the incantation. Presently, the spell was completed but for the articulation of the contingent triggers. The magic of the spell sizzled around him, awaiting his words. He thought for a moment about the nature of the spell traps he would face then whispered the triggers aloud:

"Should my body be rendered involuntarily immobile or be materially consumed by magical energy of any kind, should my soul be trapped or otherwise imprisoned, should my mind become enfeebled or otherwise unable to function."

The spell soaked into him, there to await a triggering event. Gromph had only another step or two to take before he moved against House Agrach Dyrr.

Moving his hands through another intricate gesture, he spoke the words to a spell that rendered him invisible. With another whisper, he modified the magic to cause the invisibility effect to last a full day rather than its normal duration of but an hour or two.

Finally, he called upon the ongoing transmutation that allowed him to change his shape and mentally selected the form of an incorporeal, undead creature: a literal shadow. The magic seized him, and his body grew dark, shadowy, and insubstantial. His flesh grew light but his soul grew heavy. He was suffused with dark energies. Prath disappeared; a living shadow replaced him.

Gromph felt his existence stretched across multiple realities. He felt solid to himself, as did all of his equipment, but his "flesh" tingled, and most of his senses felt dull. He could not hear or smell and the loss of sensation disconcerted him. Too, he could not touch anything on the physical world, at least not in the way he was used to. He was solid; the world was shadow. He perceived the touch of physical objects more as a distant pressure change than a tactile sensation. He "sat" in Prath's chair only as matter of will, not because of the physical properties of the chair. He could have passed through it had he wished. The archmage perceived no colors—only varying shades of gray—but his visual acuity grew sharper. Solid objects looked *solid*, the lines between them as sharp as a razor. He knew that he could walk on the air as easily as on the ground. He knew too that he could still cast spells in his shadow form. His equipment and components had transformed with him, so they were solid to him.

He was ready.

Literally sheathed in an armor of protective magic, Gromph floated up from Prath's chair and rose through the stone ceiling above him. Passing through the solid stone of the ceiling blinded him while he was within it, but he simply kept willing himself upward until he passed through it. The wards in Sorcere's structure did not impede his progress. Gromph had cast most of them and knew the gestures and words—his voice sounded hollow when he spoke—to bypass them safely.

Soon, he was in the air above the school, with a breathtaking view of all of Tier Breche: the spider-shaped, curving walls of Arach-Tinilith, the stout pyramid of Melee-Magthere, the soaring spires of Sorcere. Smoke rose from the tunnels to the north and explosions, and shouts still rang through the area. He took only a moment to enjoy the view before he turned and flew south along the cavern's ceiling, moving amidst the stalactite spear points that hung from the cavern's roof.

He passed over the bazaar, where he had fought the lichdrow, over the Braeryn, and headed directly toward Qu'ellarz'orl and besieged House Agrach Dyrr.

On her knees before the altar of Lolth in the otherwise empty temple, Yasraena prayed to the Spider Queen, not for deliverance—Lolth despised such weakness—but for opportunity. She knew that unless something changed, and soon, the siege of her House must eventually succeed. She needed to locate the phylactery and decide whether she would honor her bargain with Triel. The damned thing could have been under her very feet and she would not have known it. She cursed the lichdrow for the thousandth time, and cursed herself for allowing her House to pursue schemes concocted by a male.

She looked up to the altar, hoping for a sign of Lolth's favor. Nothing. The light from a single holy candle flickered on the polished body of the majestic widow sculpture that stood behind the altar—in reality, a guardian golem. The statue stared down at her with eight emotionless eyes.

In the distance, Yasraena heard an occasional shout from the forces arrayed atop her fortress's walls. Hours before, thunderous explosions had shaken the complex, booming along the walls. Yasraena found the relative quiet ominous. She knew the Xorlarrin forces had pulled back well beyond the moat bridge to plot a strategy for another assault. Tension sat thick in the air. She saw it in the eyes of her troops, her mages, her daughters. The next Xorlarrin attack would be more forceful than the last. She was confident that House Agrach Dyrr would hold it off, but what of the one after that or after that? What would occur when a second House joined Xorlarrin? A third?

Her House had only days left to live, unless she found the phylactery and arranged a peace. Or returned the lichdrow to life and thus bolstered, demanded a peace.

So far, Larikal and the huffing oaf Geremis had been unable to locate the phylactery, yet Yasraena was convinced that it was within the stalagmite fortress. The lichdrow had seldom moved outside its walls. He would not have secreted the vessel for his soul anywhere but within the manor.

She called upon the power of the amulet at her breast and projected to Larikal, *My patience grows thin.*

She sensed her daughter's anger through the connection afforded by their amulets.

The search continues, Matron Mother. The lichdrow was no mere conjurer. He has hidden his treasure well.

Yasraena let venom leak into her mental voice. *Do not offer me excuses,* she said. *Offer me the phylactery or I will offer your life to the Spider Queen.*

Yes, Matron Mother, answered Larikal, and the connection went quiet.

Yasraena's threat was sincere. She had killed progeny before to make a point. She would do so again, if necessary.

From behind, she heard the beat of footsteps on the temple's portico. She rose and turned just as Esvena sprinted through the open double doors and into the temple. The links of her adamantine mail tinkled like slave's bells. She held her helm in her hand, and her face was flushed.

A hundred possibilities flew through Yasraena's mind, none of them good. Her grip on her tentacle rod tightened.

"Esvena?" she asked, and her voice echoed through in the vaulted temple.

"Matron Mother," Esvena huffed and ran up the aisle between the pews. She offered a hurried supplication to Lolth before broaching the apse and bowing before Yasraena.

Esvena's otherwise plain face was as animated as Yasraena had ever seen it.

"We have him, Mother!" she said and stood, smiling.

Esvena did not need to say whom she meant by "him." A thrill went through Yasraena, and she grabbed her taller daughter by the shoulders.

"Lolth has answered our prayers," she said. "Show me."

Together, mother and daughter hurried from the temple, past exhausted troops and sunken-eyed wizards, though empty halls and chambers, until they reached the vaulted scrying chamber and its stone basin.

The two homely male wizards, both in dark *piwafwis*, awaited them there. One of them—the one Yasraena previously had choked for smiling—greeted them with a bowed head and lowered eyes. He did not smile, instead eyeing Yasraena's tentacle rod with dread. The other male stood over the scrying basin, his furrowed brow covered in sweat, his hands held over the still water, palms downward.

Without acknowledging the male, Yasraena pushed past her daughter and hurried to the edge of the waist-high basin. Esvena followed in her wake.

A wavering image showed itself in the waters. Gromph Baenre sat at a huge desk of bone, his gaze fixed intently on an unusual crystal set before him. Yasraena took the crystal to be a scrying device, though it showed only a gray mist at the moment.

Across from the archmage sat another wizard, a fat Master of Sorcere whose name Yasraena did not know. From time to time, they exchanged words. They appeared frustrated and tired.

"This is very good," Yasraena said to the room. "Very good, indeed."

She knew that she still had time to locate the lichdrow's phylactery. The archmage remained at Sorcere. Perhaps his spell duel with the lichdrow had drained him so much that he would not make an attempt on the House at all.

"The work was long, Matron Mother," said the male she had choked. "The archmage's wards were powerful. But we persisted."

"You saved yourself a painful death," Yasraena said. After a pause, she added, "Well done."

The male almost smiled, but one look at Yasraena's tentacle rod kept the corners of his mouth from rising.

The wizard went on, "Notice the gray mist present in the archmage's scrying crystal, Matron Mother. If the archmage is attempting to scry House Agrach Dyrr through that crystal, as we suppose, the mistiness indicates that he has not yet breached our anti-scrying wards."

She nodded. The lichdrow had well warded the fortress, better, apparently, than the archmage had warded his own chambers.

Yasraena saw that the archmage and the Master of Sorcere were speaking intently. From their body language, Yasraena thought that Gromph too easily tolerated impudence in his inferiors.

"Why can we not hear what they are they saying?" she asked the room.

Silence answered her. She looked up, and Esvena barked, "Answer the Matron Mother!"

The male Yasraena had choked cleared his throat and said, "Matron Mother, the basin does not allow for the transmission of sounds. I humbly apologize."

Yasraena stared at the top of the male's head for a moment before turning back to the image. The vision wavered too much for lip readers to be of much use. She would have to rely on observation to keep her apprised of Gromph's plans.

She eyed the sweating male wizard who leaned over the basin, maintaining the image. He would not be able to hold the image for much longer. She looked to Esvena.

"Rotate our mages so that this image is constant. It is imperative that we know what Gromph Baenre is doing at all times."

Esvena nodded.

Yasraena was beginning to think that the temporary Xorlarrin withdrawal was part of some larger ploy by the archwizard. Perhaps he would time his own assault with that of the Xorlarrin, hoping to sneak in under cover of the battle.

We've got you, Baenre, she thought, eyeing Gromph through the basin. With the Dyrr wizards' scrying eye on him, the archmage would not be able to surprise them. If he came, they would be ready.

Yasraena took a deep, satisfied breath. She had asked the Spider Queen for an opportunity. She had been given more time, and that was opportunity enough.

Conscious of his companions' eyes upon him, Pharaun pulled a swatch of bat fur from his *piwafwi*, positioned his fingers in a circle, and spoke a couplet.

An incorporeal, silvery orb took shape before him. With an exercise of his will, he saw through the ball as though it were his own eyes. At his mental command, the ball sped back through the chwidencha tunnel, up the vertical shaft, and through the wall of stone that Pharaun had created to cap the tunnel.

Through the eye, Pharaun saw the surface.

It was night. And raining. Spider carcasses and limbs dotted the landscape. The chwidencha bodies they had left behind lay torn in pieces. Pharaun saw no movement, no spiders. He ceased concentration on the orb, leaving it where it was, and returned his vision to his own eyes.

Quenthel stood near him, waiting. Danifae stood a few steps behind her, her expression veiled. Jeggred hulked over the battle-captive, staring at Pharaun with undisguised hunger.

"It is night, Mistress," Pharaun said to Quenthel. "And raining lightly. The Teeming appears to have abated."

Quenthel nodded as though she had expected nothing less.

"Then we go," she said. "Open the way."

Pharaun nodded. A simple spell would suffice to move them.

He visualized the surface and spoke a magical word that opened a dimensional portal between where they stood and the surface. A curtain of green energy formed in the air.

Pharaun reached out a hand for Quenthel, and her whip serpents reared up with a hiss. Even the snakes were more tense than usual. Pharaun's confrontation with Jeggred had thrown fuel on the fire of the priestesses' war of nerve. Pharaun reminded himself not to get caught in the conflagration when it inevitably blew.

"I must touch you if you are to use the portal," he said to Quenthel.

She nodded and quieted her serpents. He put his hand gently to her shoulder. As he did, he raised his eyebrows and looked a question at her.

The high priestess's expression showed that she took his meaning. They could leave Jeggred and Danifae behind, trapped underground.

Danifae shifted on her feet, as though she sensed the exchange.

Quenthel seemed to consider it before surreptitiously signing, *All go.*

Pharaun did not let his disappointment reach his face. He looked past Quenthel to Danifae and said, "Mistress Danifae?"

At her nod, he walked over and put his hand on hers, letting it linger for a moment on her smooth skin. Her flesh felt hot to the touch.

"Jeggred too," she said with a seductive, predatory smile.

Pharaun eyed the draegloth, who offered him a fanged smile and a cloud of foul breath.

"Of course," Pharaun said, wincing at the stink. He stepped to the draegloth, who slavered at his approach.

True to his promise to Jeggred, Pharaun had put a contingency spell on his person that would automatically cast another spell should the trigger be met. Pharaun had cast the spell such that if Jeggred attacked him, even if Pharaun was incapacitated or otherwise made unable to speak or cast, the draegloth would instantly be attacked by a giant, crushing hand of force. The hand was bigger than the draegloth, stronger, and would squeeze him until his bones broke.

"Gently, mage," Danifae warned.

Pharaun said over his shoulder, "Jeggred already knows how gentle is my touch. I won't hurt him, Mistress Danifae."

"Of that I have no doubt," she answered.

In whispered Infernal, the tongue of demons, Jeggred said, *"Only her command keeps me from ripping your head from your shoulders, contingency or not."*

Pharaun understood the demonic tongue, as he did many other languages, and he answered in kind, *"Should you even attempt to do so, your end will be rapid and painful. In fact, I wish you would."*

He stared a challenge into the draegloth's face. Jeggred's lips peeled back from his yellow fangs, but he did nothing else.

"Enough," Quenthel commanded.

Without another word, Pharaun slammed his fist into the draegloth's shoulder—hard. He might as well have been punching a wall of iron.

Jeggred only smiled

"Mistress," Pharaun said, backing away from Jeggred. "Your nephew remains, as always, an excellent conversationalist." He looked to Quenthel and added, "I believe we're all ready, now."

He stepped near Quenthel, and she took him by the arm.

"Us, first," she said.

"Of course," Pharaun answered.

Together they stepped through the dimensional portal.

They materialized instantly on the surface. All was quiet, and pieces of spider were everywhere. After the chaos of the Teeming, the surface felt eerily still. Eight bright stars like the eyes of a spider beat down on them from the otherwise jet black sky. A light rain pattered against the rocks.

Pharaun hissed, "Do you not think Danifae would look better dead, Mistress? And your nephew would be a fine trophy for—"

Quenthel silenced him with an upraised hand. Her whip serpents hissed.

"Of course she would," said the high priestess, "but she will look better still as a sacrifice. The insolent bitch dies when I will it, mage. And my nephew, for all of his stupidity, remains a Baenre and the matron mother's son."

Before Pharaun could reply, Danifae and Jeggred appeared beside them, both in a fighting crouch. Seeing no ambush awaited them, they relaxed their stances. Jeggred snorted with contempt, as though disappointed that his aunt had not attacked.

Quenthel didn't bother to disguise her own sneer. She held her whip in her hand and nodded at something one of the serpents, Yngoth, whispered in her ear. She looked up to the line of souls in the sky and followed them with her eyes in the direction of the distant mountains. Their darkvision did not extend far enough, and the jagged peaks were lost to the night.

Quenthel said, "Lolth bids us to hurry onward."

The wind gusted; songspider webs sang above the falling rain. Quenthel nodded absently as though the webs had spoken to her.

Pharaun perked up at Quenthel's statement. He asked, "Mistress, if Lolth bids us hurry, perhaps it is time that we make our way across this unfortunate landscape via magical means?"

He was more than a little tired of walking Lolth's wasteland.

"Indeed it is time, Master Mizzrym," answered Quenthel.

Mentally, Pharaun checked through his spells. "With all of the stray energies present here—" he gestured at the vortices of power that still dotted the sky—"I would not recommend teleportation. But I have other spells that might—"

Quenthel held up a hand to silence him and stared at Danifae.

"Call what aid you can, priestess," Quenthel said, "if you would accompany me. Lolth demands the quick arrival of her *Yor'thae*."

"Is that the reason, Mistress Quenthel?" Danifae asked with a cryptic smile. She threw back her hood. Spiders crawled along her hair, her brow, her lips. "Or are you concerned that Lolth's mind might change over the course of a longer journey?"

Anger brewed behind Quenthel's eyes. Her whip serpents lunged at Danifae but did not bite. All five of them hissed into the battle-captive's gorgeous face,

"Impudent whore!" said one of the females, K'Sothra.

Jeggred snatched at the heads with an inner arm, missed as they retracted. The draegloth growled. Pharaun couldn't remember ever having heard the serpents speak aloud.

Danifae only smiled innocently and said, "I intended no offense with my question."

"Of course you didn't," Quenthel said, and her whips swirled around her head.

Jeggred growled, as though he could he hear the serpents' mental projections to their mistress.

Pharaun felt very tired all of sudden. He just wanted the whole affair completed. If Lolth wanted it done quickly, all the better.

"Mistress," he said to Quenthel. "I have spells that—"

"Silence!" Quenthel ordered, without removing her gaze from Danifae. "Use what spell you will to follow me, Master Mizzrym, but you are to transport only yourself. Do you understand?"

For emphasis, her whip serpents turned their gaze from Danifae, stared at Pharaun, and flicked their tongues. Pharaun bowed his head in acquiescence.

To Danifae, Quenthel repeated, "I said, summon what aid you can, priestess, if you wish to accompany me further."

Pharaun saw it then and was not sure what to make of it.

Quenthel was taking Danifae's measure, testing her abilities as a priestess. That was why she had ordered Pharaun to transport only himself. All in the group had at least a sense of Quenthel's personal power. No one knew the scope of Danifae's except Danifae. Quenthel meant to find out before sacrificing the battle-captive.

The two priestesses stared at one another for a moment longer, Quenthel's challenge hanging between them. The wind blew. The rain fell. The webs sang.

"Very well, Mistress Quenthel," Danifae said, and she inclined her head slightly.

Jeggred stared at Pharaun and said to Danifae, "I could remove the ring of flying from the wizard's corpse and—"

Danifae held up her hand for silence, and the draegloth trailed off.

Pharaun answered Jeggred's stare with what he knew to be an annoying smirk. He held up his hand and waggled his fingers to show the draegloth the ring.

Quenthel turned her back on the junior priestess and her nephew and prepared a summoning. She moved away a bit and used her jet disk holy symbol to trace a circle on the blasted rocks—not a binding circle but a summoning circle. Power trailed behind her movements, leaving a distortion in the air. Throughout, she softly chanted a prayer, which Pharaun recognized as the initial words to a spell that would reach into the Abyss.

Quenthel was calling a demon to transport her.

Danifae watched Quenthel's back for a time, listening to her spell. Perhaps Danifae understood Quenthel's play and was attempting to determine an appropriate response. Presently, she began her own spell.

Holding her holy symbol to her breast, Danifae used her heel to trace a second summoning circle into the dirt, away from Quenthel's. She too chanted the while.

Pharaun and Jeggred stood a few paces apart between the dueling priestesses, doing nothing. Pharaun moved a few steps farther from the draegloth. The wind was carrying his stink to Pharaun, and the damp only magnified its foulness.

The voices of the priestesses mingled with the call of the wind and the patter of the rain. Quenthel's voice rose as she began the actual summoning. Danifae's voice, still in the midst of a preparatory chant, rose in answer.

The wind gusted hard and for a moment sang above them both, favoring neither.

Pharaun spared a glance at Jeggred, expecting to see the drooling oaf trying to threaten him with his glare, but the draegloth had eyes only for Danifae. He looked rapt. Pharaun could only shake his head at the simpleton.

Power gathered. Quenthel had started her casting first, and she would finish it first.

Orange sparks flared within Quenthel's summoning circle, little mirrors of the vortices that still littered the sky.

Danifae completed her preparations and started the final stages of her summoning.

Quenthel, sweating, chest heaving, stood at the edge of her circle, pronounced the final phrase of her spell, and shouted a name: "Zerevimeel!"

Pharaun didn't recognize the name, but it hung suspended in the air like fog, a foul echo reverberating in Pharaun's ears. A final shower of sparks sizzled in the center of Quenthel's summoning circle and left in its wake a glowing line of orange. The line expanded, and grew into a tall oval. A very tall oval.

A portal.

Through the portal, Pharaun caught a glimpse of night on another world, another plane.

A lush jungle of twisted trees, grasses, and bushes waited beyond the gate, growing from a soil the color of blood. Yellowed bones of all types and sizes jutted from the earth, as though the whole plane was a graveyard. Turgid rivers covered in a brown foam squirmed their circuitous way through the befouled landscape. Thin, twisted forms moved furtively in the shadows, mortal souls trying desperately to hide from something. Pharaun could see the terror in their eyes, and it made him vaguely uneasy.

A blast of humid air escaped the portal. It smelled like a charnel house, as though tens of thousands of corpses lay rotting in the jungle heat. It bore groans with it, the soft susuration of agonized souls.

"Zerevimeel, come forth!" Quenthel shouted.

The view in the portal changed as its perspective whipped across the landscape, passing ruined cities of crimson stone, lakes of watery sludge, huge, twisted things prowling the jungle in pursuit of the souls.

A form took shape in the portal, a towering muscular form that dwarfed even Jeggred and blotted out Pharaun's view of the demon's home plane.

Nalfeshnee, Pharaun recognized from the silhouette. Quenthel had summoned a fairly powerful demon. Not as powerful as she could have but powerful nevertheless.

Pharaun readied to mind a spell that would shroud the demon in lightning should Quenthel not be able to convince it with her offer. He knew that demons, even powerful ones, were vulnerable to lightning.

The huge demon stepped through the portal and solidified fully in Quenthel's circle, naked and slicked in something sticky and red. The creature smelled sickly-sweet, like half-cooked meat.

Behind them, Danifae continued her own summoning, her voice rising. She would complete her own spell soon, but for the moment, Pharaun ignored her and focused on Quenthel's demon.

Huge tusks erupted from the nalfeshnee's muzzle. Burning red eyes dominated its bestial face. With each breath the demon's huge chest, covered in dark, coarse fur, rose and fell like a bellows. Two ridiculously small feathered wings sprouted from its back. Clawed hands at the end of muscular arms clenched and unclenched reflexively. The demon inhaled deeply, nostrils flaring, and wrinkled its snout.

"The Pits of the Spider Bitch," he spat, his voice deep and resonant. "It is bad enough that her stink infests all of the Lower Planes, but now I must abide it directly?" He fixed his eyes on Quenthel, who stood before him, seeming small and insignificant. "You will pay for this, drow priestess. I was swimming in the gore pits of—"

Quenthel's whip cracked, and five sets of fangs sank into the sensitive flesh of the demon's thigh, very near its genitals. The blow was meant to be more a painful threat than injurious.

The nalfeshnee roared and grabbed at the whip heads but was too slow.

Quenthel spoke in a low tone. "Speak another heresy, demon, and I'll offer your manhood to Lolth as penance."

Zerevimeel's burning red eyes narrowed. He looked around for the first time, as though to evaluate his situation. His eyes moved to Pharaun, to Jeggred (at whom he sneered in contempt), to Danifae, who was finalizing her own spell.

Pharaun felt the tingle of divination magic against his skin. The demon was attempting to measure their power, to get a sense of their souls. Pharaun did not contest the spell, though he could have easily enough.

Gently, as though expecting a backlash, Zerevimeel tested the boundaries of the summoning circle. He seemed surprised when it did not hold him within its confines.

He smiled, dripping huge droplets of saliva, and said, "You have left me unbound, drow whore."

He stepped out of the scribing on hoofed legs, towering over Quenthel. Pharaun readied his lightning spell, but the Baenre priestess gave no ground.

"My spell was a calling, dolt," she said. "Not a binding. Are males such fools even among demons?"

All five of her whip serpents stared up at the nalfeshnee, hissing with laughter.

The demon regarded her with the arrogance endemic to his kind and said, "You are either a great fool or have much to offer."

"Neither," Quenthel replied. She brandished her holy symbol, stared up at the towering demon, and said, "You just cast your divination. You know the scope of my power. The Spider Queen once again answers the prayers of her faithful, and I can destroy you at my whim. You can perform willingly, or I can shred your body and summon another of your kind."

The demon rumbled low in his deep chest, a sound reminiscent of Jeggred, but did not dispute Quenthel's claim.

The high priestess went on, "If you accept willingly, you will be recompensed fairly in souls, upon my return to Menzoberranzan."

"*If* you return," the demon said, and his face twisted in an expression that Pharaun took to be a tusked grin. The creature looked skyward and for the first time seemed to notice the line of souls floating high above them. He eyed them with a predatory gaze and licked his thick lips.

"Souls, you say," he said, returning his gaze to Quenthel.

Quenthel cracked her whip and said, "Souls, yes. But not those. Those belong to Lolth. You will be paid with others, after you have flown me to the base of the mountains thence, to the Pass of the Reaver."

She pointed her whip in the direction of the far mountains, still hidden by night.

Pharaun cocked his head. He had never before heard Quenthel mention the name of their destination at the base of the mountains, though he had long suspected she knew what they would find there.

"You cannot attempt the pass and live," the demon said.

Quenthel put her hands on her hips and said, "I can and will. As will those who accompany me."

The demon licked his lips, seeming to consider his options. Finally, he said, "I am not a beast of burden, drowess."

"No," Quenthel replied, "but you will bear Lolth's Chosen and be honored to do so."

The demon's lips peeled back from oversized, yellowed canines. He turned his head to the side and spat a glob of stinking spittle onto the dirt. He crossed his arms over his huge chest and said, "Perhaps you are the Chosen, priestess, but perhaps you are not. In either case, let the Reaver claim you in his pass. But for the indignity you ask, my price shall be sixty-six souls."

Pharaun raised his eyebrows. Sixty-six souls was a very modest demand. Quenthel had cowed the demon effectively.

"Done," Quenthel agreed. "Attempt to betray me and you die."

"No betrayal, priestess," said the demon in a low voice. "I am looking forward to the feel of your soft flesh against mine. And when I return again to the blood pools of my home, I will think fondly of your soul being devoured by the Reaver."

Quenthel sneered and her whips laughed.

"Let us leave now, priestess," the demon said. "I wish to return to the familiar gore of my home."

"Not yet," Quenthel said. She turned her back to the demon—a show of supreme confidence—and watched as Danifae finally finished her own calling.

Danifae stood before her summoning circle, her arms outstretched, and called out a name: "Vakuul!"

Power flared in Danifae's circle. The air tore open. A circular portal, outlined in blue light, took shape. Through it, Pharaun could see only a swirling, thick blue mist. Some of the mist leaked from the portal and brought with it a cloying stink reminiscent of rotting mushrooms.

"Charistral," observed the Nalfeshnee with unconcealed contempt.

Pharaun assumed the word to be the name of the Abyssal plane viewable through the portal.

"Vakuul!" Danifae called again.

A buzzing sounded. It grew louder, louder . . .

"Chasme," said Zerevimeel and somehow managed still more contempt.

Pharaun saw that Quenthel was smiling. The flylike chasme demons were a relatively weak type, weaker than the nalfeshnee. Either Danifae had deliberately underutilized her abilities or she simply could summon nothing more powerful.

A winged, insectoid form filled the portal. The blue mist vanished, and the portal closed, leaving a buzzing chasme demon within the summoning circle.

Quenthel's smile vanished when she saw the creature. Pharaun drew in a sharp breath.

The chasme Danifae had summoned was the largest of the type that Pharaun had ever seen, fully as large as four pack lizards.

"Big one," Zerevimeel said.

"Silence," Quenthel ordered, and her whips hissed at the demon. To Danifae, she called, "Is calling the dregs from the bottom of the Abyss what passes for a summoning spell in Eryndlyn?"

Danifae did not turn to reply, but Pharaun read anger in her bunched back.

The chasme ignored Quenthel's taunt, and its compound eyes, each as big as Pharaun's two fists, swept the surroundings, lingering for a moment on Jeggred and the nalfeshnee. Its wings buzzed in agitation.

"Why have you disturbed Vakuul?" the chasme demanded of Danifae. Unlike Zerevimeel's baritone, the chasme's voice was high-pitched, interspersed with vibrations and buzzing.

In appearance, Vakuul reminded Pharaun of a giant black

cavefly, the kind that troubled rothé and whose bite resulted in pus-filled wounds. The demon stood on six legs. The rear four looked insectoid, with hooks and hairs sprouting from the upper segments, while the front two resembled oversized drow arms, both of which ended in hands that jerked and clenched spasmodically. A huge double pair of wings, much larger than those of the nalfeshnee's, sprouted from the chasme's back and buzzed at intervals. Each time they did, a breeze that smelled of corpses wafted over Pharaun. The chasme's head and face sprouted like a tumor from its thorax, and its face combined the features of a fly and a human to form a grotesque profile. Bony black ridges filled its otherwise toothless mouth, and a long horn jutted from where its nose should have been. Thickets of short, coarse black hair stuck out of the demon's body in irregular bunches.

Danifae stood before the demon and said, "You are to bear me to the far mountains there and the pass at their base."

The demon turned a circle, its movements jerking and insectoid, and looked in the direction Danifae indicated.

It turned back to her and said, "This is the Demonweb Pits."

Its wings buzzed again in agitation.

"And I am a priestess of Lolth," Danifae said, holding forth her holy symbol.

Jeggred stepped up beside Danifae, his eyes boring holes into the fly-demon. Big as it was, the chasme's wings twittered. It rubbed its human hands together, the same way a fly sometimes rubbed together its front two legs.

"You ask for a service but make no mention of payment," Vakuul said. "What is to be Vakuul's payment, priestess of Lolth?"

Quenthel watched intently, as did Pharaun. That would be a true indication of Danifae's power. The offer and acceptance of payment was a formality inherent to the casting, but the particulars of the bargain reflected the relative power of summoner and summoned. The higher the cost paid, the weaker the summoned believed the summoner to be. Could Danifae compel a favorable offer through threat, as had Quenthel?

Danifae eyed Quenthel before she took a step toward the chasme.

She entered the summoning circle, reached up, and ran her finger-tips along the horn of the chasme's nose. The demon's wings buzzed uncontrollably. His mouth fell open, showing a long, hollow tongue, wet with stinking saliva.

"I believe we will be able to come to some . . . amicable arrange-ment," Danifae purred.

A thick, dark fluid leaked from the chasme's mouth. The demon shifted his gaze past Danifae to Jeggred—himself the spawn of a drow-demon coupling—buzzed his wings, and leered at Danifae. Something long, thin, and dripping slipped out of his thorax.

Pharaun found the scene grotesque but fascinating.

Danifae only smiled, wrapped her hand around the demon's horn, and said, "I trust you find my offer appealing?"

"Most appealing, priestess," the chasme answered. With his thick, yellow tongue, Vakuul licked the ridges that served as his teeth. "I will carry you within my arms, carry you close. And afterward," his wings buzzed with excitement, "closer still."

Danifae released the demon's horn and said, "My draegloth must accompany us."

The chasme's wings beat in agitation. His voice rose still higher. "No, priestess, no. He is too big, his smell too foul. Just you."

Jeggred said nothing, merely stared.

Pharaun found it mildly amusing that a giant fly-demon found Jeggred too foul for transport. A cutting quip seemed in order, but he restrained himself.

Danifae smiled and put her hand on Vakuul's head. The chasme's wings beat fast as she ran her fingers along the bristles of the demon's hair.

"You cannot begin to comprehend what I am prepared to do for you," she said, low and husky, "if you but do this for me and my servant."

The thing protruding from the creature's thorax managed to squirm out just a little farther.

"Both then," the chasme said, drooling from his open mouth. "Come. Come, now."

Danifae turned and gestured Jeggred forward.

"Come, Jeggred," she said, even while signing to the draegloth:

When we arrive at the mountains, tear off anything that is sticking out of it, then kill it.

Jeggred smiled at the demon and stalked forward.

When Danifae turned back around to face the chasme, she again wore a seductive smile.

Pharaun could not help but admire her. The woman was not as powerful as Quenthel—that was clear—but she was as skilled a manipulator as Pharaun had ever encountered. Pharaun thought back to his encounter with Jeggred in the chwidencha tunnel. Pharaun had said that Danifae was manipulating the draegloth; Jeggred had answered that Danifae was instead manipulating Pharaun and Quenthel.

Pharaun began to suspect that both were likely true. Where Quenthel was raw power, Danifae was skillful subtlety. Both women were dangerous. He was coming to believe that either could be the *Yor'thae*, or perhaps neither. In truth, he did not care, as long as he came out of it with his life and his position.

Danifae looked back to Quenthel and Pharaun and said, "To the mountains then, Mistress Quenthel?"

Quenthel nodded, her face a mask of impassivity that poorly hid her anger.

Jeggred took the smiling Danifae in his arms, and the chasme wrapped both of them in his legs. Vakuul's wings beat so fast that they became a barely visible blur.

"Heavy," the demon said, in his whining voice but managed to get off the ground. "So heavy."

Quenthel turned to the nalfeshnee and allowed him to scoop her up in his huge arms. His wings too began to beat, and somehow those absurd little appendages bore his huge bulk aloft.

"Follow, wizard," Quenthel called.

Pharaun sighed, called on the power of his ring, and took flight behind them.

They soared high over the Demonweb Pits, flying into the teeth of the wind. They stayed below the souls but above the highest of the tors. The nalfeshnee cradled Quenthel against his mammoth chest. Her hair whipped in the wind. The chasme held Jeggred and Danifae close.

The creature pawed at Danifae as best he could while they flew.

Despite their respective loads, the demons moved at speed, and Pharaun struggled to keep up. He could hear nothing over the roar of the wind other than the muted buzz of the chasme's wings. Rain pelted his face.

Taking flight allowed them to avoid the difficulties of the harsh terrain, and they devoured the leagues quickly. On foot, they would have had a five or six day trek to the mountains. Flying at the rate they were, Pharaun expected to reach the mountains around daybreak, perhaps a bit after.

He surveyed the plane below him as he flew. From above, the surface of the Pits looked like diseased skin—blistered, scarred, pockmarked. Lakes of acid dotted the ground, spider carcasses lay everywhere, and great crevasses split the landscape like scars.

He looked ahead toward the mountains but they remained invisible in the darkness. He could see the glowing souls, though, flying toward the mountains' base, toward the Pass of the Reaver.

He replayed the demon's words in his mind: *You cannot attempt the pass and live,* Zerevimeel had said. Then, *I will think fondly of your soul being devoured by the Reaver.*

Pharaun decided that he would rather keep his soul than not, but he still flew on.

The night was hours old, and still Halisstra had not disturbed her sisters' Reverie. She knew she should. They ought to have used the night to travel, in case the slaughter renewed with the dawn, but Halisstra knew her sisters needed rest. They would have little opportunity for it after they left their makeshift temple atop the tor. Besides, Halisstra wanted them to have a few more hours of peace, alone with her faith. They soon would have little opportunity for that too.

She sat near the edge of the tor praying to the Dark Maiden for the strength to face the challenges ahead.

Above her, swirling vortices of colored energy still dotted the sky. With each passing moment, one or another of the vortices ejected a glowing soul into the air. With each moment, a worshiper of the Spider Queen died somewhere in the multiverse and the soul found its way to the Demonweb Pits. The process was as regular as a clockwork. Halisstra watched it happen time and again, and each time the newly arrived soul fell into the never-ending line of spirits floating toward their dark goddess, their eternal fate.

It would go on that way until the multiverse ended.

Unless Lolth died.

She watched the souls moving methodically toward their doom and wondered if Danifae was among them. With the Binding between them severed, Halisstra would not have sensed Danifae's death. She fervently hoped that her former battle-captive still lived.

Thinking of Danifae sent a surge of hope and fear through Halisstra. Danifae had told her once, as they stood together in some ruins in the World Above, that she had felt Eilistraee's call. The battle-captive had spoken those words when she had come to warn Halisstra that Quenthel had sent Jeggred to kill Ryld.

Danifae had *warned* her.

There was a kinship between them, Halisstra knew, something born in the Binding that once had joined them as master and slave. She *knew* that Danifae could be redeemed. And since Halisstra had given herself fully to the Lady of the Dance, she would be able to help Danifae along the path of redemption—as long as she wasn't already dead.

An overwhelming sense of regret tightened Halisstra's chest, regret for a life ill-spent inflicting pain and engaging in petty tyrannies. She had wasted centuries on hate. Tears threatened, but she fought them back with a stubborn shake of her head.

The wind gusted, sliced through her prayer, cut through the song-spider webs, and called out for the *Yor'thae*.

The word no longer held any magic for Halisstra. She felt no pull.

She looked up at the eight stars that seemed so much like the eyes of Lolth and vowed, "No one will answer your call."

Halisstra didn't know what Lolth intended for her *Yor'thae*, and she didn't care. She guessed that killing the *Yor'thae* would hurt Lolth, possibly weaken her. And she knew that Lolth's Chosen could be only one person: Quenthel Baenre.

"I'll kill your Chosen, then I will kill you," she whispered.

The wind died down again, as though quieted by her promise.

Halisstra looked out over the blasted landscape of Lolth's realm, over the piles of torn spider parts and carcasses. She wondered where Quenthel was at that moment. She suspected that the Baenre priestess was already in the Demonweb Pits, making her way to Lolth, just another of the damned drawn to the Spider Queen.

"I'm right behind you, Baenre," she whispered.

She sat for a time in silence, alone with her goddess, staring up at the infinite stream of spirits floating to Lolth. After a while, she took out Seyll's songsword, put its flute-hilt to her lips, and played a soft dirge, an honorarium for the lost souls above her. The notes carried over the barren landscape, beautiful to her ears.

If the souls heard her, they made no sign.

The wind rose, as though to overwhelm her song, but Halisstra played on. Though she knew it was not possible, she hoped that somewhere, somehow, Seyll heard her song and understood.

When she finished, she sheathed Seyll's blade and stood. Looking into the sky, she held forth her hand, palm up, and curled her fingers—making the symbol of a dead spider, blasphemous to Lolth.

She could not help but smile.

"This is for you too," she said.

On impulse, she shed her armor and shield, drew the Crescent Blade, and danced. High atop a ruined tor on Lolth's blasted plane, Halisstra Melarn whirled, spun, stabbed, and leaped. Except for the wail of the wind, there was no sound to which she could move, so she danced to a rhythm that pounded only in her head. Joy filled her, more and more with each step, with each turn. She became one with the weapon, one with Eilistraee. She was sweating Lolth from her skin, shedding her own past with each gasping, joyous breath.

Her hair whipped behind and around her. She could not stop grinning. The Crescent Blade felt no heavier in her grasp than a blade of grass, the tiny green plant that covered much of the World Above. The weapon whistled through the air, creating its own tune, playing its own song.

Halisstra danced until sweat soaked her and her breath came hard. When she finally finished, exhausted and elated, she collapsed, the ground on her back. Grace filled her. She felt she'd been purified, worthy at last to wield the Crescent Blade.

Thank you, Lady, she thought to Eilistraee and smiled when a cloud temporarily blotted out Lolth's eight stars.

She lay there for a time, doing nothing more than reveling in her freedom.

Sometime later she rose, walked back near the edge of the tor, and re-donned her armor. As she was strapping Seyll's blade to her back, a hand closed on her shoulder, momentarily giving her a start.

"Feliane," she said, turning to face the kind, almond eyes of the surface elf.

Feliane smiled warmly. "You did not wake me for a watch. I slept through the day. How late into the night is it?"

"The night is several hours old," Halisstra said, securing Seyll's blade in its scabbard. "We should awaken Uluyara."

Feliane nodded. She said, "It was your laughter that awakened me."

"I'm sorry," Halisstra replied. She was not aware that she had been laughing aloud.

"Don't be," Feliane replied. "It allowed me to watch you dance."

To her surprise, Halisstra felt no embarrassment.

"It was beautiful," Feliane said with a smile. "I saw the Lady in it, as clearly as I've ever seen her in anything."

Halisstra didn't know how to reply, so she dropped her eyes and said only, "Thank you."

"You have come far in only a short while," Feliane said, stepping past her to look down on the tor.

Halisstra nodded. She had indeed.

"May I ask you something?" Feliane asked.

"Of course," Halisstra said, and something in Feliane's tone caused Halisstra's heart to race.

Feliane asked, "What drew you to the worship of Lolth in the first place? The faith is . . . hateful, ugly. But I can see that you are none of those things."

Halisstra's heart thumped in her chest. She wasn't sure why the question affected her so. A tiny seed in the center of her being stirred, but no immediate answer came to her.

She thought for a moment and finally answered, "You give me too much credit, Feliane. I was hateful. And ugly. Nothing drew me to Lolth. Nothing had to. I was raised to worship her, and I enjoyed the benefits associated with my station. I was petty and small, so awash in spite that it never occurred to me that there might be another way. Until I met you and Uluyara and saw the sun. I owe you both much for that. I owe the Lady much for that."

Feliane nodded, took her hand, and squeezed it. The elf said, "May I ask something else?"

Halisstra nodded. She would hold nothing back from her sister in faith.

Feliane took a breath before asking, "Did you ever think that what you did in her name was . . . evil?"

Halisstra consciously decided not to hear an accusation in the question. Feliane's face held no judgment, merely curiosity. Halisstra struggled to articulate a response.

"No," she answered at last. "I'm ashamed now to say it, but no. Faith in the Spider Queen brought power, Feliane. In Ched Nasad, power was the difference between those who ruled and those who served, those who lived and those who died. It's not an excuse," she said, seeing Feliane's expression grow clouded, "just an explanation. What I did then, what I was, it shames me now."

Staring thoughtfully into the darkness, Feliane nodded. The silence stretched.

Finally, the elf said, "Thank you for sharing yourself with me, Halisstra. And do not be ashamed of what you were. We are made anew each moment. It is never too late to change."

Halisstra smiled. "I like that very much, Feliane. It gives me hope that someone else I know might be redeemed."

Feliane smiled back.

They stood quietly for a moment, listening to the wind.

"We should awaken Uluyara and start moving," Halisstra said.

Feliane nodded but did not turn to go. Instead, she said, "I'm afraid."

The words surprised Halisstra. She had never before heard such an admission from another female.

After a moment, she put her arm around Feliane, drew her close, and said, "I am too. But we'll find strength in our fear. All right?"

"All right," Feliane replied.

Halisstra turned to her, held her at arms length, and said, "The Lady is with us. And I have a plan."

Feliane raised her thin eyebrows. "A plan?"

"Let's awaken Uluyara," Halisstra said.

Feliane nodded, and they walked back toward the temple. Before they reached it, Uluyara emerged.

"There you are," said the high priestess. "Is everything well?"

"It is," Feliane said with a smile. "Halisstra has a plan."

Uluyara frowned. "A plan?"

Halisstra wasted no words. "I believe I know why Eilistraee put the Crescent Blade into my hands."

Uluyara's brow furrowed, and she said, "We already know why, Halisstra. You are to use the blade to kill the Queen of the Demonweb Pits."

Halisstra nodded. "Yes, but we've been thinking that I would use the blade only against Lolth herself. But I think Lolth would be weakened if her Chosen never answered her call. I need to deny her her *Yor'thae*. I need to kill Quenthel Baenre."

Her sisters looked at her, confused.

Halisstra said, "Don't you see? I was meant to meet Quenthel Baenre during the fall of Ched Nasad. I was meant to learn of her quest to awaken Lolth. Eilistraee's hand is in all of this. I see it now. Quenthel Baenre is Lolth's *Yor'thae*. If I kill her . . ."

Then maybe I can kill Lolth, she thought but did not say.

"Then Lolth will be vulnerable," Uluyara said, nodding.

"Are we certain?" Feliane ventured. "The prophecy of the Crescent Blade did not speak of the Spider Queen's Chosen."

"I am as certain as I can be," Halisstra replied, knowing that she was not certain at all.

Feliane did not hesitate. She said, "Then I am convinced."

Uluyara looked from Feliane to Halisstra. After a moment she blew out a sigh, touched the holy symbol of Eilistraee she wore around her neck, and said, "Then I am also convinced. How will we find Quenthel Baenre?"

Halisstra wanted to hug the high priestess.

"She is here, somewhere in the Demonweb Pits," Halisstra said, "trying to reach Lolth. I am certain of that too."

"Then we must find her before she reaches the Spider Queen," Feliane said. "But how? Follow the souls?" She indicated the damned souls streaming high above them.

"No," Halisstra said. "We must locate her more precisely."

Uluyara understood Halisstra's meaning, and said, "The Baenre will be warded. A scrying spell will not work."

"She will be warded," Halisstra conceded, "but she bears an item that once was mine, a healing wand that she took from me after the fall of Ched Nasad. That will aid the spell." She looked her sisters in the face. "It will work, and that it does will be a sign from the Maiden."

"She may sense the scrying," Uluyara said.

Halisstra nodded and replied, "She might. Let us trust in the Lady, High Priestess. Time is short." Halisstra felt the moments slipping from her.

"I am with you, Halisstra Melarn," Uluyara said with a smile. "But to scry, we must have a basin of holy water."

Halisstra scanned the top of the tor, looking for any standing pool of water left over from the rain. Uluyara and Feliane spread out to help search.

"Here!" Feliane called after only a few moments.

Halisstra and Uluyara hurried over and found Feliane standing over a small puddle of foul water that had pooled in a declivity in the rock.

"That will do," Halisstra said.

"I will hallow it," Uluyara said, taking out her holy symbol.

She held the medallion over the water and offered a prayer of consecration to Eilistraee. As she chanted the imprecation, she took a small pearl from her cloak and dropped it into the water. The pearl dissolved as if it was salt, the rime of filth vanished, and the water cleared. Uluyara ended the prayer and stepped back from the puddle.

"It is ready," she said.

Halisstra could not help but smile. Between the raising of the temple and the consecration of a holy water font, the three priestesses

185

had carved off a little piece of Lolth's plane in Eilistraee's name. It felt good; it felt *defiant*. She wondered how long the temple and font would last before the evil of the Pits reclaimed them.

It will stand forever once Lolth is dead, she thought.

With renewed determination, she knelt before the font and saw her dim reflection in its clear waters. Lolth's eight stars, though they hung directly above her, did not show in the reflection. Halisstra was pleased. Even on her own plane, the Spider Queen could not befoul Eilistraee's font.

Touching her holy symbol, Halisstra sang the song of scrying.

As the magic took shape, she conjured an image of Quenthel Baenre in her mind—her tall stature, her angry eyes and harsh mouth, the long white hair, the whip of serpents, the wand she had stolen from Halisstra . . .

The clear water darkened. Halisstra felt her consciousness expand. She continued the musical prayer, her voice growing more confident. Though she was not an especially skilled diviner, the words of the scrying spell poured easily from her lips. She knew that Quenthel's wards could protect the Baenre priestess, but she knew with a certainty born of her faith that they would not. Eilistraee's will would be done; Halisstra would be the Dark Maiden's instrument.

An image formed in the font, wavering at first but clearer with each note that Halisstra sang. There was no sound, but when the image came fully into view it was as clear as a portrait. Uluyara and Feliane crowded close to see.

The image showed Quenthel Baenre in the air, clutched to the chest of an enormous creature covered in muscle and short, coarse fur. The rest of the monster's body was not visible. Halisstra's spell conveyed an image of only Quenthel and her immediate surroundings. Anything beyond that appeared as an indistinguishable gray blur.

Quenthel looked forward, a tight smile on her face, her intense eyes burning. Her long hair streamed behind her in the wind. Her mouth moved as if she was shouting something to the creature that held her.

Uluyara said, "She rides in the grasp of a demon. Look at the size of it, the six fingered hands and claws . . . it is a nalfeshnee."

Halisstra nodded. Quenthel must have summoned and bound the nalfeshnee to her will.

The demon suddenly wheeled higher—Halisstra caused the scrying sensor to follow—into the midst of a swarm of drow souls. The spirits wheeled all around the image, flitting in and out of the spell's "eye."

"The river of souls!" Feliane exclaimed and looked skyward to the shades flowing through the sky. "She is here in the Demonweb Pits, at least."

Halisstra nodded but maintained her concentration, keeping the image focused on Quenthel. The high priestess of Lolth barked something at the demon and freed a hand to brandish her serpent-headed whip. The demon decreased its altitude, and the souls disappeared from the image.

"Where are her companions?" Uluyara said.

Halisstra shook her head. "Possibly just out of view," she said, though she felt a stab of fear for Danifae.

Halisstra had no doubt that Quenthel would kill anyone or anything if it served her purposes. She bit her lip in frustration. Her spell was not revealing enough. They knew Quenthel was flying with a demon somewhere in the Demonweb Pits but nothing more.

"Uluyara," she said through her concentration. "You must help me. We need more information."

Uluyara nodded. "Now that I have seen Quenthel Baenre, there is a spell I can use to aid us. It will take some time to cast. Hold the image another moment. Let me fix the Baenre's appearance in my mind."

The high priestess studied the image for a time then rose.

"Enough," she said. "Release it, Halisstra, before she senses the scrying. There is nothing more to see. Other divinations will serve us now."

With a gasp, Halisstra let the spell dissipate. The image vanished, and the water once more grew clear. She stood, but her knees trembled.

Uluyara touched Halisstra's shoulder with affection and said, "Well done, priestess. You have started us on the path. My own spell can learn how far the Baenre priestess is from here but little else. We will need that and more. While I discern her location, you two shall commune with the Lady and ask her for guidance."

Words failed Halisstra. Her heart raced. Commune with the Lady! When she had been a priestess of Lolth, she sometimes had communed with the Spider Queen as part of her temple's bloody rites, but the experience had never been pleasant. A mortal mind was easily overwhelmed by the divine. She found the thought of communing with Eilistraee both terrifying and exhilarating.

She shared a look with Feliane and saw acceptance in the elf's fair-skinned face. Both nodded at Uluyara.

"Good," said the high priestess. "Let us hurry. As you said, Halisstra, time is short."

"Not here. In the temple," Halisstra offered.

Uluyara nodded and smiled. "Yes. In the temple. Very good."

Under Lolth's sky, the three priestesses hurried back to the hallowed ground of their makeshift temple. There, they cast their spells.

Uluyara sat cross-legged on the floor, her holy symbol cradled in her lap. She closed her eyes, steadied herself, and slipped quickly into a meditative trance. Whispered prayers slipped from her lips, snippets of songs in a language both beautiful and alien to Halisstra.

Halisstra and Feliane sat away from Uluyara, facing each other and holding hands to form a circle. Halisstra's larger hands engulfed those of the elf priestess. Both of their palms were clammy. Feliane placed her holy symbol medallion on the floor between them.

"Ready?" Feliane asked and retook Halisstra's hands.

"Ready," Halisstra acknowledged. She knew the spell they were to cast would create a short-lived connection to Eilistraee. The answers to the questions they would ask would be short and possibly cryptic. Such was the nature of direct communication between gods and mortals.

"I will offer the questions," Halisstra said, and Feliane nodded without hesitation.

With that, they closed their eyes and began the spell. The spell required a prayer offered in song. Halisstra opened, Feliane joined, and soon they sang in time with one another, their voices as one. Power gathered, and windows opened between realities.

Propelled by the spell, their minds reached up and out, through the planes, to the otherworldly home of their goddess.

In the no-place created by the spell, Halisstra could not see, but she could feel—and feel with a vibrancy unlike anything she had previously experienced. Despite herself, she mentally cringed as she awaited contact with the mind of her goddess. She felt Feliane with her, also waiting.

A presence suffused the no-place, and Halisstra braced herself. When the contact came, when Halisstra's mind met that of her goddess in a place-between-places, it was not at all what she had expected. Rather than the overwhelming spite and judgment she had felt when communing with Lolth, she instead felt a sense of overwhelming comfort, love, and acceptance. It was as if she was immersed in a warm, soothing bath.

Ask, daughters, said a voice in her mind.

The grace in the voice, the gentle love, brought tears to Halisstra's eyes.

Lady, projected Halisstra. *You know our purpose. Please tell us what Quenthel Baenre seeks and to where the nalfeshnee bears her.*

Halisstra sensed approval of the question.

She seeks to become the vessel of my mother's resurrection, replied the goddess. *Without the* Yor'thae, *Lolth's rebirth will be stillborn.*

As the weight of that statement settled on Halisstra's shoulders, Eilistraee continued, *The demon carries Quenthel Baenre to the Pass of the Soulreaver beneath of the Mountains of Eyes. My mother waits on the other side.*

An image of high peaks formed in Halisstra's mind, dark spires that rose until they reached the roof of the sky. She had seen the mountains in the distance when first she had materialized on the Demonweb Pits. At the mountains' base stood a dark opening, the sole means of passing through the range—the Pass of the Soulreaver. The name of the pass triggered some old memory in her, as though she had once read of it during her studies in House Melarn, but the particulars escaped her.

How long before she reaches the pass, Lady? asked Halisstra.

A pause, then, *She will reach them before the tired sun of my mother rises anew.*

The connection grew tenuous. The spell was soon to expire. Halisstra felt her goddess moving away from her. She tried to grab on, but Eilistraee slipped through her fingers.

Before the spell dissipated entirely, she mentally blurted, *Does Danifae Yauntyrr still accompany Quenthel Baenre?*

She sensed a hesitation and instantly regretted asking such a selfish question. Still, Eilistraee offered an answer, as though from far away, and the words gave Halisstra hope.

Yes. A pause, then, *Doubt is her weapon, daughter.*

The connection went quiet. Halisstra opened her eyes, found herself again clad in her cumbersome flesh, sitting across from Feliane. The elf's eyes too were rimed with tears.

"The Lady favored us," Feliane whispered.

"She did," Halisstra answered. "She did, indeed. If Lolth has no Chosen . . ."

"Then she will die," Feliane finished.

Halisstra could only nod.

Spontaneously and at the same moment, the two sisters in faith stretched out their arms and embraced, lit with the afterglow of contact with the divine.

"We will succeed," Feliane said, and to Halisstra it sounded more question than statement.

"We will," Halisstra affirmed, though Eilistraee's last words troubled her. For whom was doubt a weapon? Whose doubt? She had no answers.

In short order, Uluyara emerged from her trance, and Halisstra and Feliane related the substance of their communion.

Uluyara took it in with a nod, then said, "The Baenre is three leagues from here. Her route follows the souls. We'll track her, find her, and kill her."

"Her route leads to the mountains," Feliane said. "To the Pass of the Soulreaver."

"Then that is where we are going too," said Halisstra. "We must reach it before the sun rises."

They would once more ride the foul wind of the Demonweb Pits. Halisstra knew they would catch Quenthel and Danifae before they reached the Pass.

"We should assume that Baenre is accompanied by more than the nalfeshnee and Danifae," Uluyara said. "The wizard, the draegloth, and the mercenary you told us about may yet travel with her."

"Agreed," Halisstra said.

As they prepared to set off, Halisstra thought of Danifae, hesitated, then said to Uluyara, "Danifae Yauntyrr said to me once that she had been called by Eilistraee. I would . . ." She trailed off. "She saved me once, from the draegloth. I would like to give her another chance to answer the Lady."

Uluyara's face showed incredulity. "Is not accompanying Quenthel Baenre answer enough?" she asked. Her face softened at Halisstra's frown, and she reached out a hand as though to touch Halisstra, though she did not. "Halisstra Melarn, your guilt over your life before Eilistraee is affecting your judgment. I know the feeling well. But no one called by the Lady would travel with a priestess of Lolth. If Danifae is with the Baenre, then she is *with* the Baenre."

Halisstra heard sense in Uluyara's words, but she did not want to throw Danifae away so quickly.

"You may be mistaken," Halisstra said. "Let us see what events bring. If she is to be a servant of the Lady, she will show it when she sees me."

Feliane's gaze shifted anxiously between them.

Uluyara's brow furrowed. She started to speak, stopped, and finally said, "Let us not argue about this, not now. As you say, we will see what we will see. I will be pleased to be wrong."

Halisstra stared at the high priestess a moment longer and decided to let the matter rest.

"Gather near me," Halisstra said.

She sang the prayer that would again change them all to mist and let them ride the wind. When she finished the spell, their bodies metamorphosed into vapor. As it had before, Halisstra's field of vision swelled and contracted in a way that made judging distances difficult. Still, she felt in control of her body. They rose from the spire, heading skyward toward the souls high above.

As they ascended into the cloud-roofed sky, Halisstra spared a glance back at the temple, on the tor they had claimed in Eilistraee's name. She knew she would never see it again.

The three priestesses fell in amongst the souls, just three more insubstantial forms amidst the thousands. At Halisstra's mental command, they increased their speed until they were streaking through the air faster than any of the shades, as fast as a bolt fired from a crossbow.

We have you, Quenthel Baenre, she thought. *And we're coming.*

Deep in the bowels of Corpsehaven, Inthracis stood in an anteroom off to the side of his assembly hall, separated from the finest regiment of his army by ornate double doors. Like the rest of his keep, he had fashioned the doors from carved bone and sheets of flesh. Beyond them stood the five hundred mezzoloths and nycaloths of his elite Black Horn Regiment, all veterans of the Blood Wars. Nisviim had sounded the muster and the Regiment had answered. The nycaloth leaders had already briefed the troops on their assignment and worked them into a killing frenzy with promises of glory and payment of twenty soul-larvae each.

The troops beat the hafts of their glaives, tridents, and poleaxes against the floor, sending shivers through the walls and floors, giving Corpsehaven a pulse that temporarily overwhelmed the wind's incessant howl. In time with the thumping, the troops shouted aloud for their general, turning his name into an incantation.

"Inthracis! Inthracis! Inthracis!"

Inthracis smiled and let the excitement build.

Even through the tumult Inthracis could hear the roars of the nycaloth sergeants. He pictured the assembly in his mind—row upon row of armed and armored yugoloths—and reveled in their adoration. Yugoloths were mercenaries to their core, and Inthracis had treated his army well over the millennia, rewarding them with glory, souls, treasure, and flesh. He had augmented their loyalty with subtle binding spells, quietly cast. He had built his army with care over the centuries, and its fearsome strength and unswerving loyalty had elevated him nearly to the top of the Blood Rift's hierarchy. He had only to unseat Kexxon the Oinoloth and he would sit atop Calaas's spire.

Vhaeraun had commanded Inthracis to bring an army to the *Ereilir Vor*, the Plains of Soulfire, in Lolth's Demonweb Pits. Inthracis could not muster his entire army without leaving Corpsehaven unguarded, but he could do the next best thing—bring the Black Horn Regiment, and lead them himself. He would leave Nisviim, his arcanaloth lieutenant, in charge of the fortress until his return. Inthracis knew the bound arcanaloth would not betray him.

Besides, he was certain the Black Horn regiment would be enough—more than enough—to slaughter the three drow priestesses and whomever or whatever might accompany them. And when the three priestesses were dead, Vhaeraun might actually reward him.

"Inthracis! Inthracis!"

The rhythmic beat of weapon hafts on the floor grew louder, faster, building toward a crescendo. Beside Inthracis, snarling and drooling, stood Carnage and Slaughter, his canoloth pets. The rising volume of the chanting agitated the four-legged, houndlike yugoloths—both were dumb but quite powerful, quite loyal—and their long, barbed tongues lolled from the fanged sphincters of their mouths. Their claws dug into the floor, and both uttered low growls.

Inthracis reached up to pat them each on their huge, armored flanks.

"Be at ease," he said and let arcane power creep into his voice.

The power of his magic eased their tension. The canoloths uttered satisfied murmurs and visibly relaxed.

For the sake of appearances, Inthracis had armored Carnage and Slaughter in their war gear—spiked plate barding covered the coarse, black fur of their wide backs and broad chests. He had even armored himself, though he would consider it a personal failing to be forced to engage in melee combat.

Still, the troops enjoyed seeing their general outfitted for war.

His light, magic-absorbing mail shirt and helm, both forged in one of Calaas's furnaces from a magic-soaked ore unique to the Blood Rift, glimmered in the light of the anteroom's yellow glowball. His spellblade, Arcane Razor, through which he could cast his spells and cut through the spells of others, hung at his belt from a scabbard made of barbed devil hide. An arsenal of metallic wands and three bone rods hung from a quiver at his thigh.

"Inthracis! Inthracis!"

As it had with the canoloths, the noise agitated the stacked corpses in the walls of Corpsehaven. Limbs squirmed, wide eyes stared, and flesh oozed. Hands reached from the walls as though to touch him, either out of excitement or perhaps out of a need for reassurance.

Carnage turned his huge head, casually ripped a grasping forearm from the wall, and devoured it, bone and all. Seeing his sibling feasting, Slaughter eyed the wall-corpses to see if another such tidbit might be forthcoming.

None were. Hands and arms retreated into the wall. Eyes stared out in semi-sentient fear.

Inthracis smiled at his pets, even as he ran his plan through his mind. He had been unable to scry any of the three priestesses—he did not know why—and Vhaeraun's avatar had not shown himself again. Still, he dared not disobey the Masked Lord's command.

Inthracis would use a simple spell to show the Black Horn Regiment where it was to go—the fiery, blasted heath of the Plains of Soulfire, in the shadow of Lolth's city and the Infinite Web—and go they would. Inthracis knew the plains to be uninhabited but for the tortured souls that burned in the sky above them—and perhaps a few of Lolth's eight-legged pets.

"Inthracis! Inthracis!"

The time had come.

Without another word, he threw open the doors and strode forward onto the high balcony that overlooked the assembly hall. The cheer that greeted him from below sent flakes of skin raining from the ceiling, shook the walls of Corpsehaven like one of the Blood Rift's frequent earthquakes.

He looked down on the regiment. Rows of squat, beetle-like mezzoloths looked up at him with their red, compound eyes. They stood on two legs, using the other four to wield their polearms. Plates of armor draped their black carapaces. Their mandibles offered soft clicks. The larger nycaloths moved amongst them, calling for quiet.

Muscles rippled under the green scales of the gargoylish nycaloths as they moved. Huge axes hung from their backs. Four clawed hands erupted from their muscular chests, and their sleek heads sported two horns, limned black, of course.

Inthracis raised his hands, and the multitude fell silent. Only the howl of the wind outside disturbed the moment. In its shriek, Inthracis still heard the echo of Lolth's call, but softer: *"Yor'thae."*

Inthracis ignored it, except to hope that the diminishment of the call indicated the diminishment of Lolth.

He willed a spell to amplify his voice. When he spoke, his softly uttered words sounded as loud and clear in the ears of his troops as if he had stood beside them.

"There are drow priestesses that we must kill," he said. "And we must do it under the eyes of the Spider Queen herself."

A ripple ran through the lines. All knew that something had been happening recently with Lolth.

Inthracis spoke the words to his spell and called up a towering image of the *Ereilir Vor*. A green mist hung over a pockmarked landscape. Pools of caustic fluid bubbled their stink into the air. Glowing souls burned in arcane fire in the sky.

Beyond the plains, Lolth's city loomed, a great, crawling citadel of iron set among the Infinite Web. Millions of arachnids scurried along its strands.

Another ripple ran through the lines. No doubt some recognized the locale.

"That is where we will do battle," he called. "And here is our prey."

Drawing upon the mental image placed in his mind by Vhaeraun, he spoke aloud the words to another spell and caused an image of the three priestesses to take shape before the regiment.

"All three must die," he said, "and an extra twenty-five souls from my cache to those who strike the killing blow."

A roar answered him and he nodded.

The Black Horn Regiment was ready. If Vhaeraun was right, and one of the three drow priestesses was or was to be Lolth's *Yor'thae*, then the Spider Queen's Chosen would never reach her goddess's side.

C h a p t e r

E L E V E N

Day was drawing near. The nalfeshnee and chasme flew on. The mountains grew larger and larger in Pharaun's sight. Though perhaps a league away, they stood so tall they looked like a wall of black rock that never ended. He knew that no one could ever go over them. There was only one way through—the Pass of the Soulreaver.

Souls streamed overhead, angling downward and flowing toward the base of the mountains. The nalfeshnee eyed the glowing souls hungrily as they passed, but his fear of Quenthel kept him from doing anything other than looking. The chasme continued to whine at the heaviness of his load.

As the mountains loomed closer and closer, Pharaun caught Quenthel looking back, not at him but at the horizon line. Pharaun turned to watch it too, expecting to see the light of the rising sun once again summon forth Lolth's children for the Teeming.

The sun peeked over the edge of the world, casting its dim red light across the landscape. To Pharaun's surprise, nothing happened.

The light oozed over the rocks, holes, and pits, but no spiders came forth to greet it.

It appeared that the Teeming was over. Strange, that so great a degree of violence could erupt and end with such suddenness. Pharaun had a peculiar sense that the Demonweb Pits was holding its breath, waiting for something.

When he turned back around, he found Quenthel staring at him. With exaggerated gestures, she signed, *Be prepared when we land. But do nothing except at my command.*

Pharaun nodded in understanding. The time for the confrontation had come at last.

He let himself lag a bit behind the chasme. There, he began surreptitiously to cast defensive spells that had no outward visible effect—he did not want some aura or emanation to alert Danifae and Jeggred to Quenthel's intent. He sprinkled diamond dust over his flesh and turned his skin as strong as stone. He whispered sequential incantations that made his body resistant to fire, lightning, and acid.

The Master of Sorcere could not contain a smile as they flew. When they reached the mountains, Quenthel would kill Danifae, and Pharaun would kill Jeggred.

It is about time, he thought.

Halisstra, Feliane, and Uluyara streaked through the air, riding the wind. They flew amidst the river of souls, though Halisstra did not look any of the glowing spirits in the face. She was afraid she might encounter someone else she had known.

The mountains were visible ahead, a titanic wall of sheer stone. They looked like the fangs of an unimaginably huge beast. The flow of souls angled downward, heading toward the bottom of one of the mountains.

Behind them, the sun rose over the horizon. Halisstra looked earthward, expecting to see another day of violence, but it appeared as if the only violence that would happen on the Demonweb Pits that day would happen between drow.

Far ahead, Halisstra caught sight of two large forms descending toward the base of the tallest of mountains—demons, she saw.

Quenthel Baenre was there, she knew. So was Danifae.

Her heart began to race.

The souls swirled around the demons as they descended toward a hole in the mountains that could only be the Pass of the Soulreaver.

Halisstra and her fellow priestesses sped onward, slowly gaining.

Flying in shadow form near Menzoberranzan's stalactite-dotted ceiling, Gromph reached House Agrach Dyrr. Looking down, he saw that little had changed from when he had scried the fortress an hour or so before.

Agrach Dyrr's defenders still paced the tall, stalagmite walls, peering down through their fortifications at the attackers. The violet-plumed helms of the officers and the blades of the soldiers' polearms and swords bobbed along behind the crenellations. Banners with House Agrach Dyrr's heraldry festooned the walls, charred but largely whole. Scores of orc and bugbear crossbowmen bolstered the drow forces.

Gromph could not smell the battlefield due to his incorporeality, but he could see the clouds of black smoke gathered near the cavern's roof and could imagine the stink.

On the plateau before the stalagmite castle gathered the massed forces of House Xorlarrin. The army numbered perhaps eight hundred all told and encircled the complex at a distance of a long crossbow shot from the moat-filled chasm. Gromph noted the makeup of the Xorlarrin soldiery: half a score drow wizards, a few hundred drow warriors, two score war-spiders, and numerous platoons of lesser creatures, all of whom stood assembled and ready. Several siege engines fashioned of magically hardened crystal and iron stood amidst the ranks.

All was quiet. The Xorlarrin appeared willing to wait for reinforcements before making another attempt on Agrach Dyrr. Gromph was mildly surprised. He knew Matron Mother Zeerith to be as ambitious for her House as any matron mother. He would have expected her to hoard the glory of Dyrr's capture all to herself. Yasraena must have been mounting an impressive defense to so temper Xorlarrin ambition.

Gromph floated down and saw scores of bodies and body parts floating in the water-filled chasm that surrounded the manse's walls. A few toothy reptiles—giant aquatic lizards, no doubt—swam in the moat and fed on the remains. Gromph saw that the dead ogres and their battering ram, which he had seen while scrying the House, no longer lay before the adamantine doors. No doubt some Agrach Dyrr necromancer had animated their corpses and turned them back against the Xorlarrin.

Until he had evaluated the fortress's network of wards up close, Gromph dared go no closer than the line delineated by the moat. With a minor effort of will, he activated the permanent dweomer on his eyes that allowed him to see magical emanations.

House Agrach Dyrr lit up like the sun of the Green Fields, the ridiculous "halfling heaven" to where the lichdrow had banished him during their spell duel. Gromph had expected as much, but seeing the wards of House Agrach Dyrr through the muted lens of his scrying glass had been something different than seeing the blazing spiderweb of defenses in person. Unlike the rest of the physical world, which appeared to his transformed eyes only in shades of gray, the wards blazed red and blue. Their power reached across the planes and would affect even incorporeal creatures.

More out of pride than necessity, Gromph decided that he would walk through the front doors, just to spite Yasraena. In truth, it did not matter where he made his assault. The wards and defenses were shaped as spheres, concentric circles of power, not walls. They covered every avenue of approach. He would face everything that protected the House whether he attempted the adamantine doors or the lizard stable wall.

He sat cross-legged on a large rock, near the far end of the adamantine bridge. He was perched almost exactly halfway between House Agrach Dyrr and the besieging Xorlarrin army. He was pleased to see that his presence went unnoted by both the Dyrr and Xorlarrin forces. He knew that the mages among them would have various divinations in effect, including some that would allow them to see invisible creatures. Gromph's nondetection ward must have thwarted them. The victory still brought him only small pleasure.

As a preliminary measure, he withdrew his ocular and held the milky gem to his eye. Though incorporeal, the magic of the ocular continued to work. Looking through the lens of the gem, Gromph saw things as they truly were—undisguised by illusion, disguise, or shapeshifting magic. The ocular's power could have been thwarted by spells like those which protected Gromph, but such protections were atypical.

He eyed the complex and saw nothing out of the ordinary except that two putative male drow officers were actually polymorphed demons. Gromph's magical lens showed their actual form, that of towering, muscular, bipedal, vulturelike creatures with hateful red eyes and large feathered wings.

Vrocks, Gromph knew. Yasraena must have bought the services of a pair of the fiends.

Gromph pocketed the ocular and softly spoke the words to a spell that modified his magic sensing vision so that it excluded from its effect the anti-scrying wards and the spells that offered House Dyrr structural reinforcement. For his purposes, those spells were irrelevant. He was interested only in those wards that would prevent his physical intrusion into the complex and those that would kill or capture him once he was within.

When the modification took effect, perhaps half of the lines of power vanished, though the fortress still glowed brightly, encased in a net of red lines. Spell traps lurked within the network, killing spells that would be triggered by the breach or inartful dispelling of a ward. For a time, Gromph used a series of divining spells to examine the intricate lattice of spells visible from where he sat. He wanted to understand the interconnections between the wards before he tried to penetrate them.

Gromph would have to peel the wards back, spherical layer by layer, as though flensing a slave to the bone.

He pulled out his eye-capped wands and with their more pointed divining spells deepened his analysis. Among the multitude of spell traps set within the network he discovered the tell-tale traces of magical symbols—one of pain, two of death. He confirmed the presence of glyphs that emitted fire and lightning, forcecages to trap him, contingency spells to bind his soul, barriers that forbade passage in any physical or incorporeal form.

And he saw something else. Knifing through the entire network was the thin, almost unnoticeable line of a ward that tied all of the other wards together and that augmented them all—a master ward.

Gromph had no doubt that the lichdrow had cast it.

Essentially, Dyrr had tied a knot around a knot, lacing his master ward through the interstices of the other wards until all of them were irretrievably intertwined. As a result, the ordinary protections put in place over the years by the various Agrach Dyrr matron mothers would, upon being triggered, become all the more deadly from an influx of power from the lichdrow's spell.

Gromph studied the line of the master ward more closely. He pulled out another wand and used it to carefully analyze the ward's dweomer. Its complexity suggested that it did more than simply augment the other wards, but Gromph's spells could not divine anything more, at least not from where he sat. He would have to get within the ward network itself before he could do a more detailed analysis from another angle.

He sheathed his wand and frowned. His ignorance of the master ward's full purpose gave him pause but he knew there was nothing for it. He could not turn back, and delay was his enemy.

He floated to his feet and faced his first challenge, a simple detection spell that would alert the caster if anyone, in any form, crossed the adamantine bridge. Gromph looked along the ward's bulky, glowing lines, saw no spell trap connected to it, and dispelled it with a whispered counterspell.

He flew across the adamantine bridge. Blood stained it in several places. From atop the walls, Dyrr soldiers and the two demons looked through and past him. To them, he did not exist. He was alone with the wards.

Hovering before the gate, he studied the lines of magic crisscrossing its surface. The lines not only prevented physical passage, their pattern formed two magical symbols that would kill anyone whose flesh touched the doors without first speaking the password, having the appropriate item on their person, or the right blood in their veins. A further analysis with one of his wands showed Gromph that the symbols were permanent. They did not vanish upon a single discharge. Instead, they would continue to reset and kill unless they were eliminated.

He spoke the words to a counterspell and focused the magic of the spell into his forefinger. Gently, he ran his shadowy fingertip over the lines of the first symbol. Though his finger was incorporeal, the magic reached into the physical world. Where his finger touched, his spell erased the symbol. Soon, it was effaced.

Gromph cast another counterspell and repeated the process with the second symbol. It proved more stubborn than the first. Gromph's magic met the magic of the symbol and did nothing. His counterspell had no effect. Biting back his frustration, he prepared another spell, a more powerful, focused version of the counter.

Sudden motion from above drew his eye. A swarm of crossbow bolts rained down at something behind him. Gromph turned to see a half-score of giant trolls charging across the bridge. They wore piecemeal armor strapped haphazardly to their gray-green, warty hides. The smallest stood three times as tall as Gromph, with over-long limbs, a mouthful of fangs, finger length claws, and rippling muscles. In their huge hands, the giant trolls held a mammoth sta-lagmite, shaped by magic into a fearsome battering ram. Gromph's magic-detecting vision told him that the ram had been powerfully enspelled.

Green disks of magical energy hovered over the huge creatures— cast by distant Xorlarrin wizards—protecting the trolls from the rain of bolts that poured from the walls. In ten strides, the giant trolls had crossed half the bridge.

From the Xorlarrin lines behind them, a platoon of orog crossbow-men and their shield bearers ran up to the edge of the moat-chasm and fired a volley of arrows at the defenders on the wall. An answer-ing volley streaked down at them. Fire and lightning fired from Dyrr wands exploded in the midst of the orogs, and several of the bestial creatures burst into flames or exploded into pieces.

Drow soldiers stood lined and ready fifty paces behind the orogs, ready to charge forward should the giant trolls penetrate the doors.

The huge creatures lumbered forward, the bridge vibrating under their weight. Fire exploded in their midst but did not divert their charge.

A wall of conjured ice, taller than the giant trolls and an arm's span thick, formed before the creatures, blocking their rush across the bridge. They did not even slow. In stride, they swung the magical stalagmite ram into the wall, and the ice exploded in a blast of shards. They charged onward.

Cursing, Gromph started to fly upward. Though incorporeal, magical energies could still harm him, as could appropriately enchanted weapons. He did not want to get caught in any crossfire.

A cloud of vapor—poisonous vapor, Gromph assumed—formed before the doors. The giant trolls gulped clean air and charged in, swinging the huge ram as they did—right at Gromph.

He dodged aside but his incorporeal flight was cumbersome and slow. The magical ram clipped his shoulder, and its enchantments reached through realities to affect his insubstantial body. Agony exploded in his brain. The impact spun him in a circle and knocked him toward the gate and the killing symbol.

He struggled to right himself and contorted his body to avoid contact with the magically charged gates. Gromph regained control a heartbeat before careening into the gate, and he flew upward and off to the side of the bridge, hovering over the moat chasm. His entire right side flared with pain, but his ring began immediately to repair the wound.

Still holding their breath, the giant trolls reared the ram back and slammed it again into the doors. Sparks flew from its tip, flecks of stone showered the bridge, but the adamantine doors showed not even a scratch. More and more crossbow bolts poured down on the trolls, some getting through the magical shields and finding flesh. One of the creatures, struck in the cheek by a bolt, exclaimed in pain and inadvertently drew a breath of poisonous air. He fell writhing to the bridge and was dead in moments.

The rest continued on, futilely battering the gates as bolts poured down. Gromph found the scene surreal. He could hear nothing, smell nothing. He felt as if he was looking at the imperfect illusion of a first year apprentice.

Gromph assumed the giant troll assault to be only a feint, with the real attack occurring elsewhere, but he had no way to confirm his guess. Apparently, he had been mistaken about Xorlarrin complacency. Matron Mother Zeerith had not yet decided to surrender the glory of sacking House Dyrr. Either that or she simply wanted to keep the Dyrr defenders off guard and force them to expend resources on fodder troops.

To their credit, the Dyrr defenders were using mostly mundane weapons to deal with the giant trolls. They had wasted only two spells and a few discharges from their wands. Crossbows were doing most of the work. Already four of the trolls lay dead. The remaining six continued to swing the ram, though with less force.

An idea struck Gromph.

Moving quickly, he wove his hands in an intricate gesture and spoke aloud the words to a spell. The magic generated a field of force as an extension of Gromph's will. With it, he gripped one of the foremost giant trolls—the creature's eyes went wide, though it did not shout for fear of inhaling the poisonous gas.

Gromph forced the giant troll to loose its grip on the ram and reach forth an arm to touch the doors. The beast seemed to sense its danger and its great strength warred against Gromph's will—but the Archmage of Menzoberranzan's will was the stronger. The giant troll held out a clawed hand, touched the gate, and triggered the remaining symbol.

Gromph averted his gaze as the symbol flared. The magic entered the giant troll, and the creature opened its mouth in a scream. It fell to the bridge, dead. Gromph gave it no further thought.

The rest of the giant trolls, seemingly stunned at the stupidity of their companion and unable to easily manage the weight of the ram without him, broke. First one, then another loosed their grip, turned, and ran. Crossbow bolts chased them back across the bridge. A sphere of magical darkness formed around the head of one. Blinded, the creature ran off the side of the bridge and fell into the chasm.

Gromph studied the gate and saw with satisfaction that the symbol was gone. For a precious few moments, it would remain so.

Moving quickly, Gromph hovered before the door, in the midst of the poisonous cloud, above the giant troll corpses. With the delicate touch of a skilled chirurgeon, he bent aside the lines of the ward that prevented physical passage and slipped through. He did not like leaving the intact symbol behind him but figured he would be able to leave House Agrach Dyrr much more easily than he would be able to enter it. Wards typically barred entry, not exit.

He flew through the adamantine doors and found himself standing in the gatehouse tunnel of House Agrach Dyrr, in the midst of two score spear-armed, lizard-mounted drow cavalrymen. Many of their spear tips glowed with magical power in Gromph's sight, power enough to harm Gromph, had they known of his presence.

They stood in a cluster around him, not seeing him. They must have been stationed there in the unlikely event of a breach or perhaps in preparation for a counterattack.

Gromph could not hear their voices, but he could see the sweat on their faces, the determination in their eyes. Some of the soldiers shifted their mounts and passed right through him. He flew into the air to the tunnel's ceiling to avoid their touch. The negative energy associated with his shadow form might damage one of them and alert them to his presence, or worse, one might inadvertently wound him with an enchanted spear.

Safely up against the ceiling, he allowed himself a smile. He had beaten the first challenge. He was in.

Looking to the end of the gatehouse tunnel beyond the cavalry, he saw that another ward awaited him there.

The glowing lines of the master ward charged the air around him, around the soldiers. Magic literally saturated the air around the Dyrr defenders, but they saw it no more than they saw him.

Having bypassed the first line of defense, Gromph had another perspective on the structure of the master ward. He pulled out one of his wands, triggered its dweomer, and examined the line of the master ward.

The wand showed that it had many threads within it. He frowned.

One of the threads was a contingent dimensional lock. Its latent magic likely had been triggered by the destruction of the lichdrow's physical form, to prevent easy entry into House Dyrr and consequent access to the lichdrow's phylactery. The presence of the dimensional lock complicated matters.

A dimensional lock prevented all forms of magical transport. Even if Gromph disabled or dispelled all of the ordinary wards in House Dyrr, he would not be able to teleport out of the Dyrr complex unless he first dispelled the master ward, or at least the dimensional lock that was part of it. Even the powerful contingent evasion spell that Gromph had cast on himself would not work in the presence of a dimensional lock.

Gromph could see that the master ward was too intricate for him to be able to dispel with any ease. It would take hours, and he could not spare the time. He had to keep moving.

He floated over the Dyrr soldiers toward the far end of the gate-house tunnel. A flash from behind him turned him around, a defensive spell on his lips.

A violet pulse ran through the master ward and traveled to the area of the discharged symbol on the adamantine doors. The magic circled the area, redrew the symbol, recharged it, and reset it.

To Gromph's surprise and admiration, the power in the master ward then circled the point where Gromph had dispelled the first symbol and redrew it too, essentially recasting the spell. Gromph's dispelling dweomer should have eradicated the symbol forever.

The lichdrow's spellcraft was masterful. It was unfortunate that such knowledge would be lost forever when Gromph destroyed the lich's phylactery.

Without further waste of time, he turned and began his attack on the ward at the end of the tunnel.

Chapter

TWELVE

Up close, the mountains were among the most majestic things Pharaun had ever seen. Sheer and jagged, they soared so high they appeared never to end, an infinite wall of rock ejected from the ground to reach for the sky. Like the rest of the Demonweb Pits, cracks, jagged openings, and tunnels dotted the face of the peaks. Spiders scuttled in and out of the holes, preying on each other. Lolth's sun gave the otherwise dark rock a peculiar reddish cast, as though the mountains were dusted with rust, or perhaps blood.

Souls streaked around Pharaun, near enough that he could have reached out and touched a dozen as they flew past. He hoped soon to add Jeggred's spirit to their number.

The nalfeshnee and chasme eyed the souls with hungry eyes as they passed. Only the barked orders of Quenthel and Danifae kept the demons from feasting on Lolth's dead.

The stream of souls flowed toward and into a jagged black hole at the base of the tallest peak. Pharaun presumed the opening to be the

Pass of the Soulreaver, though it was less pass than tunnel. To Pharaun, it looked like a rough tear in the mountain, a malformed mouth open in a scream.

The pass's opening was as dark and impenetrable as pitch. The light of Lolth's sun did not touch it, let alone enter it. The hole was a literal wall of black.

A creeping realization struck Pharaun: the Pass of the Soulreaver was *on* the Demonweb Pits but not *of* the Demonweb Pits. To enter it would be to enter something . . . *other*.

Untroubled by Pharaun's realization, the souls poured into the hole and vanished the moment they broached the entryway, as though they had been extinguished, swallowed by the mountain.

Pharaun licked his lips.

Quenthel pointed downward with the handle of her whip and shouted an order to Zerevimeel. The nalfeshnee headed lower. So too did the chasme bearing Danifae and Jeggred. Pharaun followed.

Zerevimeel set down fifteen or so paces to the right of the pass. Pharaun landed beside the towering nalfeshnee. Danifae steered the chasme down perhaps ten paces to the left of the tunnel. The river of souls flowed between them, and the Pass of the Soulreaver devoured them all.

Quenthel straightened her robes and stared through the line of ghosts at Danifae. Pharaun could see the calculation in Quenthel's eyes.

The nalfeshnee, his feeble little wings still beating, bent down to Quenthel's ear and said, so softly that Pharaun could hardly hear, "I could be of assistance to you for the right price. The draegloth would be an enjoyable kill."

Pharaun could not have agreed more.

Out of the side of her mouth, still staring at Danifae, Quenthel said, "I require no assistance, creature. And this is to be decided by priestesses. You are dismissed. Begone."

The demon hissed in anger. His muzzle peeled back from his fangs, and he reared up to his full height. Pharaun put his hand to the iron wand of lightning at his belt, just in case. He need not have worried. The demon had no desire to challenge Quenthel Baenre.

Pharaun wondered if Danifae still did.

"Remember our bargain, priestess," the nalfeshnee said. "You owe me sixty-six souls. I will expect payment when next we meet."

Quenthel waved a hand dismissively. The nalfeshnee's eyes narrowed, but he gave no further expression to his irritation. He triggered the innate ability of his kind to teleport and disappeared in a blink.

A short distance away, Danifae and Jeggred stood near the chasme. The fly demon beat its wings and turned a circle in excitement.

"Perhaps my payment now, lovely priestess?" the demon said, and a long tongue emerged from a toothless mouth. Something else long and dripping emerged from his thorax.

Danifae smiled sweetly at the chasme, and he beat his wings harder. The charnel reek from the wings caused Pharaun to wrinkle his nose.

Danifae sidled a step closer to the demon. She licked her lips and said, "Kill this wretch, Jeggred."

At first, the words did not seem to register with the demon. His wings beat in agitation, and his malformed brow creased in confusion.

"What did you say, priestess?"

Jeggred bounded forward, and the demon at last understood his peril. He flew into the air but Jeggred leaped up and grabbed him by his human forelegs.

The chasme squealed in pain.

"You lied!" he screamed at Danifae, trying to shake Jeggred free.

Danifae laughed and said, "Of course."

Jeggred, partially lifted into the air by the chasme, grunted and yanked at the demon's arms. The chasme squealed and whined; Jeggred roared and tore.

With a wet ripping sound, the draegloth pulled the chasme's forelegs from its body. Jeggred fell to the ground in a crouch, clutching the two gory sticks of the chasme's arms.

The chasme wailed with agony, and the sound was so ridiculous Pharaun almost smiled. The demon buzzed in circles overhead, showering them all with gore from the bleeding stumps of its front shoulders.

"You will pay, lying drow bitch!" the demon screamed through its pain. "You will pay. Vakuul does not forget!"

Jeggred threw one of the demon's arms at it, but the chasme whined indignantly and wheeled aside. The bloody limb landed at Pharaun's feet.

With one final glare at Danifae, the chasme disappeared, teleporting back to whatever layer of the Abyss it called home.

Jeggred sniffed the other arm, wrinkled his nose, and tossed it away.

Still smiling, Danifae looked through the river of souls to Quenthel. The priestesses stared at one another for a long moment before Quenthel said, "Lolth awaits her *Yor'thae* beyond the Pass of the Soulreaver."

Jeggred must have sensed something in the air. He stepped in front of Danifae, his eyes fixed on his aunt. Pharaun drew nearer to Quenthel.

"Mistress Quenthel states the obvious," Danifae said.

Her small hand was on Jeggred's back. It took Pharaun a moment to realize that she was signing against his skin, telling him something.

"Mistress . . ." Pharaun began, but Quenthel cut him off.

"I state the obvious, battle-captive, because the obvious has escaped you since first we set foot on Lolth's domain." She punctuated her point with a crack of her whip.

Jeggred's breath came faster. Danifae removed her hand from his back. She had told him whatever it was she had wanted him to know—or wanted him to do.

Tension sat as thick as mist. Pharaun brought to mind the words to a spell. Quenthel had told him to attack only at her command so he stood ready and waited.

Jeggred stared through the souls and alternately eyed him and Quenthel with undisguised hunger. His battle with the chasme had only whetted his appetite, no doubt.

Danifae touched her holy symbol and said, "And what obvious point have I overlooked, Mistress Quenthel?"

Quenthel's serpents hissed hate at Danifae.

"Just this," Quenthel said. "That Lolth requires a sacrifice before her *Yor'thae* enters the pass."

She reached back with her whip as though to strike but Jeggred moved faster. Before Quenthel could move, before Pharaun could cast a spell, the draegloth charged Quenthel.

He covered the distance in four bounding strides.

"Do not!" Danifae shouted, but her words did not match the pleased expression on her face.

Taken aback, Quenthel managed a weak swing with her whip but Jeggred caught the serpents in a fighting claw and held them away from him. He shouldered Quenthel's shield aside and lashed out with a vicious claw strike at her chest.

Armor links flew. The impact knocked Quenthel back two steps.

Jeggred followed up with savage speed, still clutching the hissing whip serpents, which tried futilely to sink their fangs into his iron-hard flesh. Roaring, the draegloth slashed with his free claw. Quenthel recovered herself and batted it aside with her shield, reversed her parry, and struck the draegloth in the face with her shield rim. Several of Jeggred's teeth flew. The strength of the blow momentarily stunned him.

Taking advantage of the respite, Quenthel yanked the whip serpents free of Jeggred's grasp with a grunt. Pharaun marveled at the strength granted her by her magical belt. She leaped back a step, spun the serpents over her head, and lashed them at the draegloth. Propelled by the force of her strength, the serpents struck home. Bloody furrows opened along Jeggred's ribcage. He roared in pain and dived aside, coming to his feet in a low crouch.

Growling, spraying spit, Jeggred pounced forward and unleashed a flurry of blows against Quenthel, blows that would have shredded a rock wall. Quenthel's shield answered, and there was her armor, but the force of the blows drove her backward. Her whip snapped again, and fangs sank into the draegloth's flesh.

Pharaun realized that he had been watching the combat too long. He quickly pulled a small leather glove from his *piwafwi*, moved his closed fists through an elaborate gesticulation, and spoke aloud the words to a spell.

When he finished, a gray disembodied fist as large as a titan's formed before him. At his mental command it flew at Jeggred. The draegloth never saw it coming, and it struck him on his flank with force enough to crack stone.

The impact cut short Jeggred's roar and sent him flying through the air. He landed in a roll ten paces from Quenthel, amidst the souls. He found his feet and clawed at the passing spirits to no effect.

With a roar, he charged Pharaun, but the Master of Sorcere interposed the magical fist.

"I'll kill you, mage!" Jeggred shouted and rent the construct with his claws. "I'll kill you both!"

"Jeggred!" Danifae said, and for the first time in Pharaun's memory her words did not get through.

Battle mad, the draegloth continued to claw at the fist.

Pharaun smiled and readied the fist to deliver another blow.

"Jeggred, *stop!*" Danifae shouted.

That registered.

Jeggred stopped in mid-rampage, looked to Danifae, then back to the fist. His chest rose and fell, his eyes glared, and slobber dripped from his fangs. He fixed his gaze on Quenthel, on Pharaun, on the magical fist of force Pharaun had summoned.

"She was going to attack us, Mistress," Jeggred hissed to Danifae.

Pharaun inched the magical fist closer to the draegloth. He could strike Jeggred again anytime he wished, but he was enjoying the draegloth's growing frustration.

"You underestimate your aunt," Danifae said, smiling sweetly at Quenthel.

Pharaun said, "She ordered Jeggred to attack, Mistress."

The Baenre priestess, only mildly winded from her exchange with Jeggred, smiled and said, "You overestimate our battle-captive, Master Mizzrym."

Pharaun thought not but said nothing.

Jeggred, voice low and dangerous, said to Danifae, "Mistress, I should be allowed to kill—"

"Silence, male," Danifae snapped.

The draegloth fell silent. Pharaun admired the obedience she had instilled in the dolt.

Quenthel examined the small hole in her armor caused by Jeggred, then said to the draegloth, "Nephew, you have just named yourself as a sacrifice to Lolth."

Jeggred spat a glob of yellow saliva in Quenthel's direction. It spattered on the magical fist and dangled there before falling to the rocky ground.

"Are you certain that my mother would approve, aunt?" he said.

That hit home. Jeggred was the son of Matron Mother Baenre. Perhaps Quenthel would risk Triel's wrath by sacrificing him, but perhaps she would not. Pharaun had his answer with Quenthel's next words.

"I shall enjoy administering your punishment, nephew," she said.

Disappointed, Pharaun decided that changing Quenthel's mind was worth another try.

In the most cavalier tone of voice he could summon, he said "This shaggy dolt has repeatedly disobeyed your instructions, has sided with a minor priestess—" he nodded with contempt at Danifae—"and has shown himself unworthy of the Baenre name. His folly is exceeded only by his stink. If you will not sacrifice him, please allow me to kill him. It would be a favor to intelligent life in the multiverse."

Jeggred glared hate.

Quenthel didn't look at Pharaun but answered, "You will do nothing unless I allow it, Master Mizzrym."

"Mistress . . ." Pharaun began.

"*Only* if I allow it, male," Quenthel snapped, and her serpents fixed Pharaun with a stare.

The mage ground his teeth in frustration but managed a half-hearted bow.

"The mage's insolence and the influence of that cursed whip is what shows your weakness, aunt," Jeggred growled.

Pharaun brought the magical fist to his side.

"Enough," Danifae said. She looked to Quenthel and withdrew her holy symbol.

Quenthel did the same. They stared at one another for a moment.

"Perhaps some protective spells before we attempt the pass?" Danifae said.

Quenthel nodded.

Both began to cast, eyeing the other the while.

Pharaun saw the look in each of their eyes and was not certain that defensive spells were what either had in mind.

Gromph moved methodically through the unending series of wards. Sometimes he used brute magical force, dispelling or destroying them; sometimes he used subtlety and misdirection, bending or warping the magical defenses for a time while he slipped past.

He focused entirely on House Agrach Dyrr's arcane defenses, barely noticing the passing Dyrr soldiers or the second foiled attack on the bridge by the Xorlarrin.

With each ward he overcame, he moved nearer to Lolth's temple, nearer to the golem and the phylactery.

The wards and spell traps cast in days or years past by Yasraena or a previous matron mother provided little challenge for Gromph's counterspells. Only those cast by the lichdrow proved difficult to bypass or dispel, but always Gromph prevailed.

And always the lichdrow's master ward, the thread that strung all of the others together, reactivated those that Gromph deactivated. Gromph opened and unlocked two score magical "doors" on his way in, only to watch the master ward close and relock them behind him. He did not fully understand the lichdrow's purpose and had no time to think on it more.

Time passed, but Gromph had no way to measure it. He assumed he had been at the wards an hour and a half or more. Soon, the spell that allowed him to change shape—the spell that had allowed Prath to take his form and him to take that of the shadow—would expire. He would no longer be incorporeal. Prath would no longer look like Gromph.

At that point, Yasraena would surely recognize the deception, assume that Gromph was within the complex, and muster all of the resources at her disposal to find him.

He put that possibility out of his mind and focused on the next defense, a spell trap that would imprison him in a cage of force if he attempted to bypass the ward's outer border. The forcecage could hold him even in incorporeal form.

Just as he prepared to dispel it, he noticed a subtle twist to the ward.

It was not one ward but two, the second cleverly masked by the first.

The hidden ward would be triggered by dispelling the first and held a latent spell that caused a few moments of agonizing pain before stopping the target's heart.

Gromph admonished himself for his carelessness. He was mentally exhausted, and fatigue was making him sloppy. He had almost made a fatal mistake.

He took a moment to refocus before dispelling the wards in the proper sequence. As he passed through the area, the master ward reactivated them both behind him.

Gromph continued on.

The temple doors, themselves heavily warded, stood tantalizing near. He moved rapidly through the two wards that stood between him and the temple as Dyrr soldiers hurried past.

Constructed of finished stone, the temple sported a domed ceiling and a stone-flagged portico with a colonnade. A pair of open bronze double doors, darkened with age and inlaid with electrum spider motifs and prayers to Lolth, opened onto the nave.

Within, Gromph could see stone benches lining either side of the center aisle, which led up to the apse and the altar. He could not quite make out the golem, though he knew it to be positioned behind the altar.

The temple appeared unoccupied. The House was too busy defending itself to spend time in worship.

Several powerful wards and spell traps shielded the doors. The master ward twisted through all of them and extended into the temple, straight up the center aisle, presumably right into the spider golem.

Gromph floated before the lines of power and cast several spells that enabled him to analyze the wards' natures. He removed one of his divining wands and stared through its tip while he cast.

He saw that the wards on the doors were heavily intertwined, heavily interdependent. He was not sure he could unravel them.

Frustration made his pulse pound. He tried to calm himself, but then he sensed something behind him and turned around.

A drow female, Yasraena's daughter Larikal, walked toward the open doors of the temple. Her mesh armor hid her overlarge frame. A large mace hung from her belt. Her bland, unattractive face wore an angry scowl.

A balding, portly male walked beside her, his hands stuffed in the pockets of his black robe—Geremis, Gromph remembered, and thought that he looked much like Nauzhror.

Both Larikal and the wizard glowed various hues in Gromph's sight. Personal protective spells sheathed both of them. Magical trinkets and weapons adorned each. Gromph read their lips as they walked.

"I will not tolerate your failure much longer, male," Larikal said.

Like all drow males, Geremis had the good sense to accept the admonishment without comment.

"The phylactery is within the fortress," the priestess continued. "You and your undermages must find it within the hour. Or the next time you enter this temple with me, it will be as a sacrifice to Lolth."

"Yes, Mistress Larikal," Geremis replied.

Larikal and the mage walked right through Gromph's incorporeal form—it felt to Gromph as though a breeze passed through him—and stepped through the temple's open doorway. The wards on the doors shimmered at their passage, briefly encapsulating each in crimson light as they walked across the threshold. Neither had spoken a command word or made any sign so Gromph reasoned that the wards must be attuned to something they wore or perhaps to their very bodies.

Just beyond the doorway, Geremis stopped. He turned, a curious look on his round face, and looked back at the space Gromph occupied.

Gromph cursed and froze. Fearing that the mage had sensed him somehow, he prepared a spell that would immolate Geremis, assuming it could get through the mage's personal wards.

Gromph relaxed when Geremis turned away and hurried up the

center aisle after the Dyrr daughter. Gromph shifted his position so that he could better see within the temple.

The priestess walked up the aisle, crossed into the apse, and kneeled before the black altar. Her manner suitably reverent, she used a tinder-twig to light the single candle atop it. Shadows leaped up around the temple. Spiders, some as large as Gromph's fist, crawled over the altar.

In the candlelight, Gromph could see the silhouette of the golem. It was huge.

Geremis maintained a discreet distance from Larikal; males were forbidden to enter the apse of a temple of Lolth. He took a seat in the front bench and bowed his head.

Without preamble, Larikal lowered herself to her knees, likewise bowed her head, and prayed. Gromph could not hear the words but he could imagine her murmuring voice carrying through the temple.

The candlelight danced across the smooth finish of the spider golem. The huge creature loomed over the altar, over Larikal. She was less than five paces from the subject of her prayers and did not realize it. Gromph almost smiled through his exhaustion. The Spider Queen certainly had a sense of humor.

Gromph turned back to the wards. He had to—

An idea struck him, and finally he did smile.

He did not have to unravel the wards after all.

Quenthel held her holy symbol in her shield hand and hurried through the words to a spell. When she finished, she grew to nearly twice her size, as did her whip, armor, and shield. A violet glow suffused her and leaked from her eyes—the divine favor of Lolth made manifest.

Danifae completed her own spell, and a gray shield of magical force surrounded her entire body—her faith in physical form.

The priestesses eyed one another across the broken ground while Lolth's dead streamed between them and into the Pass.

Those are not defensive spells, Pharaun thought as he prepared again to send his magical fist against Jeggred.

Quenthel's whip hissed. Danifae shifted on her feet, her hands near the haft of her morningstar.

"An interesting choice of spell, Mistress Quenthel," Danifae said.

Quenthel sneered.

Pharaun thought open combat inevitable at that point, but no. Both priestesses held their ground and began again to cast.

Though he knew arcane magic far better than that granted by the gods, Pharaun had seen enough spells cast by clerics such that he would be able to identify most of the invocations that were being performed.

Danifae finished her spell first. The magic had no visible manifestation, but Pharaun determined from her gestures and words that the spell had augmented her physical strength.

Pharaun appreciated Danifae's subtlety. Quenthel's first spell had made her large and strong but obviously so. Danifae had made herself stronger too but without it being apparent.

Quenthel finished her own prayer, and a faint, green glow formed around her skin.

Resistance to spells, Pharaun recognized.

With that, the two priestesses eyed each other anew.

"The pass?" Danifae asked but took a threatening step toward Quenthel. "Or . . . something else?"

Quenthel smiled, took a step toward Danifae, and said, "Something else."

Pharaun too smiled. If Quenthel and Danifae came to blows, he would take the opportunity to kill Jeggred, Baenre or no.

Halisstra's heart caught in her throat. Ahead, at the base of the mountains, Danifae and Quenthel Baenre stood facing each other. A shimmering shield of gray force surrounded Danifae, while Quenthel Baenre stood twice her normal size.

They were doing battle, or about to.

The draegloth Jeggred, watched from one side, and the wizard Pharaun, with some kind of conjured fist before him, watched from another. The souls of Lolth's dead streamed around and between the combatants, flowing into the jagged opening at the base of one of the tall mountains—the Pass of the Soulreaver.

Halisstra had to move quickly. She flew down behind a rock outcropping thirty paces from the scene. Feliane and Uluyara followed. With an exercise of will, Halisstra ended the spell that had transformed them to vapor. She crouched behind the rocks and spoke with urgency.

"You see?" she said to Uluyara. "Danifae is fighting Quenthel Baenre. The Baenre priestess must have learned of her allegiance to Eilistraee."

She turned to go, but Uluyara grabbed her by the shoulder and turned her around.

"Halisstra, they do not appear yet to be fighting. We should prepare defensive spells. The Baenre priestess is not a trifling opponent."

"There is no time," Halisstra said, pushing Uluyara's hand away. If Danifae had finally heeded Eilistraee's call, Halisstra did not want to leave her to face Quenthel alone. "We will use our spells in combat. It will be enough."

She looked her sisters in their eyes, demanding with her gaze that they obey her.

"The draegloth and wizard?" Feliane said. "What of them?"

Halisstra drew the Crescent Blade.

"Quenthel Baenre is our enemy," she said. "Assume the draegloth and wizard are too, unless they give you reason to believe otherwise."

"And what of Danifae?" Feliane asked.

"Leave her to me," Halisstra said.

With that, she turned and charged toward the combat. Uluyara's horn rang out behind her.

THIRTEEN

From somewhere behind Pharaun, the bray of a battle horn sounded.

For a moment, the tension between Quenthel and Danifae subsided. Both turned in the direction of the clarion.

At first Pharaun thought it a trick of his eyes, but Quenthel's words dispelled his misconception.

"Melarn," Quenthel said, her voice low. The whip serpents hissed and writhed in agitation.

Pharaun spared a glance behind him to see Danifae open her mouth as though to speak, but she said nothing. Shock showed in her expression, but she recovered quickly.

"It appears Lolth has provided a different victim for the sacrifice," she said.

Pharaun turned back to see Halisstra Melarn, accompanied by another drow female and a female surface elf, charging toward them across the rocky ground. Each wore armor and bore swords. The symbol on Halisstra's shield drew Pharaun's eye—an upright silver sword, around which swirled a silver ribbon.

He knew it to be the symbol of Eilistraee. He needed to see nothing else. Somehow, Halisstra had tracked them through the Demonweb Pits. And she had brought two allies with her, presumably also priestesses of the same cursed goddess.

"She bears the symbol of Eilistraee, Mistress," Pharaun said, even as he called upon the power of his ring and took to the air.

"I am not blind, male," Quenthel barked.

"She thinks me her ally," Danifae said to Quenthel and backed off several paces. "I will cause her to doubt."

With that, Danifae shouted, "Mistress Melarn! To me! We will stop Quenthel Baenre together. In the Lady's name, to me!"

Quenthel frowned. The heads of her serpent whip alternated between looking at Danifae and looking at Halisstra.

In response to Danifae's words, Halisstra smiled and whirled a glowing blade above her head. The other drow priestess sounded her horn again.

Jeggred answered with a roar.

Pharaun was as confused as the serpents. He did not know for certain whether Danifae was manipulating Halisstra or Quenthel or both. Like the pragmatist he was, he decided to err on the side of prudence and treat them all as his enemies.

With his mind made up, he chose his course quickly. Halisstra and Danifae might have been dangerous, but Jeggred was perhaps the most deadly opponent on the field.

Halisstra and the two other priestesses headed toward Quenthel. Jeggred charged in Quenthel's direction too, but whether to attack his aunt or the priestesses, Pharaun could not be sure.

With a mental command, Pharaun flew the fist of force at Jeggred. The draegloth saw it coming and tried to dodge aside, but the fist caught him full force in the head and chest. The impact knocked the huge draegloth into a headlong tumble, and he lay on the earth unmoving, apparently stunned.

Pharaun grinned. Sometimes his mastery of spellcraft surprised even him.

Danifae shot a glare up at Pharaun and backed farther away from Quenthel.

"Here, Halisstra!" Danifae said brandishing her morningstar.

As the three Eilistraeens charged, they called aloud to their goddess. Their prayers were as much song as chant.

Halisstra finished her prayer, and a black ray shot from her fingertips at Quenthel. The Baenre priestess sidestepped it, and it slammed into the rocks.

The other drow priestess completed her prayer, and a rosy aura surrounded her. The elf priestess targeted Pharaun with her spell. She pointed her finger, and a sphere of light blazed into being around him.

He gasped and threw his forearm over his face. The sudden illumination sent needles of pain into his eyes. Without opening them, he gritted out the words to a counterspell, and the welcome dimness of day in the Demonweb Pits returned.

He opened his eyes and saw only spots for a moment. Tears poured from his eyes, but he blinked them away. When he could again see, he located his magical fist—hovering over the stunned Jeggred—and sent it speeding for the elf priestess.

All three priestesses spread out as they ran. The fist moved to intercept the elf.

The elf aborted her charge and braced her tiny shield for the fist's impact.

But Pharaun did not cause it to strike her.

At his mental goading, the fist stopped before her, opened its fingers, and made to grab her. She was fast, and her blade slashed into the conjuration, but the hand was inexorable.

Its huge fingers wrapped her up. Only her head was visible. Before she could scream for aid, Pharaun caused the hand to squeeze.

The elf's mouth opened in a scream but she had no breath with which to utter it. Instead, she suffered in silence.

Pharaun turned to see Halisstra veer toward Quenthel.

"Aid us, Danifae," Halisstra shouted.

Danifae said, "Of course, Mistress," but made no move to help.

The other drow priestess, wielding a long bladed sword in two hands, came at Quenthel from the side opposite that of Halisstra, but she stopped when she glanced back and saw her comrade trapped in Pharaun's magical fist.

"Feliane!" she shouted.

The drow priestess located Pharaun in the air and sang a spell.

Pharaun flew toward her, drawing his wand of lightning and voicing his own spell.

She finished first.

A sword of magical force formed in the air to Pharaun's right, flying along beside him. It attacked the moment it appeared, striking at the mage's head.

He spun away from it, but it doggedly pursued, stabbing and slashing. He rolled in the air, spun, twirled, but the damned thing kept pace with him. Twice the blade managed to penetrate his magical protections and opened the skin of his shoulder, his forearm. He lost the thread of his own spell and cursed aloud.

He spun a series of circles, opened a bit of space between him and the sword, and quickly uttered the words to a counterspell, pitting his magic against the priestess's.

His prevailed. The sword of force winked out. He touched his shoulder and found the wound to be more bloody than deep.

Pharaun looked down and saw the drow priestess advancing on Quenthel from one side, while Halisstra advanced from the other. The Baenre priestess stood her ground, serpents hissing, whip cracking.

Pharaun pulled a piece of quartz from his *piwafwi*, formed a dome with his hand, and rattled through the words to a spell that would even the odds.

When he completed the conjuration, a hemisphere of armspan thick, semi-opaque ice materialized out of nothing, taking shape over and around Halisstra, imprisoning her.

He could see the Melarn traitor moving frantically within it, hammering at it with her weapons. It would not hold her long, Pharaun knew, but it would buy Quenthel time.

Seeing the opportunity, Quenthel took it. She charged the other drow priestess and swung her whip in a wide arc.

The priestess of Eilistraee, still surrounded in a rosy hue, did not retreat or hesitate. Instead, she danced and spun between the serpents of Quenthel's whip, at the same time unleashing a backhand slash that sliced open Quenthel's armor across the chest. Quenthel, still enlarged from her spell, countered with a shield bash, but the Eilistraeen sidestepped it, and stabbed her blade at Quenthel's stomach.

The Baenre priestess leaped back to avoid the blow, but the Eilistraeen followed hard after, spinning, whirling, her blade a blur.

"Danifae Yauntyrr!" the Eilistraeen called. "Answer the Lady and aid me."

But Danifae did not answer, Pharaun saw. She stood apart, seemingly content to watch the conflict, perhaps to await a weakened winner whom she could then finish.

Breathing hard and bleeding, Quenthel swung her whip in a flurry of vicious attacks. A glancing blow knocked the Eilistraeen off balance, and Quenthel managed to put her shield into the Eilistraeean's chest.

Quenthel's strength and size sent the Eilistraeen careening, but she somehow managed to turn the stagger into a graceful recovery. She found her feet and raced at the Baenre priestess, her blade stabbing and slashing.

Spinning her whip high, Quenthel lashed at the Eilistraeen. The priestess dodged right, left, ducked, opened a gash in Quenthel's arm, and—

One of the serpents sank its fangs into the Eilistraeean's arm. She grunted with pain, and the Mistress of Arach-Tinilith took the opportunity to follow up with another shield bash. The Eilistraeen priestess rolled with the impact, but the strength of the blow drove her back five paces. The wound in her arm was already beginning to blacken.

"It's over," Quenthel said.

The high priestess advanced, her whip serpents hissing and whirling.

The Eilistraeen danced backward, still spinning. She reached for her holy symbol and sang a spell.

A beam of silver light flew from her outstretched palm, penetrated Quenthel's protective spell, and struck Quenthel in the chest. Groaning, the Baenre priestess staggered back.

"Hardly," answered the Eilistraeen, and she charged Quenthel.

Before the priestess reached her, Quenthel held her whip aloft and demanded, "Speed."

The whip serpents whirled around and echoed, "Speed."

The adamantine handle of the whip flashed violet, and the high priestess's movements became faster. Her whip was a blur in the air.

The Eilistraeen priestess darted in, blade low. Quenthel deftly slipped aside, drove the priestess's blade into the ground with her whip handle, spun, and lashed the priestess across her back with all five serpent heads.

Grunting, staggering, the Eilistraeen still managed to keep her feet. She whirled aside from a follow-up lash that would have torn her head from her shoulders.

The priestess of Eilistraee began to cast again, but Quenthel was too fast. The whip cracked once more, found flesh through the Eilistraeean's armor, and her scream of pain ruined her spell.

Pharaun could see that the combat was over. The Eilistraeen was no match for Quenthel Baenre.

Halisstra must have seen it too, through the ice wall. Her muffled shout carried through the barrier: "Uluyara! Danifae, help her!"

But Danifae did nothing, declared her allegiance to no one.

Desperate, the priestess of the Dark Maiden rushed Quenthel, spinning, slashing, and stabbing. Quenthel parried the blows and answered with a shield smash that sent the Eilistraeen reeling.

Moving with her whip-enhanced speed, Quenthel withdrew from an inner pocket of her *piwafwi* a silvery rod of metal as long as her forearm. She pointed it at the prone Eilistraeen, and it discharged a mass of some kind of sticky, semiliquid substance. The stuff soaked the priestess and quickly hardened. The Eilistraeen struggled against it for a moment but could not move.

Quenthel grinned and walked over to the prone, immobilized priestess.

Pharaun, pleased that things had gone so easily, took a moment to survey the field. Jeggred remained stunned, though one of his hands was spasming. The elf priestess remained immobilized and squeezed in Pharaun's magical hand. Halisstra was temporarily trapped in a hemisphere of ice, though Pharaun could hear her weapon working at breaking through—and she would soon succeed.

Quenthel belted her whip and took from her robes a small, adamantine knife with a stylized spider hilt.

A sacrificial knife, Pharaun knew.

She maneuvered behind the prone priestess so that Halisstra Melarn would have a clear view.

"I am not afraid," the immobilized Eilistraeen said, though Pharaun could not tell whether she meant the words for Halisstra or Quenthel.

"Of course you are," Quenthel said as she raised the blade high.

Halisstra's blade poked through the ice wall. "No!" she shouted.

Pharaun incanted a quick spell and sent five darts of magical energy from his fingertips and through the small hole Halisstra had opened in the ice. They slammed into the Melarn priestess, and she exclaimed with pain.

Meanwhile, Quenthel offered a quick prayer to Lolth and slit the priestess's throat open. The Eilistraeean's blood poured onto the rocky ground of the Demonweb Pits, and she died gurgling.

"No!" shouted Halisstra.

Quenthel rose, smiled at Halisstra, then at Danifae, and called up to Pharaun,

"Come, Master Mizzrym. The Pass of the Soulreaver awaits. My sacrifice to the Spider Queen is complete."

Pharaun caught Danifae absently signing, *And mine soon will be.*

The mage spared a last look back at the elf priestess, still clutched helplessly in the magical hand. His spell would expire soon. Perhaps she would be dead by then, perhaps not. Pharaun did not care. The Eilistraeeans were no match for them.

He flew down to Quenthel's side. He did not so much as a glance at the sacrificed Eilistraeen. Together, the two of them strode toward the pass.

Behind him, Halisstra finally chopped a large enough hole through the globe of ice that the rest of the barrier collapsed around her.

Too, Jeggred uttered a soft growl. Apparently, he was returning to sensibility, at least inasmuch as he was ever sensible.

"Turn and face me, Baenre bitch," Halisstra challenged from behind.

Spellcasting sounded from behind—it was Halisstra. Pharaun listened to the words and nodded—a strike of flame.

Almost absentmindedly, he voiced the words to a counterspell and foiled her casting.

He could imagine Halisstra's consternation.

"Stop, Baenre!" Halisstra roared her voice desperate, angry. "Face us and let's see which goddess is the stronger."

Quenthel ignored her. She and Pharaun reached the very threshold of the Pass of the Soulreaver. The hole in the rock was as black and impenetrable up close as it had been from afar. Souls entered it and vanished one by one.

Halisstra sped after them, her boots crunching against the rock.

From behind, Quenthel seemed almost in a trance. To Pharaun she said, "The Reaver exists at the sufferance of Lolth. It is bound within and does her bidding."

Pharaun eyed the tunnel entrance as the souls continued to stream into it.

"What is her bidding?" he asked.

Quenthel did not look at him when she replied, "As it always is, male. To test those she wishes to test. Some souls pass through unchallenged. Some do not."

She turned to look him in the face, though her eyes remained unfocused.

"I will be tested," she continued, then nodded back at Danifae. "And if she dares enter, so too will she. As for you and my nephew, the challenge of the pass is not for you. Though I expect the Reaver will take his tithe nevertheless."

"Mistress, why don't we simply kill her?" Pharaun asked, meaning Danifae. "And your nephew?"

Quenthel's eyes were distant, her mind already on the challenge of the pass.

"They no longer matter," she said.

Before Pharaun could ask anything more, Quenthel stepped into the black hole. The darkness swallowed her utterly. Souls continued to stream around him and enter the pass. They too vanished.

Halisstra was closing, ten strides away, eight.

"Face us, coward!" Halisstra challenged.

Pharaun stood there for a moment, staring into the darkness, undecided. Finally he took a breath and stepped into the Pass of the Soulreaver. He felt a slight resistance as he broached it, as diaphanous as a spiderweb.

Halisstra watched as first Quenthel then Pharaun stepped into the tunnel and vanished. She ground her teeth in anger, clutching the Crescent Blade in a white-knuckled hand.

She halted her charge and stared at the hole in the mountain. She could see nothing beyond the darkness.

Breathing heavily, she exhaled rage and frustration with each breath.

Souls streamed around her, Lolth's dead.

Quenthel and Pharaun had escaped. Uluyara was dead, sacrificed. Feliane was—

Feliane!

She whirled around and saw to her relief that the magical hand had disappeared. Feliane walked a weaving line toward her, cradling her ribs.

Danifae had walked over to Uluyara, and crouched over her, concern in her eyes. She met Halisstra's gaze.

"I could not save her, Mistress," she said.

Halisstra could only nod.

"I tried to assist you, Mistress," Danifae said and walked to Halisstra's side. "But the wizard twice countered my spells. Next time, I will better serve you."

Halisstra was too tired to speak.

A scrabbling from her right drew her eye. The draegloth was climbing to his feet. His red eyes burned with anger, and Feliane watched him warily.

The draegloth eyed Danifae then the slight elf, and growled.

Halisstra looked the fell creature in the face and said, "Your mistress has abandoned you for the wizard. She has left you to me. And I'll have your heart for killing Ryld Argith."

The draegloth smiled a mouthful of daggers, looked at Halisstra, and said, "My mistress has not abandoned me, heretic."

Before Halisstra could answer, Danifae slammed the head of her morningstar into Halisstra's back. Ribs cracked, and flesh punctured. Her breath went out in a whoosh. Blood poured down her back. She stumbled forward and fell.

Halisstra understood it all then.

Danifae had manipulated her, feigned a calling by Eilistraee. Danifae had simply wanted Halisstra to kill Quenthel for her. And Danifae had arranged for the draegloth to kill Ryld.

Halisstra had been blind, seeing what she had wanted to see.

Now she would suffer the consequences.

"Halisstra!" exclaimed Feliane and ran toward her.

Standing over Halisstra, Danifae said, "Jeggred, kill that tiny elf bitch."

The draegloth roared and charged at Feliane, cutting her off before she reached Halisstra.

Wracked with pain, weighed down by the burden of her own stupidity, Halisstra nevertheless managed to get to her hands and knees. In her mind, a series of words kept repeating, words aimed at Eilistraee:

You could have warned me. You could have warned me.

Halisstra looked up as the draegloth tore into Feliane, his claws slashing and stabbing. Feliane answered with her own blade but Halisstra saw the fear in the small elf's eyes.

"Don't," she tried to say to Danifae, but the word barely made a sound. She had no breath in her lungs.

Danifae again slammed her morningstar into Halisstra's back. Her armor absorbed much of the blow, but pain still knifed through her, and she fell back to the ground.

Her former battle-captive grabbed Halisstra by her hair and jerked her head back. Halisstra tried to bring the Crescent Blade to bear, but Danifae tore it from her grasp and cast it aside.

"You have something to say, Mistress Melarn?" Danifae hissed into her ear. "No? Then watch," she commanded.

Halisstra closed her eyes and shook her head.

"Watch!" Danifae ordered and shook her head by the hair.

Halisstra opened her eyes as the draegloth tore a claw across Feliane's face. The elf staggered back but spun away from the draegloth's follow up strike. The elf's blade opened a gash on the half-demon's stomach, but it did little damage.

Roaring so loud it hurt Halisstra's ears, the draegloth rushed Feliane. She answered valiantly, but she was too small, too slow, too weak. The draegloth tore a gash in her chest, nearly jerked an arm from its socket, and finally knocked her to the ground.

Feliane lay there, breathing heavily but stunned, unmoving.

Halisstra suddenly remembered Feliane's words to her atop the tor: *I'm afraid.*

The draegloth loomed over her. Without preamble, he pinned her arms to the ground and began to feed. Her screams of pain were lost in the half-demon's hungry snorts.

Halisstra bowed her head. Tears leaked from her eyes, angry tears, tears of regret. She could not find her breath.

Danifae saw them and mocked her. "Tears, Halisstra? For the weakling little elf?"

She slammed her fist into Halisstra's temple. Sparks exploded in her head. Unconsciousness threatened but did not come.

Danifae kicked Halisstra over onto her back. She lay there on the ground of Lolth's Demonweb Pits, bleeding, gasping, her former battle-captive standing over her.

Danifae spat on Halisstra's breastplate, fouling Eilistraee's holy symbol. Halisstra did not care. Eilistraee had fouled her own symbol by failing to warn Halisstra. Her priestesses had been no match for the servants of Lolth.

Eilistraee was weak. And Halisstra was foolish to have followed a weak goddess. She looked up at the blurry image of Danifae above her.

"Why?" she mouthed.

Danifae's mouth curled with contempt. "Why?" She reached under her cloak and withdrew a chunk of amber in which was encased a spider—her holy symbol of Lolth. She held it before Halisstra's face.

"This is why, Melarn. You were always weak. It's fitting that you served a weak goddess in the end. I, however, do not."

Halisstra stared hate at Danifae and managed, "You are still a Houseless battle-captive"

Danifae sneered, stepped back, and raised her morningstar for a killing blow. When it came, Halisstra summoned all of her strength and rolled aside.

The head of the weapon smashed into the rocks.

Halisstra found her knees and scrabbled after the Crescent Blade. She couldn't see clearly, and the pain in her ribs sent stabs through her.

The morningstar slammed into Halisstra's ribs and sent her sprawling to the rock. The pain was nearly unbearable.

Danifae loomed over her again, holding her morningstar high.

Sickening sounds came from behind Halisstra—the draegloth feeding on Feliane, lapping her blood, chewing her flesh.

"Why do you toy so with your food, Jeggred?" Danifae said, smiling. "The Pass of the Soulreaver and the vintage blood of Quenthel Baenre await."

At that moment, Halisstra wanted death, wanted it more than anything. She closed her eyes and waited for it.

Eilistraee had failed her.

Halisstra had killed them all.

"Good-bye, Halisstra," Danifae said, and smashed her morningstar down on her former mistress's face.

Halisstra felt a flash of pain then nothing.

Danifae stared down at the bloody body of her former mistress. She had made her sacrifice, and so she could enter the pass.

"Praise Lolth," she said, and gave Halisstra a final kick. She looked to Jeggred, who was feeding on the elf priestess's flesh. The elf's hand closed, opened. Soft moans escaped her. Danifae smiled at the pain she must have been enduring.

"Come, Jeggred," she said. "It is time to follow after your aunt."

The draegloth looked up from his feast. Blood soaked his muzzle. Shreds of flesh hung from his teeth.

"Yes, Mistress," he said.

He rose and loped to her side, obviously reluctant to leave off his still living meal.

"How long before you kill her?" Jeggred asked. "Her and the mage?"

"In due time," Danifae answered.

Together, they walked into the Pass of the Soulreaver.

Chapter

FOURTEEN

Gromph stood on the portico outside the temple's doors and used a divination to analyze Geremis's personal protections. One after another, Gromph moved gently through the mage's protective spells: elemental wards, a spell that made the Dyrr wizard's flesh as hard as stone, a death ward, and . . . a feedback ward. Gromph raised his eyebrows at that last. The archmage rarely saw feedback wards; the lichdrow must have taught it to Geremis himself.

The feedback ward would turn back on Gromph the effect of any directly offensive spell he cast on the Dyrr wizard. The archmage would have to get rid of it.

Unfortunately, casting a spell on Geremis would cause Gromph to become visible—a foible of the invisibility spell—so he moved off to the side of the doors, amidst shadows that would camouflage him when the magic was terminated. From there, he quietly whispered the words to a dispelling dweomer, targeting only the feedback ward.

When the magic took effect, Gromph felt a tingle over his skin as he became visible. Safely hidden in darkness, a shadow within shadow, Gromph guided his magic against Geremis's feedback ward.

As delicately as a cutpurse lifting a coin pouch, the archmage assaulted Geremis's ward. Gromph's counterspell met the magic of the Dyrr wizard and oozed over it.

In the span of only two breaths, Gromph's magic prevailed. Geremis's ward winked out.

I have you, the archmage thought.

While drow were inherently spell resistant, almost no dark elf in Menzoberranzan could resist the power of Gromph's spells without augmentation to their natural resistance. He had detected no such augmentation on Geremis. The Dyrr mage was vulnerable.

Geremis raised his bowed head and spared another glance behind him. Though he looked over and past Gromph, suspicion was writ clear on his face. He reached into his pocket to search for something, no doubt a spell component.

Gromph prepared to cast his own spell but cursed when he realized that he would need a pinch of dust to cast it. He didn't make it a habit to carry mere dust as a component because it was always readily available—at least when he could touch the corporeal world.

With nothing else for it, Gromph called upon the power of the shapechanging spell and transformed himself into the form of a drow male, though not his own form. His flesh hardened, his body grew heavy, and soon he felt his feet on the floor. Sound and smell returned to him. The stink of stale incense wafted through the temple doors. Larikal voiced her prayers to Lolth in a low tone.

Gromph crouched low in the shadows outside the temple's doors, and Prath's *piwafwi* hid him almost as well as his shadow form.

Moving slowly, he removed a small lodestone from his robe, gathered a pinch of rock dust from the temple's portico, and quietly recited the words to a powerful spell. He infused a bit of additional Weave energy into the casting, to make it more difficult for Geremis to resist.

The Dyrr wizard pulled a clear lens from his pocket and raised it to his eye. He looked at the temple doors, right at Gromph, and the lens fell from his hand.

"M-mistress!" he sputtered, stumbling to his feet and beginning to cast. "We are not alo—"

Gromph finished his spell. A green beam shot from his finger and hit Geremis in the chest. The mage's warning died on his lips as the spell engulfed him in a green outline and reduced him to dust. Larikal stood and whirled just in time to see Geremis obliterated. She already had her mace in hand.

To her credit, she did not cry out for aid. Instead, she put her off-hand to the platinum spider holy symbol at her neck and started to cast. The symbol glowed briefly at her touch, as did her eyes. As she chanted her spell, she scanned the doorway with her obviously enhanced vision and fixed her gaze on Gromph.

She saw him. She could not recognize him as the Archmage of Menzoberranzan, of course, but she knew him to be an enemy. She probably thought him a Xorlarrin mage.

With no time to sift through his pockets for the gem he ordinarily would have used as a component, Gromph snatched the ocular from his inner pocket—it was ready to hand—and uttered the words to a spell.

Larikal charged down the aisle, mace at the ready, while continuing to cast a spell that Gromph recognized. It would charge her hand with death-dealing energy. She would have but to touch him with it and he would likely die.

He held his ground and hurried through his own spell.

Larikal finished first. A globe of sizzling black energy formed around her off hand, and she closed on him.

He backstepped away from the doors and finished his own spell just as she lunged through the threshold and reached forward to touch him.

The magic of Gromph's spell transferred his soul into the gem at the end of the ocular's chain just as Larikal closed her hand over his wrist.

With his essence in the gem that had become a magic jar not unlike the lichdrow's phylactery, the death spell could not affect him. His soulless body would appear dead, though, so Larikal would surely believe she'd slain him.

Her guard would be down.

Within the gem, Gromph possessed only one sense—a visceral ability to detect nearby life-forces. He sensed Larikal near him, no doubt bending over his apparently dead body.

The magic of the spell allowed him to attempt, through sheer force of will, to displace a soul in a nearby living body and force it to take his place in the gem. He had taken a risk in casting it, but he needed to get through the wards quickly.

Extending his consciousness, the archmage reached out for Larikal and sought her soul.

He caught her by surprise. He sensed her alarm. She resisted his attempt, but he pressed, and pressed, fought through the resistance, and at last . . .

Sensation returned to him. He was looking down at the body of a drow male—his transformed body—and in his hand he clutched the ocular, which sparkled softly, alight with Larikal's soul.

"Thank you, priestess," he said to the gem and was surprised to hear the feminine lilt in his voice.

The spell allowed only the caster to displace other souls. Larikal could do nothing but stew inside the gem. She would be trapped until Gromph allowed her to escape.

While occupying yet another new form—especially a female one—was disconcerting, Gromph retained all of his mental faculties, including his spellcasting ability. And he had full use of Larikal's stronger physique. That pleased him. It would assist him when he faced the golem.

He spared a glance around and saw no one. The nearby Dyrr structures appeared empty. No doubt most of the House was occupied with the defense of the walls.

His smile of satisfaction vanished when the spell that had allowed him to change shape expired. His soulless body reverted back to its normal form. He was looking at his own face through Larikal Dyrr's eyes, staring at the vacant, stolen eyes of a Dyrr son.

Gromph cursed. Prath too would have reverted back to his normal form, or soon would.

Yasraena would be searching for him, if she wasn't already. He had little time.

Moving quickly, he took the duergar axe from his belt and removed his robe, loaded with his spell components, and his ring of regeneration. He donned the robe, the ring, belted the axe, and cast two spells on his soulless body. The first spell shrank his body to the size of his hand. The second turned it invisible to normal sight, though he could still see it through his magically enhanced vision. Gromph dared not carry his body, which still held the tiny ocular gem, through the warded doorway for fear of triggering the words with his Baenre flesh. Instead, he hid it off to the side of the door, in a crack in the stone of the portico. He would have to hope that it was overlooked.

He turned and—

The amulet on Larikal's body—on his body—caught his attention. He held it in his hand—it was electrum, with amethysts inset in a spiral. He knew it for what it was—a telepathic amulet.

He took a moment to attune his consciousness to it. He knew he had succeeded when a voice he recognized sounded in his brain: *Larikal! Larikal!*

Gromph smiled. Larikal had not called out for aid because she had done so telepathically.

Larikal, answer!

Gromph knew he should have said nothing but he could not resist.

Your daughter currently is indisposed, Yasraena, he projected.

He felt consternation through the amulet.

Gromph Baenre? Yasraena asked.

You do not sound pleased to learn of my visit, he replied.

The matron mother's mental voice leaked something akin to panic. *Listen to me, Archmage. I know why you have come. But I have entered into a bargain with Triel. I am to destroy the phylactery myself.*

Gromph thought the words a poor lie. But even if they were true, the archmage was unbound by any such bargain. Triel had never mentioned it to him.

But you do not know its location, Matron Mother. And even if you did, I would be concerned that the impulse to see the lichdrow reincorporated would be too strong for even one of your iron will. I will be pleased to destroy it in your name.

With that, Gromph terminated the connection. He knew Yasraena would be coming, so he took a deep breath and stepped across the heavily warded temple threshold. The wards did not trigger. Gromph would never know whether it was something Larikal wore or her very blood, but he did not care. He was in.

From the dome above, Lolth stared down. The center aisle extended toward the apse, toward the black altar, behind which loomed the forbidding body of the spider.

The golem was waiting.

Yasraena rushed through the halls for the scrying chamber, heedless of the indignity of her pace. She dared not communicate through the telepathic amulet for fear that Gromph Baenre would eavesdrop.

In her mind, Esvena's voice sounded, *Matron Mother! We are deceived. The image in the basin is not what it appeared to be. Gromph Baenre—*

Is in our house, Yasraena finished for her. She sent her next projection to all of her daughters and sisters, *Cease using the amulets immediately. The archmage is in the complex and wears Larikal's amulet. He can hear me even now.*

The connection fell silent, and for the first time since the siege began, real fear took hold in Yasraena. If Gromph got to the phylactery before her, all was lost.

She had to get to him first.

When she reached the scrying chamber, no one dared look at her. The two male wizards stood near the scrying basin, heads bowed. Esvena could not make eye contact.

To Esvena, Yasraena said, "Where is Larikal?"

Esvena fumbled for an answer.

"Your sister!" Yasraena said. "Where was she last searching?"

One of the male wizards in the chamber offered, "Geremis last reported that they were to search the temple, Matron Mother."

The temple. Yasraena could hardly believe her ears. Had the

lichdrow secreted his phylactery within the *temple?* She cursed him for the arrogant, scheming fool he was.

Yasraena clenched her fists, then her jaw. Her body shook. Anger and fear threatened to overwhelm her.

Through gritted teeth, she said to Esvena, "Go to the walls and retrieve the vrocks and any House mages you can find. Then meet us at the temple. Go, now."

Esvena streaked from the chamber.

Yasraena looked to the two males still with her and said, "You two, accompany me to the temple. The Archmage of Menzoberranzan awaits us.

When the shapechange spell expired on Prath, Nauzhror swore aloud. Prath studied his hands, saw them grow larger, and looked wide-eyed across the desk at Nauzhror.

At that moment, the Dyrr wizards had learned of Gromph's deception.

For a heartbeat—but only a single heartbeat—Nauzhror wrestled with what action he should take. Nauzhror coveted the archmage's position, but his fear of failing Gromph Baenre outweighed his ambition. If Gromph succeeded and learned that Nauzhror did nothing more after the shapechange spell expired, Nauzhror knew he would suffer. If Gromph failed and died, he knew too that Triel Baenre would investigate herself, and again, Nauzhror would suffer.

In the end, the Master of Sorcere knew that he could do nothing but play his part to the best of his abilities and hope that Gromph succeeded.

To Prath, still sitting in the archmage's chair, he said, "Get up, boy."

Prath leaped from the chair as though it was on fire. Nauzhror circled the desk and slid into the chair. With an expertise born of decades of training, he attuned Gromph's chrysoberyl scrying crystal and caused it to show him the Xorlarrin forces gathered outside of House Agrach Dyrr. The soldiers and wizards were massed but standing idle.

Nauzhror studied the locale for a time, fixed the image in his mind, and let the scrying crystal go inert.

"What should we do now, Master Nauzhror?" asked Prath. The apprentice's voice betrayed his nervousness.

Nauzhror replied, "Now, we assist the archmage's efforts by seeing to it that Yasraena will be faced at the same time with enemies within and without."

Without further explanation, he spoke a word of power and teleported into the midst of the Xorlarrin army.

FIFTEEN

Pharaun's mind fogged the moment he stepped onto the Pass of the Soulreaver. His equilibrium failed him. He felt as though he were moving back and forth, up and down, all at once.

Staggering, he held out a hand until it touched the cool wall of the narrow pass. He stood still, leaning against the stone and trying to recover himself.

The mage knew he wasn't moving but still felt a sensation of motion and perceived the rapid passage of time. He stood at the center of the world as it streaked around and past him.

Pharaun closed his eyes, gritted his teeth, and clutched at the wall with a death grip.

Time and motion stopped so suddenly he almost fell forward.

He opened his eyes and saw no souls, no Quenthel, nothing but stone walls to either side of him rising toward infinity. Darkness shrouded the pass, but ordinary darkness through which Pharaun could see. A smooth, narrow path stretched before him, disappearing into the far distance. He turned around and saw the same path extending backward to the limits of his vision.

But he had taken only one step. Hadn't he?

Pharaun had teleported, gated, dimension doored, and shadowwalked enough to understand that the Pass of the Soulreaver was not a physical place with spatial dimensions so much as it was a metaphor, a symbol for whatever bridged the time and distance between the ruined land he had just left behind and Lolth's personal realm that lay ahead.

For a disconcerting instant, though, he wondered if the entirety of Lolth's plane was no more than metaphor, if the minds of he and his companions had given form to something otherwise formless.

The thought disquieted him, and he pushed it from his brain.

"Quenthel," he called and did not like the quaver he heard in his voice. The word echoed off the stone, and when it came back to him, the voice was not his own.

A scream of terror: "Quenthel!"

Hysterical laughter: "Quenthel."

A despairing mumble: "Quenthel."

A wail of pain: "Quenthel!"

Pharaun's skin crawled. Sweat beaded his forehead. His skin was clammy. He kept his mouth shut and walked down the path—slowly.

He saw nothing and heard nothing but the twisted echo of his own voice, but . . .

He was not alone.

And it was not Quenthel he sensed.

From ahead—or was it behind?—whispering began, hissings, the remnant of ancient screams. The inarticulate mutterings soaked into his soul. He felt itchy, soiled. His breath came fast.

"Who is there?" he called and cringed when the words rebounded to him, screaming in terror.

He reached into his robe and withdrew a wand for each hand: the iron shaft that discharged lightning in his right, the zurkhwood wand that fired bolts of magical energy in his left.

He walked on. The walls whispered and muttered in his ears.

"Reaver," they said.

He felt eyes on him from behind, boring into his being. He whirled around, both wands brandished, certain something was there.

Nothing.

The whispers turned to hissing laughter.

Breathing heavily, he put his back to the wall and tried to gather himself. Ghostly hands as cold as a grave reached through the wall and covered his mouth. Panic sent his heart hammering. He pulled himself free, fell to the ground, turned and fired three magic missiles into the wall.

There was nothing there.

He scrabbled to his feet.

What was happening? He was not himself. A spell was affecting him. Surely he—

A sudden shriek rang off the walls, a hopeless wail filled with despair and rage. Pharaun tensed, his knuckles white on his wands.

Ahead of him, a vast, spectral form flew out of the wall on one side of the pass and into the wall on the other, like a fish swimming through the waters of the Darklake. The form moved fast, but he caught a good glimpse of it before it vanished into the stone—a vast, bloated, serpentine body of translucent gray, within which squirmed and screamed hundreds or thousands of glowing drow souls.

The Soulreaver.

Its black eyes were bottomless holes; its mouth a cavern. It dwarfed the nalfeshnee; it dwarfed ten nalfeshnees.

It was a living prison for failed souls.

Pharaun imagined his own soul trapped within it, and a pit formed in his stomach. He tried to ignore the shaking in his hands as he put one of the wands back in his robe and withdrew a pinch of powdered irtios, a clear gem. He cast the sparkling powder into the air while speaking aloud the words to a powerful evocation.

He maintained his concentration even when the arcane words echoed back at him as wails.

When he finished, the irtios powder swirled around him, formed a sphere about fifteen paces in diameter, and transformed into an invisible, impenetrable sphere of force that could keep out even incorporeal creatures.

Pharaun prayed to Lolth that it would keep out the Soulreaver. Even it if did, however, Pharaun knew the solution was only a temporary one. The spell would not last overlong, and he could not move the sphere. Still, he needed some time to gather himself. He was agitated, nervous.

The shriek of the Soulreaver repeated but sounded muffled, as though from deep in the ground.

Secure within his sphere, Pharaun tried to settle his racing heart and develop a plan.

The soles of his feet began to tingle. He looked down and saw a distortion in the floor of the pass. He watched in horror as the rock turned translucent under him and the distortion took shape: an enormous open mouth lined with teeth.

The Soulreaver was coming up through the floor directly under him, mouth open, wide enough to swallow both Pharaun and the sphere.

Pharaun stared downward, wide-eyed with terror. He tried to find the words to a spell but failed, stuttering incoherently.

Deep down in the Soulreaver's gullet, he saw the tiny forms of wriggling souls, their eyes filled with a terror that mirrored his own.

The walls of the inside of the Soulreaver's mouth rose around him, and he could do nothing but watch as he was engulfed.

He did not even have time to scream before the jaws snapped shut and he joined the damned.

Quenthel stood alone on the Pass of the Soulreaver. She knew that anyone who would brave its trials must do so alone.

She knew too that the Soulreaver was the lone survivor from the mythology of a long dead world. Lolth allowed it to exist in the Demonweb Pits because it amused her, because it provided a final test for some of her petitioners.

The high priestess did not know why some petitioners were tested and others not. She attributed it to the chaotic whim of Lolth. When Quenthel had died at the hands of a renegade male in the Year of

Shadows, her soul had passed into Lolth's city without test by the Reaver.

She knew she would not go untested a second time.

With her whip in hand, Quenthel stalked down the narrow pass. The wind whistled between the walls, calling Lolth's *Yor'thae*. The heads of her whip rapidly flicked their tongues in and out, listening, tasting the air.

It comes, Mistress, said Yngoth.

Quenthel knew. Her skin went gooseflesh.

When she heard the Soulreaver's sinister hissings, sensed its maddening mumbles deep in some primitive part of her brain, she had to fight to keep putting one foot in front of the other.

She was Lolth's Chosen, she reminded herself, and she would not be deterred.

The Soulreaver slithered up out of the floor ahead of her, passing through stone as though through air, a sinuous, huge, translucent serpent. Souls squirmed within its long body, trapped, desperate, tortured. The Reaver was the final resting place and torture chamber for thousands upon thousands of failed souls.

Quenthel did not intend to add her own soul to their number.

Be wary, Mistress, said K'Sothra.

But Quenthel did not intend to be wary. That time was past. She would take what the Soulreaver offered.

Gripping her holy symbol in her hand, speaking Lolth's praises from her lips, she charged forward toward the apparition. It opened its mouth and hissed, showing her the squirming, twisted faces of innumerable trapped souls lodged in its gullet. Without hesitation, Quenthel dived through its teeth and into its jaws.

Hate pulled Halisstra back to consciousness. Rage opened her eyes. She fought her way through the pain and stared up into Lolth's sky. It was night, and she felt upon her the weight of the eight stars of Lolth.

Souls streaked above and past her, on their way to their dark mistress, heedless of her agony.

She fought through the pain and sat up.

Dizziness made her vision swirl, but she steadied herself with a hand on the ground until the feeling passed.

Feliane lay in a bloody pile not far from her, glistening in the dim light. Spiders crawled over the elf's small body, tasting her flesh and blood. Uluyara's corpse lay not far from Feliane. The substance that had held her immobile had dissolved. She lay on her back, facing the sky, and the slash in her throat gaped. Arachnids crawled in and out of the hole.

To her surprise, Halisstra felt no sympathy for her fallen sisters. She felt nothing but anger, a white hot flame of rage burning in her gut.

As she watched, Feliane's body spasmed, and she emitted a wet gurgle. She was still alive.

Halisstra rode her rage to her feet and retrieved the Crescent Blade. Pain wracked her body. Crusted blood coated her ruined face. Her jaw was cracked, innumerable ribs were broken, and she could not see out of one eye. She could well imagine how she must appear.

The souls flew past her into the Pass of the Soulreaver, uncaring. Lolth's seven stars and their dim eighth sister looked down from the cloudy sky, also without a care.

Halisstra called to mind a prayer of healing but stopped before the words formed on her swollen lips.

She would not call on Eilistraee, not ever again. The Dark Maiden had failed her, had betrayed her. Eilistraee was no better than Lolth. Worse, because she purported to be different.

"You could have warned me," she managed, through the bloody mess of her lips.

Halisstra realized then, fully and finally, that she had embraced the weakness of Eilistraee's faith out of guilt. She had worshiped a weak goddess out of fear. She was pleased that she had learned wisdom before the end.

She was through with Eilistraee. The part of Halisstra that had worshiped the Dark Maiden was dead. The old Halisstra was resurrected.

"You are weak," she said to Eilistraee.

Gritting her teeth against the pain, she took her lyre from her pack and sang a *bae'qeshel* song of healing through her torn lips. When the magic took effect, the pain in her face and head subsided, the punctures closed. She sang a second song, a third, until her body was once more whole.

But the spells did nothing to close the emptiness in her soul. She knew how she could fill it, how she would fill it—she felt Lolth's pull stronger than ever. Since Lolth's Silence first began, Halisstra's faith had moved like a pendulum between the Dark Maiden and the Spider Queen. Like all pendulums, it must ultimately come to rest in its natural state.

She looked at the dark opening of the Pass of the Soulreaver. Souls flew in and vanished, swallowed by the mountain. Halisstra knew what lay beyond it: Lolth.

And Danifae.

She was going to kill Danifae Yauntyrr, kill her without mercy. She pushed from her mind everything that she had learned from Eilistraee. She had no more room in her soul for sympathy, understanding, forgiveness, or love. She had room for only one thing: hate. And hate would give her strength.

It was enough.

She consciously gave herself over to the seed of her former self that had long lain dormant within her. From that point on, she would behave as a drow should. From that point on, she would be as merciless a predator as a spider.

Halisstra looked down at her breastplate and saw there the symbol of Eilistraee inset into the metal. She used the Crescent Blade to pry it loose. It fell to the ground, and she crushed it under her boot as she walked toward Feliane.

The elf lay on the ground, a bloody pile of torn skin. Her eyes were open and staring. Her mouth moved, but no sound came forth save the labored wheeze of her failing breath. The draegloth had fed on the soft parts of her flesh.

Halisstra knelt over her former fellow priestess. Feliane's almond eyes, glassy with pain, managed to focus on her. The elf's hand moved, as though to reach up and touch Halisstra.

Halisstra felt nothing. She was a hole.

"We are made anew each moment," she said, recalling the elf's words to her atop one of Lolth's tors.

Feliane's body shook with a sigh, as though in resignation.

Without another word, Halisstra put her hands to Feliane's throat and strangled the elf. It took only moments.

Praise Lolth, Halisstra almost said as she stood. Almost.

She walked toward the Pass of the Soulreaver amongst the flow of Lolth's dead, falling in with the rest of the damned.

Still occupying Larikal's stout body, Gromph pulled closed the temple doors and stripped off the priestess's chain mail hauberk, shield, and mace. They would interfere with his spellcasting.

Unencumbered, he channeled arcane power into his hands, placed them on the two door latches, and said, "Hold."

His magic passed into the bronze slabs. The spell would make the doors impossible to open without first dispelling his dweomer, a difficult task for any of Yasraena's House wizards. And the lichdrow's dimensional lock would prevent Yasraena and the Dyrr forces from using teleportation or similar magic to get into the temple. They would have no choice but to enter through the doors—which Gromph had since warded himself—or the windows.

The archmage turned, looked up, and examined the windows. Four of the half-ovals lined each wall of the nave, about halfway up the stone walls. They were large enough that a drow could easily pass through them. Gromph would have to seal them off.

From his robes, he withdrew a small piece of granite. With it in hand, he spoke the words to a spell and summoned a wall of stone. Its shape answered his mental command, and it formed up and melded with the stone of the temple wall, filling in the window openings in the process. He did the same with the windows on the other side.

The temple felt like a tomb.

The wall of stone would hold a skilled wizard or a determined attacker for only a short while, though, so Gromph took from his robes another component, a pouch of diamond dust. Casting on first one side of the temple then the other, he reinforced the walls of stone with invisible walls of force. Yasraena and her wizards would have to bypass both to get in through a window.

"That should give me enough time," he muttered in Larikal's voice and hoped he was right.

Gromph started up the aisle and stopped about halfway. The spider golem stood behind the altar, dark and forbidding. The pulsing master ward extended through Gromph and into the golem's thorax like an umbilical cord. They were connected, at least metaphorically.

Gromph knew golems. He had created several over the centuries. Mindless and composed of inorganic material, even the most ordinary of them were immune to virtually all forms of magical attack.

And the spider golem was no ordinary construct. Composed of smooth jet, it was the guardian of the lichdrow's phylactery. Gromph had no doubt that the lichdrow had augmented its immunities to magic. He knew that the spider golem could be destroyed only by physical attacks with enchanted weapons.

Unfortunately, Gromph was not a highly skilled fighter—his battle with Nimor had demonstrated that amply—but he nevertheless planned to chop the golem down with the duergar axe. He had spells that would assist his strength, speed, stamina, and aim, but still. . . .

At least it was Larikal's body that would suffer, he thought, but the realization gave him only small solace. He occupied the body, so he would feel the pain.

And he was growing weary of pain.

Gromph unbelted the axe and got comfortable with its heft. Eyeing the golem, he took a piece of cured lizard hide from his robes and cast a spell that sheathed his body in a field of force—essentially a suit of magical armor. Next, he spoke the words to a spell that caused eight illusionary duplicates of himself to form around him. The images shifted and moved—it would be difficult for the golem to determine which was the real Gromph and which an illusion. He followed that with a spell that formed a shield-sized field of force before him that would deflect attacks. An illusory shield appeared before all of the duplicates.

Almost ready, he thought.

He took a specially prepared root from his robe, chewed it—the taste was sour—and articulated the words to a spell that sped his reflexes and movement.

He had one more spell to cast—one from his scroll— but after casting it, he would not be able to cast another until it had run its course. Most mages were loathe to use it. Gromph had no choice.

First, he had to awaken the golem.

He held the scroll ready in his hand, took a wand from his pocket, aimed it at the spider golem, and discharged a glowing green missile of magical energy. It struck the golem in its chest, below the bulbous head. While it did no harm, the attack animated the construct.

The huge stone creature stirred. Light animated its eight eyes. Its pedipalps and legs stretched.

Gromph unrolled the scroll and read the words to one of the most powerful transmutations he knew. As the words poured from him, the magic took effect, bringing with it an understanding of how to use the duergar axe, an understanding of how to fight. Gromph felt his skin harden, his strength increase, his speed increase still more. A vicious fury seized his mind.

By the time the spell had transformed him fully, Gromph felt nothing but a powerful compulsion to chop the golem into bits. He reveled in the spell-induced ferocity. The knowledge imparted to him by the spell crowded out his understanding of the Weave, but he did not care. He would not have cast spells even if he could have. Spellcasting was for the weak.

The axe felt weightless in his hand. He crumbled the suddenly blank parchment in his fist and spun the axe around him with one hand, so fast it whistled.

The golem fixed its emotionless gaze upon him and bounded over the altar. The creature moved with alacrity and grace, unusual for a construct. Its weight caused the temple floor to shake.

Gromph brandished the axe, roared, and charged the rest of the way down the aisle.

Quenthel sat cross-legged on the floor of her room, praying by the light of a sanctified candle, asking for some revelation that would explain this *absurdity*. She clutched her holy symbol in her hand and ran her thumbs along its edges.

Lolth did not answer. The Spider Queen was as silent as she had been immediately before her rebirth.

Merely thinking of that obscenity caused Quenthel to shake with rage. The serpents of her whip, laying by her side, sensed her anger and swirled around her in an attempt to comfort their mistress.

She ignored them, rose, and took the whip and candle in her hand. Quenthel threw open her door, exited her chambers, and stalked the great hall of House Baenre, seething. Her wrath went before her like a wave and cleared her path.

Servants saw her coming, bowed their heads, and scurried into side halls and off chambers. Her forceful strides caused her mail to chime and the candle flame to dance.

How could Lolth have chosen another? Quenthel was—*had been* she reminded herself with heat—the Mistress of Arach-Tinilith. Lolth had brought her back from the dead.

But the Spider Queen had chosen *her,* an upstart whore!

The serpents of her whip offered soothing words in her mind but she ignored their soft hissing.

You are still the First Sister of House Baenre, K'Sothra said.

True, Quenthel acknowledged. But she was no longer Mistress of Arach-Tinilith. *She* had seen to that.

Quenthel knew it was blasphemous to think ill of the *Yor'thae,* but she could not stop herself. Quenthel would have preferred the dignity of a clean death to the shame of being removed from Arach-Tinilith. Triel regarded her differently since her removal; everyone in the House did.

Why would Lolth have cast her so low? After all she had done and endured?

No one had been better suited to be Lolth's *Yor'thae.* No one. Especially not *her.*

A cobweb caught Quenthel's eye. Her rage subsided, and she stopped in the middle of the hallway. She saw nothing unusual about the web, but it seemed meaningful to her.

It hung in a corner, strung between two tapestry-covered walls, silvery in the candlelight. It was big.

A stonespider's web, Quenthel decided. She had seen stone spiders grow half as large as her hand.

A few desiccated caveflies hung from the strands like tiny marionettes.

She walked to the web, head cocked, and held the candle aloft.

She studied the strands, thinking them beautiful in their intricacy. Every strand had a reason to exist in the web, every strand served a purpose.

Every strand.

The web made sense in a way that her life, death, and resurrection did not.

She looked more closely at the web, moved the candle around it, but saw no spider. She lightly brushed it with her finger, hoping the vibration would draw the creature out of hiding.

Nothing. The caveflies bounced on their strings.

For no reason that she could articulate, Quenthel hated the web. An impulse took her, and she could not stop herself.

She lifted the candle and held its flame to the strands. She knew it was blasphemy but she did it anyway, unable to contain a crazed grin.

The strands curled and disintegrated, vanishing into fleeting streams of smoke. The caveflies rained to the floor. Warming to her work, Quenthel continued until she had obliterated all sign of the web. She kneeled and burned each of the caveflies, one by one.

The serpents of her whip were too stunned even to hiss.

Mistress? K'Sothra finally managed.

Quenthel ignored her and stalked off, her rage inexplicably abated.

"The timing is not coincidental," she said but did not explain. She assumed the attack to be designed to protect the archmage. His allies surely knew that the matron mother had learned of his deception.

Anival looked up and down the line, at walls of adamantine and stone. They had stood for millennia. Surely they would not fall now?

Dyrr solders lined the battlements, and Anival could see from their hard expressions that all of them sensed the impending attack. A tense rustle rippled through the ranks.

"We will hold," Anival said, speaking to herself as much as to Urgan.

The weapons master said, "We will."

Anival thought she heard doubt in Urgan's tone but let it pass. She wondered whether she should hope for her mother's success or failure in stopping the archmage. If the matron mother died and the lichdrow's phylactery was destroyed, Anival might—*might*—be able to negotiate an end to the siege.

But first, she needed to hold her walls, and without either her vrocks, or her House wizards.

Xorlarrin war trumpets sounded.

"Here they come," Urgan said.

🕷   🕷   🕷

Each of the spider golem's forelegs ended in a sharp claw of jet as long as a short sword. Its mandibles churned with fangs as long as Gromph's hand.

Gromph did not care. Transformed into a skilled warrior by the power of his spell, he charged straight at the golem's front, axe held high in both hands.

The golem crouched at his approach, and two claws lashed out in rapid succession before Gromph got within reach. Anticipating the move, Gromph spun aside and partially parried one blow with his axe. The other claw struck at one of the mirror images, hit it, and caused it to vanish with a pop.

Using the force of his spin to add momentum to his swing, Gromph whirled in close, slashed with the duergar axe, and cut a wedge of jet from the construct's thorax. With his spell-augmented speed, he followed up with another, cleaving a furrow in one leg.

The spider leaped backward—crushing a bench under its weight—and struck at Gromph with one claw, then another. Gromph ducked and dodged, trying again to get in close. Two more images vanished. The construct moved with astounding rapidity, despite its weight.

For a moment, the two circled, a few paces apart. The golem stepped over the benches, cracking stone as it moved, waving its pedipalps hypnotically. Its clawed feet thumped into the floor with each step.

Gromph followed it with his eyes, light on the balls of his feet.

A boom against the temple doors turned Gromph's head. Someone was trying to get through his holding spell. Yasraena had located him.

Seeing his distraction, the golem lunged at him, knocking over benches in its haste. Gromph dived aside and rolled. Claws thumped into the ground around him—one, then another, and another—and three images vanished in rapid succession. A claw nicked his shoulder, drawing blood. His ring began to heal the wound.

Gromph leaped to his feet and intercepted a decapitating claw strike with his axe. The parry severed one of the golem's legs, and a shaft of jet as large as an ogre's arm crashed into a nearby bench.

Another boom against the door. His spell held but Gromph had little time.

Dodging first one blow, then another, he darted inside the golem's reach and struck at its head with his axe. He cut a sliver from it, but it backed off, toppling benches. Gromph pressed but the creature responded by exhaling a cloud of black mist.

Acid, Gromph realized, but could not avoid it. The personal wards that would have protected his own body did not protect Larikal's. Agony lit his skin. His nonmagical clothes disintegrated—which thankfully didn't include the enchanted robe in which he carried his essential spell components—and his exposed flesh burned and blistered as the mist sloughed away flesh. The stone of the floor and surrounding pews smoked and pitted. An acrid stink filled the air as the cloud dissipated.

Gromph gritted his teeth against the pain, leaped over an acid-slicked pew, and struck another leg from the golem. Another.

The golem answered with a flurry of claw strikes that drove Gromph backward and dispelled all of his images.

Blood and pus leaked from Gromph's skin. His breath came fast and heavy. The pain was slowing him. If the golem was like others of its kind, he knew it would be able to use its acid breath again after only a short time. It had but to gather more of the caustic substance within its enchanted body, and the archmage doubted he would survive a second coating of the stuff. Gromph had to destroy it first.

He parried another claw strike, reared his axe back and—

A blow from the golem hit him squarely in the chest. Only the magical shield of force and conjured armor kept the impact from splitting him open. Still, the force of the blow sent him careening backward. He stumbled, flailing, and tripped over the broken remnants of a bench. Gromph fell on his back.

The spider lurched at him, crushing the broken bench. Its mandibles opened wide. Its pedipalps reached for him. Gromph swung his axe furiously from his back, rolled, and tried to regain his feet. A claw descended for his throat, but the shield of force turned it, though the force knocked him down again.

He scooted backward, found his feet, and swung his axe defensively. The golem pressed him, drew in close and snapped its jaws. The bite snagged Gromph's cloak and pulled him off balance. A claw strike knocked him to all fours, and he nearly dropped his axe.

Gromph reared up and struck a glancing blow on the golem's head, just above its eye cluster. Flecks of jet flew and the golem backed off, pedipalps waving menacingly. Gromph regained his feet and backed off a bit too.

Breathing heavily, Gromph knew that he could not waste time. Soon, the golem would be able to use its acid breath again. Soon, Yasraena and her wizards would find a way into the temple.

The vein of the master ward stuck out of the spider's abdomen like some grotesque entrail. At the end of it, Gromph knew, within the golem's body, was the phylactery. He had to press the attack.

He backed off toward the altar, axe held defensively. The spider followed, clambering over broken and acid-scarred pews.

Gromph feigned a stumble and the spider pounced. The archmage dived aside, regained his feet in an instant, and unleashed a vicious downward slash that severed one of the golem's legs at the shoulder.

The golem struck at Gromph with another leg as it tried to turn to face him—the blow opened the archmage's thigh—but Gromph bounded between two of its remaining legs and chopped furiously. Chunks of the golem flew into the air as it clambered around.

Another blow struck Gromph, cracking ribs and driving the breath from his lungs, but he dared not stop his attack. His ankle caught under the golem and snapped.

Stars exploded in his vision. Agony raced up his leg. Shouting, spraying spit, he continued his onslaught. His axe rose and fell, rose and fell. Pieces of the golem lay scattered about the temple like so much Darklake flotsam.

After an indeterminate time, Gromph became aware that the spider golem was not moving. Fueled with spell-induced ferocity, he chopped at it several more times before he was sated.

When he came back to himself, the pain nearly caused him to lose consciousness. The bulk of the golem lay before him, cracked and broken. Its bulk pinned his leg. Pieces of it lay all around, scattered amidst the broken benches.

Another boom sounded against the temple's double doors, fairly shaking the whole of the structure. Yasraena and her wizards had not yet been able to breach Gromph's holding spell. They would try the windows next.

Gently, hissing at the pain, he pried up the golem's body with the duergar axe and slid his foot free. Bone ground against bone, and the pain caused Gromph to vomit the mushrooms he had eaten in his office earlier. He did not look at the break. His ring was working to heal his wounds, but too slowly. He reached into his robe—its magic had protected it from the acidic breath of the golem—and extracted two healing potions, both ordinarily serving as material components to his spells. He tore their seal with his teeth and drank the warm fluid down, one after the other.

His ankle reknit and the gash in his thigh and shoulder closed. Even most of the acid burns healed.

He sighed, tested his ankle, found it fine, and climbed atop the golem's body. There, he found his footing and straddled the point at which the rope of the master ward vanished into the golem's body. He raised the axe high and started to chop.

With each swing he grew more and more eager and the light from the phylactery's dweomer grew brighter and brighter in his sight.

After half-a-score swings, the axe blows revealed a hollow within the spider golem's thorax. Gromph stopped, sweating, and stared.

There, floating in the air, intertwined with the vein of the master ward, was a shimmering, fist-sized sphere of red.

The sphere turned yellow. Then green. Then violet.

Gromph watched the globe cycle through seven colors before beginning the sequence anew. In a distant way, he knew the globe for what it was—a prismatic sphere. The colors lay atop each other, alternating spheres within spheres, like the layers of a flakefungus. The lichdrow must have found a way to make a prismatic sphere permanent. He had placed his phylactery within it and placed the whole within a specially constructed golem.

Gromph knew how to bring down a prismatic sphere. Certain spells defeated certain colors. Touching certain colors without dispelling them resulted in harm or death. He would have to defeat all of the colors to get at the phylactery within.

It would take time. Time he did not have. Besides, he had another problem.

The transformative spell that had turned him into a warrior had temporarily modified his mind, closing the door on that part of him that interacted with and drew on the Weave. He knew that he could cast spells, but the knowledge that allowed him to link with the Weave was gone, temporarily crowded out by the knowledge imparted to him by the transmutation spell.

He could not end the spell early. It had to run its course. Only after it had would he be able to bring down the sphere.

Above him, a portion of the conjured stone wall before one of the temple's windows shattered, destroyed by some spell cast by one of

Yasraena's wizards. The stone rained down on the temple floor.

Gromph had only the wall of force between him and the forces of House Dyrr.

He was almost out of time.

A scrabbling sound turned him around. What he saw caused a pit to form in his stomach.

Each of the pieces he had chopped from the golem—the legs, the chunk of thorax, the claw, the piece of abdomen—cracked and split. Eight legs of jet sprouted from the cracks, a pair of mandibles. The threescore chunks of golem that Gromph had left scattered around the temple had been reanimated as buds of the main golem. The battle was not over.

For the tenth time in the last hour, Gromph cursed the lichdrow.

Danifae looked through the tiny, unglassed window of her garret in the Braeryn. Narbondel glowed red two-thirds of the way up its shaft. It was late in the day.

Danifae had lost track of time. For her, one day seemed much like another, one hour bled into the next.

She found it easier to measure time not with Narbondel but with corpses. It had been thirty-seven corpses since Lolth had selected *her*—Danifae could not so much as think her name—as *Yor'thae*.

Though Danifae had never been to Menzoberranzan before Lolth had selected her *Yor'thae*, she had come to know it well since. And to hate it.

To her right, far across Menzoberranzan's cavern Danifae eyed the mammoth steps of the great stairway that led up to Tier Breche. She could see it at such a distance only because of its enormous size and the violet faerie fires that illumined its steps. On the high plateau beyond the stairs—invisible to her at that distance—stood Lolth's grandest temple, Arach-Tinilith, the heart of the Spider Queen's faith. Danifae had never set foot within it and never would.

Within Arach-Tinilith presided the bitch, Lolth's *Yor'thae*.

Anger still boiled in Danifae, hate without end for the *Yor'thae*. She vented it on the males who came to her.

Danifae had created her own temple to Lolth, her own Arach-Tini-lith: a tiny, stinking garret deep in the Braeryn. There, she spun her web and fed on her prey in Lolth's name.

She leaned out of the window—her holy symbol still dangled from her neck, the amber smudged with grease and soot—and looked down to the street below. Addicts haunted the alleys like sunken-eyed, dazed ghosts. Fellow whores loitered in the doorways below her, soliciting anyone and anything that passed them by.

Groups of filthy orcs and bugbears leered at the fallen drow females. Danifae could see that the whores had sold their dignity along with their flesh. Not her. She served the Spider Queen still and ever would, despite the *Yor'thae*.

A thick sludge of sewage and trash coated the street. "The Stenchstreets," they were called, and rightly. Danifae could not but think of the whole of the Braeryn as an open sewer that she could not escape.

She would not let Danifae escape.

The odor of freshly emptied chamber pots carried up to the window and made Danifae wrinkle her nose. The expression felt awkward around the stiff scars that marred the left side of her face. Thinking of her disfigurement brought another flash of anger. She willed hate through the air and across the cavern to Tier Breche.

She had long ago given up trying to hide her scars. They were part of her, as much as her faith, as much as her hate.

After Lolth had made her choice, the Spider Queen's resurrection had been completed and the *Yor'thae* had come to Menzoberranzan in triumph. She had promised to usher in a new age for the Spider Queen and her worshipers.

But not for all of her worshipers.

The *Yor'thae* had punished Danifae for her presumption, forcing her to live a houseless life, dispossessing her of almost all of her property, marring her features to make her ugly, denying her the dignity of an execution.

Even Lolth herself appeared to have turned her back on Danifae.

The goddess no longer granted the former battle-captive spells and instead merely haunted her dreams. When she slept, Danifae saw visions of eight spiders, eight sets of fangs, legs, eyes, and poison.

Despite it all, Danifae refused to accept the label of apostate. She worshiped Lolth still, though she was a congregation of one.

Poor and disfigured, she sold her body to males to earn enough coin to eat. Though the *Yor'thae* had scarred her face, men still lusted for her body and were willing to pay for its use. Danifae abhorred their touch, despised making them feel as though she were subjugated to them, but nevertheless did what she had to to survive—like any good spider.

The *Yor'thae* had laughed when she'd cast Danifae into squalor, thinking that a life of penury would make Danifae weak. But Danifae was a survivor, like all spiders, and her trials were but another test in a long line of tests. She had and would survive it. She would grow stronger. She could not be broken, not ever.

If Danifae had learned but one tenet from Lolth's worship, from her life as a slave to Halisstra Melarn, it was that existence was a test. Always. The strong preyed on the weak and the weak suffered and died. There was nothing more to know.

And though Danifae was not the *Yor'thae*, she refused to be weak.

She left off the window, turned, and looked upon her sparsely furnished garret. She preferred to think of it as her web, an unassuming web, like that of the widow, within which lurked a predator.

A mushroom fiber pallet strewn with soiled blankets sat against the near wall. Every day, she carried the sheets to the shores of the Darklake to launder them—the routine had long ago taken on the significance of a religious ritual—but the smell of sweat and sex always lingered. She slept on the floor, refusing to take rest in the same bed that she shared with a male. A clay oil lamp sat on a stool near her bed, its tiny flame guttering in the stagnant air. In the corner stood a stone chair, upon which she hung the few articles of clothing she owned. A chamber pot and washbasin sat on opposite walls.

Danifae owned nothing of significant value except her faith, her holy symbol, and the blackroot distillate that she kept in a vial at her sash. She refilled the vial every fourth tenday by giving her body to an old, half-drow apothecary who worked out of the bazaar. She had made herself immune to the poison long ago through slow exposure.

She had sunk far, she knew, much farther even than when she had been a battle-captive. But she refused to surrender her faith. Most thought her nothing more than an insane whore or a cast-off hag afflicted with grand delusions. But she was neither. She was a spider, and she was being tested, nothing more and nothing less.

She had failed Lolth back in the Demonweb Pits—that was why she had not been chosen to be the *Yor'thae*—but she would atone for that failure and someday again find favor in the Spider Queen's eight eyes.

In the meantime, Danifae murdered in Lolth's name. Every eighth client that came to her garret fell prey to her. The Spider Queen might not have been answering Danifae's prayers, but Danifae offered sacrifices nevertheless.

She disposed of the corpses by selling them to an elderly drow fungus farmer. Danifae's prey ended up fertilizer in the mushroom fields of the Donigarten.

The weak fed the strong, she thought, and smiled through her scars.

A knock on her door turned her around.

" 'Fae," said a slurred voice from behind the door. "Open up. I want to taste your flesh."

Danifae knew the voice. Heegan, the second son of a failed merchant, who always stank of pickled mushrooms and mindwine.

"Hold a moment," Danifae said, and the male did as he was told.

Heegan was number eight.

Danifae pulled the vial of blackroot distillate from her pouch, daubed her finger, and coated her lips. Donning a smile, she moved to the door and opened it.

There in the hallway stood Heegan, his white hair mussed, his filthy shirt partially unbuttoned. Danifae stood two hands taller than the male. She looked at his watery, dull red eyes and thought, You are one of the weak.

"Well met, 'Fae," he said, leering at her breasts, covered only in her threadbare shift. "Aren't we a pretty pair?"

He dangled a pouch of coins under her nose.

Danifae snatched the coins and slapped him across the face. He smiled through his bleeding lip, seized her in his arms, and pressed his lips to her. His breath was foul, his excited grunts fouler. She abided, knowing that with each kiss he became more ensnared in her web.

She allowed him to steer her toward the bed. He tried to lay her down but she used her superior strength to turn him around and force him down instead. He grinned drunkenly, muttering some ridiculous endearment.

She straddled him and he licked his lips in excitement. His hands fumbled with her shift, her sash, and she could tell from his movements that more than mindwine was clouding his mind. His hand passed over the blackroot vial and never paused, so eager was he to get at her skin.

Smiling into his face, she teased him for another thirty count—until his eager expression grew confused, then alarmed.

"What's happening to me?" he said, his speech thick and sloppy. "What have you done to me, bitch?"

He tried to shove her off him but the drug had already taken hold. His strength was gone, and he managed only to paw at her shoulders. In moments, he was fully paralyzed and could only stare up at her in horror.

She eyed him coldly, still smiling, and began her incantation. Her voice called upon Lolth, offering the male's death for her amusement. When she finished her prayer, she put her hands on his throat and throttled him.

He died with bulging eyes and a wet gurgle.

"You are the weak," she whispered in his ear. "And I am the spider."

SEVENTEEN

Halisstra stepped into the Pass of the Soulreaver and felt her body stretch through time and space. She gritted her teeth and forced herself to keep moving forward. Vomit raced up her throat, but she fought it down.

A narrow path stretched before her and behind her. Sheer walls rose to either side. A mist cloaked her ankles.

The mist screamed at her and hissed.

She clutched the Crescent Blade. She was not alone and she knew it.

"Come out," she said, her voice low and dangerous.

Ahead, the mist swirled and formed into a vast serpent whose body stretched behind it to infinity. Black, empty eyes stared into Halisstra's soul and pinioned her in place. The serpent opened its mouth and hissed. The sound turned Halisstra's legs to water.

Deep within the serpent writhed the tiny, partially consumed essences of millions of failed souls. Their screams, rich with despair, fat with terror, bombarded Halisstra. She struggled to stand her ground. She saw her own fate in them—she too was a failed soul—but instead of causing her despair, it raised her anger.

"Face me," she said and did not know whether she was talking to the creature or to someone else.

The serpent hissed again and slithered sinuously forward. The souls wailed their pain and terror with each movement of the creature.

Halisstra stared at the glowing souls and wondered for a moment if Ryld was trapped within the creature. She decided that she did not care and moved forward.

She roared, lifted the Crescent Blade, and charged, meeting the serpent's advance with one of her own.

The miniature golems swarmed forward at Gromph. The transmutation that allowed him to fight prevented him from casting any spells to stop them, and he refused to abandon his station over the prismatic sphere atop the main body of the golem.

The smaller constructs scrabbled and leaped up the body of the golem to get a Gromph, thirty of them, forty. The archmage roared and brandished his axe.

A spider golem landed on his back, then another, and both bit into his flesh. Others clambered up his legs to beat at his chest. His armor spells deflected some but not all of their bites, and he grunted with pain over and over again.

He grabbed one of the creatures by a leg, threw it atop the body of the golem, and chopped it with his axe. He chopped another, and another, all the while waiting for the transformative spell to abate so that he could focus on the real issue—the prismatic sphere.

To his horror, the miniature golems that he struck split into smaller fragments and within a five count sprouted eight legs each and came at him again.

He cursed, swung at more of the spiders, again and again. Each time he struck, the small constructs burst into pieces, and each piece itself became another, smaller spider golem. Killing one made five more.

He was surrounded by a roiling swarm of constructs. They came at him from all sides, a swarm of fearless, remorseless killers. Eventually, he stopped chopping at them with his axe and instead tried to throw or push them off of the main body of the golem. But he could do only so much and in moments was covered in them, their weight so heavy that he could hardly move.

He tried to trigger the levitation power of his House Baenre brooch but the weight of the golems crawling over him was too much. He could not get airborne.

Their fangs and claws ripped through his defensive spells and into his flesh. He screamed with rage, pain, and frustration. His ring struggled to heal the wounds inflicted by the spiders, but there were too many. For every spider that he jerked from his body or threw down from atop the golem, another three took its place. He shook them from his hands, pried them from his face, pulled them from his legs. Agony lit him. He roared as he fought. If not for the regenerative magic of his ring, he would have been dead.

With the suddenness of a whipdagger strike, his transformative spell ended.

Knowledge returned to him in a rush. Physical strength drained out of him, and he sagged under the burden of the golems. His understanding of combat—swings, feints, and footwork—faded out of his memory like a half-remembered dream. His normal understanding of the Weave—the necessary gestures, component admixtures, the language of the arcane—refilled his mind.

Gromph was himself again, and he was in agony. A hundred holes pockmarked his flesh. Blood soaked his robe. In theory he could again cast spells, but the pain was too much.

Thinking fast, he did the only thing he could. He leaped from atop the golem and hit the ground in a roll. The impact jarred many of the spiders loose. With fewer attached to him, he triggered the levitation magic inherent in his brooch and went airborne.

He shook free the remaining spiders and hung in the air, gasping and breathing, dripping blood.

Below him, a thousand eyes stared upward, tiny mandibles clicking, tiny pedipalps waving. His broach allowed him only vertical movement, so he took a feather—a spell component difficult for him to procure in the Underdark—and spoke the words to a spell of flying. When he finished, he floated to his right.

As one, the swarm of spiders followed him, eyes turned upward. An idea occurred to him—

A sizzling sound from above and behind turned Gromph around. Green veins of magical energy arced along his wall of force. The Dyrr wizards were attempting to dispel it but their first attempt had failed.

Gromph had to move fast. He flew farther to his right, drawing the swarm of golems away from the body of their destroyed parent. He took from his robe a finger-shaped lodestone, one end of which was covered in iron shavings.

Hovering above the swarm of golems, he incanted the words to a powerful transmutation. When he finished the casting, the shavings moved from one end of the lodestone to the other and within a cylindrical area that ran from floor to ceiling and included Gromph and all of the spider golems, up became down.

Under the effect of his flying spell, Gromph simply adjusted his internal bearings, flipped over, and remained hovering in the air. The golems, however, fell up toward the ceiling, just as if they had stepped off a cliff. Gromph dodged them as they fell past. Two latched onto him, but he shook them free, and they too fell upward. All of them crashed into the ceiling, but it damaged them little.

With the entire swarm treating the ceiling as if it was the floor, Gromph spoke the words to another wall of force and ringed the area of effect in which he had reversed gravity. The golems would not be able to walk out of the affected area of his spell and fall to the floor. They were hedged in.

Gromph allowed himself no time to enjoy his victory. He flew down, flipped again when he left the affected area of his spell, landed atop the body of the parent golem, and looked down at the prismatic sphere, at the twine of the master ward that fed into it. He could have used one of his more powerful spells to disjoin the magic but doing so would negate all magic within the temple, triggering the master ward, freeing the golems, forcing his soul back into his body, and negating his walls of force.

Instead, he would cancel the sphere with the methodical application of specific spells. Each of the seven colors of the sphere was negated by casting a certain spell on the sphere when the appropriately colored layer appeared.

In his mind, Gromph thought through the spells he would need to eliminate the sphere's layers. Some of them would require material components. He reached into his robes and withdrew the materials he would need: a tiny cone of glass, his lodestone, and a pinch of dried mushroom spores.

He stared at the prismatic sphere as it cycled through its colors. He had to down the colors in sequence, starting with red and moving to violet. The master ward complicated things potentially, but Gromph had no more time to worry about it.

He readied his spells.

The sphere showed red. Gromph incanted a couplet, put the glass cone to his lips, and exhaled a cone of freezing cold that slicked the floor in ice. The prismatic sphere froze in the ice. Gromph tapped it with his finger, and the red layer shattered and disappeared, revealing the orange layer.

Another assault on the wall of force. The angry clicking of the golem swarm from above. Gromph ignored both.

He spoke another series of arcane words and summoned a powerful gust of wind. The magic of the spell whipped his hair into his face and tore the orange layer from the sphere, where it dissipated into nothingness. The yellow layer was revealed.

He picked up his lodestone, gathered some of the dust from the floor, and spoke the words to the same spell that he had used to disintegrate Geremis. The spell annihilated the yellow layer, exposing the green.

Gromph heard voices from outside the window. The screech of something powerful and predatory.

Yasraena must have brought the vrocks, he thought, recalling the shapechanged demons that had stood on the walls.

He picked up the mushroom spores and spoke aloud the words to a spell that ordinarily would have opened a hole through solid walls. Instead, the magic opened a tiny hole in the green layer, which rapidly expanded until the layer was consumed. The blue layer lay open to him.

Almost there.

The vrocks screeched again.

He whispered the words to a simple evocation, pointed his finger, and discharged a bolt of magical energy. It struck the blue layer and consumed it, revealing a scarlet layer.

He was nearly done.

Behind and above him, another assault on his wall of force brought it down. A shower of sparks announced its fall. A victorious cry sounded from outside the window. Gromph could not halt his attack on the sphere to erect another defense.

Looking at the next layer, he closed his eyes and pronounced the words to the next spell. When it took effect, light as bright as the sun in the World Above illuminated the temple. Gromph's eyes watered even through his closed lids.

Shouts of dismay sounded from outside the window. House Dyrr's forces no more liked light than did Gromph.

Darkness spells quickly countered the light, but the spell's work was done. The light had burned away the scarlet layer. Only one remained—violet.

Gromph uttered the words to the spell he had used so many times over recent hours, the spell that dispelled other magic. When he pronounced the final syllable, the violet layer disappeared.

He held his breath.

There, exposed but for the twisting embrace of the master ward, lay the lichdrow's phylactery. It glowed so brightly in his magic-attuned vision that he had to again blink away tears.

The phylactery looked like nothing more than a sparkling, fist-sized beljuril, a hard green gemstone. Tiny runes covered it.

Within it, Gromph knew, was the lichdrow's essence.

Gromph hefted the duergar axe. Not only would a blow from the axe destroy the gem, it would drink the lichdrow's soul, such as it was. The thought pleased Gromph.

Behind him, the vrocks streaked through the window and into the temple. Gromph spared a look back. The demons had assumed their natural form: that of muscular, giant, bipedal vultures. Vicious talons ended their legs, and large, tearing beaks jutted from their twisted faces. The beat of their enormous wings carried the stench of carrion.

"She is here!" they shouted back out the window, and Gromph heard exclamations of excitement from outside the temple.

Yasraena appeared in the window, levitating high and stepping onto the sill. For a moment, she stared down with a confused expression at the ruined temple and Gromph—he still wore the body of her daughter—but her expression quickly changed to one of rage.

She guessed who he was.

"Archmage!" she screamed.

Gromph shot her a smile and raised the axe high.

The vrocks flew toward him as fast as arrows, mouths open wide and shrieking. Yasraena voiced the words to a spell.

"Good-bye, Dyrr," he said, and drove the axe into the beljuril.

The gem shattered into countless glittering fragments, emitting a foul puff of smoke. A vague, distant howl sounded somewhere deep in Gromph's mind, and the axe shook in his hands. The lichdrow's soul rushed into the metal. It glowed, vibrated, and displaced the previous souls that the axe had claimed. A score or more spirits exploded from the axe head, exclaimed with joy at their freedom, and vanished into the aether. Henceforth, the axe would house only the lichdrow.

"No!" Yasraena screamed and lost the thread of her spell.

The vein of the master ward turned a burning orange.

Before Gromph could reason out the meaning of the change in the master ward, before he could turn to face the onrushing vrocks, a tremor shook the temple, shook all of House Agrach Dyrr. The force of it knocked Gromph off of the remains of the golem, and the vrocks shrieked past him overhead.

Speaking as quickly as he could, Gromph uttered the incantation to one of his most powerful spells.

Time stopped for everyone but Gromph.

Silence fell. Motion ceased.

The vrocks hung frozen in mid-air, mouths agape. Yasraena stood in the window, frozen in the middle of another casting.

Gromph studied the vein of the master ward. A bubble of power distorted its otherwise straight line, just where it passed through the temple doors.

It took Gromph a moment to determine what had happened. He cast a series of divinations to confirm his suspicions. When he saw the results, he almost laughed.

The lichdrow's defenses never ended. And it appeared he would have his revenge, after all.

The master ward had reset the wards behind Gromph not to prevent a second intruder from entering but to provide a power source for its real purpose. The destruction of the phylactery had triggered the lichdrow's final spell, a cyclic reaction that fed on the reset wards.

Power would race back along the vein of the master ward, absorbing the energy of all of the wards in its path. When it reached the start of the spell network, it would rebound back to its place of origin—the location of the phylactery, the temple—bringing with it all of the pent-up power of the absorbed wards.

The explosion would be enormous, perhaps large enough to level the entire stalagmite fortress complex of House Agrach Dyrr.

Gromph could not flee. The dimensional lock prevented magical travel, and he could never get out on foot in time.

The lichdrow had ensured that he would not go alone into oblivion.

"Well done," Gromph said to the axe, though he knew the lichdrow could not hear him.

The archmage smiled at the symmetry. He had destroyed the lichdrow's body by breaking and exploding his staff of power. The lichdrow would destroy Gromph's body by breaking and exploding all of House Agrach Dyrr.

There was nothing else for it. Gromph's timestop spell was about to end. He decided that he would rather die in his own body than that of some Dyrr priestess. He decided too that he would die amused. The battle of spells and wits, of moves and countermoves, had been as good as any *sava* game he'd ever played.

He spoke the words to a minor transmutation and transformed Larikal's body to look more like his own—shorter, slimmer, with shorter hair and sharper features. The likeness was rough but probably good enough.

Despite his timestop spell, he sensed the master ward collecting power.

With an exercise of will, he returned his soul to the ocular, forcing Larikal back into her own form. Once inside the gem, he quickly moved back into his own shrunken, invisible body. He came back to himself outside the temple, small and unseen, awaiting his death.

Yasraena blinked in surprise but managed to hold onto the thread of her spell. For a moment, Gromph Baenre had appeared cloaked in an illusion as her daughter Larikal, but the illusion had expired, and the Archmage of Menzoberranzan stood revealed.

The vrocks streaked in, biting with their beaks and tearing with their claws. The archmage appeared disoriented, reaching for weapons at his waist that did not exist, lashing out with fists rather than spells. His screams sounded like those of a woman. He found the axe he had used to destroy the lichdrow's phylactery and swung it awkwardly at the circling vrocks.

Yasraena continued her spell. She would annihilate the archmage. A bottomless ocean of pent up anger flowed into the casting, powering it—rage at Gromph for his deception, rage at the lichdrow for the foolish, short-sighted plotting that had brought her House down.

Another tremor nearly shook her from the window perch, but still she continued the chant. Flecks of stone rained from the temple dome. Glass cracked. The entirety of House Agrach Dyrr was shaking.

She saw it then.

With a sense of certainty that opened a hole in her stomach, she knew that House Agrach Dyrr was destroyed. The archmage had destroyed the phylactery, and the fool lichdrow had triggered some retaliative magic that would bring the entire complex down.

No matter, she thought. She would kill the archmage. Matron Mother Yasraena would die with at least that satisfaction.

The words poured out of her, and power gathered with every

syllable. The vrocks continued to attack, harrying Gromph from either side. He comported himself well with the axe. He fought back the vrocks and looked up at Yasraena. His expression went wide-eyed.

He shouted something but she could not hear it over the shaking temple, over the boom of her own voice.

She finished the spell, pointed her holy symbol at the archmage, and let its energy take root in his body. She knew he would be warded, but she also knew his wards would fail him. She had put all of her power into the spell. No one could resist it.

Still staring at her, the archmage began to shake. His entire body quaked as much as the temple and the rest of the fortress. Sounds poured from his mouth but Yasraena could not understand them. The vrocks backed off, unsure of what had occurred. Yasraena touched her House brooch and used its levitation magic to lower herself to the shaking temple floor. She wanted to watch Gromph die up close.

"You are but a male, Archmage," she said. "And I will watch you did before Lolth claims me."

The magic took deeper root. Gromph struggled to say something to her but could not control his body. His tongue flopped between his lips. He gagged, bit down on his tongue, and sprayed spit and blood. A horrible gargling noise escaped his lips as his body began to shrink in on itself.

For a moment, as the body collapsed, Yasraena saw Gromph's features contort to reveal . . .

"Larikal?" Yasraena rushed forward and took the archmage's imploding body in her hands. "Larikal!"

She could see the archmage—no, her *daughter*—trying to nod through her spasms. The quaking grew more and more intense.

Yasraena could not stop the spell. It was too late.

Mother, Larikal croaked through the connection of their telepathic amulets.

Yasraena could not respond before her daughter's mental voice became a prolonged scream, then turned into an incoherent, pain-riddled gobbling. With a wet, tearing sound, her body folded in on itself over and over and over again until it was nothing more than a densely packed ball of flesh at Yasraena's feet.

Yasraena stared down at her daughter's remains and clenched her fists in rage. The archmage had deceived her again.

Above her, the dome began to crack. She stared up and looked into Lolth's eyes.

Blood-spattered and gasping for breath, Halisstra stood on the landing outside the doors of Lolth's pyramidal tabernacle. To her left and right lay the corpses of Danifae and Quenthel. Halisstra had killed them both, cut them nearly to shreds with the Crescent Blade. In her rage, she had left Danifae little more than a pile of bloody, shapeless flesh.

She had stopped them both from entering the tabernacle. Neither would be Lolth's *Yor'thae.*

She unstrapped her shield and cast it to the stone landing. The rattle sounded loud in the silence. Except for the occasional sigh of the violet fires on the Planes of Soulfire behind and below her, the entirety of the Demonweb Pits seemed to be holding its breath. Even Lolth's wind had died down.

She looked up at the massive, pyramidal structure before her—Lolth's tabernacle, composed of black metal and acrawl with spiders. At its base, the towering double doors stood open and beckoning. Violet light leaked from within. Halisstra saw arachnid silhouettes in the light—huge, predatory forms.

Now she would do what she had come to do.

She paused.

What had she come to do?

She shook her head—her thoughts were confused—and stepped across the threshold.

Webs covered the slanting walls of the temple's interior, their collective pattern suggestive of something disquieting but indiscernible. Spiders of all shapes and sizes skittered through the webs.

Columns dotted the structure, slender spires fashioned of hardened, twisted web strands. She could not see the source of the violet light.

At the far end of the web-strewn temple, standing on a raised dais of polished, black granite, stood the eight bodies of the Spider Queen.

Seeing her former patron goddess in the flesh, Halisstra found it difficult to breathe.

Lolth was in her arachnid forms and appeared as eight giant widows, graceful and deadly—one goddess, eight aspects.

Seven of the widows crawled over each other, hissed at each other, as though fighting for position. But all of them stood behind the eighth, the largest, who sat quiescent in her web. The eyes of the eighth impaled her.

A yochlol stood to either side of the dais, their forms like melted wax, their waving arms like ropes.

Creatures that Halisstra had never before seen lined a processional directly between Halisstra and Lolth. Their tall, graceful forms—nude drow females sprouting long spider legs from their torsos—loomed over Halisstra. Halisstra felt their eyes on her too, and the weight of their expectations. She marveled at the grace of their forms.

"I am not the one!" she shouted, and the webs swallowed her voice.

The eighth spider stirred.

A rustle ran through the ranks of the temple.

As one, the drow-spider creatures responded, "But you could be. The eighth awaits the *Yor'thae.*"

"No!" she answered.

They hissed and bared their teeth, revealing a spider's fangs.

The eight bodies of Lolth clicked as one, and the widows fell silent.

They cocked their beautiful heads, listening to their goddess.

Halisstra brandished the Crescent Blade, drew in a deep breath, and took another step into the temple.

The doors swung closed behind her with a boom. She stopped for a moment, uncertain, trapped, alone. She looked down the aisle at Lolth and somehow found a reserve of courage.

"I will face you for what you have done to me," she said.

The widows rustled. The yochlols waved their ropy arms.

You have done it to yourself, Lolth answered in Halisstra's mind.

The goddess's voice—*voices,* for Halisstra heard seven distinct tones in the words—nearly drove Halisstra to her knees.

Holding the Crescent Blade in both sweating hands, her knuckles white, Halisstra took another step, then another. The blade shimmered in her grasp, its crimson fire a counterpoint to the temple's violet light. Halisstra might have no longer served the Dark Maiden, but Eilistraee's sword still wanted to do the work for which it was designed.

The strange drow-spiders eyed her as she walked between them but made no move to stop her. They shifted uneasily with each step that she took nearer to Lolth's forms.

Halisstra was shaking, her legs felt leaden, but she kept moving.

Seven sets of mandibles churned as Halisstra got closer. The eighth body of Lolth stood still, waiting. Halisstra stepped to the base of the dais, before the bodies of Lolth, and looked into the emotionless eye-cluster of the eighth spider.

She saw herself reflected in those black orbs and did not care for how she appeared. Her heart pounded in her breast, so hard it surely must burst.

Sweating, gritting her teeth, she lifted the Crescent Blade high.

Lolth's voices, soft, reasonable, and persuasive, sounded in Halisstra's mind.

Why have you come, daughter? Lolth asked.

I'm not your daughter, Halisstra answered. *And I've come to kill you.*

She tightened her grip on the Crescent Blade. Its light shone in Lolth's eight eyes, reminding Halisstra of the satellites in the sky of the Demonweb Pits that had watched her from on high.

The yochlol to Lolth's sides slithered toward Halisstra, but Lolth's forms stopped them with a wave of their pedipalps.

You could not even if you willed it, Lolth said. *But I see your heart, daughter, and I know that you do not will it.*

Halisstra hesitated, the Crimson Blade poised to strike.

It is not me that you wish to kill, child, said Lolth. *I am what I am and you have always known that. I kill, I feed, and in that killing and feeding I am made stronger. Why does your own nature trouble you so? My daughter's worship ill-suited you. Why do you fear to admit what you want?*

The Crescent Blade shook in Halisstra's hand. Tears welled in her eyes. She realized it then.

It was not Lolth that she wanted to kill. She wanted to kill the uncertainty, the dichotomy in her soul that had spawned her weakness. She knew it lingered there still, a guilty, fearful hole. She had raised a temple to Eilistraee in the Demonweb Pits, had slain countless spiders holy to Lolth, had wielded the Dark Maiden's own blade. Her final rejection of Eilistraee was inadequate penance.

She loved Lolth, longed for the Spider Queen, or at least the power that Lolth brought. That was what she wanted to kill—the longing—but she could not, not without killing herself and who she was.

Embrace what you are, child, Lolth said in a chorus of seven voices.

But it was eight sets of mandibles that opened wide.

Chapter

E I G H T E E N

Billions of eye clusters burned holes into Inthracis's back. He felt their gazes through his robes like a thousandweight. The clicking of countless arachnid mandibles rang in his ears.

He could sense the nervousness in the regiment. The fiends shifted uneasily, stealing looks over their shoulders. Souls or no souls, they had not expected this.

Stand your ground, he projected to the nycaloth leaders.

He kept his back to the Infinite Web and Lolth's mobile city. Inthracis did not want to look again upon the unending abyss, the chaotic strands of the web that never ended, the grotesque undulation and metallic groans of Lolth's metropolis.

And the eyes.

Millions upon millions of spiders and other arachnids—including thousands of abyssal widows and hundreds of yochlols— thronged the far edge of the plains, looking toward the mountains, toward the Pass of the Soulreaver, toward Inthracis and the regiment. Inthracis had never before seen a horde of such size, not even during the Blood Wars. It seemed that every arachnid in the Demonweb Pits had gathered there, in a line before their goddess's city.

Several tense moments had passed before Inthracis felt certain that the throng would not attack. Apparently, they had gathered not to fight but to bear witness.

Still, the realization caused Inthracis concern. It meant that Lolth had planned for, or at least foreseen, Inthracis's involvement. He comforted himself with the reminder that Lolth was a demon, chaos embodied, and that she would not—*could* not, by her very nature— accept a predetermined outcome. Matters were still subject to chance.

Perhaps Inthracis's attack would facilitate the creation or emergence of the *Yor'thae*. Perhaps he would kill all three priestesses and Lolth herself would die. Perhaps, perhaps, perhaps.

He considered reneging on his promise to Vhaeraun and returning to the Blood Rift, but he knew that the Masked God's vengeance would be swift. Perhaps Vhaeraun was watching him even then.

Inthracis resigned himself to play his part. If Lolth was going to allow him to attack the priestesses, then he would attack the priestesses. If she was not going to allow it, then he would not.

He showed none of his doubt to the regiment, of course. To them, he projected, *If they were going to attack, it would already have come. Remain steady. It will not be long.*

He patted Carnage and Slaughter, and they growled softly in response. They too seemed restless. He looked around and wondered how in all the planes he had allowed himself to become involved in the workings of the gods.

The Plains of Soulfire spread out around him, a cracked, broken plateau of rock that bridged the half-league between the mountains and the Infinite Web. Open tears in the rock spat sprays of arcane fire and blasts of acid into the sky. A thin haze of green gas cloaked the terrain, not enough to be opaque but enough to create wrinkles in Inthracis's perception.

Before him, the plains ended at the mountains. Behind him, the plains just . . . stopped, as though wiped clean. And where they stopped, an infinite abyss yawned, a black, empty hole in reality that never ended. Spanning the abyss, and extending out to forever, was the Infinite Web of Lolth.

Inthracis did not turn, but he pictured the web in his mind: strands of silk, most of them fifty paces in diameter or more, stretched across the void forever.

Lolth's city sat amidst the strands, an architecturally chaotic metropolis that somehow appeared like an enormous spider, on equally enormous legs, crawling along an even more enormous web. Its glacial, groaning movement across the web vibrated even the hugest of the strands.

The city was a mammoth cluster of metal and webbing, with one web-cloaked structure piled on another, and no order, reason, or uniformity to the layout. Only the position of Lolth's pyramidal tabernacle made sense: it capped the city, glowing like a beacon with violet light. Transformed souls stalked the city's walks, webs, and ways, damned insects in a hive. The glowing spirits of those not yet transformed into their eternal flesh flitted around the metropolis like frustrated fireflies.

Billions of spiders prowled strands of the Infinite Web around the city. Some lived in holes, and tunnels bored into the strands. Others skittered along the surface. All of them fed upon the others. Only the strongest survived for very long.

Inthracis put the city out of his mind and focused on his task.

Before him rose the titanic peaks of jagged stone whose tops scraped the sky. Cracks and holes marred the sheer mountainsides, and millions more spiders crawled in and out of the openings.

The Pass of the Soulreaver, like a black mouth in the stone, parted its lips three spearcasts up the sheer side of the tallest of the mountains. A ledge jutted from the mountainside at the pass's opening, and only a single, twisting, rock-strewn path—a ramp, really—led down the steep mountainside.

The pass vomited souls. A steady line of glowing spirits streamed out of the opening and streaked into the air for Lolth's city. Few made it unharmed.

Curtains of magical energy rose from the cracks in the broken rock of the plains and engulfed the souls as they soared over. The ghosts burned everywhere in the sky, so numerous they looked like sparks cast off from a blazing fire. After squirming for a period of time that varied from a few heartbeats to a two-hundred count, the flames released the captive soul, and the spirit flew free toward Lolth's city. Inthracis assumed that the burning served as some kind of purgation.

To his nycaloth sergeants, Inthracis sent, *Order up the troops. When the drow priestesses emerge from the Pass of the Soulreaver, we ambush them with spells as they exit. They will have no cover. That should force them down, and we can finish them here.*

If the priestesses survived the initial onslaught of spells, they would have to walk or fly down the narrow path. Inthracis and his troops would attack them as they descended and be waiting for them if they reached the Plains of Soulfire.

The nycaloths, flying above the assembled host of mezzoloths, growled orders, and the latter shifted into formation. The regiment assembled into a roughly crescent moon shape at the base of the ramp leading down from the Pass of the Soulreaver. The barbed tips of their glaives shone with magic. The nycaloth commanders continued to circle the troops, eyeing the pass. Each bore a powerfully enchanted axe.

Inthracis stood near the rear of his forces, rods at his belt, canoloths at his side.

Given the audience gathered behind him, Inthracis assumed the priestesses would soon cross from the other side of the pass. He cast a series of defensive spells on his person and attuned his vision to see magic, invisible creatures, even ethereal forms. Nothing on the mountainside could escape his sight.

Soon, the Pass of the Soulreaver would spit out Lolth's priestesses. And when it did, Inthracis would be ready. He intended to give his audience something to watch.

Pharaun came back to himself on what he assumed to be the other side of the Pass of the Soulreaver. The dark opening yawned behind him. Souls exited and flew over and past him. He thought of the

Reaver, of the souls that would never leave the pass, and shuddered.

After being swallowed by the creature, he had felt nothing more, seen nothing more. He did not remember moving through the pass at all. Moments or hours had been lost to him. He recalled a whispered voice, vague screams, and agonizing pain, but the events were so distant in his memory that they might as well have happened to someone else.

The challenge of the pass is not for you, Quenthel had said. From you, the Reaver will take only a tithe.

A tithe.

He did feel somehow diminished in a way he could not quite articulate. He tried to conjure a witty observation but came up with nothing. Perhaps that in itself was reflective of his diminishment.

In his mind's eye, he saw the Reaver's chasmal maw, its insidious whispers. He could not help but wonder what Quenthel had experienced.

He lay on the rocky ground, on the other side of Lolth's mountains, facing the cloudy, gray sky. He saw no sun, though dim light illuminated the land. He felt as though he had traveled through the mountains to find himself on another world, another plane. He knew that where he lay at that moment was related to the land he had left only in that Lolth ruled both, only in that the Pass of the Soulreaver connected them.

He put his hand to his temple and found that small spiders crawled over him. He heard a sizzling, like cooking meat. He could not pinpoint the source. A soul flew over him, then another.

He turned his head and saw that Quenthel lay to his right, her eyes closed. Her face looked drawn. She held her holy symbol in her hand. Her body had returned to normal size.

He swallowed but found his throat dry. Dusting off the spiders, he sat up and—

To his left, Jeggred and Danifae lay unconscious. He stared for a moment before the reality struck him.

How had they ended up there, at that moment? They must have entered the pass well after Pharaun and Quenthel.

He toyed with the idea of quietly killing Jeggred but swallowed the impulse. Quenthel had allowed him to live even after the draegloth had attacked her. Pharaun dared not act so presumptuously.

Frowning with frustration, he reached out and put a hand to Quenthel.

"Mistress," he hissed and shook her.

She frowned, mouthed something incomprehensible, but her eyes did not open.

Jeggred uttered a growl. The draegloth's fighting hands clenched into fists. Pharaun wondered for a moment about what Jeggred might have seen in his journey through the Pass of the Soulreaver, then decided that such things were better left unknown.

He climbed to his feet and stood on wobbly legs.

Fire exploded all around him, soaking the ledge in light and heat. His magical protections shielded him from substantial damage from the flames, but the explosion blew the breath from his lungs, seared his exposed skin, and knocked him flat.

He sat up, blinking, looked to Quenthel, and saw that she too had come through the fireball relatively unharmed, partially because she had been prone. Unfortunately, Danifae and Jeggred too looked blackened but alive.

Another explosion rocked the ledge, then another. The heat was melting the rock. Smoke made Pharaun's eyes water. Crisped spiders fell from the heights like black snow.

What in the name of the Abyss is happening? he thought.

A lightning bolt ripped across the face of the ledge, shattering rock. Fragments of stone buried themselves in Pharaun's face, in Quenthel's hands, in Jeggred's flesh.

Quenthel's serpents came hissing to life, followed by their mistress.

From Pharaun's left, Jeggred too awoke fully, his inner hands brushing away the stone shards stuck in his flesh. Danifae propped herself up on one of arm and looked around, dazed.

For a long moment, the four of them stared at one another.

Another explosion rocked the mountainside.

"What's happening?" Jeggred growled, as he climbed to his feet.

Danifae stood and said to Quenthel, "It seems we've both passed the trial of the Soulreaver, Mistress Quenthel."

Quenthel's serpents hissed at the former battle-captive.

"So it appears," Quenthel acknowledged.

Pharaun started to crawl toward the lip of the ledge, but before he reached it, an impenetrable cloud of white vapor cloaked the edge, and veins of superheated embers suffused it. Pharaun recognized the spell—an incendiary cloud. The embers sank into Pharaun's skin, burning their way through his protective spells.

Pharaun threw the hood of his enchanted *piwafwi* over his head. The embers still found his hands, and he gritted his teeth against the pain.

The stink of burning flesh and hair filled his nostrils.

Jeggred roared with pain. The priestesses grunted against the burning.

Pharaun could not see through the fiery mist more than an arms-pan in front of him.

A second lightning bolt split the fog, rocked the ledge, and sent Pharaun crashing into the mountainside. The embers swirled in the explosion, rooting for exposed flesh.

"Dispel the cloud, Mistress!" Pharaun shouted and did not care which of the priestesses heeded him. "I will give us cover."

From his left and right he heard both Danifae and Quenthel chanting spells. Their voices sounded as one, eerily disembodied in the burning cloud. Jeggred growled low, the pained, angry rumble of a wounded animal.

Pharaun waited until the priestesses were well into their spell before beginning his own. He took a pinch of diamond dust from his *piwafwi* and rushed through the gestures and words to a spell that would raise a sphere of magical force around them. He could not tell exactly where Quenthel stood—the explosions had sent both of them careening about the ledge—so he worded the spell to make the sphere as large as possible.

The priestesses finished their spells simultaneously, and one or both of the counterspells dispelled the magical cloud. One moment the cloud was there, the next it was gone.

Both priestesses were brandishing their holy symbols on opposite sides of the ledge. Jeggred crouched in a huddle near Danifae, his arms encircling her protectively, his mane and skin still smoking.

The priestesses stared at each other, Danifae holding her chunk of amber, Quenthel her jet disc.

Pharaun had no way to know whose spell had successfully dispelled the cloud, and the uncertainty troubled him. Everything about the recent past troubled him.

Still, he kept his concentration and finished his own spell. When he pronounced the final word, a transparent sphere of magical force took shape around the ledge, covering all of them.

Another fireball and lightning bolt slammed up against the sphere and exploded in light, but neither breached Pharaun's spell.

Jeggred stood to his full height, eyeing Quenthel. Dried blood caked his claws and ringed his mouth. Pharaun imagined it to belong to one of the Eilistraeeans.

"Mistress," Pharaun said, "my spell will not hold long."

"Of course it won't," Quenthel answered. "You are a male."

Pharaun ignored the barb, crept forward the rest of the way, and looked out over the ledge. The others did the same.

A twisting path, bounded on its sides by sheer drops, led down the steep mountainside to a plateau riddled with chasms, craters, and pools of acidic venom. A green haze filled the air, and Pharaun blinked at the acridity. Through the haze, Pharaun saw . . .

An army waited below.

"Yugoloths," the mage observed. "Five hundred, at least."

"Mercenaries," Quenthel spat, following his gaze. Her serpents hissed.

Scaled, four-armed, nycaloths swooped through the air above an assembled force of insectoid mezzoloths. The squat, beetle-like mezzoloths bore long polearms in their four arms, while each of the nycaloths held an enchanted battle-axe. They were arranged in a crescent shape at the bottom of the path, a wall of armor and flesh. Pharaun knew the yugoloths to be resistant to most forms of energy. He assumed that most would have used magic to bolster their inherent resistances. Dealing with them would not be as easy as simply burning the lot with a fireball, but he had killed fiends before.

He scanned the army for the ultroloth that he knew must be

leading them. Nycaloths and mezzoloths were followers, servants to the archwizard yugoloths.

The haze in the air made it difficult to discern details, but . . .

There.

Toward the back lurked a gray-skinned, bald ultroloth. Even from that distance, Pharaun felt the weight of its huge, black eyes. Two overlarge canoloths, both armed with spiked barding, stood to either side of him. The ultroloth wore dark robes, a sword at his belt, and a quiver at his thigh filled with rods. He held another rod in his hand.

Souls continued to stream out of the pass behind them and soar over their heads. When the spirits reached the plains, the air itself caught them up and exploded in sheets of violet fire. They burned there for a time, writhing in the air above the yugoloth army, before being released. The flames reminded Pharaun of faerie fire, the harmless sheath of flame that most all drow could summon.

"The Purging," Quenthel said, seemingly more interested in the spirits than the yugoloth army.

"Where weakness is seared away," Danifae added.

Looking down at the yugoloth army, Pharaun said, "Speaking of searing . . ."

Even as they watched, several of the mezzoloths held up their palms and balls of fire appeared there. They hurled them up toward the ledge, where they hit the wall of force and exploded.

Instinctively, the drow sheltered behind the ledge, but no fire pierced Pharaun's spell. They peeked back over.

The army remained in place.

"Why aren't they coming?" Jeggred asked.

"Why would they?" Pharaun answered. "They would bottleneck themselves on the path."

Pharaun knew that the four drow could have held for days the narrow path that led to the ledge. The yugoloths hoped to either force them down by bombarding them with spells or simply wait them out. It was no mystery that the four of them had not gone all the way to the very gates of Lolth's city only to turn back.

"We cannot go back," Danifae said, giving voice to Pharaun's next thought. "And we must go forward."

"Of course we will," Quenthel said with undisguised contempt. "They are the final test."

"Are they?" Danifae asked.

Pharaun thought an army of yugoloths to be quite a test but kept his observation to himself. He let his gaze wander and for the first time looked beyond the army, beyond the ruined plains, to Lolth's city.

"Look," he said and could not keep the awe from his voice.

Half a league away, the plains ended—just ended, as though cut off with a razor—at a gulf of nothingness that went on forever in all directions.

A web of monstrous proportions somehow spanned the void, its far ends lost in infinity. All of Menzoberranzan could have sat insignificantly upon its strands.

Lolth's city, a heaped clump of metal and webs and souls and spiders as large as a hundred Menzoberranzans, sat near the edge of the web. Mammoth legs—a grotesque amalgam of the organic and the metallic—sprouted from the city's base and held it in the web strands.

A roughly pyramidal temple capped the metropolis. Intuitively, Pharaun knew the pyramid to be the tabernacle of Lolth. Its great doors appeared closed.

"The children of Lolth. . . ." Danifae said, and it took Pharaun a moment to understand her meaning.

At the border where the Plains of Soulfire ended and the web began, an entire host had gathered: abyssal widows, driders, yochlols, billions and billions of spiders, more even than Pharaun had seen during the Teeming.

"Her web covers all," Quenthel muttered and touched her holy symbol.

"And the world is her prey," Danifae finished. "Her host has come to bear witness."

"We must get through the yugoloths," Quenthel said.

"They should all die," Danifae added. "Their presence here is heresy."

Jeggred eyed the army below and growled in the way that Pharaun knew to be a prerequisite to his entering a battle frenzy. But for the wall of force, the draegloth looked as though he would leap over the ledge and charge down the path at any moment.

Quenthel's serpents haloed her head, and she nodded at something they communicated to her.

"We must pass," Quenthel said again.

Danifae smiled broadly and said to Quenthel, "Indeed we must. Summon what aid you can, priestess."

Each eyed the other for a moment, then both stepped back from the ledge, out of the sight of the yugoloths, and began to cast.

Back in his own body outside of Agrach Dyrr's temple, Gromph dispelled the dweomer that had reduced him to a fraction of his size. Still invisible, he watched the mighty stalagmite fortress begin to shake itself apart. Buildings cracked from their foundations to their roofs. The great stalagmite and adamantine walls vibrated. Dyrr soldiers scurried frantically along the walls for the stairways, sprinted across the grounds or leaped from the walls and levitated to earth.

Gromph would have laughed but for his own impending death. He might have tried to fly into the air and away from the fortress, if he had not left his spell components in his robe on Larikal and if he had thought it would allow him to escape. He did not think it would.

The explosion would be too big. There was no outrunning it.

With his dweomer-sensitive eyesight, he watched the pulse of power run along the master ward and saw it extinguish the lesser wards and draw their power into itself. It was a beast, devouring all of the magical power in House Agrach Dyrr's intricate defensive structure. In moments, it would vomit it all out in an explosion that would shake Menzoberranzan's cavern.

The gathering energies caused Gromph's ears to pop.

The wave of power reached the outer wards on the gate and walls, gathered them in, and rebounded back, moving fast.

Roofs collapsed on the buildings around the archmage. Drow screamed. Priestesses shouted unheeded orders.

Another great tremor shook the temple behind him, and the central dome collapsed in a shower of crashing stone and glass. Gromph presumed that Yasraena, Larikal, and the vrocks died under its weight.

Fitting, he thought, that in the end Lolth had crushed the traitors.

Gromph stepped off the portico and away from the temple. He wondered distantly if the Xorlarrin forces would be caught in the blast. Certainly enough power seemed to be gathering. The energy from all of the wards would power the explosion. It would consolidate at the trigger, in the center of the collapsed temple, and explode outward from there. Gromph thought it possible that all of House Agrach Dyrr would be destroyed.

He looked toward the gates and saw the wave surging back—a great, glowing wall of arcane power. The ground rippled before it.

An idea fluttered around the back of Gromph's mind. The wave was gathering and extinguishing all of the wards as it moved.

All of them.

Even the dimensional lock?

His heartbeat accelerated.

Could the lichdrow have made such a mistake?

Gromph thought it might be possible. He studied the surviving wards as the wave of power drew nearer. The dimensional lock was still in place and he could not tell if the master ward would draw on even it. If so . . .

If so, Gromph might be able to time a final spell just right. Fortunately, the spell he would use required no material component.

He waited . . . waited.

The wave of power surged along the master ward and passed him, knocking him from his feet.

There! The wave subsumed the dimensional lock and hit the ruined temple. The whole structure glowed, pulsed a blinding white.

Gromph shouted the words to his spell as rapidly as he could without risking a mispronunciation.

Blinding beams of energy shot from the temple in all directions. An explosion was imminent.

He hurried through the spell. A word. Another. Another.

The temple burned as bright as the sun of the World Above as it exploded in a unequalled blast of magical energy. Gromph did not complete his spell.

Pain seared his body, a brief moment of agony unlike anything he had ever felt, and Gromph Baenre knew pain.

Then it was over.

On the Plains of Soulfire, the mezzoloths shifted into battle formations. The nycaloths flew above the host, axes in hand. The ultroloth pulled out a second rod, likely to bring down Pharaun's wall of force.

Jeggred stood at the top of the path that led down to the plains, growling with rage.

"Get rid of this wall, wizard!" the draegloth roared, veins and tendons visible under his leathery skin.

Beside Pharaun, the priestesses voiced spells of summoning. Quenthel didn't bother with a summoning circle. Neither did Danifae. Each cradled her holy symbol to her breast and called on Lolth for aid. Their voices rose into the darkened sky, boomed over the blasted plains.

And the Spider Queen answered.

Quenthel called out a name. The word hit Pharaun like a physical blow, skipped off his brain, and was lost to his memory.

A roll of thunder boomed. Quenthel repeated the name.

Above them, the sky opened. An enormous shadow filled the hole, winged and awful.

Pharaun knew it for it was, but he could scarcely believe his eyes.

A klurichir. One of the most powerful demons in the Abyss. Quenthel had taken a great risk in summoning it. She was either very confident or very desperate.

Except for the lonely sound of Danifae's voice, silence fell over the Plains of Soulfire. Even Jeggred quieted. A nervous shuffle ran through the yugoloth army. The nycaloths hurriedly flew back down to stand with their troops. Pharaun caught the magically augmented telepathic projection of the ultroloth.

Stand your ground, he ordered, and the yugoloths obeyed.

The klurichir circled downward, growing larger with each pass. A roar escaped it, and the sound shook the mountains.

It alit on the mountainside, just outside of the invisible wall of Pharaun's sphere of force.

The klurichir's powerfully muscled body, covered in coarse grayish skin and hair that looked more like quills, stood four times the height of Jeggred. The membranous red wings that sprouted from its back extended out to twice that and cast the entire ledge in shadow. Its short legs looked as thick and sturdy as stone columns. Four powerful arms, all of them in constant, twitchy motion, erupted from a torso that was little more than a gobbling, cavernous mouth that could have swallowed two ogres whole. An insectoid pincer on each side of the mouth spasmed hungrily. A flood of incompressible prattle and drool leaked from between its rows of grinding teeth.

Pharaun thought the babbling would drive him mad. He vomited down the front of his *piwafwi*. He couldn't help it.

The mammoth head that sat atop the demon's torso looked vaguely orclike, though more bestial. A second, smaller mouth opened in the face, below a pair of black eyes. In one of its hands, the demon held a rune-inscribed axe as long as Jeggred was tall.

The bass voice that emerged from the mouth in the klurichir's face nearly knocked Pharaun down with its power. The huge mouth in its torso continued to gobble and drool while the other mouth spoke.

"You should not have summoned me, child priestess," the demon said, the implicit threat in its words all the more terrifying because it was unspoken.

To her credit, Quenthel's body did not shake, though Pharaun knew that not even Quenthel Baenre could match the klurichir in power.

For a moment, Quenthel seemed at a loss for words.

At last she said, "Ten thousand souls are yours if you but perform a single service for me."

Both mouths erupted in laughter.

"Ten thousand souls are a pittance to me," the klurichir answered. Its wings beat in agitation, sending a hail of scree into the air.

"Name your price," Quenthel said, blinking in the gust.

Pharaun could hardly believe what he had heard. Even Jeggred gasped.

Quenthel had offered one of the Abyss's most powerful demons whatever it wished.

The demon too seemed stunned. For a moment, its huge mouth ceased its senseless gobbling. A giant tongue emerged from the mouth and licked its lips.

"Your desperation intrigues me," it said. "Name your service and I will consider it. For payment, I shall have such other, fleshly payment as I may see fit."

Quenthel did not quail, and Pharaun could not believe it.

"Done," she said, and gestured down at the plains. "Assist us in destroying the yugoloth army below."

The demon grinned, gobbled, and took wing, soaring high into the sky. Quenthel watched it go, smiling, breathing heavily, sweating.

Danifae's voice sounded behind him, reminding him that she too was summoning aid.

As the former battle-captive finished her casting, her voice rose, imploring Lolth for assistance. When she finished, she turned to face the mountain. At first nothing happened.

Then the mountainside began to seethe.

Millions of spiders, billions, boiled forth from every crack, crag, hole, and opening. The sound of their legs and pincers was like a rainstorm, almost worse than the gobbling of the klurichir.

Danifae shouted something that Pharaun could not make out above the hissing din, and the spiders crawled together, massed, clustered. Churning sickeningly, they piled themselves into a swarm as large as the klurichir. The swarm took the rough shape of a giant spider.

Danifae swept her arm out wide and gestured down toward the yugoloths.

As one, billions of arachnids boiled down the mountainside.

"Now, Master Mizzrym!" Quenthel shouted to Pharaun.

"Lower the wall of force!" Danifae ordered.

Pharaun did exactly that and immediately took wing.

Jeggred tore down the mountainside, roaring with rage. Quenthel and Danifae followed at a run. The klurichir roared, raining drool on the Plains of Soulfire, and descended downward. The arachnid swarm boiled toward the yugoloths.

To their credit, the yugoloths responded quickly. They were a practiced force.

Though they often were loath to do it due to the price, Pharaun knew that extraplanar creatures had the ability to summon others of their kind, usually due to some pre-existing cooperative arrangement. The mezzoloths and nycaloths were no exception. A hum of arcane syllables wafted up from below, and more and more mezzoloths and a handful more nycaloths teleported in with a soft sizzling sound and the stink of vomit. An army of five hundred became an army of eight hundred in a three count.

The nycaloths hurriedly deployed the new troops, trying to prepare for the klurichir's attack, Jeggred's charge, and the swarm's rush.

The ultroloth rose into the sky, his presence there offering a clear challenge to Pharaun. Half a score nycaloths rose with him.

The klurichir roared, the yugoloths clicked and shouted, the swarm hissed and boiled.

The battle was joined.

Jeggred pelted down the narrow path, heedless of the long fall to either side, heedless of the army that awaited him at the bottom. His clawed feet dug furrows in the stone with each stride. Rage burned in him. He could already taste blood and flesh. He roared for joy.

Below him, two score mezzoloths awaited his charge, glaives at the ready. Several of them gestured, calling upon their innate magical abilities, and clouds of stinking green gas formed before him.

He ran through the killing fog without a pause, inhaling the foul fumes, feeling the sting on his flesh. He ignored the discomfort on his skin and in his lungs and charged on.

Some of the mezzoloths in the second rank summoned balls of fire to their palms and threw them at him as he ran. Most missed and exploded harmlessly on the rocks or in the air, but even those that struck him had no effect on his flesh. He was demonspawn after all. Low intensity fires could not harm him.

He threw back his head and roared again.

Another explosion nearly knocked him from his feet. He dug his fighting arms into the rock to keep his balance and ran on.

A shadow fell on him, but he did not spare a glance up. The giant demon summoned by his aunt soared overhead, toward the rear of the mezzoloths.

Jeggred was twenty strides from the first of the creatures. Fifteen. Ten. He looked into their compound eyes, brought his fighting arms up to rend. Five. He could hear their clicks, the ring of their armor.

He leaped high off the path and landed into their midst. His momentum carried him into two of the mezzoloths' glaives, and both sank deeply into his skin.

He barely felt the pain, even as his blood began to flow.

He let fury take him over fully. His claws rose and fell, slashed and tore. Sometimes he struck carapace, sometimes he struck nothing. He had arms in his mouth, bodies, heads. Anything that came within his reach was bitten, rent, torn. Yugoloth blood dribbled down his chin.

Glaives slammed into him but he did not care. Balls of flame exploded against his skin and he still did not care. He felt his blood flowing down his back, his chest, his arms. He was swarmed with mezzoloths. He roared and killed, roared and killed.

Impenetrable darkness suddenly sheathed him. Blind, he continued to rake and slash at anything within reach. He didn't know if the mez-zoloths could see within the darkness, and he did not care. He slashed and killed even as he began to grow weaker.

Pharaun watched Jeggred tear down the narrow path and leap into a mass of waiting mezzoloths. The draegloth vanished under an avalanche of black bodies, and Pharaun gave him no further thought.

The klurichir set down toward the rear of the yugoloth army and cut a great swath through their number with its axe. Nycaloths and mezzoloths swarmed it, axes and glaives thumping into its flesh. Its roar rang across the battlefield.

The spider swarm poured down the mountain like an avalanche and crashed into the front of the yugoloth lines. The mezzoloths responded with clouds of green killing gas, which left piles of spiders dead, but the swarm churned forward, devouring everything in its path.

The ultroloth floated over the battle toward Pharaun, perhaps a long crossbow shot distant. Eight nycaloths accompanied the power-ful ultroloth, four to either side. Each of the nycaloths called upon an innate magical power and caused multiple mirror images of themselves to form around them. Eight became over thirty, and Pharaun could not tell which was real and which an illusion.

Half of the nycaloths beat their wings, brandished their enchanted axes, and flew for Pharaun. The ultroloth followed them, holding a sword in one hand and two crystal rods in the other. The other nycalo-ths veered aside and flew toward the ledge, toward the priestesses.

"Beware, Mistress!" Pharaun shouted down to Quenthel.

She heard him and looked up.

Quenthel saw the scaled, green yugoloths streaking toward her. She stopped her charge down the path, pulled her holy symbol, and began to incant. Beside her, Danifae too began to chant a spell.

Yugoloths are inured to lightning, Mistress, Yngoth said in her ear. *And to fire and ice.*

Quenthel nodded as she cast. She knew all about yugoloths and assumed that they had augmented their innate resistances with magical protections. She had no intention of using any of those energy types. Instead, when she completed her spell, a sheath of blue energy flared around each of the approaching nycaloths. The magic of the spell destroyed all of the moisture within the nycaloths' bodies—water, saliva, blood. The creatures had only a moment to scream their agony before Quenthel's spell reduced them to shrunken husks of flesh and bone that fluttered to the ground.

And the high priestess had only a moment to enjoy their destruction before Danifae cut short her spell by slamming her morningstar into the back of Quenthel's head.

Sparks erupted in her brain, pain in her skull. Her vision went dark, and she stumbled forward.

But she did not fall. The blow would have killed most anyone, but Quenthel's protective spells muted much of its force.

She lashed out blindly with her whip behind her and hit nothing. The serpents hissed angrily.

Danifae's voice from behind said, "Here is the final test, Baenre bitch. You for me, and me for you. Let us see who is to be the *Yor'thae.*"

Quenthel felt the back of her head—it was warm and sticky with blood, but already her vision was clearing. She turned around, whip and shield at the ready.

"You should have made certain to kill me with that blow, child," she said.

Danifae whirled her morningstar and answered, "I will remedy that mistake right now."

Halisstra awoke on the other side of the Pass of the Soulreaver. The sounds of battle—the ring of steel, the screams of the dying—brought her back to herself.

The din gave way to the words from her vision, which still echoed in her brain: *Embrace what you are.*

She would. And with the power granted her by Lolth, she would kill Danifae Yauntyrr.

Her hand closed over the hilt of the Crescent Blade, lying beside her on the rock.

She sat up and found herself on a ledge, high up on the mountain-side. The Pass of the Soulreaver yawned behind her. Souls streamed out of it and past her.

Fire had blackened the rock of the ledge, melted it in places. Burned spiders littered the ground, their charred legs curled under their bodies, the hair of their carapaces singed.

"A sign, Spider Queen?" she asked of Lolth.

Nothing.

Then a breeze stirred the dead spiders, caught them up in a tiny whirlwind. She watched them, transfixed by their tiny bodies floating randomly, chaotically on the eddies of the wind. She sympathized with them.

Staring at the dead spiders, she felt a thrill charge her soul. She grinned, a fierce, hateful smile. She understood at last.

Lolth had told her to embrace what she was.

Eager, she climbed to her feet and studied the face of the mountain.

There. A narrow, deep crack, like a slot.

"I understand now," she said.

Halisstra stuck the blade halfway into it, took the hilt in both hands, and jerked downward. The blade resisted her attempt. She tried again. Again. She roared and tried again.

The Crescent Blade snapped in a flash of crimson light. When its steel broke, something in Halisstra broke as well. Tears flowed down her face, and she did not know why. The tiny seed of doubt, of hate, the power-loving kernel that sat in her center, bloomed fully and flourished. She felt as she had before the fall of Ched Nasad, as though the past days had been a dream.

No, she realized. Not a dream. A test.

And she had finally passed it.

She was Halisstra Melarn, First Daughter of House Melarn,

servant of the Spider Queen, and she knew what she had to do.

She would kill Danifae.

She *needed* to kill Danifae, as much as she once had thought she needed to see her former slave redeemed.

Halisstra watched the blade of the broken sword blacken and shrivel in her hand, curl up and die like the dead spiders that littered the ledge.

She had her new holy symbol. She had her sign.

The prayers she had memorized in Eilistraee's name, the magic she had stored in her brain for use against Lolth, flowed out of her in a rush. She sighed, sagged, and kept her feet only by leaning against the mountainside.

Halisstra was empty, bereft.

A small black spider emerged from a crack in the stone and crawled onto her hand, the hand that held the broken sword. She watched it as it sank its fangs into her flesh.

She felt no pain, but a coldness suffused her being. The venom entered her veins, and as it spread through her body it brought—

Halisstra arched her back and screamed as the spells that Eilistraee had stripped from her mind were restored by Lolth. Tears flowed again, but at least she knew why.

Overflowing with power, she wiped her face dry and hurried to the lip of the ledge.

A battle raged below her between demons, yugoloths, and drow. Lolth's city beckoned in the distance, an infinite web shimmered over a bottomless gulf, and Lolth's damned burned in violet fire in the sky above the plains.

Halisstra paid little heed to any of it. She had eyes only for Danifae Yauntyrr, who fought Quenthel Baenre on a narrow path that led down from the ledge.

Holding her holy symbol in her hand, Halisstra chanted a prayer to Lolth. When she completed the spell, she felt her strength increase. She smiled at the feel of again casting spells in Lolth's name.

She sang the words to a *bae'qeshel* spell-song and turned herself invisible.

Ready, she drew Seyll's sword from the scabbard on her back and hurried down the path toward her former battle-captive.

Pharaun hovered in the air and watched the nycaloths bearing down on him. He pulled a small glass flask of alchemist's fire from his *piwafwi*, coated his fingers in the sticky, flammable substance, and hurriedly recited the words to a powerful incantation. When he finished, he mentally selected several points in the air next to the nycaloths flying toward him, beside the nycaloths flying toward the priestesses, and a few points at random amidst the mezzoloths on the ground.

Little balls of fire appeared at the loci he had selected and exploded into small but incredibly intense bursts of flame and heat. The nycaloths roared. The explosion sent them all spiraling off course. One of the four coming at him fell smoking to the ground, trailing its mirror images.

Yugoloths were resistant to fire but not fire of the intensity that Pharaun could summon.

The mezzoloths below answered Pharaun's spell as three score balls of flame exploded in the air around him. His protective spells partially shielded him, but his non-magical clothing burst into flame and his skin charred.

The explosion spun him around, and he struggled to recapture his bearings. At last he found the three nycaloths as they streaked toward him. Just as he prepared another spell, all three of the nycaloths winked out.

Teleportation, Pharaun realized with a curse.

Before he could respond, they appeared beside him.

He caught only a chaotic glimpse of muscular, scaled bodies, fanged muzzles, black horns, beating wings, armor, claws, and axes.

Steel and claws rained down on him. His enchanted *piwafwi*, as hard to penetrate as plate armor, turned most of the attacks, but a claw rake opened his shoulder, and the wound poured blood.

He went straight up into the air and spun a long, vertical loop—his field of vision went from ground, to mountains, to sky and back again. The nycaloths and their illusionary duplicates pursued, harrying him the while, but he was more agile in the air than they.

While he flew, he spoke the arcane words to his next spell. Midway through the incantation, he produced a small glass mirror and held it in his palm.

One of the nycaloths flew past him and caught him by his ankle. Another crashed into him from the other side. The three of them went into a mad, twirling spin. Centrifugal force stripped the grip of the nycaloth on his ankle.

Pharaun could not tell up from down. He turned from ground to sky, ground to sky, ground to sky.

A lightning bolt from the ultroloth ripped into him. It had no effect on the nycaloths—yugoloths were immune to lightning, he knew—but its power sliced through his protective wards, burned holes in his skin, and set his hair on end. He gritted his teeth and continued his casting.

The nycaloth grappling him growled in his ear, its wings and claws beating frantically. Pharaun held it off as best he could while holding the rhythm of his spell.

Claws tore through Pharaun's *piwafwi,* ripped the skin of his midsection. Blood leaked from the wound, but Pharaun managed to mouth the final word of his spell while simultaneously slamming the mirror against the flesh of the nycaloth holding him. Green energy flared, and the nycaloth's roar was cut abruptly short as the magic took effect.

The creature's entire body turned to clear glass.

It started to fall, along with its illusionary doubles, dragging Pharaun with it.

Pharaun wriggled free of its stiff grasp and watched with satisfaction as the transformed creature shattered on the rocky ground below. The other two nycaloths and their illusionary duplicates circled back at him, roaring.

Pharaun turned and flew away from them, speeding around a series of burning drow souls, gathering for another spell.

He spared a glance to his right, over at the ultroloth. Already, a shimmering globe of magical energy surrounded the yugoloth wizard, and the creature was in the midst of casting yet another spell. Pharaun knew the globe would make the ultroloth invulnerable to a whole host of Pharaun's less powerful spells.

Pharaun pulled up hard and wheeled to his right. The clumsy nycaloths flew past him, cursing.

Hoping to disrupt the ultroloth's casting, Pharaun pulled a crystal cone from his *piwafwi* and hurried through an incantation.

The ultroloth finished first and pointed his open palm at Pharaun.

Almost all of the protective spells on Pharaun's person winked out at the same time, dispelled by the yugoloth's counterspell.

Pharaun cursed. The ultroloth must have been powerful to have so disposed of Pharaun's protective magic.

Pharaun put his vulnerability out of his mind and finished his own spell. He flew at the ultroloth, pronounced the final word, put the cone to his lips, and blew.

An expanding blast of ice and freezing air erupted outward and engulfed the ultroloth. The creature spun backward, coated in a sheath of freezing cold.

Pharaun could see that his spell had harmed the ultroloth, but far from mortally.

He rotated a circle in the air, looking back for the nycaloths.

He saw them nowhere. Either they had abandoned the field or they had turned invisible.

He accelerated upward, anticipating an axe blow with every breath, and at the same time triggered his ability to see invisible creatures. The power took effect just in time for him to see the nycaloths swooping in from either side, axes high.

He veered aside but too slow. An axe sank deeply into his shoulder. The other would have split his skull but he managed to duck under it at the last moment, so it only tore his scalp.

Wings beat in his face. The nycaloths grabbed at his *piwafwi*, clawed at his flesh. Their weight dragged him downward. He used the ring of flying to resist their pull, but he was slowly drifting down.

Below, hundreds of mezzoloths waited.

Bleeding, mildly dazed, Pharaun voiced the single word to one of his more powerful spells. The incantation used sound as a weapon, and Pharaun thought it unlikely that the yugoloths would have protected themselves against sonic energy.

When the magic took effect, he felt it gather in his throat. He let it build, then exhaled it in a high-pitched scream that resounded over the battlefield. The magic of the scream tore into and through the nycaloths, killing them both, and continued downward in an invisible wave until it smashed into the waiting mezzoloths and killed fully half of them where they stood.

He righted himself in the air, bleeding profusely from the wounds inflicted by the nycaloths' claws, and turned to face the ultroloth. Souls burned in the air between them, writhing in pain.

Pharaun, burned and torn, sympathized.

Chapter

TWENTY

Inthracis shook off the last lingering effects of the drow wizard's cone of cold. His ears still rang from the wizard's banshee wail, but he had been too far away for the magic to affect him otherwise. His nycaloths had not been as fortunate.

Things were not going as Inthracis had hoped. The klurichir and swarm of spiders were churning through the regiment. His troops were fighting well, but the huge demon and spider swarm were more than he had anticipated. The dead littered the battlefield. He could have summoned his own additional aid, of course, but nothing to match either the klurichir or the swarm.

He had to keep the klurichir and swarm occupied, at least until he could kill the priestesses.

He pulled a thin rod of basalt from his thigh sheath and summoned its power.

A pulse of black energy went out and down from him and rippled across the battlefield. Where it passed, slain mezzoloths and nycaloths clawed and shambled their way to their feet, even those just killed by the drow wizard. The undead yugoloths would not be as effective combatants as his living troops, but they would be of help against the swarm of arachnids and perhaps even the klurichir.

He sent his mental projection across the field, commanding the newly risen undead: *Attack the klurichir and spider swarm until they are destroyed.*

The dead moved to obey, joining their living comrades in the desperate melee. Satisfied, Inthracis considered his options.

Vhaeraun wanted him to kill the three priestesses. He saw only two. They were battling each other on the path leading down from the mountain. He decided that he would see them dead quickly or not at all. Vhaeraun would be satisfied or he would not. Inthracis had seen enough.

To every surviving nycaloth in the Black Horn Regiment, he projected, *Two of the three priestesses are on the ledge leading down from the Pass of the Soulreaver. Teleport there, kill them, and retreat from the field.*

That done, Inthracis's thoughts returned to the drow wizard. He called to mind the words to one of his more powerful necromantic spells.

Quenthel lashed out with her whip at Danifae. The battle-captive dodged aside but too slow. The serpents tore into the flesh of her arm and injected their venom. The poison had little effect—the battle captive must have been protected against poison—but Quenthel took satisfaction in the bloodshed. So too did the whip serpents, who laughed and hissed.

Danifae gritted her teeth and charged, swinging her morningstar for Quenthel's head. Quenthel took a step back, parried the blow with her shield, and answered with her whip. The serpents bounced off of Danifae's mail. Danifae spread her grip on the morningstar and drove the haft under Quenthel's shield and into her abdomen.

The blow stole Quenthel's breath, and she backed off. Danifae bounded forward—

And screamed in pain.

A blade erupted from the right side of her chest, spraying Quenthel with blood. Danifae's shocked eyes opened as wide as coins and stared down at the arm's span of steel jutting from her chest.

Standing behind Danifae, her invisibility spell terminated by her attack, stood a drow female. Hate so contorted her face that it took Quenthel a moment to recognize her.

It was Halisstra Melarn.

The traitor priestess put her mouth to Danifae's ear and whispered, "Good-bye, battle-captive."

Pharaun knew he was vulnerable—his protective spells had been countered—but he could do little about it. And the wounds from the nycaloths continued to leak blood, much more than Pharaun would have expected for the relatively minor wounds. He could do little about that too, and the blood loss was causing him to grow weaker. He could not afford a prolonged spell duel.

He and the ultroloth circled at a distance, eyeing each other. The slaughter went on below. The bellows of the klurichir rang through the air. The seething of the swarm sounded like the waves of the Darksea.

The ultroloth began to incant, his fingers tracing an intricate gesture through the air. Pharaun answered with his own spell.

The ultroloth finished first, and a black beam streaked from his outstretched fingertips. Pharaun swerved but too slowly. The beam hit him in the arm.

Negative energy soaked him and siphoned off his soul. His lungs froze for an instant. His body went weak. His mind clouded. The spell wiped half a dozen of his most powerful spells from his mind.

He struggled to maintain enough coherence to continue his own incantation. Blinking, dazed, he spat out the arcane words. When he managed the final syllable, he waved a weakened hand at the ultroloth, and a green field of energy enshrouded the creature.

It did not harm the yugoloth wizard, Pharaun knew. Instead, it merely prevented the ultroloth from teleporting or otherwise using magic to travel. It was a strange spell to cast, but the mage had an idea.

While the ultroloth puzzled over the spell his dark elf opponent had cast, Pharaun fought through the numbness and pulled a tiny ball of bat guano and a pinch of powdered quartz from his *piwafwi*. He would need to cast two more spells in rapid succession for the stratagem to work. He held the guano between thumb and forefinger and spoke the words.

The ultroloth drew his blade and slashed at the green field that enveloped him. Pharaun assumed the blade must have the ability to absorb or dispel magical effects that it touched.

The blade met Pharaun's magic, cut a visible slash in the energy field, and set the whole to vibrating.

But it did not fail. Pharaun breathed a sigh of relief and finished the first of his two spells. The ball of guano transformed into a small bead of fire. He pointed a finger at the ultroloth and started his second spell.

The bead followed his finger and streaked away. It stopped right in front of the ultroloth without exploding. There it spun, building energy.

The ultroloth knew the bead for what it was—a fireball with a delayed blast. The creature moved his long-fingered hands through the gestures that would effect his own spell, possibly to counter the fireball.

Hurrying, Pharaun cast the quartz powder into the air and rushed through his second spell. He completed it at the same moment the ultroloth completed his.

Pharaun's dweomer encapsulated both the ultroloth and the bead within a sphere of force. At the same time, the ultroloth's spell—not a counter to the fireball; perhaps he thought his words would protect him—caused a field of black energy to flare around the drow wizard. The magic gripped Pharaun's body and held it rigid. He could not move even his little finger, though his ring still allowed him to fly. He was a floating statue.

The two stared at each other across the battlefield, the dark elf immobile and vulnerable, the ultroloth trapped and unable to teleport out.

Pharaun started a mental count: Four . . . three . . .

The bead near the ultroloth spun faster, glowed brighter.

The ultroloth understood his danger and frantically cut at the wall of force with his blade. The weapon's edge slashed a tear in the dome but not large enough for the creature to slip through.

The bead spun faster, began to hum. The ultroloth cut another slash, crosswise, and tried to squirm out.

Two . . . one . . .

The ultroloth's squeezed his head and shoulders out of the globe of force as Pharaun's bead blossomed into fire.

A momentary inferno burned within the globe. A tongue of flame shot from the slash in the sphere's side, engulfed the ultroloth's head, and extended twenty paces into the sky.

From the battlefield below, a cry of shock went up from the yugoloths.

Within the sphere, the explosion turned back upon itself time and again. Pharaun did not doubt that the ultroloth had been shielded against fire and heat, but no wards could protect against the firestorm in the globe. The heat devoured the yugoloth wizard's body, charred his head and shoulders into blackened cinders.

When the fire abated a moment later, a curled and blackened husk lay halfway in, halfway out of the sphere. Nothing more remained of the ultroloth.

Pharaun would have smiled if only he could move.

TWENTY-ONE

Halisstra twisted Seyll's sword in Danifae's arched back, and the former battle-captive gasped with pain. Halisstra took satisfaction in each of Danifae's bubbling, labored breaths. Behind Danifae, Quenthel Baenre looked on with surprise. Halisstra ignored her. She had eyes only for her battle-captive. The high priestess was irrelevant.

Danifae's morningstar fell from her hand.

"Mistress . . . Melarn," she said, her voice soft.

Halisstra decided that she wanted to look Danifae in the face before she died. She released her grip on Seyll's sword and allowed her former battle-captive to turn around.

One third of Seyll's blade jutted like a bloody pennon from the side of Danifae's chest. Danifae's beautiful gray eyes stared out of an incongruously gentle expression. She looked upon Halisstra and smiled a mouthful of blood-stained teeth.

"Do not call me Mistress ever again," Halisstra said.

Danifae's full lips twisted with pain. She raised a hand as though to touch Halisstra's face. The effort caused her to wince.

"Halisstra," she said, each word divided by a pained breath. "I'm . . . sorry."

It took a moment for Halisstra to understand the words. When she did, tears welled in her eyes; she could not stop them. In a rush, she thought of all that she and Danifae had shared, the secrets, the ambitions. They had been through so much together, had come to know each other so well through the Binding. She surprised herself by regretting what it all had finally come to.

"Sorry?" Halisstra said, and her voice broke. "Sorry? It never should have come to this!"

Danifae nodded. Blood seeped around the blade sticking out of her body. Halisstra had missed her heart.

"I know," Danifae said, still holding out her hand.

Despite herself, Halisstra started to raise her own hand but stopped.

"I missed you, Mistress," Danifae said.

Halisstra blinked away tears and finally took Danifae's hand.

"I missed you t—"

As quick as an adder, Danifae grabbed Halisstra with her other arm and yanked her close, impaling her on the point of her own blade.

Halisstra gasped as the steel penetrated first her mail then her flesh. She felt the point scrape against her ribs and exit her back. Warm blood soaked her *piwafwi*.

She should have known. She should have known.

Her eyes looked over Danifae's shoulder to Quenthel.

The Baenre priestess smiled, gloating, whip in hand.

Danifae wrapped her arms around Halisstra and squeezed her tight. Pain knifed through Halisstra.

"I am sorry *for nothing*," Danifae hissed in her ear.

Halisstra fought through the pain and returned Danifae's embrace, just as hard.

Both of them gasped with agony.

Their bodies were melded, joined by steel. Their blood flowed as one. A Binding of a different sort once again united them.

Halisstra rested her head on Danifae's shoulder, a strangely soft gesture.

"I hate you," she whispered.

Danifae reached up and stroked Halisstra's hair, something she had done countless nights before.

"I know," Danifae answered.

Halisstra loved her too, despite it all.

"I know," Danifae said again, and her embrace softened.

Halisstra could bear no more. With a grunt, she pushed Danifae away, screaming as the blade exited her flesh. The effort knocked them off balance, and both sprawled to the ground, Danifae still stuck through with steel. They both sat on Lolth's ground, bleeding and gasping.

Quenthel Baenre eyed them both.

"Here is where it ends," she said, and advanced on Danifae. The whips of her serpent glared.

A hiss and sizzling sound turned Halisstra's head, turned Quenthel's head, turned the heads of the whip vipers.

Nycaloths appeared around them, teleporting in from the battlefield below. One, three, eight, a dozen—the smallest of them towered over even Quenthel. Their muscles rippled under their scaled skin. Each bore a rune-inscribed axe. Their muzzles twisted into snarls.

Desperation contorted Quenthel's face. She looked at the nycaloths, at Danifae, at Halisstra. Halisstra could see the indecision in her eyes. It resolved into an expression of utter hate.

"It is not you," the Baenre priestess said to Danifae, her voice shrill.

She ignored the danger of the nycaloths and raised the whip high for a killing strike when high atop the grotesque heap of Lolth's city the double doors to the Spider Queen's tabernacle flew open. Rays of violet light poured from the temple doors.

For Halisstra, time seemed to stop. Motion ceased. Every being within sight of Lolth's city—yugoloths, drow, demons, and draegloth—stayed their hands. All eyes turned toward the unending web, toward the Spider Queen's city.

A ripple ran through the arachnid host gathered at the far edge of the plains, an anticipatory shuffling. The sound of their motion reminded Halisstra of the downpour of rain she had heard while in the World Above.

Her heart hammered; her breath came fast. She clutched the broken Crescent Blade in her fist so tightly she feared her skin would split. She barely felt her wound. Danifae lay a few paces from her, facing the city, eyes wide, breathing shallow, her cloak soaked with blood. A whispered prayer of healing, a powerful one, leaked from the battle-captive's lips. Seyll's sword slid from her flesh, and the wound closed. Halisstra echoed the prayer and closed her own wound.

Quenthel didn't notice either of them. She stood and stared back at Lolth's city, frozen, her whip still held high for a strike.

Souls hung sizzling in the air over the Plains of Soulfire, writhing in agony, bleeding weakness from their eternal forms.

A sudden breeze picked up, blowing outward from the tabernacle. It turned to a gust, to a screaming gale, and in its scream Lolth's voice spoke, the sound that of multiple voices, the seven voices of Halisstra's vision: *"Yor'thae."*

Around them, the nycaloths shared a look. Halisstra saw the fear in their eyes, the uncertainty.

Without warning, they blinked out, teleporting back from whence they came. The retreat spread rapidly to the rest of the surviving army, and they too fled. The klurichir, its flesh torn and one of its pincers severed, nevertheless gathered another mouthful of mezzoloths and blinked out himself. The swarm of spiders dissipated, and the creatures made their way back to their mountain dens. The undead mezzoloths animated by the ultroloth fell to the ground, as inert as the soil.

Corpses lay everywhere over the still Plains of Soulfire. Pharaun Mizzrym hung in the sky over the broken land, strangely motionless. Halisstra did not see Jeggred Baenre anywhere.

"She has chosen," Danifae said as she rose to her feet.

Halisstra did the same.

A ripple went through Quenthel Baenre's body, though whether from ecstasy or fear, Halisstra could not tell.

Pharaun couldn't move or speak. He controlled his flight with his ring, which followed his mental urgings. Blood continued to pour down his sides from the wounds inflicted on him by the nycaloths.

He had heard Lolth's call, had seen her temple open, but none of that concerned him. If he did not get aid from one of Lolth's priestesses, and soon, he would die of blood loss.

He maneuvered his posture in the air so that he could see the ground. Movement from below drew his eye: Jeggred rose, staggering, from underneath a heap of mezzoloth corpses, his flesh bloody, one of his inner arms torn off at the elbow, one of his eyes little more than a bloody hole. The draegloth looked not to Lolth's temple but back up the path toward the Pass of the Soulreaver, to where the *three* priestesses stood.

Halisstra Melarn had followed them, somehow.

Quenthel, Danifae, and Halisstra stood high above the field of slaughter, staring up at Lolth's tabernacle. They reminded Pharaun of queens surveying their realm.

In the air around Pharaun, souls still burned in violet fire. After undergoing purgation for a time, they flew on to Lolth's city.

Pharaun knew that the priestesses too had undergone purgation. So had he. So, in his way, had Jeggred.

He flew toward them, marveling that they did not kill each other.

Pharaun supposed that Lolth's call was bigger than their hate for each other. The Spider Queen's voice controlled their conflict, just as her worship controlled the conflict endemic to drow society.

His vision blurred, but he fought back the oblivion of unconsciousness. He was weakening. He wanted to call out to Quenthel but he could not speak. He flew toward the path.

The priestesses saw him coming. Halisstra retrieved a sword from the ground, but none of them moved to help. He set himself down before Quenthel.

Behind and below, he heard Jeggred loping up the ledge.

"Your male has returned," Danifae said with a smirk, though Pharaun took satisfaction in her wince of pain.

"And yours is returning," Quenthel said over her shoulder, meaning Jeggred.

The Baenre priestess studied Pharaun for a time, a peculiar look on her face. The Master of Sorcere saw in Quenthel's expression that his life sat on a blade's edge.

"You can fly due to your ring but are otherwise immobile?" she asked.

Pharaun could not answer.

"A counterspell will do," Quenthel said.

Pharaun would have breathed a sigh of relief, if he could have.

Quenthel incanted her spell, and when she finished, Pharaun still could not move.

A dark smile split the high priestess's face.

"No more flying," she said.

He tested her words, mentally calling upon the ring to lift him. It did nothing.

The bitch had countered the magic in his ring!

"The goddess summons me, Master Mizzrym," she said. "You have served your purpose, as all males do. But now your soul belongs to her."

Jeggred loped up, panting, bleeding, the ragged flesh of his arm stump seeping crimson.

"Mistress," the draegloth said to Danifae and eyed Quenthel and Pharaun with undisguised hate.

Danifae looked at Jeggred, looked at Pharaun, looked out over the Plains of Soulfire.

"The goddess summons *us*, Quenthel Baenre," she said to Quenthel. To Jeggred, she said, "Carry Master Mizzrym down to the plains and leave him there. As Mistress Quenthel said, his soul belongs to the Spider Queen."

Pharaun wanted to curse, to cast, to rail, but he could do nothing. His heart beat fast in his chest.

Jeggred did not question. He leered into Pharaun's face and reached out to take him in his fighting arms.

A surge went through the mage. The ultroloth had not dispelled Pharaun's contingency spell. The moment the draegloth touched him,

a magical fist would come into effect. Pharaun could control it mentally. He tensed, ready.

Jeggred cocked his head and pulled back.

"He said he would cast a contingency spell, so that if I touched
him. . . ." Jeggred trailed off, staring at Pharaun.

Pharaun's heart sank. Why had the draegloth only just then
decided to show some intelligence?

Danifae tsked. "You've always been too obvious, Master Mizzrym,"
she said and chanted a counterspell. When she finished, Pharaun's
contingency spell dissipated.

"Now, Jeggred," she said.

"Farewell, male," Quenthel added, her voice devoid of any trace
of emotion.

Jeggred gathered him up in his fighting arms and ran down the
path. When he reached the plains, he manipulated Pharaun so that
they were face to face.

"I would have preferred to kill you myself," the draegloth said.
"What? No insulting response?"

The draegloth laughed, and his vile breath flew into Pharaun's
face.

The Master of Sorcere could not believe that one of the last sensory
impressions of his life would be to inhale Jeggred's wretched breath.

Jeggred loped a ways farther out and cast Pharaun to the rocky
ground. He landed on his side, staring at the Infinite Web, at Lolth's
city, at the arachnid host gathered on the Plains of Soulfire.

From above and behind, he heard Danifae's voice: "Save yourself if
you can, Jeggred Baenre. I am called to the tabernacle."

With that, Pharaun heard the sound of spellcasting. After a few
moments, each of the three priestesses flew over him, in the form of
gray vapor. As fast as quarrels, as though racing, they sped to Lolth's
presence at last.

As the priestesses vanished into the distance, the host of spiders at
the far end of the plains began to stir. Pharaun was reminded of the
Teeming, and the image disquieted him.

Without warning, the spiders surged forward. Pharaun watched
them approach, a wall of eyes, claws, legs, and fangs. Their coming

sounded like the rush of water. They fed on the fallen as they moved, reducing flesh to bone in moments. He hoped that his wounds would bleed him out before they reached him.

Behind him, he heard Jeggred curse, followed by receding foot-steps as the draegloth ran back up the path toward the Pass of the Soulreaver.

The oaf finally learned some sense, the mage thought.

Pharaun could not even close his eyes. He could only watch the approaching wave and wait to be eaten alive. The bleeding was not killing him fast enough.

He watched the horde strip the flesh from one corpse after another. He knew then that his last sensory impression would not be Jeggred's stink. It would be pain.

TWENTY-TWO

Together but apart, Danifae, Halisstra, and Quenthel rode the wind over the Plains of Soulfire, over Lolth's host, over the Infinite Web, and up to the top of Lolth's city. The priestesses alit on the stone walkway that surrounded the pyramidal tabernacle and returned to flesh.

Quenthel shot Danifae a hateful glare.

Staring up at the mammoth pyramid, Halisstra had an eerie sense of having done it all before. She looked through the temple's doors and saw that it appeared almost exactly as it had in her vision. Webs covered slanted walls. A processional of the drow-giant widow crossbreeds lined an aisle that led to a raised dais. Yochlols stood to either side, their misshapen, slimy bodies strangely elegant, their eight tentacle arms slack at their sides. The yochlols had no faces, but a single red eye glared out at the priestesses from near the top of their columnar, amorphous bodies.

Lolth sat atop the dais in the form of eight spiders, eight giant widows. The power exuded by her presence nearly knocked Halisstra to her knees. Webs extended from her bodies in all directions, reached to the walls, through the walls, and into the multiverse.

Her web covers all, Halisstra thought.

Beside her, Danifae and Quenthel stared in awe. All three abased themselves.

Lolth's voices rang in Halisstra's head, no doubt in all of their heads.

Enter, Yor'thae.

Almost as one, the priestesses rose and stepped over the threshold. Halisstra was not certain who had taken the first step.

Side by side, they walked the aisle. The abyssal widows shifted as they passed. Lolth's eight sets of eyes watched them approach. Halisstra could not take her gaze from the eyes. The largest of the eight spiders sat centermost. As it had in Halisstra's vision, it seemed strangely quiescent, as though waiting.

She realized that she was praying, whispering supplications under her breath with each step. Danifae and Quenthel were doing the same. All three held a hand on their respective holy symbols—their *different* holy symbols.

They reached the dais and stood, small and insignificant, before the eight bodies of their goddess. Each of the eight spiders was as large as Jeggred, with the eighth half-again as huge. Halisstra could not stop staring into the empty eyes of that eighth spider.

The eight embodiments of Lolth stared down at them, the ultimate predators. No flaw marred the carapaces of their glistening, black bodies. Each of the bodies' long, graceful legs ended in a spike as long as Halisstra's forearm. The black flecks of her eye clusters reflected what they saw, revealed nothing, and contained no mercy. Seven mandibles churned slowly in seven fanged mouths. The eighth stood still, waiting.

Lolth's eyes fell first on Danifae, then on Halisstra, on Quenthel.

Each of the priestesses fell to her knees in turn. Each bent her head and stared at the floor. None dared speak.

Sweat soaked Halisstra's body. Her breath was labored. She felt lightheaded.

Had Lolth chosen her? The thought both thrilled and repulsed her.

Only one of you will leave my tabernacle alive, Lolth projected, her seven voices driven like spikes into Halisstra's temples.

Each of the priestesses looked sidelong at the others.

With fearsome suddenness, the eighth body of Lolth lurched into motion, lunging forward and taking Danifae in her mouth.

The battle-captive screamed once.

The Spider Queen lifted Danifae from the floor, impaled her on her fangs, and drank her dry. Blood and fluid leaked from the goddess's maw and pooled around Quenthel and Halisstra. Danifae's legs kicked spasmodically as she died. After feasting on her fluids, Lolth devoured her flesh and bones and cast her clothing and gear to the floor with a clatter.

The other seven spiders watched, as still as had been the eighth.

Halisstra thought she might pass out, so fast was she breathing. She felt Quenthel looking at her and turned her head to see. The Baenre priestess wore an ecstatic grin, even as she continued her supplications.

Only one of you will leave the tabernacle alive.

The eighth spider slid to her side until she stood over Halisstra. Halisstra could have counted the hairs on Lolth's legs. She squeezed shut her eyes and continued to pray. She realized that she still had Seyll's sword in her hand. The other seven spiders took a step forward, an eager step.

Halisstra clutched the blade so tightly it made her knuckles ache.

She awaited the touch of fangs. Long moments passed.

A cracking sound. Wet tearing. Lolth screamed in her head, the sound enough to flatten Halisstra and Quenthel to their bellies on the blood-soaked floor. With effort, she pulled herself to her hands and knees, opened her eyes, and looked up. She had to bear witness

Before her, the seven bodies of Lolth were tearing apart the eighth, feeding on their sister. With their own mandibles, Lolth's bodies sliced into the legs of their eighth sister. The eighth spasmed on the dais, shaking the webs, sending a quiver through the multiverse. Her exoskeleton cracked in a hundred places.

Behind Halisstra, the abyssal widows shuffled anxiously. The seven spiders stepped back, pieces of the eighth still hanging from their jaws. Two yochlols hurried forward to the torn body of the eighth. They slid atop the dais and wrapped their eight tentacles around the eighth's legs, her thorax, her abdomen. They began to split her apart, moving methodically from one leg to the other, to her thorax, her head.

Lolth screamed again—the sound of eight female voices. Dark liquid leaked from the cracks in the flesh of the eighth spider, ichor that drained to the floor around Halisstra and mixed with Danifae's blood. Pieces of Lolth's carapace fell way in chunks.

Halisstra lurched to her feet, horrified. What was happening? She fell back a step, staring wide eyed at her goddess. Quenthel too climbed to her feet and staggered back a step, uncertainty in her eyes.

A whisper ran through the ranks of the abyssal widows. The yochlols returned to their station beside the dais.

Lolth's carapace gave way with a wet crack and was still. Ichor poured from the arachnid body, soaking Halisstra's feet.

The tabernacle went silent.

Halisstra did not know what to say, what to do. Quenthel looked aghast.

Halisstra opened her mouth to speak and—

Movement on the dais, a stirring amidst the pile of hair, carapace, and gore.

With a lurch, the Spider Queen pulled her new form from the old, separating from the shell of her eighth body with an even louder wet, tearing sound. She stepped out of her divine molt and stood, wet and glistening before Halisstra and Quenthel.

Her shining black body was still that of a giant black widow, but instead of a spider's head and face, a drow form jutted from her thorax, a beautifully featured face, a full figured torso. . . .

Danifae Yauntyrr.

Yor'thae.

The Eighth Face of the Queen of the Demonweb Pits.

Lolth was transformed.

Halisstra could not move, could not think.

Only one of you will leave here alive, Lolth had promised.

Halisstra fell to her knees and waited for death.

A tapping on his cheeks brought Gromph back to consciousness.

"Archmage," said a voice, Prath's voice. "Archmage, open your eyes."

Gromph blinked open his eyes and found himself staring up into the concerned face of Prath Baenre. Gromph was on the floor of his office, facing the ceiling.

Prath's youthful face split in a smile, and he said, "You appeared from nowhere, burned all over, and fell to the floor. You have been this way for over an hour. I was afraid to move you or to leave your side. I am pleased to see you alive, Archmage."

Gromph smiled, and his burned lips cracked.

The archmage said, "I share your sentiment, apprentice. But . . . ?"

Prath only shook his head, still smiling.

The last thing Gromph remembered he had been trying to cast a teleportation spell to escape the explosion of the master ward. He had failed to get the spell cast in time, so how . . .

It struck him: His contingent evasion spell. He had forgotten about it in the rush of events, but the absorption of the dimensional lock by the master ward had allowed the evasion to function.

But only after his body had been "materially consumed by magical energy." And he had no ring to heal him. He'd left it on Larikal's body. "Now that you are awake, Archmage," Prath said, "I will send for a priestess."

Gromph shook his head, and the motion caused shooting pain along his neck.

"No." He didn't bother to explain his reasons. "No, apprentice." Gromph had an eerie sense of reliving previous events. He had been in much the same state not so long before, after his battle with the lichdrow, but it had been Nauzhror bent over his burnt body then.

Events had come full circle.

Prath looked down on him, ran his eyes over Gromph's body, and said, "You are badly burned, Archmage."

Gromph knew that well enough. His skin felt as stiff as leather. He didn't want to look at his hands. He didn't want to move, not for a long while.

He said, "Prath, I have healing salves in metal tins in the first dimensional shelf in the third drawer on the left side of my desk. Retrieve them."

Prath rose, and Gromph almost grabbed him.

"Wait!" he said instead. "What of House Agrach Dyrr?"

A soft rush of air announced the operation of a teleportation spell.

Gromph would need to put his wards back into place. No one should have been able to teleport into his offices.

"Archmage!" exclaimed a voice.

Nauzhror.

Footsteps, then the pudgy Master of Sorcere appeared over the Archmage. Gromph saw him steel his expression when he looked upon his master's burns.

"You are alive," Nauzhror said. "I am pleased." Over his shoulder, he ordered, "Apprentice! Send for a priestess!"

Gromph shook his head. "He is retrieving healing salves from my desk, Master Nauzhror. I would just as soon be spared the attentions of another priestess of Lolth."

He tried to laugh, but it turned into a painful cough.

Nauzhror smiled and nodded in understanding.

"I assume the phylactery is destroyed?" the master asked Gromph.

The archmage managed a nod. "Destroyed," he said. "I was just asking Prath about House Agrach Dyrr."

Nauzhror nodded and said, "The temple was utterly consumed in the blast, Archmage, along with many of the House's forces. In the aftermath, House Xorlarrin breached the walls at last. It seemed as though House Agrach Dyrr would fall, annihilated by the Xorlarrin. But . . ."

"But?" Gromph prompted.

"But Matron Mother Baenre arrived with a contingent of Baenre troops and halted the assault. She met with Anival Dyrr, now apparently Matron Mother of House Agrach Dyrr, and it appears they reached an understanding. House Agrach Dyrr will survive as a vassal House to House Baenre."

Gromph smiled through his pain. Anival and House Agrach Dyrr would be beholden to Triel for centuries, essentially an extension of House Baenre. His sister once again had surprised him. He reminded himself never to underestimate her again.

"You have done the city a great service, Archmage," Nauzhror said.

"Indeed," Prath echoed, looking up from his search.

Gromph nodded. He knew that. But the healing would be long, for himself and the city. For a moment, he wondered what had happened to the duergar axe with which he had destroyed the phylactery and taken the lichdrow's soul. He had left it behind in the temple.

He put such thoughts from his mind. The lichdrow was destroyed for good.

He hoped.

"The healing salves, apprentice," he called to Prath.

Quenthel stared up into Lolth's face, into *Danifae's* face, and tried to control her anger, her disappointment, her shame.

Danifae Yauntyrr, a Houseless battle-captive, was Lolth's *Yor'thae*.

Quenthel's rage burned so hot she could scarcely breathe. Her shame weighed so much she could hardly stand. Halisstra lay on her face beside Quenthel. The high priestess looked at her, looked at the eight bodies of Lolth, at Danifae's form sticking out of the body of the largest, and slowly, with great difficulty, put her head to the floor.

Quenthel might not have been the *Yor'thae* but she remained a loyal servant of Lolth.

When she looked up, she dared ask, "Why?"

Anger crept into her voice, and once it started, it poured out.

"Why bring me back from the dead?" she demanded. "Why make me Mistress of Arach-Tinilith if only to do . . . this?"

She thought back to the many times she could have killed Danifae outright and rebuked herself for her mistake. She had been a fool, an arrogant fool.

Lolth's eight bodies surged forward, with the eighth at their center. Quenthel thought she was going to die, but instead Danifae—*Lolth!*—reached forth with a drow hand and stroked Quenthel's hair, an inexplicably gentle gesture. When she spoke, her voice was eight voices, but Danifae's was loudest.

"You seek reasons, daughter, purpose, and that is your failing. Do you not see? Chaos offers no reasons, has no purpose. It is what it is and that is enough."

Quenthel heard the words and in them understood how she had failed her goddess. In that failure, she had failed her House and herself.

She did not have it in her to cry at her failure, not in front of her goddess, especially not in front of her goddess. She would not give Danifae, or what was left of Danifae, the satisfaction.

She lifted her head and looked into Lolth's gray, drow eyes—Danifae's eyes. "Kill me, then. I will not beg for my life."

She almost added the blasphemous, "from you," to the end of her statement, meaning Danifae. But Danifae was no longer just Danifae, and Quenthel had to come to terms with that. Danifae was part of Lolth, the Spider Queen, the Queen of the Demonweb Pits, Quenthel's goddess, and in a form greater than before.

Lolth's full lips curved back in a smile to reveal not teeth but a spider's fangs.

"And that is why you will live," Lolth said.

Quenthel was not sure if she felt relief, shame, or both. She said nothing, merely bowed her head.

"Leave my tabernacle, Mistress of Arach-Tinilith," Lolth said. "Return to Menzoberranzan and continue to head my faith in that city. Tell what you have seen here."

She stroked Quenthel's hair a second time, less gently, as though controlling an impulse to kill.

"Now," the goddess said. She indicated Halisstra with a nod and added, "Leave this one with me."

Quenthel did not question. She rose, turned, and strode between the abyssal widows until she was out of the temple.

Halisstra could not move. She had heard the Spider Queen speak to Quenthel, but the words did not register, simply skipped off of Halisstra's hearing.

Danifae was the *Yor'thae*. Lolth was reborn.

After a time, Quenthel turned, gave Halisstra one final look—a mixture of hate and respect—and exited the temple.

Lolth had promised that only one would leave the temple alive. Quenthel had just left—alive.

Halisstra was going to die.

The goddess looked upon her. She felt the weight of Lolth's gazes. She awaited the bite of the goddess's mandibles, as she had seen in her vision.

It did not come.

She dared a look up into Lolth's face and saw Danifae there, but also so much more. She still clutched Seyll's sword. She released it and shoved it from her.

"I'm sorry, goddess," she said to Lolth and abased herself fully. "Forgive me."

She knew that her apostasy was beyond words. She had danced to Eilistraee on Lolth's plane, erected a temple to the Dark Maiden atop the Spider Queen's tor. She was the worst kind of heretic.

All eight of Lolth's aspects regarded her, and the silence stretched. When the goddess at last spoke, her voice was Danifae's only, but pregnant with power, thick with anger.

"You have been away from me too long, daughter," Lolth said. "I do not forgive."

Lolth leaned toward her, over her. The seven other bodies of Lolth encircled her. Halisstra could not move. Lolth bent. Halisstra's heart pounded.

Lolth's sibilant voice, more Danifae's than ever, whispered in her ear, "Good-bye, Mistress Melarn. What you could have been is not what you are."

Halisstra screamed when the goddess' fangs sank into her neck, twin rods of agony. The other seven spiders too lurched forward and sank their fangs into her flesh. The pain was agonizing, exquisite. The venom set her skin afire, turned her body red hot. Pain and an inexplicable exaltation caused a spasm to course through her body. Her vision went blurry. She opened her mouth to curse Lolth, to thank her, but she could make no sound. Her life ebbed, ebbed. Briefly, she wondered what would become of her soul in death. She longed for the same annihilation as Seyll.

She smiled as the end came for her.

But Lolth's venom did not kill her. She lingered between life and death.

"Not death, wayward daughter," Lolth said in all eight of her voices. "Your sins were too great for such an easy release. For your apostasy, you will give me an eternity of service as my Lady Penitent, my . . . battle-captive," she said in Danifae's voice, "neither living nor dead. You are charged to shed the blood of the heretics who follow my daughter, son, and once-husband. Pain will eat at you ever. Hate will fuel you. And guilt will plague you but never stay your hand. This is to be your penance. Your *eternal* penance."

Horrified, Halisstra grasped for death. Futile.

"There is no escape," Lolth said. "Like me, you too will be transformed and resurrected."

The eight body of the Spider Queen took Halisstra in her pedipalps and pulled her under her thorax. Halisstra hung limp in the arms of her goddess. From her spinneret, Lolth drew forth silken webs and with fearsome grace, spun Halisstra into them.

She was being cocooned. It started at her legs and crept up her body. She barely felt it. She barely felt anything. The strands covered her eyes, and she saw only darkness. Lolth dropped her to the floor.

Within the cocoon, Lolth's venom transformed her. She retreated from the edge of death. The venom saturated her to her soul, wracking her with pain, pain that she knew would never end. Something in the webs sank into her skin.

Lolth's power probed her heart and found there the hate that

Halisstra had never been able to extinguish, found there the forgiveness and love that she had never fully been able to nurture. Lolth's touch brought the hate to full bloom, and reduced the weakness of love and forgiveness to little more than a single spore.

Her skin grew as hard as her soul. Her strength and stature increased to match her hate. The pain of rebirth was agonizing. She opened her mouth and screamed. It came out as a hiss. She ran her tongue over her lips and felt fangs. She tore through the webs with her newfound strength and freed herself from the cocoon. She rolled out onto the floor of the tabernacle, covered in slime.

The yochlols oozed forward to her and wiped her clean with their tentacles. The eight bodies of Lolth retreated to their web, finished with her.

Beside her, Halisstra saw a sword, Seyll's sword. She closed her hand over its hilt and rose.

Violet flames rose from the blade.

Somewhere deep inside, a tiny part of her watched it all in horror. The small spore of her former self, that piece of her that had found joy dancing under the moon, could only watch and despair.

The rest of her remembered her old life, a life of sacrifice, power, and debauchery. She eyed the blade in her hand, longing to use it.

Perhaps the Velarswood, the Lady Penitent thought, and smiled through her pain.

"Welcome home, daughter," said the eight voices of Lolth.

Quenthel stood outside the temple. She did not look back, even when she heard Halisstra Melarn scream. She looked up at the sky. There, the eight satellites of Lolth burned red, and all burned equally bright. The eighth had been reborn.

She swallowed her frustration, took out her holy symbol, prayed to Lolth, and once more took the form of the wind.

She flew off the tabernacle, descended past Lolth's crawling city, and over the Infinite Web toward the misty Plains of Soulfire. Abyssal widows, yochlols, and spiders still thronged the plains.

She alit on the plains and took her normal form amidst the milling arachnids. None paid her any heed.

Little sign remained of the battle with the yugoloths. The field had been picked clean by the horde.

As before, souls exited the Pass of the Soulreaver to be caught in the violet flames of the Plains of Soulfire, burning and writhing until weakness was purged from their flesh. Quenthel wondered when next she passed through the plains how long her own her soul would hang in the air, burning, until her weakness was adequately purged.

She saw movement near the ledge before the Pass of the Soulreaver. A towering form called out to her and loped down the path—Jeggred.

She walked forward over the broken ground to meet her nephew. The draegloth picked his way over the plains, through the arachnids. Blood and gore covered him. Ribbons of yugoloth skin still hung from his claws. His own flesh, torn open by innumerable scratches, cuts, and oozing wounds, looked as broken and battered as the plains around them. One of his inner arms was nothing more than a bloody stump. He slowed as he approached, obviously surprised to see her.

His eyes narrowed in a question, and he looked up and past her, to the city, to the tabernacle.

"I knew it," he said, grinning like the idiot he was. "It was her."

Her whip stung his hide, and he whirled on her, claw raised. Her stare stopped him cold.

"You were but a fortunate fool," she said, pent up rage making her voice tight. "Lolth is reborn, and now things are as they were. You answer to House Baenre."

The serpent whips flicked their tongues and hissed.

Jeggred stared at her, indecision on his face.

"Disobedience will be punished severely, male," she added.

Jeggred licked his lips, bowed his head, and bent his knee. "Yes, Mistress."

Quenthel smiled. Cowing Jeggred brought her some small satisfaction but not enough. She stared at the top of the draegloth's head, thinking, her anger unsated.

She incanted a prayer, cast a spell that charged her touch with enough power to kill almost anything.

Jeggred heard her casting and looked up, his gaze wary. Quenthel smiled at him.

"You well served the Spider Queen, nephew," she said, and reached out to stroke his mane.

Jeggred visibly relaxed.

Quenthel's smile faded. She grabbed a handful of the draegloth's course hair and discharged into the draegloth all of her hate, all of her anger, all of the power in her spell.

It hit Jeggred like a giant's maul. His bones twisted and shattered; his skin tore itself open; blood erupted from his ears, eyes, and mouth. He fell to the ground and writhed with agony, roaring.

"But you poorly served me," she said.

She brandished her whip for a killing blow but hesitated.

She had a better idea.

The half-demon clawed his way to his feet, bleeding from a hundred wounds.

"She will kill you for this," he said, spitting blood. "I will kill you."

Quenthel was not sure whether Jeggred meant Triel or Danifae but either way, she could only smile. Jeggred understood little.

"You've served your purpose," she said into Jeggred's bloody face. "And you are but a male."

Around them, the arachnids began to gather, perhaps attracted by the smell of Jeggred's blood.

Quenthel looked into his red eyes and said, "Farewell, nephew. You are my first sacrifice to the reborn Spider Queen."

With that, she held her holy symbol in her hands and offered a prayer to her reborn goddess. Magic swirled around her, magic that would return her to Menzoberranzan.

She had much to tell her matron mother.

Just before the spell moved her away from the Demonweb Pits, she saw a thousand spiders clamber forward, coat Jeggred's body, and begin to feed.

The draegloth's screams made her smile.

E P I L O G U E

Invisible, Aliisza called upon the arcane heritage of her demon blood and transported herself in an instant to the Plains of Soulfire, in Lolth's Demonweb Pits.

She appeared on the broken, cratered landscape amidst caustic pools, steaming fumaroles, and clouds of green vapor. Her demon blood prevented the environment from harming her. She was alone on the plain.

Behind her, Lolth's Infinite Web stretched over a limitless abyss and outward toward forever. The Spider Queen's city, capped with its pyramidal tabernacle, crawled the strands. So too did more spiders than there were demons in the Abyss.

Before her rose sheer jagged mountains as tall as Aliisza had ever seen. Spiders crawled all over them too. Aliisza didn't know what Lolth saw in spiders. The alu-fiend thought them hideous creatures, as ugly as a dretch.

She still did not know exactly what had transpired. She knew only that Lolth had been reborn as something greater than she had been.

And that Pharaun Mizzrym was dead.

The acknowledgment stirred a strange sensation in her, not unlike the way she'd once felt after going without food for a few days. Her stomach hurt, and her legs felt weak. She felt a sense of loss, or at least of missed opportunity. She would miss Pharaun's companionship, his ready wit.

And I bedded him only once, she thought with a pout, though she supposed that was better than not at all.

All around her lay the signs of a great battle. Severed limbs, broken weapon hafts, rent armor, dented helms, broken earth. She had learned through divinations that Pharaun had died there, fighting Inthracis and his ridiculous Black Horn Regiment. She kicked a nycaloth's helm and sent it spinning into the nearest steaming pool.

Though she was invisible, she felt the eyes of the city on her, lurking the way spiders did, watching, waiting for any sign of weakness. She found herself moving slowly across the landscape, as though she were traversing a web and wanted to keep it still lest the vibrations caused by her movement awaken the spider.

The things I do for lust, she thought and smiled through her anxiety.

In the shadow of Lolth's city, alone on the Plains of Soulfire, Aliisza methodically scoured the site of the battle. She used spells to assist her search from time to time but mostly relied on her own eyes and ability to see enchanted items.

Several cast-offs from the battle glowed in her sight but nothing of interest to her until . . .

There.

There was almost nothing left. His robes lay in tatters. His flesh, even his bones, were mostly gone, consumed by some rabid yugoloth or arachnid—a swarm of either or both.

But something had survived. Aliisza bent and retrieved it. She held it before her face.

Pharaun's severed finger, its flesh intact, still wore his Sorcere ring, which glowed in Aliisza's sight. She looked at the digit for a time, at the smooth skin, the manicured nail. She wondered what it might feel like to have those fingers on her body again.

Laughing, she slipped the finger and the ring into her pocket.

"Well, dearest," she said to the air, "It looks like I'll get a piece of you after all. I'll have to think about what to do with it."

With that, she teleported away.

Valas Hune crouched near the top of the magnificent, natural staircase that led up from the floor of Menzoberranzan's cavern to Tier Breche. Magical traps and wards glowed on the stairs, and two guards from Melee-Magthere stood at the top.

Valas skirted the wards, and the guards looked over and past him. Shrouded in the shadows, he looked down on Menzoberranzan.

Already the city had mostly returned to normal.

Behind him, slaves labored on Tier Breche, rebuilding the damage done to Sorcere and Arach-Tinilith by the duergar stonefire bombs. Many of the slaves were themselves duergar, former soldiers captured rather than slaughtered by the Menzoberranyr.

Across the cavern, Qu'ellarz'orl stood in all its faerie fire-limned majesty. It looked the same as it had for centuries. With House Agrach Dyrr removed from the Ruling Council, Valas could well imagine the scramble among the lesser Houses to seize Dyrr's position in the hierarchy.

Things had indeed turned back to normal, he thought.

Flesh peddlers, spice merchants, narcotic dealers, and more ordinary sellers thronged the booths and shacks of the city's rebuilt Bazaar. Pack lizards and trade carts crawled along Menzoberranzan's streets.

Qu'ellarz'orl might have been Menzoberranzan's head, but the Bazaar was the city's heart. Valas knew that the marketplace reflected the status of the city at any given time. He could see that trade was thriving, which meant that Menzoberranzan was coming back to life.

Rumors had been swirling through the city, most merely hard-to-believe, but some patently absurd. Valas didn't know what he believed but he did know what he saw: Quenthel Baenre was once again

Mistress of Arach-Tinilith and neither Pharaun, Jeggred, Danifae, or any of the others had returned. Valas heard the unspoken message in that. Of the band that had been sent to find Lolth, none but the high priestess had returned.

Valas was leaving the city, lest he too disappear. He had arranged with Kimmuriel, his Bregan D'aerthe superior, to take a scouting mission far from Menzoberranzan. He would return again, but only after enough time had passed so that Quenthel Baenre had forgotten all about him.

To his surprise, the thought of leaving the city turned him maudlin.

Strange, that he would feel nostalgia over such a pit. Menzoberranzan was an ugly, black-hearted bitch who devoured the weak and made bureaucrats of the strong. Still, she managed to evoke a certain attachment in her surviving citizens.

Valas supposed that was the secret of her survival. Mean as she was, the drow who lived there called her home and fought like demons to preserve her. He stared at Narbondel, glowing red in the darkness, signaling another day.

Another day of violence, infighting, murder, and betrayal.

Lolth and the city deserved each other, he decided, and smiled.

With nothing else for it, he turned, melted into the shadows, and headed away from the city for his next mission.

Inthracis the Fifth opened his eyes. Nisviim stood over him, the jackal-faced arcanaloth's expression slack and distant. Without a word, Nisviim turned and exited the chamber.

Inthracis lay there, his new mind racing. He had failed. His last memories were of searing pain. The drow mage had captured and incinerated him with a clever combination of spells. Inthracis resolved to remember the tactic so that he might use it himself one day.

He presumed that Lolth's *Yor'thae* had reached the Spider Queen. He did not know which of the three priestesses had been the Chosen One, and he did not care. He cared only about the possibility of facing

Vhaeraun's wrath. If the Masked Lord discovered that Inthracis lived again. . . .

He pushed such thoughts from his mind.

He would simply have to hope that Lolth's wrath with her son would keep Vhaeraun occupied long enough that the Masked God would forget about Inthracis. Meanwhile, the ultroloth would stay in the background for a few decades and allow Nisviim to take a more active hand in the affairs of Corpsehaven.

He sat up, reveling in the feel of his new body. For a moment, he wondered if Lolth too was adorned in new flesh.

He put that thought from his mind, too. He'd had enough of gods and goddesses to last him a long while.